THE SHADOW

by SHELLEY MUNRO

Jewel Imprint: Ruby
Medallion Press, Inc.
Printed in USA

DEDICATION:

For Paul.
Your love encourages me to strive for dreams.

Published 2006 by Medallion Press, Inc.

The MEDALLION PRESS LOGO
is a registered tradmark of Medallion Press, Inc.

Names, characters, places, and incidents are the products of the author's imagination or are used fictionally. Any resemblance to actual events, locales, or persons, living or dead, is entirely coincidental.

Printed in the United States of America

10 9 8 7 6 5 4 3 2 1
First Edition

THE
SHADOW

by SHELLEY
MUNRO

CHAPTER 1

Some girls attend society balls to snag a rich husband. Not me. I was stuck in work mode with beginner's nerves lurking not far under the surface. Katherine Fawkner—cat burglar in training.

The women in the chatty cluster nearest to me wore diamonds, emeralds, and sapphires, mostly with classic gowns, although one woman wore a radical leather sheath from a new star on the designer front. I hummed along with the Robbie Williams pretender who fronted tonight's band while my gaze wandered from jewel to jewel. No rubies yet. A pity because Father's contact had requested red stones.

Turning to broaden my vista, I intercepted the shocked look of a new acquaintance. Jessica, no . . . Jemima. I'd met her at two society bashes so far, and no doubt we'd keep bumping into each other for the rest of the season.

The horrified look on the woman's face was worthy of a photo. I would have laughed, but I sensed Jemima was going to make a scene.

"Kate Fawkner! *What are you putting in your mouth?*"

The spoon I held in my left hand came to an abrupt halt three inches from my lips. The chocolate confection on the spoon wobbled precariously.

"Kate!" Jemima screeched.

Heads snapped around while I froze like a virgin comedian in front of a hostile audience. My ears vibrated. I swear Jemima's shriek of horror swept to all four corners of the Ritz Ballroom on Piccadilly, probably halfway across London as well. My nerve elixir was creating the disturbance.

Hell's teeth! After the terrible trio's lectures on the correct behavior for a fledgling cat burglar, I'd still slipped. "Do the blond-bimbo act," Father had said. "That always works. They'll think you're too stupid to execute a job." *Yeah, right, Father.* While my looks fit the stereotype, I wasn't doing so well on the execution.

I shrugged inwardly, knowing I was "it" whether I wanted the job or not. Father owed money to loan sharks. They wanted it back. Ergo: I was jammed smack in the middle of the mess. It was my duty to keep my family safe.

Jemima stared at my dessert as though it harbored a nasty cockroach. How was I supposed to remember blond bimbos only ate lettuce leaves? Mental note for next time—I'd just add it to the other dozen or so.

I placed my spoon down and stared at the double serving of Death by Chocolate with real regret. Chocolate was a weakness. Tonight it might be my downfall.

"I like a woman with a healthy appetite," a newcomer said. His voice held humor and the twang of the Antipodes.

Curiosity ignited, I turned to face him, clutching the offending dessert plate to my chest. As I stared, his gaze swooped, taking in the chocolate confection, rising fractionally to my 36C breasts, and finally lifting to my face. His grin was infectious.

"Looks tasty," he murmured, brown eyes twinkling in a naughty boy fashion.

The surge of heat to my face took me by surprise. At age twenty-five, I was past that flirty girl/boy stuff. Kate Fawkner handled everything the world tossed her way, rolled it in a tidy ball, and lobbed it back. I blinked at the dark-haired stranger. His grin widened. A dimple winked in his cheek, highlighting his amusement. Irritated by the flash of warmth that had zapped to my toes, my gaze traveled down the length of his rangy body before making a return slow-boat-to-China journey and doing some sightseeing on the way. Evening clothes: black trousers and cummerbund, pristine white shirt, and a black bowtie. Muscles gave the clothes a great shape. A vision appeared in my mind—one with far fewer clothes. Imagination connected the dots. Actually, "tasty" was a lackluster description for this specimen, but I hated to create an ego

3

problem so I kept my poker face intact.

The man chuckled, not put out in the least by my lei-surely survey.

"I'll take that for you." Jemima wrenched the plate from my hands and set it on the buffet table with a thump. "Have you broken up with Seth?" she demanded.

My father hadn't raised a fool. I clutched the excuse with both hands and ran. "Fight," I said, thinking of my childhood pony, Cuddles, and his death at the ripe age of twenty-five. The tears welled while I mentally apologized to my good friend and neighbor, Seth Winthrop.

"Maybe I can help take your mind off . . . your prob-lems. Would you like to dance?" the stranger asked.

I blinked to clear my tears and thrust out my hand. "My name is Katherine Fawkner. You are?"

"Kahu Williams." His large hand enfolded mine in warmth. "Pleased to meet you, Lady Katherine."

A surge of acute pleasure shot along my arm and sped to my lower belly. The sensation distracted me for an in-stant before his use of my title registered. He knew me? Or had seen me and asked questions? My brows shot up before I realized I wasn't doing such a stellar job keeping the blond-bimbo image intact.

A short, sharp giggle erupted. "You naughty boy," I trilled. "Seth and I will make up." My gaze settled on Seth in the far corner of the ballroom. My best friend was a closet gay. We'd made a deal to help one another

4

by attending social functions together. Nothing romantic about our relationship at all. I allowed my smile to widen to a flirtatious, toothy grin and aimed it at Kahu Williams. "But if you're game, I don't mind making him jealous."

The distaste on his bronzed face made me want to cheer, but I didn't, now firmly in blond-bimbo mode. I seized him by the arm and dragged him onto the dance floor, chatting nonstop. I'd resume my surveillance of the attendees and their lovely jewels while we danced.

When I slid into Kahu's embrace, I considered the irony. Even though I wore an expensive red Valentino gown matched with the requisite accessories, the noble Fawkner family was flat broke. I'd been horrified to learn the financial situation when my daughter and I returned from Europe a few months ago. Financially embarrassed, my father was suffering from arthritis—a real crimp in his lifelong career, and the family estate was falling about our ears. As I said to Father and his good friend and some-times-assistant, Ben, when they talked about the necessity of doing another job, "How many successful cat burglars do you know with creaky, swollen joints?"

It was up to me to correct the downturn in the fam-ily fortunes and assure our safety. A tough assignment with the goons sent out by the loan shark muttering dire warnings about our overdue payment. A shudder skipped through my body as I recalled the oily voice on the phone only this morning. "Pay up or else."

"Or else what?" I'd quipped, ever the smartass.

"Or else your daughter suffers," the man had growled. And he'd meant it.

Unfortunately, a qualified waitress didn't earn the sort of money we required to cement our future—a secure and safe future where we lived to enjoy our twilight years. That was when Father, Ben, and Hannah—the terrible trio— had suggested I take over the role of *The Shadow*.

So, here I was after much argument and discussion. Katherine Fawkner, cat burglar with training wheels, seeking a target to hit later in the week. Jeez! Sounded like some awful B-grade movie. But the alarming calls from the loan shark's goons and the bills in the overflowing mailbox put a realistic spin on the situation.

I inhaled deeply and moved closer to Kahu Williams, savoring his silent strength when my thoughts were in such turmoil. If I were looking for a man, he'd make the finalist list: intelligent, easy on the eye, with the slight kink in his nose hinting at an interesting history. The man was a natural on the dance floor, moving like a . . . well . . . a cat burglar. A real joy to partner. And tall, dark, and striking; smelled good, too. Pity I wasn't shopping.

Raising my head, I looked deep into a pair of chocolate-brown eyes. He had the sort of eyes a girl could fall into, if she had the time or the inclination.

"What sort of a name is Kahu?" The question came out as a breathy sigh. I gave myself a swift mental kick.

"Family name," he said. "Means Harrier hawk."

"The accent?"

"I'm from New Zealand."

Good. That was good. It meant he didn't live in London, and I'd probably never see him again. "Here on holiday?"

"No." His gaze zeroed in on someone behind me.

Irked by his reticence and the lack of attention, I pushed for more. "So what are you doing over here?" The second the demand left my mouth, I sighed. Move over, blond bimbo—I want to get out. This wasn't the way to secure family safety! Concentrate. Pick a jewel. Any jewel.

"I'm on a case," he murmured, not taking his gaze from the object that had snagged his interest.

My feet stopped moving. "Case? What sort of case?"

"What's wrong?" His eyes narrowed, milk chocolate turned to dark.

"Thought I saw someone I knew," I muttered. My feet resumed the basic one-two-three pattern but I promptly stood on Kahu's foot. "Sorry!" I chirped. "Old boyfriend. Ended badly, you know." Okay, that was better. I sounded dizzy blonde again.

In silence, we recommenced dancing while my mind worked frantically. A cop! In all the gin-joints, why the heck did he have to pick mine? "Caught any crooks lately?" The blond bimbo leapt out with vengeance and stepped on his foot again.

"Will you watch where you're putting those heels?"

Even exasperation sounded good coming from his mouth. Sorta slow and sexy in his antipodean drawl. Oh, boy! I needed to get a grip. I mean I didn't even have the excuse of being drunk since I didn't drink and hadn't done so since the eighth of December six years ago. The mere thought of that night made my brain sharpen, my lusty senses dead to the man who held me in my arms. The vapid smile on my face died and grim purpose gave my backbone steel. In that moment, I became *The Shadow* on a job.

As we danced, I checked the men and women standing around the fringe of the dance floor. They chattered carelessly like twittering birds, hands gesturing while gemstones winked and glowed, drawing the eye. Drawing my eye as I settled into the serious business of choosing my mark. Glittering diamonds, sparkling sapphires, emeralds, pearls. Mmm, which would it be?

I caught a flash of red from the corner of my eye. Ah, a ruby. My gaze shot up to the face of the woman who wore the lustrous red stones around her slender neck. Nope, didn't recognize the face. Who was the man she was dancing with? He looked familiar. Perhaps Seth would know.

Just then Kahu swung me around, and I lost sight of my quarry. Damn and blast. The ballroom was crowded tonight with every aristocrat and wannabe in attendance.

"Can I cut in?"

Kahu's hands tensed fractionally around my waist before he let go. I regretted the loss of contact immediately, and that pissed me off.

"Thanks for the dance," he said and wandered away without a backward glance, leaving me to the mercies of the other man.

"Lady Fawkner. Kate. I've been looking for you." The voice was smooth and one I'd heard via telephone yesterday when he'd requested a meeting with Father.

Drat. I pinned a polite smile into place and swung about to face Richard Beauchamp. When I'd pressed, Father had admitted he owed the man money. Beauchamp wanted to arrange collection, no doubt. I tossed my head. One of the blond curls that dangled on my bare shoulders danced a jig. "So now you've found me." I needed to tread delicately until I found out what he wanted. After all, it was possible he owned the mouth that controlled the goons.

"Shall we?" he murmured. With polished, gentlemanly manners, he took me in his arms and started to move to the sounds of a Shania Twain ballad. Clammy hands clutched my bare arm and curled around my waist, drawing me close. His protruding belly bumped and jostled. The lead singer sang on. It was going to be a long four minutes.

"We need to discuss money," he said finally.

I played dumb, hoping to fill the gaps in my knowledge. And if I found he was behind the threat to my daughter, he was toast. "Oh?"

"Your father owes me money." The sophisticated veneer dropped enough to show the shrewd businessman behind.

"He's behind on payments. The interest is mounting."

As he spoke, his hands slipped to squeeze my butt. I put up with his familiarity for the minute. It wasn't the place to show my self-defense skills. "What do you want me to say, Mr. Beauchamp? Should I congratulate you?"

A bark of laughter sounded. "You're a cool one." He studied me intently until I felt like a juicy steak cooked to perfection and ready to eat. "I wonder if you'll be as cool in bed."

My eyes narrowed. "I have a boyfriend, Mr. Beauchamp. I'm happy with Seth. I'm not on the market for further, shall we say, activity."

"I like that. An old-fashioned girl with scruples."

Huh, if only the man knew. Although I looked like Playmate of the Month in my clinging red dress, I was celibate. I didn't do sex, so he was wasting his breath trying to persuade me into his bed. The ballad cruised to an end. I wrenched away, giving him an icy glare when what I really wanted to do was let loose with a shriek and a kick to his smug upper-crust head.

"I must find Seth," I said, wanting to reinforce my previous words. I wanted to quiz him about the woman with the ruby necklace anyway.

"But we need to talk. I want to make arrangements." He paused, seeing what I'd already noticed. The band was leaving the dais. As the last couple standing on the dance floor, we stood out like pimples on an adolescent boy.

"Hell, too public. Meet me in the gardens in half an hour."

I nodded, not trusting myself to stick to language bimbo if I spoke. "Mr. Beauchamp," I finally gritted out. I had a job to do and time was wasting. There'd be no rendezvous in the garden, but he didn't need to know that right now.

"Oh, Lady Katherine?"

"Yes?"

"Make it Richard. We're going to be very good friends."

Eew! I paused mid-step and turned back to check his expression. He'd better not mean what I thought he meant. Damn, he did. My eyes narrowed. Just let him try.

Feeling the weight of a stare, I glanced up and connected with a pair of chocolate-brown eyes. Kahu. For a mere acquaintance, he looked a little too interested in our conversation. Was he investigating Beauchamp? I glanced from Williams to Beauchamp.

"I thought you didn't double-dip," Beauchamp growled.

"I don't. I hardly know the man." Interesting. Apart from the snide reaction, he didn't appear to know the cop. But instinct told me something was afoot. Beauchamp might be clueless, but I was betting Williams was on his game.

Just then I saw the woman with the ruby necklace heading in the direction of the restrooms. It's right what they say about women and restrooms. Women really do require escorts. It's lonely in those places—much friendlier if

11

there's someone with whom to chat about the latest gossip.

◇ ◇ ◇ ◇ ◇

Perdita Moning, one of the Lancashire Monings, owned the rubies. She and her husband, the Honorable James Moning, were staying at their London residence in Hampstead. I researched the Moning family, obtained a copy of the security plans at great expense, and hightailed it back to Oakthorpe in Surrey.

"Father, what do you think? Is this job a go?"

My father and Ben, who also happened to be married to our housekeeper, Hannah, exchanged glances. It wasn't difficult to see they wanted to muscle in on my job. For a cowardly heartbeat, I considered it before grimacing. Father's arthritis was slowing him down. He'd had a good patch lately, but I couldn't take the risk. Despite the loan-shark business being Father's fault, I had to help. I didn't want him captured, not after he'd eluded the cops for so long. He'd earned his retirement even though it chaffed him. And I felt guilty for staying in Europe for so long without checking on Father.

"No, you are not going along with me," I said, making my voice firm. "You can help with the planning and organize a receiver for the goods. That's as close as either of you are getting."

My father scratched his head through sparse white hair

and frowned. "But you haven't done a job before."

"But I have good teachers. I'll be fine." Christ, and maybe if I said that often enough even I'd come to believe. I was petrified, scared stiff I'd trip a silent alarm and summon the cops. They'd whisk me away and I'd never see my daughter, Amber, again. Things were dangerous enough for Amber without me adding further risk to the situation. An icy shiver of pure fear swept my body despite the lingering warmth of the summer day. I made a mental note to plead with Hannah to keep an extra-close watch over her when I couldn't be at Oakthorpe.

"She's physically fit, Charles," Ben said. "And clever."

My father sniffed. "That's no substitute for experience." He squinted at me, a flash of alarm suddenly shooting across his face at what he saw on mine. "You're not having problems with ethics, are you?"

Ben and my father shared a panicked glance; then Ben said, "That Robin Hood geezer was nuts giving away hard earned money. You won't do that."

"Certifiable," my father agreed. "These people are insured. Fawkners have been cat burglars for five generations. Family honor at stake, you know. If you're squeamish then Ben and I will do the job."

"You can't. Look at your hands." We all looked until my father jerked them out of sight behind his back. "And you know it's not just honor at stake this time," I continued. "I'm the only Fawkner left to do the job. If I decide to give

13

away some of the proceeds to ease my conscience, then I will," I said, settling the argument. "Let's start planning." Shoving aside all feelings of remorse, I concentrated on the instructions given by Ben and my father.

"Right," I said about an hour later. "I can't force any more details inside my head. It's crammed to capacity. I'm going to put Amber to bed and read her a story."

"But—"

"Let her go, Charles," Ben said. "The lass is right. Any more and we'll make her nervous."

Damn straight, I thought, scurrying for cover while the going was good. I headed straight past the kitchen, with its enticing waft of roast chicken, and up the stairs to Amber's bedroom. My daughter was in bed, chatting to her doll, Margery, and her stuffed dog, Toto.

"You've already had a bath," I said, disappointment rocketing through me when I studied her pixie face and damp brown curls. Bath and bedtime ranked high among my favorite times spent with my daughter. Regret burdened me along with a sliver of guilt. I'd missed quite a few since taking on the role of *The Shadow*.

She grinned, and my heartstrings tugged with a wave of love. "Hannah helped me, Mama. I had bubbles. Pink ones that came right up to my chin."

"Did you?" I tucked a stray curl behind her ear and pressed a quick kiss to her satin-soft cheek, savoring her scent of flowers and little girl. "Would you like a story?"

Her head bobbed with enthusiasm. "I've picked one out," she said, reaching for a battered book of fairytales. "Cinderella with all the voices, please."

A bittersweet moment. I sent a silent prayer winging skyward when I opened the pages to Cinderella. *Please help me keep her safe.*

One hour later, I was back in my battered blue Mini on the road for London. My destination was the Kensington home of Father's receiver. As I drove down the A24, I thought over what I was about to do and how much I had to lose. I relaxed my hands on the steering wheel, knowing that despite my qualms and spiraling fears, I was fresh out of options.

The drive into London didn't take long. It was half past eight when I drove down Kensington High Street. People still walked the paths in Kensington Gardens, admiring the flowers and gawking at Kensington Palace. While I waited for the lights to change to green, I watched the antics of a chubby gray squirrel that was performing for a bunch of Japanese tourists. Minutes later, I pulled up outside a block of flats flanking Kensington Square. I stopped the car and climbed out, wiping moist hands on my jean-clad thighs.

Showtime. Maybe. Probably, I decided, knowing in truth I had to go through with this job. Alistair Seagrove, my father's old friend, would help me run through my plan again. And with his contacts, I'd liquidate the jewels with no questions asked.

The hunter green door to number six flew open before I had time to grasp the heavy iron knocker.

"Katie, girl. You're early."

I smiled weakly, feeling like a kid again. "Hi, Emily. I've got the jitters," I confessed when I stepped inside.

"Alistair will be pleased to hear it," Emily said. "A little of the old adrenaline gives an edge. Don't you worry, Katie, girl. Your father, Charlie, is the best, and he's trained you extensively. You've done the prep with Charlie and Ben. You'll be fine." She grinned, revealing a flash of gold from one front tooth. "Besides, Alistair has promised me a week in the Caribbean with his share of the proceeds. I want that holiday. I'm counting on you, Katie, girl."

Alistair appeared behind Emily. "Nothing like a little pressure to make a job go well," he said in a wry tone. "Leave the dear girl in peace. I can see she's nervous enough without you adding to the load."

"Do you want a cup of tea? Something to eat?" Emily asked as she shoved me gently in her husband's direction.

The thought of eating made my stomach somersault. "No, thanks," I said, fighting down a shudder.

Alistair smiled gently. "A cup of tea, Emily. Bring the girl some tea."

Now that I was in London, my decision to continue in my father's footsteps seemed even more final. I wondered if I would manage to force down even a cup of tea.

Nevertheless, I nodded and watched Emily waddle in the direction of the kitchen.

"Come along," Alistair instructed in a crisp upper-class accent that reminded me of my childhood and time spent with Father's friends. "I want to run through the plan with you to make sure you have it down pat."

I followed the thin, upright man into his office, nerves doing a real number on my knees. For a moment, I wondered if I might buckle, so I zeroed in on Alistair's desk and fell against it for support.

Alistair produced a set of blueprints and unrolled them on the wooden desktop, pinning the plan down at the corners with two books, a stapler and an empty china mug.

"Run me through your plan, Katie."

I pictured the eighteenth-century house in Hampstead. The security system was top of the line, except for one thing. The owners hadn't alarmed the house past the second floor, thinking no one would be foolhardy enough to enter through the old servant quarters on the third floor. Unluckily for them, I was that fool. I concentrated on the plan we had worked out after my reconnaissance. "Arrive in Hampstead around midnight, double-check that Perdita Moning isn't at home. Her husband is away in Brussels on business," I added, anticipating Alistair's query. He nodded, and I continued. "Deal with the security cameras at the entrance and also the neighbor's cameras—the ones that scan the street. Circle to the rear of the property and climb to the third floor. Jimmy lock. Enter building. The jewels are kept in a safe in the Monings' bedroom on the second floor. If I can't open the safe manually, I'll blow it. Take jewels and leave."

"Don't get cocky, Kate. Tell me where the alarm sensors are. One mistake, that's all it will take, and you'll have the cops or a security company there in minutes."

I sighed inwardly, but rattled off the details.

"Excellent," Alistair said. "Do you have all your equipment?"

Talk about being back at school. I bit back a smart retort. "Yeah. All present and accounted for as per our plan."

"Good. Good. You're more organized than Charles. He was forever forgetting his gear." He paused, the good humor evaporating from his face. "How is he?"

"Good days, bad days."

The door flew open without warning. "Charlie not too good, then?" Emily *tsk-tsk*ed as she placed the tea tray on the desk. "Terrible thing, arthritis."

Alistair accepted the steaming mug of Earl Grey tea and his wife passed him with a slight smile. "Eavesdropping again, Emily?"

"Wanted to make sure my holiday in the Caribbean was still looking good. And to tell Kate not to worry. I consulted the cards. This job will go smooth as silk."

CHAPTER 2

I parked my Mini about four streets away and made my way by foot to the Georgian mansion at number twelve, Admiral's Walk. I slunk along the quiet streets, dressed in full cat-burglar gear: black leggings and black jumper, my long blond hair bound up in a tight French braid and tucked under my clothing, out of sight. My head was covered by a close-fitting black balaclava that doubled as a mask when pulled low. I carried a black nylon pack on my back, filled with every conceivable tool required by the well-dressed cat burglar. All dressed up and places to go.

After spraying black paint across the lens of every camera I passed and checking the street in both directions, I scaled the London plane tree that grew outside number ten. I crawled along a sturdy limb until I had a good view of the Moning house and the garden. The air smelled damp, making me suspect a mist would roll in tonight and cover the nearby heath. After I watched for the requisite ten minutes followed by another five minutes for safety's sake, it was still quiet. I wriggled along the limb and dropped into the garden at number twelve. Crouching low, I crept across the manicured lawn, past an archway draped with old-fashioned scented roses, making sure I stuck to the looming shadows cast by the stand of English oaks.

A low growl was all the warning I received. I froze. Another growl made the hairs at the back of my neck stand and salute. Hell! A freaking dog. My heart thundered as I slowly turned.

The dog stood a few feet from me. Black. All teeth and fangs. Damn and blast. The damned thing hadn't been here the three times I'd checked out the premises. And if the dog had a kennel, I hadn't seen it. With slow, careful movements, I eased the pack from my back and fumbled with the zip. My hand closed around the doctored cheeseburger, and I let it fall to the ground at my feet. The dog sniffed the burger. It woofed the treat down in two bites before staring fixedly, perhaps debating if I were the second course. It growled. Father had assured me the sleeping pills would do the trick without hurting the dog. I hoped he knew what he was talking about. No sooner had the thought passed my mind than the dog swayed.

I bolted. The dog gave a feral growl and sprang. Fabric ripped. My steps faltered. For an instant, I panicked, but suddenly the dog let go. Without looking back, I sprinted to the back of the house, my legs pumping like a hundred-meter sprinter at the Olympic Games. I scampered up the sturdy vine I'd chosen and only then looked back, my chest burning for air. The dog lay still on the ground. I turned to survey the rip in my leggings and shifted uneasily. My backside smarted like the devil.

Smooth as silk.

Huh? Emily had read someone else's cards, not mine.

I scaled the wall in no time at all, stubbornly ignoring the pain in my ass, and after pulling on a pair of gloves, entered the building via the nursery room window. Lucky for me the nursery was empty of all save the lingering scent of lemon furniture polish. I crept down to the next floor, but that's when luck deserted me again.

A footfall sounded.

I froze, my heart hammering with alarm. There was someone at home. Laughter—both male and female. Had the husband returned? Why were they there with the lights off? Duh! Stupid question. It was obvious why the room was dark. Abort my mission or risk it? As I hesitated on the landing, I heard footsteps on the stairs. The front door opened.

"Darling, tomorrow night?" the man asked.

"Yes. James isn't back until Friday," Perdita replied.

Kissing followed—loud enough to make me roll my eyes. After what seemed like ages, the door shut again and soft footsteps sounded on the stairs.

What the hell was I going to do now? I thought about hitting her over the head, snatching the jewels and running. I mean, she was fooling around; she deserved everything that was coming. I considered the idea a bit longer and rejected it as stupid. A girl had to have some scruples. Physical violence was one of mine.

Before I'd made a decision, I heard the front door open again. Jeez! The place was like Paddington Station at rush hour. I hunkered down in my hiding place on the landing and waited to see what developed.

Stealthy footsteps padded up the stairs toward the bedroom where Perdita had entertained her lover. Surely not another one?

"What do you want?" I heard Perdita demand.

I crept from my dark corner but couldn't see a damned thing. What now? I wondered in frustration. Did I try to get closer?

A scream. A gunshot. I heard the sound of a rapid retreat. The front door slammed; then there was silence. No more laughter. Not a single bloody sound. I hovered indecisively. Dithered, really. When everything remained silent, I cautiously crept toward Perdita's bedroom.

When I was a few feet from the doorway, a cuckoo burst from its clock, nearly giving me a coronary. I leapt in fright but managed to hold back on the accompanying squeak. After my heart settled back into place, I slunk closer to the bedroom.

A little moonlight seeped in from outside, but I didn't need illumination to tell something was badly wrong. I could smell it. An indescribable scent, layered with expensive perfume and sex, that I didn't want to smell again in a hurry.

"Hello?" I whispered. It was no surprise to me that I sounded shit-scared. And not much of a surprise when no one answered. I fumbled for the light switch, not because I wanted to but because I had to know.

Blood.

Everywhere. It really stood out on the white satin sheets. I swallowed when I observed the very dead woman sprawled on the king-sized bed, and then gulped again when my stomach threatened to revolt. It was Perdita Moning, all right.

Strangled laughter sounded, and I was a bit surprised when I realized the noise had come from me. Slightly hysterical. A little crazed. But hell, not every day a girl witnesses a murder.

I stepped closer and stopped abruptly. If I were wise, I'd be out of here. Although I'd heard the murderer leave, they might return and realize I'd been in the house. The thought stopped me short. I had a daughter who was in enough danger as it was—a hell of a lot to live for. I whirled about in a frenzy to leave the scene. Amber was only five, and I wanted to see her reach adulthood.

The light caught the ruby necklace. I stopped, mesmerized by the lustrous sparkle, and then shook myself. More red. But I scooped it up anyway, along with a pair of matching earrings and a rather nice diamond-and-sapphire choker. I hardened my heart. Perdita Moning was dead. She wouldn't need them anymore.

About to leave, one more thing caught my notice. My heart started to pound. I shivered from head to toe.

It was a photo of four children. Innocent fun preserved from a happy, carefree day at the beach. I started to wheeze. I tore at my jumper trying to loosen it around my neck, but the gloves were useless. I ripped one off and yanked at my buttons. Concentrate. Breathe.

When I had myself under control, I looked back at the photo. My trembling hand reached out to brush one finger across the face of the girl in the picture. She wasn't my daughter, but she was a dead ringer. I swallowed my shock.

A clue—at last.

You see, I didn't know the identity of my daughter's father, but now that I'd seen this photo I intended to discover the truth.

CHAPTER 3

I don't remember much of my journey back to the flat in Kensington. I know I used my prepaid mobile to ring the cops and report the murder. I drove on automatic pilot while my mind refused to move past the photo I'd seen.

And the memories the photo brought back . . .

The implications.

December 8, a Christmas ball six years ago. Eighteen and fresh from boarding school in Switzerland, I was ready to party with my friends. I remember the ballroom with the Christmas decorations, the mistletoe, the bouquets of balloons, the huge Douglas fir tree covered with silver balls, shimmering tinsel, and twinkling lights. I remember giggling with my girlfriends, flirting with the men. Snatching a kiss under the mistletoe. I even remember

SHELLEY MUNRO

sipping glasses of champagne and sitting on Santa's knee. But that's where my memories faded.

I woke up the next morning at the Mayfair Hotel. Naked. Alone in a bed with no idea of how I'd come to be there. Or what had happened.

I crawled from the bed. My body ached, my head pounded, and my mouth felt like an arid desert. The move from the bed was a bad idea. My stomach retaliated. I groaned and staggered to the bathroom where I hurled until my throat burned and my sides ached for relief.

Shivering, I hugged the cool porcelain of the toilet bowl. I'd never felt so ill in all my life. Or felt so used and dirty. It was obvious what had happened, even to someone in my confused state.

I'd had sex.

Tears burned at my gritty eyes. Although I'd flirted and had numerous boyfriends, I didn't believe in casual sex. It wasn't that I was saving myself for Mr. Right, but I'd wanted my first time to mean something special.

I concentrated hard, trying to remember the previous night. It was all a blur. I remembered nothing of leaving the ballroom, of entering this room. I had no idea who I had been with after the party. A man. A woman. Or a combination thereof. I swallowed, biting back hysterical laughter.

Get a grip, I thought, dragging myself from the floor. I staggered to the shower, turned it on and stepped under the water heedless of the fact the water still ran cold. Gradually, the water heated. Steam filled the shower cubicle. I reached blindly for the luxurious citrus shower gel provided by the hotel and scrubbed my skin, my hair.

About half an hour later, I felt more alert and my brain started to function. I needed to find out who had done this to me. I needed to talk to my friends, the group of people I had sat with during the evening. I wanted answers.

I shut off the shower and grabbed a towel. Drying myself briskly, I avoided my reflection in the myriad of mirrors in the well-appointed bathroom, not ready to face myself.

Back in the bedroom, I found the clothes I'd worn the previous night scattered all over the floor—an electric-blue gown designed especially for me by one of my friends, my wispy underwear, and thigh-high stockings. A shudder swept through my body while I stared at them. Although I was reluctant to don the clothes, there was no option.

Fully dressed, I hunted for my shoes and bag. My bag lay by the bed. One shoe sat by the door, but the other was on the dressing table. I plucked the shoe off the dressing table and froze. The shoe had been used to weigh down a wad of money. Six crisp fifty-pound notes. If I hadn't felt like a tramp before, I did now.

A sob of shame escaped. God, whoever I'd been with last night really wanted to rub my nose in the muck at the bottom of the gutter. The need to level the playing field burned deep in my gut. In that instant, I wanted revenge. I needed revenge, and I intended to get it.

Laying aside my pride, I shoved the money in my bag and let myself out of Room 210.

I marched to the lift and pounded on the down button. When it arrived, I stomped inside to join two women passengers. The doors clanked shut, and they both edged back against the walls as if I harbored an insidious disease. Uncomfortable silence greeted the man that entered the lift on the next floor down. His brows rose when he saw me.

"What are you staring at?" I snapped.

A smile hovered about his perfect mouth. "Nothing, sweetheart."

"I am not your sweetheart," I snarled. The lift reached the ground floor. I swept out, heading for reception and joined the line. Tapping my left foot on the carpeted floor, I waited for my turn.

The receptionist was a young man. Sandy hair. Earnest face. He sported a pimple on the end of his large nose. "Are you checking out?" he asked, his tone expressing doubt as his gaze swept me from head to waist.

I sensed the high level of interest behind me so kept my voice low and polite. At eighteen, I had learned manners gained more than a show of rudeness. I'd slipped earlier in the lift but had myself back under control. "Yes, please," I said pleasantly. "Room 210."

He tapped on his keyboard. "All the charges have been paid."

"Yes, but by whom?"

28

His brows drew together. "Don't you know?"

Behind me, I heard a chuckle. My cheeks burned. "No," I said swallowing my pride. "I would like to know so I can . . . ah . . . thank them."

He tapped on the keyboard again. "They paid cash," he said, loudly enough for everyone in the growing line to hear.

"Who paid cash?" I struggled against the urge to place my hands around his scrawny neck and choke the life out of him.

"I'm sorry, miss. But we can't give out that information. Don't worry, the charges for the room are paid." He looked to the next person in line. "Next please."

"Wait a minute," I burst out in frustration. "Why can't you tell me who paid for the room?"

"Hotel privacy rules."

"Are you finished?" the man behind me demanded. "I have a taxi waiting."

I stood my ground. "But I want to know who paid for the room."

"Lady, it's obvious what you do for a living," the man behind me snarled. "I presume you were paid. Why don't you leave it at that and go home?"

My face burned afresh. For a moment, I thought about telling them what had happened. I was not a woman of the night. I was an eighteen-year-old convent girl, and someone had taken advantage of me. The whispers and amused contempt behind me made shame grow. The young man at the desk exhibited not a shred of sympathy. Finally, my head hung in defeat, and I left the hotel. I hailed a cab and used the money I'd been left to pay the fare home to Oakthorpe.

I remained in seclusion, unable to talk about that night or see my friends. That should have been the end of the ordeal. I mean, I certainly wanted to put the whole shameful episode behind me, but the gods decided I was a wicked girl and must be punished. Two months later, I finally faced up to the fact I was pregnant with no idea of the father's identity. It was another three weeks before I plucked up the courage to talk to Hannah, our housekeeper.

My father, Ben, and Hannah were brilliant. They never shouted or expressed their disappointment. They asked minimal questions for which I was thankful. Not that I had answers. I was an emotional mess. In the end, it was decided I would go to my godmother, Renee Girard, in France. I would have the baby and put it up for adoption; then my life could move forward.

The moment of Amber's birth is vivid and clear in my mind. The nurse dropped her in my arms and that was it. One glance at the dark fuzzy head of hair, the red, blotchy face, and a pair of unfocused blue eyes, and I was in love. I refused to give my daughter up.

I've learned to live with the circumstances of my daughter's birth and try not to dwell on the method of her conception. Of course, at five, Amber's getting to the stage she asks the odd question. I've made up an acceptable story and tell Amber her father died in an airplane crash. And despite the lies, I'm a good mother.

I glanced at the photo on the passenger seat. I hadn't realized I'd grabbed it before I left. It was a different one from the first one I'd seen, but the truth was there nevertheless. Whoever had fathered the child in this photo was probably Amber's father.

The brakes on my Mini squealed when I pulled up outside the Kensington flat. Lights shone through several of the windows. Alistair and Emily had waited up for my return. No doubt Emily was concerned about the viability of her Caribbean holiday. I scooped up my backpack from the passenger side of the car and picked up the key Emily had given me earlier. The green door flew open before I had time to use my key.

"How did it go?" Emily's brown eyes shone bright with expectation.

"Is that Kate?" Alistair called.

I couldn't resist. "No, it's the Loch Ness Monster."

"She made a joke. See, I told you she would be fine," Emily hollered back at her husband. She stepped a little closer. "My God! What happened to you? It looks like a vampire has drained your blood. You look pale and interesting." Her face creased in a frown. "You okay?"

Was I okay? Had the heist gone well? Good questions. And where to start . . . ?

My left butt cheek ached like the devil. I'd had no idea

a frou-frou mutt could inflict such damage. I'd witnessed a murder, and my past had come back with vengeance to bite me in my uninjured buttock. Yeah, things were peachy keen.

Alistair appeared beside Emily. I noticed his gaze flickered down to study the rip in my black leggings.

"Dog bite," I said tersely. "But that's not the worst of it."

"Come through to the study," Alistair said. "We can talk there."

"I'll make tea," Emily said, already heading for the kitchen. "Wait till I get there. Better yet, have a quick shower and dab some iodine on that bite."

"Yeah, okay," I said. "I don't think the skin is broken too badly. It's just bruised."

Fifteen minutes later, we met in the study.

"Perdita Moning is dead," I said baldly. There was no other way to report bad news but straight out and direct.

Emily gasped. The teapot thumped to the table. "You didn't . . ."

"Of course she didn't," Alistair snapped. "Did you?"

"No," I retorted. I limped the length of the library and back again.

Emily sighed loudly. "There goes my trip."

"Emily," Alistair warned. "Katie, tell us what happened."

"I entered the house, just like we planned. Apart from the mutt—"

"The cheeseburger worked, then?"

"Emily, hush."

"I was on the landing when I heard noises. Mrs. Moning was entertaining her lover." I explained the rest of my close call with murder but left out the bit about the photo since that was private business. I hadn't talked to anyone about my past, and I wasn't about to start now.

"A gunshot," Emily blurted.

"Are you sure she was dead?" Alistair chipped in.

"Oh yeah. I'm sure." A person couldn't lose that much blood and live, but the bullet hole between Perdita Moning's eyes had been a dead giveaway. "I checked for a pulse. There wasn't one."

"Did you call the police?"

"Yeah, from my cell phone after I left."

We were all silent, contemplating the crime.

"Did you tell the police you were there?" Alistair asked.

I shook my head. "No. Just told them there had been a break-in and hung up. There is some good news though."

"Do tell," Emily said. "I could do with a laugh."

I reached over and picked up my backpack from the floor at my feet. I unzipped it and pulled out the jewels I'd stashed there before I'd fled the scene. The rubies, diamonds, and sapphires gleamed in the light.

Emily's breath eased out with a hiss and she grinned. She stood, plucking the gems from my hands and holding them aloft, stretching with a cat-like grace despite her bulk. She hummed softly before bursting into triumphant song. "La, la, la, Caribbean."

33

Alistair scowled. "Emily, you're impossible." But I saw the twinkle in his eyes and the obvious love for his wife of thirty years. For a brief moment, envy kicked me in the gut, stealing my breath.

Kahu Williams came to mind. Briefly, before I thrust his image away. A cop and a cat burglar. Nope. Didn't exactly go together, not like fish and chips or gin and tonic. My lips curved in a rueful grin. *A cop and a cat burglar.* I didn't think so.

"When will *The Shadow* strike again?" Emily asked.

I settled back against the oak desk to consider my reply. The throb in my backside made me wince. I stood upright and even that hurt. "I'm considering the Khan residence in Richmond. Jaspinder Khan has a diamond-and-garnet tiara I'd like to get my hands on." And I'd heard rumors about the way she treated the hired help.

"Woo-hoo! Caribbean, here I come!"

A laugh burst from me. I couldn't help it in the face of Emily's exuberant good spirits. "On that note, I think I'll leave. I want to arrive home before Amber wakes up." Even though it would hurt to sit down and drive home, a little bit of pain was worth the opportunity to see my daughter's smile.

"Off you go now, Katie," Alistair said. "I'll have the money for you by the end of the week."

CHAPTER 4

The Gibson costume ball was one of the highlights of the social calendar. Invitations were highly sought after with many wannabes experiencing disappointment. I had one since I'd gone to school with Selena Gibson.

I showed my pastel pink invitation to the security men on the door and stepped inside the flower-bedecked ballroom with Seth at my side.

"Nice," I said to Seth, referring to the décor.

He snorted, showing his contempt in a way that only a male can, even a gay male. "A bit pink."

I grinned. "And what's wrong with pink? You don't think it goes with our costumes?" Seth was a debonair vampire. I was dressed in black with orange accessories. I fingered one of the ugly orange warts that dotted my face and smoothed the black skirts of my witch costume. "Is my wig straight?" I asked, remembering my blond-bimbo persona—the one that lay under the dark wig.

Seth studied me for an instant. "Yeah. I'm going to skip out and leave you on your own." His blue eyes held a trace of nervous excitement. I'd already noticed how fidgety he'd been tonight. "Will you be all right on your own? Do you want me to come back to collect you?"

Not likely. Being a lone ranger suited me fine. I wanted to find out all I could about the Moning family. There would be gossip aplenty, and I wanted to hear it all. They say revenge is a dish best served cold. My dish of revenge had cooled for six years, and now that I'd found a clue after all this time I was chomping at the bit. The bastard who'd drugged and raped me was on a countdown.

"No, I'll see you in the morning at the flat." The flat I referred to was Seth's. We often stayed overnight and drove home the next day. Or rather I stayed there while Seth visited with friends. "How about a dance first? Best not look too eager," I said.

Seth grimaced. "Am I that obvious?"

"Only to me."

We stepped onto the dance floor and moved into a slow dance.

I leaned into Seth so we could talk without being overheard. "Did you hear about the murder?" I'd purposely not discussed it on the drive up from Oakthorpe. Although Seth was my best friend, he didn't know of my extracurricular activities and I didn't want him to learn the truth about my family. Here at the ball, with Seth distracted, was the perfect time to gather information.

"Perdita Moning?" he murmured.

"Yeah. On the radio they said it was a robbery gone wrong. It's creepy. I spoke to Perdita in the restrooms the other night. Now she's dead." I tensed, hoping I hadn't overdone it and raised suspicion. Seth knew me better than most.

"I didn't really know them. I know of them. You know what it's like."

I did. The grapevine worked efficiently and frequently in our world. "I presume they had kids?" I tossed the important question in casually. My heart thumped so loudly I was sure Seth would notice.

"No children. Rumor was Moning shot blanks."

I stumbled in my shock, one stiletto heel landing on Seth's toes.

"Bloody hell, Kate." He let go of me to gingerly touch his foot. "I think you've broken something."

Blanks? That couldn't be right. I moved, barely missing Seth's other foot.

"Kate, watch where you're putting your feet!"

"Sorry."

"Just don't do it again. I'd like my body in perfect working order."

I batted my lashes at him. "Ohhh. Sounds kinky."

"You're incorrigible," Seth muttered, glancing about to see if anyone was listening.

By this time, we were creating a traffic hazard in the middle of the busy floor. Disgusted sounds equivalent to tooting car horns were being directed our way.

"Shall we adjourn to the bar?" I asked.

"Sounds safer than the dance floor." Seth took my arm, and directed me to the bar, his exaggerated hobble making me laugh.

I grabbed at his shoulders and planted a kiss smack on his lips. "I love you."

He grinned and squeezed me gently. "Love you too, pumpkin." He pulled out a barstool for me. "What will your poison be? Champagne? A fruity little Sauvignon Blanc? Or the usual soft drink?"

"Coke, please." From the corner of my eye, I noticed a man watching us intently. For an instant, I thought it might be Seth's special friend; then he moved. Well, well. Kahu Williams.

I smiled and raised my glass in silent salute. Probably not a bright move since he and I were on opposite sides of the law, but there was something about the man that attracted and goaded me to outrageousness.

He sauntered along the bar toward us, obviously taking my smile as encouragement. Kahu was dressed as a cowboy, and a very fine cowboy he made, too.

"We meet again," I said. "This is Seth Fleming. Seth,

this is Kahu Williams. Why aren't you dressed as a cop?"

The two men shook hands.

"He's a cop," I added.

"Oh?" Seth asked. "Are you working on the Moning case?"

"Yes," Kahu said.

He left it at a one-word answer, and straight away, I wanted to needle him. "Going to give us any inside information," I asked.

"No." Unperturbed, his brown eyes scanned my face, coming to a halt on the orange wart on the right side of my mouth.

Lots of tingles resulted from that one look. It felt as though he'd touched me with his hand and I shrugged, uneasy with the foreign sensation. "Pity." I caught Seth watching me with narrowed eyes and knew I'd given myself away. Or rather, the interest I had in Kahu. Good thing Seth had a hot date so I'd escape an interrogation. "Didn't you want to catch up with that friend from work?"

"Yeah," Seth drawled. "I did." He bent close to kiss me. "He looks like a keeper."

"I'll catch up with you later," I said to Seth, not deigning a reply. As Seth walked away, I turned to Kahu. "How many cases do you work at once?"

His dark eyes dissected my appearance. A grin flickered briefly. "Several unless there's a high profile one that comes along. Your boyfriend is very trusting."

I shrugged. "I heard on the radio that it was a robbery. Is that true?"

"Seems that way."

"What did they take?" I asked the question already knowing the answer.

His gaze sharpened. "The usual. Jewelry. Stuff."

And that was as many questions as I dared ask. The man was no slouch in the brain department. "I talked to her at the Friends of Chelsea ball." My comment sounded casual. I held my breath while I waited to see if he'd bite.

"Did you know her?"

Bingo. "A little." Meeting in the ladies' restrooms counted, right?

"Now's not the time to talk. I'll call you." He set his drink on the bar and held out his hand. "Let's dance."

A trifle bemused, I accepted the hand he offered. It engulfed my smaller one, his firm clasp sending a tiny zap akin to a mild electrical current surging up my arm. I managed not to wince. Just. It had happened every time he touched me, but my response still took me by surprise. Not that I hated men. Only the one—him, I'd castrate and throw to the wolves in a New York minute.

The upbeat song finished as we reached the dance floor and the band commenced a ballad. Kahu drew me close, and I stumbled.

"Relax," he murmured.

Chagrined, I sucked in a deep breath and willed my

traitorous body to relax.

The singer crooned of a faithless lover. We stood so close I felt Kahu's steady heartbeat. Our legs brushed, and his breath ruffled the tiny hairs at my temple. One hand trailed down over my back and pressed me close. To my astonishment, tiny goose bumps surfaced in the wake of his touch. I shivered.

This wasn't dancing.

This was torture.

"Should we dance so close?" I blurted, throwing my head back so I could see his face.

He smiled. "Relax. We look the same as the others."

He was right. The small, crowded dance floor made real dancing impossible. It was difficult to do more than shuffle. *Concentrate on his top button and keep out of trouble.* For all of two seconds my plan worked. As close as we were, I couldn't help but notice his scent. And it distracted me, reminding me of France, of long walks along the secluded beach near my godmother's house, the clean sea air and lazy summer days. My tongue darted out to moisten dry lips. I caught myself in the act and cursed under my breath, but couldn't help moving on in the thought department. From smell to the other senses. We were already touching. I had the smell, sight, and hearing thing covered. That left taste. My gaze shot up to his mouth. As I watched, his lips curved in a gentle smile.

"Kate?" Humor lurked in my name.

My heart thumped with an alarming loudness. I had a

desperate need for air. Oh, man. This was like . . . like love-making in a public place. What the hell was I thinking?

Just then there was a flourish of drums. The song ended. My sigh held huge relief. Finished. I was outta here. Time for me to mingle and find the answers I sought.

"Stay," Kahu murmured. "Dance with me again."

"No, I—"

"Beauchamp is heading this way in his Henry disguise."

Beauchamp as Henry the Eighth? The mind boggled. This I had to see.

"No, don't look now." Kahu's chuckle was low and intimate as he pressed me close. "He's still heading this way. Looks eager. Like a dog scenting game."

"Charming." I wasn't sure I should believe him, but remained in his arms anyway.

The band rocked into a number with a strong Latin beat. Several couples left the floor. Not many men were willing to attempt a Latin dance. We had a perfect excuse to exit the dance floor. Even knowing this, my right foot tapped to the beat. Longingly. I glanced at Kahu, and knew my gaze expressed doubt. "Still want to dance?"

"I think I can manage." One brown eye closed in a lazy wink and with a conspiratorial grin, he fell into step with the sexy beat. His hands skimmed my body, moving down to grasp swaying hips.

"Are you sure?"

"Don't worry about me," he said dryly.

Was that a challenge? Another glance confirmed it. Exhilaration raced through me. I wasn't one to back away from a dare. The music pulsed through my blood, dredging up primitive needs, primitive wants. I smiled at Kahu, my heart hammering harder on seeing his return grin. The rat-a-tat sound of my heels tapping the wooden floor, the singer's vocals, and the swish of my skirt added to the spell the dance wove. The people dancing around us blurred to the background as we twirled and circled, each flirting move from me counteracted by one from Kahu. Gazes touched and held as the pulsing music and sensuous dance drew us into a private world of two.

Hot blood roared through my veins, my breasts heaved in exertion. I clicked my heels and flung back my head as I anticipated Kahu's next move. His lean body spun away then strutted back toward me until we were so close we almost touched. Almost. His broad grin flashed pleasure; his avid eyes moved down my body. I felt every touch of his gaze on my heated skin.

At the back of my mind, I knew I shouldn't dance like this with him, not so flamboyantly and full of passion and not in public. I licked my lips and his eyes, dark and smoldering, lingered on the moist curves of my mouth. He wore a look I'd seen before, a look that told me he wanted to take me to bed and not surface for days.

A full-fledged ache sprang to life deep in my chest. I was out of my element, and I knew it. The sexual tension

43

I associated with his presence leapt to new, heady heights as we taunted each other, circling on the dance floor the Latin way.

The song ended in a bold fanfare of drums. I flinched, ripped rudely from the sensual spell. We froze in position, sides heaving, gazes meshed together.

"Folks, give them a hand. That was some floorshow!" The singer's breathy voice wrenched me to the present, as did the ripple of enthusiastic applause and rousing catcalls from friends.

"Drink?" Kahu asked.

"Sure." I matched him for coolness, but I suspected the intense undercurrents had rattled us both.

At the bar, Kahu ordered fresh drinks, despite our glasses being half full and sitting where we'd left them. I approved, having learnt the hard way about unscrupulous people who thought it was funny to spike drinks.

Kahu handed me my coke. The ice tinkled when I rolled the glass against my cheek.

"Are you engaged to Seth?"

My head jerked up. Coke splashed over the rim of the glass. "No, we're not engaged."

"Good." Kahu tipped back his head to drink his beer. His tanned throat worked as he swallowed. He set his empty glass on the bar. "Seth seems like a decent man. I wouldn't want to step on his toes." He brushed a kiss across my lips and stepped back. "I'll be in touch."

He strutted away before my brain engaged enough to formulate a smartass answer. I stared after him in real consternation. What the hell had he meant by that?

Richard Beauchamp popped up beside me with the suddenness of a jack-in-a-box, resplendent in his navy blue satin. A beard covered his weak chin. I sighed and stowed my questions about Kahu; they would be dragged out later, when I was alone. One look at Beauchamp's red, bloated face told me I was in for a proposition. I sipped my coke while debating how to handle him. No time like the present to start on my investigation.

"Did you hear about the murder?"

"Perdita Moning," he said. There was a break in his voice that made me study him carefully.

"Did you know her?" I asked.

"Old family friends. I went to Eton with Perdita's older brother."

"Hell of a way to go," I observed, watching him carefully over the rim of my glass. "I feel sorry for her husband and children."

"They didn't have children."

"Oh?" So why did they have all the photos in the bedroom? I arched one brow while I waited impatiently for him to answer.

He gazed off into the distance, seemingly far away. I wanted to shake him. Demand answers.

"Perdita didn't like children," he said finally.

45

That didn't make much sense either. If I didn't like children, I wouldn't keep kid's photos on my bedroom dresser. None of the rumors gelled. Didn't like children. Shot blanks. The answer probably lay somewhere in the middle. I needed to dig deeper in the gossip garden.

"I thought anyone who married into the Moning dynasty would produce the requisite heir and a spare."

Beauchamp sank onto a barstool with a loud sigh. "Perdita had several miscarriages. The baby she managed to carry to term died when he was a toddler."

God. Sympathy stirred within me. I'd give my right leg and arm up in exchange for Amber's safety even though the circumstances of her conception made my gut churn. "And then she was murdered. The lady didn't have much luck."

A strange look passed over his face. Secrets. The man wasn't telling me everything.

"Morbid subject, murder. Let's talk about us, Lady Katherine." Lowering his voice, he edged closer. "Your father owes me money. I intend to collect, one way or the other." His gaze came to a halt on my breasts.

Once again, sex reared its ugly head. "That would be blackmail," I said. "Go see my father. He's the one that owes you money." I glimpsed Selena Gibson across the dance floor. She'd be a good source for gossip. Let Beauchamp do his worst. I slid from my stool and stalked off, ignoring the whispered threats that slithered after me.

At least I didn't need to play dumb for Selena. We had met

each other as nervous five-year-olds on the first day of school. Our friendship endured through the years even though we went for long stretches without seeing each other.

"Selena, how are you?" We air-kissed before stepping back to smile broadly and study the evolutions each had made since our last meeting. "Got time for a chat? Catch up on a bit of gossip?" I silently admired her solid-gold earrings. Each time Selena moved her head, the Egyptian emblems glistened in the light.

Selena tossed her head, making the earrings dance against her Cleopatra wig. "Sure have. Fancy a quick turn about the garden? I could do with peace and quiet. It's been hectic all day."

We wandered through a pair of open double doors and paused on the patio. A soft breeze ruffled the leaves of an ornamental orange tree. Five steps led down to a floodlit garden. An erupting fountain danced on our right, the tinkle of the water soft, musical, and relaxing.

The exact thing I needed to soothe my fractured nerves after my latest meeting with Kahu "The Hawk" Williams. The man certainly took after his name. Saw everything. Noted it all. I'd have to remember to take extra care at our next meeting. The blond-bimbo image needed to stick like elephant-strength superglue.

We wandered aimlessly until we came to a secluded seat amongst the hedges. The low drone of traffic was the only discordant note in the serene garden.

"I saw you on the dance floor," Selena said as she sank onto the stone seat.

"That wasn't me," I said promptly.

"I know," she said. "That's why I'm so intrigued. Who is that cowboy?"

"No one important," I muttered, uncomfortable with the attention. People were used to seeing me with Seth since I'd arrived back in England. Prior to that rumors had circulated about my preference for women. It had never bothered me until now. "Let's talk about something juicy instead. Murder. Did you know the Monings?"

The humor bleached from Selena's face. "Terrible, isn't it? They're saying in the press that it was a burglary gone wrong. I would have handed over the jewels plus the key to the safety-deposit box with instructions to take the lot. Life's too important to risk for material possessions."

I opened my mouth to say the murder had nothing to do with theft, then snapped it shut. That information was on a need-to-know basis. And I was the only one who needed to know I'd been present at the murder. Much safer that way. The report of the gunshot echoed in my head, re-inforcing my decision. Perdita had known her murderer. If I tripped over clues while I searched for the child, I'd ring the cops with an anonymous tip. Until then, I was going to keep the info to myself.

"I suppose they had children," I murmured.

"You know, I'm not sure. I didn't know them well. I

guess they'll be at the funeral if they did."

Good point. I made a mental note to check the papers for the time of the funeral.

"Oh, hell. I knew I should have worn my glasses." Selena clutched my forearm. "Kate, is that Henry the Eighth heading this way?"

I turned to look in the direction she indicated and nodded. "Yep, I'd recognize that stomach anywhere."

"I'm outta here," she muttered, leaping to her feet. "Detain him for me, will you? Give me time to escape." She flew down the gravel path in the opposite direction leaving behind nothing but a whiff of Chanel Number Five.

Jeez. I didn't want to see the man either. I darted in the same direction as Selena but turned left where she'd turned right. I brushed past a pot of roses and ducked down another path, entering the box-hedge maze with the intention of lingering until Beauchamp disappeared.

It was much darker in the maze. I slowed, letting my night vision adjust. A series of high breathy giggles alerted me to proceed with caution. I caught a glimpse of a couple groping each other. The male had his hand up the skirt of his partner's maid costume. A lot of heavy breathing punctuated the giggles. Averting my eyes, I tiptoed past.

The sound of gravel crunching underfoot alerted me to a presence ahead. I stepped off the path onto a section of grass and my heels sank halfway to China. I cursed and yanked free of the grass while I debated which direction to head. A man's voice made me hesitate. Damn and blast! Not another clandestine tryst.

Another man replied. I froze. I knew that voice.

"What are you doing out here?"

Bloody hell. I knew *that* voice too. What were Kahu Williams and Richard Beauchamp doing out here? Together. Curious, I edged closer and settled in to listen.

"I needed a breath of fresh air." Kahu's tone was mocking, and I sensed he wanted to provoke Beauchamp. Beauchamp was a bit slower on the uptake than me.

"I'm meeting someone," Beauchamp snarled.

"I won't take up much time."

Beauchamp must have registered the determination underlying the antipodean accent. "What do you want?"

"Do you know Rick Morrison?"

A beat of silence played out. "Never heard of the man."

"Liar."

I sucked in my breath at the hardness in Kahu's voice. Just like an iceberg, I was betting there was more below the surface.

"For God's sake, quit the games and tell me what this is about." Beauchamp was becoming impatient.

I imagined him glancing at his watch. And intrigued, I wondered who he was meeting. It wasn't me, and I know it wasn't Selena since she'd fled when she saw him. His confident attitude implied the meeting was prearranged.

"Rick Morrison is dead."

This time the silence was longer and preceded by a shocked intake of air. Yep, Beauchamp knew this Rick Morrison, whoever he was. Now Kahu knew it too.

"I don't know who this Rick Morrison is," Beauchamp snapped. "Never heard of the man."

Intrigued, I crept closer. I wanted to see Beauchamp's face. Kahu's too, although if I were a betting kinda gal, I'd lay odds Kahu Williams had a hell of a poker face. As I slid to the end of the hedge, I caught the blur of movement when Kahu grabbed Beauchamp by the scruff of the neck. He thrust his face right up to Beauchamp's and shook him like a dog shakes when it's wet. Hard and vigorous.

"That's a lie. You knew my brother. He worked for you and now he's dead. Talk, dammit! I want answers."

I heard voices behind me. So did the two men. Kahu let go of Beauchamp with a muttered curse. "Keep watch over your shoulder, Beauchamp, 'cause I'll be there until I get the truth about my brother." He stalked away, luckily in the opposite direction to where I was hidden.

Beauchamp appeared shaken and stirred like the proverbial James Bond special. He smoothed his crumpled satin outfit before slinking along a third path I hadn't noticed. The man looked furtive, and I wasn't nicknamed Kat for nothing. I sneaked after him. About halfway down the path, a slender shadow separated from the hedge. A woman. The deluded soul threw her arms around his neck and kissed him. Beauchamp didn't object. Two shadows melted to one. Yuck!

"Hello." An arm snaked around my waist. "Fancy finding you out here."

Out of the frying pan, into the fire. Clichéd but oh so true.

"Doing a little spying?" Kahu drawled.

The sexy drawl got me every time and melted the heck out of my willpower. I turned, and my hand reached to touch before the warning bells even whimpered. Jeez. I needed control in the way a fat woman needed a diet. Yesterday. I snatched my hand away, millimeters before I touched warm masculine skin.

"Just out for some fresh air," I said.

"A lot of that going 'round," Kahu muttered.

I bit back a grin. "I wanted peace and quiet, but I keep tripping over amorous couples. You'd think they'd prefer a soft bed."

"Never fancied adventure?"

Oh, boy. One conversation detour coming right up. "I need a drink." Lame, very lame.

"You know, variety is the spice of life."

"I'll take your word for it," I said tartly. I whirled about and headed directly for the steps leading to the ballroom.

A soft chuckle followed me. My face burned, but I restrained the impulse to look over my shoulder and read his expression. Sometimes strategic retreat is the wisest course—the only path.

CHAPTER 5

The funeral was scheduled for Wednesday in the Monings' hometown of Kinnell Green in Lancashire. My Mini rattled up the M6, shaking and shuddering theatrically each time a truck flew past. I eyed the temperature gauge with misgiving, but the needle hovered in the middle of hot and cold. I sighed, but softly so I didn't tempt the gods to hammer me for smugness.

Apart from a childhood foray to Blackpool, I'd never visited this part of the country before. To tell the truth, I was relieved to leave Oakthorpe. I'd let my destination slip to my father and been called upon to defend my reasons for traveling north instead of heading for the jewel-rich mansions of London. Evasion and lying without blinking an eye was becoming second nature to me, but I hadn't quite got the impassive expression down because Father, backed up by Ben, had demanded details. Of course, I'd refused. The argument had heated up to shouting and cursing, and things had headed downhill from there.

A loud crash sounded overhead. A bright flash of lightning followed the thunder. The black clouds had hovered in the distance the whole journey, but now it looked as though they were about to unleash nature's wrath. Rain lashed my windscreen. I flicked the window wipers on and resigned myself to getting wet since my Mini leaked like fishing net.

I peered through the rain and finally spotted the turn-off. Half an hour later, chilled and damp, I pulled up outside the church and parked behind a dark blue Mercedes.

Two men climbed from the sedan. Although I could only see the back view of both men, my heart sank. One of them was Kahu Williams. I'd stake my left leg on it. My pulse rate kicked up, and I swallowed. Drat. I'd hoped to sneak in and peruse the attendees without any messy entanglements. But Kahu Williams was the definition of "messy," and judging by the nerves dancing happily in my stomach, "entanglement" as well.

Aghast at my reaction to seeing him, I dawdled. I had no idea why I was attracted to danger. "Maybe it's genetics catching up on you," I muttered in disgust.

The second the two men disappeared inside the church, I opened my door and stepped from my Mini. My black jacket and knee-length skirt didn't look too bad despite the dampness.

I strode up to the double wooden doors that looked old enough to date from medieval times, opened them, and slid inside the church. A gust of wind ripped the door from my grasp and the resulting crash had every head turning to stare. Most wore disapproval, although I did catch a glimpse of humor from a couple of the males.

"Sorry," I muttered, desperately searching for an empty pew to duck into.

"Kate, over here." The masculine voice held a trace of amusement beneath the huskiness.

Although heat suffused my face, my heart did an excited flip-flop. It was pleased to see Kahu Williams even if *The Shadow* wasn't. After a quick glance and nod of greeting, when my heart lurched again, I slid onto the hard wooden pew and stared straight ahead. Beside me, Kahu moved slightly, his hard thigh cozying up to mine, the warmth welcome after the chill outside.

"You're wet." His warm breath stirred a tendril of hair at my temple.

I turned to face temptation head on despite my inner qualms. "It is raining outside." The heart palpitations should have forewarned me, but his masculinity struck me afresh. Tanned skin, dark intelligent eyes that held laughter at the moment, and a lean face combined together into a dangerous package. Briefly, I closed my eyes and prayed for fortitude.

"I didn't know you were coming to the funeral," I said, opening my eyes again.

"Standard procedure these days. You'd be surprised at how many murderers attend the funeral because they knew the victim."

My brows rose at the subtle implication. "Family? Do you think one of her family murdered her?" Guilt made the words at the end of my sentence rise. I had information but was withholding it to save my skin. I was reasonably confident that the murderer wasn't related to Perdita Moning. It was more likely a crime of passion.

"Surely that doesn't surprise you," Kahu said. "A lot of victims know their murderers."

I bit my lip and debated how to answer. Forensic tests would show that Perdita Moning had had sex prior to her death. Her husband's alibi was probably tight enough that they knew he hadn't committed the crime. Finally, I settled for something generic. "I guess you'd know from experience," I said.

I turned my attention to the minister's sermon, listening to the friends and family members who read from the Bible or related personal memories of Perdita and filed away impressions to drag out later. It was hard not to get emotional. A young woman snuffed out before her prime. I wasn't the only one attempting to hold back tender sentiments. A lone tear spilled down my cheek, and I knew if I didn't do something quick, there'd be more. I groped in my jacket pocket searching for the handkerchief I'd put there this morning and came up empty. Minutes later, a large white handkerchief floated in front of me. Accepting it gratefully, I dealt with the tears and hoped that I didn't end up looking too much like a panda bear.

There were a few familiar faces at the funeral. Richard Beauchamp was in attendance, thankfully on the far side of the chapel. I squeezed closer to Kahu, and hoped like hell the man didn't see me before I saw him once we left the church. Jemima Cameron, the new friend that I kept running into at balls and charity functions, sat a few pews in front of us. I made a mental note to ask her a few questions later. Also present were a few acquaintances from school. I wasn't looking forward to the "what are you doing now?" conversation, where subtle games of one-upmanship were played, but I'd suck it in and deal. Finding out about Amber's father was much more important than false pride.

While I listened, you can bet that I took lots of mental notes. I'd tried to keep up with case developments via the newspaper, but it was a mission to get to the paper first at Oakthorpe. Father and Ben devoured the headlines before turning to the social pages to scout possible targets for *The Shadow*. Hannah used it to clean the windows, if she got to it first. This morning, I'd received the newspaper in bits since Amber had cut out pictures to take to her playschool art day. It wasn't easy being parent, detective, and fledgling cat burglar, I can tell you.

An hour passed. My damp suit started to feel distinctly uncomfortable, the crop of goose bumps that pebbled my skin growing by the minute. A shiver worked its way through my body.

"Won't be long now," Kahu murmured. "It's stopped raining so it won't be so bad outside."

The minister wrapped up the service, and everyone stood as Perdita made the final journey to her resting place.

I waited until most people had filed from the church, taking the chance to see exactly who had come to pay their respects. And to decide who I should question later. There were several children present, but it was difficult to know if they belonged to the Monings or were related to other attendees. Disappointing that none of them looked remotely like Amber, but it was possible that if the Monings had children they weren't present for one reason or another. The funeral notice had been brief with nothing apart from pertinent info relating to the service and burial. And with the newspaper situation at Oakthorpe, it was entirely possible that I'd missed the all-important stories. I'd have to make some discreet inquiries and spend some time at a library.

Behind me, I heard Kahu and his fellow officer murmuring, no doubt discussing a plan of attack. An arm curled around my waist, making me start a little. Kahu bent closer to murmur in my ear. "Ready to go?"

"Ah, sure." With my mind in a pleasant haze caused by

his citrus aftershave, I wasn't sure that attending the grave-side in police presence would be helpful or not. My usual lightning-quick thought processes were decidedly foggy. I felt a slight pressure from the arm around my waist and stepped into the aisle. *Try and ignore it*, I thought as I un-successfully suppressed another shiver.

"Still cold?" Kahu asked in a low tone. The husky voice massaged my skin and hiked desire with a suddenness that made me shudder violently.

"No, I'm fine," I answered, hoping the rain would start again. Another dousing with cold water might benefit both me and my frisky hormones.

"I need to talk to a few people." Kahu paused to tuck a lock of hair behind my ear. The move was intimate and smacked of possession. My stomach roiled but there was no distaste involved. The aforementioned frisky hormones leapt and frolicked like spring lambs as I stared into his chocolate-brown eyes. "Will I see you later?"

"Ah . . . probably not. I have to get home. My father isn't that well, and if I'm not there to supervise, he over-does things." I comforted myself with the fact that I spoke nothing less than the truth. I didn't want Father and Ben attempting a job without direction. My supervision.

Kahu nodded.

"Coming?" his partner asked with a trace of impatience.

"I'll be with you in a minute," Kahu said, waiting until the other man moved out of hearing range. "Can I ring you?"

My head started to nod before my brain fully engaged. *Oh, boy.* This was not good. How to railroad a perfectly good investigation in two seconds flat. "No," I said. Of course, I ended up making a total fool of myself, but that was nothing new where this man was concerned.

Kahu grinned, a flash of white teeth in a tanned face. "I'll give you my card," he said, amusement shading the husky voice. He whipped a plain white business card from his pocket and pulled out a pen to jot another number on the back while I stared in helpless horror. My only excuse—the man looked *really* sexy when he smiled. "My private number," he murmured, every trace of humor receding. "I look forward to hearing from you."

My head nodded even as I thought, *no way!* There was obviously something in the air surrounding him. A drug. I needed to seek fresh air, and quickly, before I did something really stupid.

"Don't get too cold, sweetheart."

Before I could unravel my brain, he kissed me. Right on the lips. Short. Sweet. Confusing. My hands crept up to touch my tingling lips the moment he turned and exited the churchyard. My gaze lingered on the man's butt as he sauntered away.

"I thought you were going out with Seth," a disapproving voice interrupted my Kahu-fueled fantasies.

My cheeks took on an embarrassed glow; or at least it felt that way. I turned to face my accuser. "Hi, Jemima. I haven't seen you since the Gibson ball."

"You haven't answered my question," she said sternly.

My eyes narrowed at her tone. Who did she think she was—my mother? I remembered the chocolate episode and amended mother to conscience. "Seth and I are friends," I said finally, not really sure why I was explaining.

"Good friends or sleeping friends?" she asked.

For Seth's sake, I tiptoed around the question. "You interested in Seth?"

"Only if he's not taken," she said with a prim note that pressed on my humor button. "I don't like to steal."

"You'll have to check with Seth," I said, my mouth quirking in the beginnings of a full-out grin. His secrets were not mine to tell. "But I don't really think he's in the market for a relationship at the moment."

Jemima nodded and jerked her head in the direction of the churchyard. "You coming?"

"Yeah. Do you know the family well?"

"My brother went to school with Perdita so she used to spend time at our house."

I hesitated unsure of how to proceed. "I met Perdita last week. I didn't know her well but . . ." I shrugged and trailed off hoping that Jemima would add information without any prompting on my part.

"They haven't arrested anyone yet."

"No. The police seem very tight-lipped. There hasn't been much in the papers. Perdita was so young."

"At least there were no children," Jemima said as we headed for the group of people loitering in the cemetery.

Frustration slammed through me. So who were the kids in the photos? How did I get more information about the portrait shots in Perdita's bedroom? It wasn't as though I could come straight out and ask without someone surmising that I'd been in her bedroom.

"Are you going to the Harlequin ball on Saturday?"

"Seth asked me to go with him a few weeks ago." And the creditors were banging on the door again. I needed to do another job sooner rather than later.

"I'll see you there," Jemima said. "I want to talk to Perdita's brother."

My spirits brightened upon hearing Jemima's words. "See you there," I echoed with a bright smile. If the child wasn't Perdita's, perhaps she was a niece. *Or a godchild*, I thought. Heck, that was going to make my investigation more difficult. I scanned the faces of the children still present. None of them was the child I sought. I'd have to think of some other way of obtaining the information I required. But what? I frowned.

"What's a pretty girl like you doing with such a big frown?" An arm slid around my waist then immediately disengaged. "Ugh. You're wet."

I turned to regard Richard Beauchamp with a cool gaze, one designed to freeze at six paces. "That would be because it's been raining."

"I know a cozy hotel that's not far from here. The owners are discreet." His hand trailed down my cheek. "No one will know we've been there."

I shrugged off his hand, suppressing a shiver even as I took in the heavy and expensive gold band on his ring finger. "I would appreciate you keeping your hands off." The temptation to relieve the pompous man of some of his wealth took flight. Perhaps, I'd do a little research. With the creditors clambering for money, Father and Ben were starting to mutter about jobs. Actually, it was more of a dull roar, but after my last adventure I wasn't in a hurry to repeat the experience.

Beauchamp's ruddy face took on a hard, determined look, one that told me he wasn't going to give up on having me. His next words confirmed my supposition.

"I'm sick of getting the run around from your father. He owes me money, and I intend to collect. You can take the time to talk to me now or face the consequences."

The underlying threat made the fine hairs at the back of my neck prickle. I shrugged and tossed off a carefree laugh. "I'm listening."

"Richard!" a woman called. She waved with an elegance that spoke of a finishing-school education.

I studied her with interest, especially when I caught Beauchamp's wince. To test the theory that flashed through my mind, I said, "Let's walk." I indicated the far end of the graveyard with a jerk of my head. "It's quiet over there.

Only the ghosts to witness our conversation."

"Not here," he muttered. "Meet me at the Admiral's Arms in the village." He checked the Rolex on his left wrist. "Four o'clock. And I'm warning you. Be there or you'll be sorry."

"Richard!" the woman called again. Up close, she appeared older than my first estimate—probably late forties. Her fur coat and diamond earrings put her in a higher income bracket than I.

"Hello," I said, extending my hand in greeting. "A terrible business, this. I feel so sorry for James."

The woman, who I assumed was Beauchamp's wife, raised well-tweezed brows and glared at my hand so hard you'd think I carried anthrax. I glowered back, raising my own brows in a silent stare-down contest. Slowly, she extended her hand and grasped my fingers for a millisecond. It was a wet-fish handshake, the sort that makes you want to run off and wash your hands.

"Millicent, this is Lady Katherine Fawkner. Lady Katherine, my wife Millicent Beauchamp."

"Lady Katherine." The woman inclined her head, the light catching the diamonds in her earrings. Her mouth didn't sneer but she might as well have hired neon signs in Piccadilly Circus. The woman had pigeonholed me as inferior and possibly a threat to her hold on her husband and that was that.

I gritted my teeth and pretended not to notice but

suddenly I was very keen on the idea of relieving the Beau-champs of their jewelry.

"I see an old school friend that I must catch up with. It was nice to meet you," I murmured to Millicent Beau-champ. Turning, I walked away, only acknowledging Richard Beauchamp with a clipped nod. The man was a worm, but he'd piqued my curiosity. I'd meet him at the Admiral's Arms and take things from there.

After a quick glance at the groups of mourners, I headed for the biggest one. I knew a few of the people on the outskirts and hoped to eavesdrop on the ones I didn't know—the mourners that stood beside James Moning.

"Hi, stranger."

I found myself scooped off my feet and wrapped in the arms of a blond man. Before I could even take a breath, he kissed me. His tongue snaked into my shocked mouth.

"My turn," a masculine voice said.

I was handed over like a parcel at a kid's birthday party and thoroughly kissed once again. This time without tongue, for which I was truly grateful.

"Put me down," I gasped. At five-foot-eight, I wasn't exactly tiny, but at the moment, I felt it, and I didn't like the sensation.

Tristram's eyes glowed like a friendly puppy. "How are you, Kate? I haven't seen you for years. My sister told me you were living in France. Are you back home?"

"Give the girl a chance to catch her breath."

Well, he was certainly in a position to know that I needed some air. Some mouthwash wouldn't go astray either. I stared at the blond who'd stuck his tongue half-way down my throat with narrowed eyes before turning back to his friend.

"Hi, Tristram. Yes, I'm back home from France for a while."

Tristram grinned in an affable way. I remembered him as a bumbling young man with good intentions. He hadn't altered, in either temperament or bad judgment, regarding his friends. Simon Grenville. The Honorable Simon Grenville. He hadn't changed much either, still full of slimy, groping moves that left a girl feeling dirty.

"So, you're living at home with your father?" Simon asked.

"That's right." My reply was short and not far from rude.

"You have a daughter, don't you?" Slime oozed from his words despite the charming grin.

I went on high alert. Although, I didn't keep Amber a secret, I didn't go out of my way to tell people about her either. It was a form of self-protection for both of us. Even now, in my aristocratic world an unmarried mother was treated as something dirty and too stupid to live. Abortion was an acceptable means of contraception, especially if it meant keeping the gene pool free of undesirables. That was part of the reason I'd resisted returning home. In France, no one judged.

"That's right," I said. I left my answer short, keeping to the facts.

"What were you doing in France?" Simon demanded. Evidently, strictly the facts weren't enough.

"Looking after my godmother." I shrugged in dismissal. "This is a terrible business. I hope they catch the murderer soon."

"I haven't seen you for years, not since the Christmas ball. Your godmother must have been very sick." Simon persisted with his questions.

"That's right," I said. A casual glance across the surrounding area made the breath freeze in my lungs. Kahu's displeasure seemed to leap across the distance separating us. I was left in no doubt he'd witnessed the kisses. Fury followed swiftly on the heels of shock. Kahu didn't own me. No man owned me. I was my own person and God help anyone who tried to tell me otherwise. Breaking the connection, I turned back to Simon and Tristram. One look at Simon's blond hair and blue eyes and my brain jolted into fifth gear. Exactly why was Simon so interested in my missing years? I wasn't so bigheaded to think that I was truly that memorable. In heart-stopping horror, I tried to superimpose my memory of Amber's features over those of Simon Grenville. The hair was a different color. But the eyes were right.

No, it couldn't be.

But the facts remained. It was highly possible. Shoving

67

aside distaste and loathing, I placed Simon Grenville on my list for future investigation. It felt good to have a name on my list, but I didn't intend to go off half-cocked with my revenge. I'd waited years—a few more days or weeks made little difference in the greater scheme of things.

CHAPTER 6

The Admiral's Arms was your traditional English pub, set in the middle of the mainly Victorian village. Befitting its name, the pub had a nautical theme with low beams, lots of paraphernalia to attract dust, and small, smoky rooms. I frowned when I stepped into the main bar and debated on where to sit. I'd decided to arrive early to scope out the place and jot down my thoughts on paper while the funeral was fresh in my mind. After ordering a coffee, I chose a recently vacated seat in a small wooden alcove facing the door.

If Beauchamp wanted privacy, he had chosen the wrong place for our meeting. The pub was doing a roaring trade since market day fell on Wednesdays. I'd had to fight my way past the men three deep at the bar and definitely wanted a space away from the traffic. I stirred a sachet of sugar into my coffee while I organized my thoughts. The teaspoon clinked against the thick white china mug when I dropped it on the table. I rifled through my black handbag looking for paper and a pen. My bank statement was the only thing at hand in the paper department. The money in my account came to ten pounds, fifty-three pence. I figured I didn't need the reminder.

I wrote.

1. No children. Niece or godchild? Need to search archives at library.

I chewed the top of my pen, and the plastic taste fueled a brainwave.

2. Search the archives at St. Katherine's House.

3. Find out if P. or J. Moning have brothers and sisters. Do they have children?

At this point, I bashed the side of my head with my right palm. I'd been that rattled about finding the photo that I hadn't taken it from the frame and looked at the back. Stupid! It might be inscribed, or at the very least, I'd find out which photographer had taken the portrait. If I had this information, I could question the photographer or if he or she proved stubborn about privacy, I'd search after hours.

Under point 4, I wrote, Suspects. S. Grenville.

I tried to think back to the Christmas party where it all happened and tried to picture the faces of the men or young boys who had been in our group. My mind came up blank. I suspected that I didn't want to remember.

"There you are." Beauchamp slid into the seat beside me, an accusing note in his voice.

I calmly folded up my bank statement and thrust it inside my handbag, zipping it closed so the list wouldn't fall out.

"I didn't hide on purpose." Beauchamp would need to be both blind and deaf to miss my annoyance. "It's busy in here today. I need to get home. Can you say whatever it is you need to say so we can leave?"

"Can I get you a drink?" he asked abruptly. "I sure as hell need one."

"No, thanks," I said, although I could understand his need. Millicent Beauchamp didn't strike me as a woman who stood for nonsense.

Beauchamp stood and brushed against me—on purpose, I'm sure. "Won't be long."

"Take your time," I replied, and I meant it. A niggling instinct screamed that the man was about to tell me something I'd rather not hear.

Beauchamp returned and moved his chair nearer to mine. He took a sip of his drink, whiskey by the smell of it, before setting it on the table.

"Your father owes me money."

"So you've said." Could he tell me something new?

"He's told you, then?" Beauchamp's eyes narrowed on me in expectation.

"Stop playing games and tell me what you want so we can both go home."

"Your father owes me five hundred thousand pounds."

The blunt answer stole my breath. I stared at Beauchamp not pretending anything other than shock. "Half a million pounds?" I whispered. That sort of money deserved the reverence. I'd never seen that amount of money, let alone borrowed it. "Are you sure?"

"Oh, yes. I'm sure," Beauchamp said. "I take it you didn't know?"

I shook my head, still having difficulty forming words. But inside my head, thoughts whirred at breakneck speed. No wonder Father and Ben were pressuring me to do another job. They were up to their necks in trouble, but did they tell me? Their innocent stooge. Oh, no.

I picked up my handbag and stood. Heads were about to roll!

"Where are you going?" Beauchamp scowled. "I haven't finished yet."

"We don't have the money." I could tell by the heat in my cheeks that my face had colored with both embarrassment and a hint of temper.

Beauchamp's voice cracked out sharp and determined. "Sit."

Like a well-trained dog, I sat. "What did you want me to do about the debt?" I asked through clenched teeth. Already, my mind was skipping ahead trying to calculate how many jobs it would take to earn a cool half million.

"The way I look at it is that if your father can't pay, you'll end up fronting the cash."

"I don't have it."

"That's what I figured," Beauchamp said. *No mistaking that tone for anything but smug,* I thought while I waited for the bomb to drop.

"We can work out a deal."

"What sort of deal?" I demanded.

Beauchamp's hand closed over my hand. He gave it a gentle squeeze. "I like you," he said. "We could help each other."

For a moment, I thought I was going to throw up. Deep breaths. One. Two. In. Out. I worked my way through the nausea before risking a glance at his bloated face. "How can I help you?"

He moved his chair closer. "I think you already know," he said. "I can be very generous with women I like."

A momentary twinge of sympathy for other women caught in the Richard Beauchamp trap simmered through me, but I thrust it aside. I needed to concentrate on extricating myself from this mess I'd found myself in through no fault of my own. One thing was for certain—I was going to do some physical damage when I arrived back at Oakthorpe. I forced my mind off that pleasurable thought and back to dealing with Beauchamp.

"Are you saying that if I become your mistress the debt

will be repaid in full?"

Satisfaction flooded his face before an affable smile settled on his mouth. "I'm afraid I can't let you off that easily. No woman is worth half a million in bed. Your father will still owe me the money, but I'll waive the interest charges. How does that sound?"

Words failed me. Many tingled on the tip of my tongue, but I was pretty sure they weren't the words he wanted to hear. I needed to stall.

"I need to talk to my father. I take it you have proof of the debt?"

"I thought you'd require proof." Beauchamp's hand slid into the inside pocket of his jacket and he pulled out a wad of papers. "It's all there." His gaze burned into me for long seconds before he finally spoke again. "I'll give you a week to make your decision."

◊ ◊ ◊ ◊ ◊

"Hi, Katie. Any job prospects?"

Despite the anger that had bubbled and grown during the drive home, I had trouble suppressing a spurt of humor. Hannah made it sound as though I'd been out hunting for a job. Similar to a normal person. The thought jerked me up short, made me focus. The sooner I confronted Father and Ben, the better. "Is Amber home from the birthday party yet?" I knew Hannah was taking extra care but wanted to see her.

Hannah wiped her hands on a towel and checked the clock on the kitchen wall. "She shouldn't be far away. Josh Green volunteered to drop all the children off at their homes afterward. I thought that would be okay."

I nodded, having known Josh since I was a child, but I'd feel better once I could cuddle my daughter.

"She'll be hyper from the sweets and fizzy drinks, no doubt. If she doesn't toss her cookies. Just like her mother, that one," Hannah added in a gruff tone that disguised a heart as big as England.

I sucked in a deep breath, knowing I'd need cunning and guile to corner the terrible trio. I wasn't under any illusion that Hannah knew exactly what was going on. If I showed the slightest hesitation in putting my foot down, the three would trample me. My daughter's future was at stake here. If there was one thing that I wanted for Amber, it was a normal life with a normal job in her future that didn't involve skirting the law.

Strength. Resolve. Determination.

The terrible trio would gang up on me, but since this was my life, my freedom on the line, they'd better produce answers. Pretty damned quick.

"Are Father and Ben around?"

"No."

Was it my imagination or had Hannah hesitated? "Where are they? I need a family meeting. Today," I added in a firm, no-nonsense voice.

Hannah fumbled with the bag of potatoes she'd picked up, and her head jerked in my direction, her blue eyes round behind the lenses of her glasses. "Is something wrong?"

Good try. "I want to speak to everyone together. No sense repeating myself."

"But if the topic is serious enough to warrant a family meeting, I might need to give the matter some thought," Hannah replied.

No flies on Hannah. My impish sense of humor almost got the better of me. "After dinner," I said. "Once Amber's gone to bed. You never said where Father and Ben were. Will they be long?"

"They're at the . . . farmers' market," Hannah said.

Apart from the hesitation, the answer was pretty smooth, but I was on to the terrible trio. Tonight, they'd never know what had hit them. "The farmers' market? Why?" I felt a little mean cornering Hannah like this but decided the practice would come in handy for tonight.

"They're . . . ah . . . doing research! We have lots of excess produce in the garden and they wanted to know if we could sell it to bring in some extra money. Lord knows, we could use it to pay some bills," she said, doing a cross over her heart.

Humph! And the moon was made of tasty cheddar. "Good idea," I said, making a mental note to nab the duo before they could get their story straight with Hannah. If the situation weren't so serious, I'd be looking forward to the verbal skirmish ahead.

◇ ◇ ◇ ◇ ◇

Unfortunately, Father and Ben arrived home while I was giving Amber a bath. I read her a bedtime story and thanks to the running around she'd done with the other kids during the party, she dropped off to sleep pretty quickly. I tugged the covers over her, buzzed a kiss over her forehead, and stepped out of the room.

I was aware of voices in the room we used to watch TV and relax after dinner in the evenings. A wry smile curved my lips. The terrible trio was ready for me, no doubt. I opened the door, and the chatter stopped mid-sentence. Three sets of eyes looked in my direction. They visibly squared their shoulders.

"It's time to do another job." Father fired the first salvo.

"We need the money," Hannah seconded.

"Oh," I said sweetly. "Didn't you make much money at the farmers' market?"

"We went for research," Ben said.

Father nodded in agreement.

I rolled my eyes before nipping in for the kill. "How much money do you owe Beauchamp?"

My father ruffled up like one of Hannah's bantam roosters. "Who said I owed money? It's a lie!"

"That would be half a million pounds worth of lie? Pretty expensive lie." My scorn sliced through Father's bluster.

"But . . . but," he spluttered before glancing from Hannah to Ben and back again.

"It's no good looking at them. I know you owe the money. I have copies of the paperwork with your signature at the bottom."

"We were going to tell you," Ben muttered.

"They're not going to the casino anymore," Hannah said. "They promised me."

"Casino!" I shrieked. I'd been that shocked by the amount of money owed that I hadn't asked the how or wherefores. "You have me running through hoops stealing—"

"It's not stealing," Father said hastily. "It's redistribution of wealth."

"You have me risking my freedom to cover your gambling debts! You're putting Amber in danger." This time it was a definite shriek. My fists clenched and unclenched, the urge to hit someone or something, a siren lure in my brain. I ended up hitting the wall, and it hurt like blazes.

"Ouch!"

Hannah bustled over to me. "Let me see," she ordered, reaching for my hand when I would have hidden it behind my back. "A right mess you've made. Hold still. You're dripping blood."

"She didn't do the wall much good either," Ben noted,

gesturing at the hole I'd made.

"Shut up," I snapped. "One more bill added to half a million is nothing." I took a deep breath, suppressing the urge to strike out at something else. "I want to know the exact total we owe—everything from household bills to gambling debts. Right to the last penny."

Father slumped back into his favorite recliner chair. "All right. We'll sort out the paperwork tomorrow."

"Now," I snapped, "if I have to steal—ah, *excuse* me— 'redistribute' wealth, I want to know the exact total. Once you're done, you can tell me how much we can expect to earn at the farmers' market if we attend every one."

"But we didn't go to the farmers' market to—"

"I know," I interrupted. "But it's a good idea, and it will keep you out of mischief."

"Perhaps the girl has a point. Our vegetables are bigger than John Cowan's. Did you see his pumpkins?"

Father scratched his ear. "Yeah, his carrots were scrawny. Looked anemic to me."

Okay. Call me a masochist, but I had to know. "So if you didn't go to look at the vegetables, what did you go for?"

Hannah huffed and rolled her eyes. "They went to gossip."

"Did not," Ben fired back.

"Did." Hannah planted her hands on ample hips and glared at her husband.

"Market research," Father said with quiet dignity.

I snorted an inelegant sound that stopped the argument short.

Ben shook his head. "That is not attractive."

My eyes narrowed. I was on to them. "Don't change the subject. Market research? All right, I'll buy that, but what sort of market research?"

"Yes, I'd like to hear the local gossip." A wave of familiar lavender water wafted from Hannah as she squeezed broad hips on the settee next to Ben.

"Well, aside from learning that our vegetables are a sight better than those at the market, there was a bit of a to-do about Sid's goat. Mabel got loose and wandered into Marian Alexander's rose garden. Helped herself to some prize specimens." Father smirked during the retelling.

"That would be Mabel you're talking about," I said, fascinated in spite of myself. Village life was the same everywhere, be it France or England.

"Serena and George McKenzie had their garden professionally landscaped. Cost them a bomb to hear George talk. Don't think he was in favor of the idea, but you know Serena."

When Father paused to take a breath, I had to restrain myself from shaking the end of the story from him.

Ben shook his head, the light catching his bald spot. "Glad I'm not married to Serena."

Hannah beat me to the question that begged an answer. "What happened?"

"Last night, someone stole the lot."

Ben nodded. "Every stone, every fancy statue, and most of the plants. I thought George was going to cry."

"Serena did cry," Father inserted. "The local bobbies don't have a clue, and gossip was running hot about who did it and why."

I took one look at their grinning faces and alarm jolted through me. "It wasn't you two?"

Their grins blanked. Hannah leaned forward, her jaw dropping in shock. Three sets of eyes gazed at me full of hurt.

"Hell, no!" Father said, straightening in his recliner. He rubbed his jaw, the stubble prickling loudly in the room. "Although I wish we'd thought of it. There's big money in plants and garden statues."

"Okay. Good." I blew out and upward, hard enough to lift my fringe off my forehead. "That's good."

"The thing is, Katie, they're offering a five-thousand-pound reward for information that leads to a conviction." Ben beamed with enthusiasm. "Charlie and I are going to investigate."

Father nodded. "That's right. You and Hannah can help. Just keep an ear open when you're out and about. Amazing what you can hear at the grocery shop in the village."

Hannah nodded, a thoughtful expression on her face. "Or at Amber's nursery school."

I studied the faces of the terrible trio. Private investigators.

The thought of them snooping around made me shudder. But at least it would keep them out of my way. Maybe. Okay, probably not. "You won't do anything illegal?"

They shook their heads in a definite "who me?" way.

I shook away my unease and returned to the debt issue. "Half a million," I mused. "That translates into a lot of jobs."

"Give it a rest, Kate," Father said.

"Family meeting again tomorrow night," I countered.

Each of the terrible trio glared at me. I grinned, and their scowls darkened.

"Meeting tomorrow night," I repeated.

"Fine," Father snapped. "We can decide on your next job at the same time."

Point and set. While I was thinking about the inevitability of putting my freedom on the line again, the phone rang.

Hannah struggled from the soft cushions of the settee. "I'll get it." She walked briskly over to the other side of the room to pick up the phone. "Hello, Oakthorpe." We all watched her expression for a clue as to the identity of the caller. "Kate? Is this business or personal?"

Hannah placed her hand over the receiver. "It's a man." Her voice held definite glee while my heart took off in a slow canter then gathered into a gallop.

The only male I could think of was Kahu. I sucked in a deep breath. There was no reason for him to ring me.

"Who is it?" Father asked.

"I have no idea." I stood and sauntered over to the

phone pretending a coolness I didn't feel. Inside I felt like a giddy schoolgirl asked out on her first date. "Hello."

"Katie has a boyfriend," Ben said.

"Kate, how are you?"

I turned away from the interested gazes of the terrible trio, closed my eyes and let Kahu's husky voice wash over me. "How did you find my number?"

"I'm a detective. That's what I do. Detect." Laughter filled his voice, inviting me to share the joke, his triumph. Instead, I felt queasy. What would happen if he discovered I was *The Shadow*?

"Hmmm," I said to give myself time to get a grip of my turbulent emotions. Joy that he'd liked me enough to track me down, and pure fear at what he could do to me. My family. My heart.

"I wondered if you'd like to go to the Harlequin ball with me."

Regret grabbed hold of my heart and squeezed. "I'm sorry, but I promised to go with Seth." I tried to tell myself it was for the best. Pity my heart refused to listen.

"Another time," he said. "Save a dance for me."

"Okay." I held the phone cradled next to my ear until I heard the decisive click at the other end. I replaced the receiver and turned to face the uproar.

"Who was that?" Father demanded.

"You've never had a man ring before," Ben added.

"His voice sent shivers up and down my spine,"

Hannah said with a wink. "I hope you said yes to whatever he wanted."

Ben and Father sent Hannah equally aggrieved glares.

"You heard her as well as we did," Father said. "She said no."

"She's going out with Seth," Ben commented.

"Huh!" Hannah snorted. "They generate about as much heat as a snowball at Christmas."

"That's enough," I snapped, quelling further comments with a decisive glare. "The man's a detective. You want *The Shadow* to get that close to a cop?"

"Holy shit," Father said. Ben and Hannah appeared suitably stunned.

"Yeah," I said, suppressing every unruly hormone in my traitorous body. "Sorta like going to bed with the enemy."

CHAPTER 7

The minute I stepped into the kitchen the next morning, the spirited conversation around the table stopped dead. The terrible trio was not about to halt their discussion merely because the subject had presented herself.

"What?" I snapped.

Father shook his head from side to side. Slowly and painfully. "I can't believe a daughter of mine would consort with the enemy."

I ignored the criticism and turned to Amber. "Sweetie, what would you like for breakfast today?"

"Eggs and bacon and toast and milk," she said. "Who is the enemy?" Although she stumbled a little over the word, she knew what it meant. I scowled at the terrible trio in a definite not now manner.

Hannah climbed to her feet. "Little pitchers have big

85

ears," she murmured sotto voice. "Katie, take a seat, and I'll get breakfast for Amber."

I settled Amber and poured her a glass of milk before taking a seat next to Father. "The nursery school is holding their Olympics today. I'm going to help out." I also intended to hit the local library for research. "What are you up to today?"

Ben busied himself slathering jam over a slice of toast. I turned to Father and caught a sliver of unease on his wrinkled face before the poker mask slipped into place. My warning antenna, honed by motherhood, kicked into high alert.

Amber looked up, a milk moustache outlining her mouth. "Grandfather and Ben and Hannah are coming to see me," she announced.

"Are they now?"

"Research," Father said hastily.

"Investigation," Ben stated.

I nodded. This was inevitable. They were going to do what they wanted, no matter what I said.

◊ ◊ ◊ ◊ ◊

The library was an old Victorian building on the outskirts of the village. I pushed open the glass door and stepped inside. Instead of a quiet atmosphere where anything louder than a whisper led the head librarian's wrath to land on your head, it was more like rush hour in Oxford Street.

"Is it always like this in here?" I gasped out after I'd finally made my way to the head of the information-desk line.

"Only on Wednesdays," the young librarian said with a slightly stressed smile. You know, one of those smiles that appear stuck on, and if a stiff wind blows, it'll drop off. "Senior citizens' day," she added.

I made a mental note never to come to the library again on a Wednesday and asked for directions to the newspaper section.

"Over there," she said, pointing with her glazed smile still firmly attached.

"Are you gonna take all day?"

I turned to behold a wizened man who came up to my shoulder.

"Some of us don't have all day," he snapped.

That, I could believe, seeing the way he tottered.

"I have one more question and then the librarian is all yours." By this time, my smile was glazed, and I felt a comradeship with the library staff. "Do you have a genealogy department?"

"In the basement," she answered.

I backed away, then threaded through the mass of aging bodies looking for the stairs. I figured they would have far less traffic than the lifts.

Inside the stairway was cooler and blissfully peaceful. Just the right place to rearrange my plan of attack. I heard the distinct tap of a walking stick. Huh! The place was infested with senior citizens. It was bad enough that I had three at home ganging up on me.

"Arianne is devastated," a woman whispered. It carried up to where I hovered in indecision. "Absolutely devastated."

"She had forgiven Perdita? Last I heard they weren't talking to each other."

Okaaay. Perhaps I'd hit the mother lode. Did I make my presence known and question them, or did I continue to hover in the hope I'd learn something important? The distinct squeak of the door at the top of the stairs forced a decision. I continued down the stairs toward the two elderly women who, judging from the loud taps, were laboriously making their way up the stairs. At the next landing, we met face to face.

Luck was with me. I knew them. "Hello, Mrs. Rodgers. Mrs. Williams. How are you?" Although I knew I'd get chapter and verse about their medical complaints, there was certain etiquette employed when it came to worming information out of neighbors.

"Katherine Fawkner! How are you, dear? I heard you were home from France. How's your dear wee daughter?" Her brown eyes twinkled with curiosity.

Footsteps behind me stalled the questions trembling on my lips. I moved back to let a teenage girl pass. "I'm fine and so is Amber. We're both enjoying being back at Oakthorpe."

Mrs. Rogers nodded and so did her double chins. I tore my eyes from the fearful sight. "I'm sure Charles is glad to have you home."

"Hmmm," I said, although I was positive Father had second thoughts about my being home again. He'd been forced to give up his job, and now I was bossing him around, demanding to know the financial state at Oakthorpe. Nope, it was a pretty safe bet he had a few niggling regrets.

"Father said that the McKenzie's new landscape garden was stolen the other night," I said. May as well steer the conversation in the direction of crime.

"Yes," Mrs. Williams said.

Mrs. Rogers and her chins nodded vigorously.

"I hear they've offered a reward. Has anyone come forward with information?"

"Not that I've heard of but Janet, the landscape gardener is upset. This is the third theft from gardens that she's designed and planted. Business is starting to suffer."

Revenge? Since it was so often in my thoughts, the idea leapt out. A distinct possibility. I'd get Hannah researching on the Internet about local competitors. We could certainly do with the reward money.

"A body's not safe these days," Mrs. Williams stated. "Arianne Jessup's great-niece was murdered last week. Shot in cold blood, and they haven't caught the murderer yet."

"The woman in London?" I asked.

"That's the one," Mrs. Rogers said. "Arianne despaired

of her. We went on a senior citizens' trip into London to take in a show. Who should we see in the theatre but Perdita Moning with another man? Arianne didn't say much, but it definitely wasn't her husband. I hear she used to run around with other men. Quite openly."

"No?" Wow. I'd known she was seeing another man. His identity was still a secret but what if she made a habit of one-night stands? Could some sort of family feud be in play? What if James Moning—no, I discarded the idea almost straight away. The husband would be under immediate scrutiny. Kahu would check that first. My eyes widened at the thought. Exactly when had I started thinking of him as Kahu? I wasn't involved with a man. Uh-huh. Not me.

"Are you all right, dear?" Mrs. Rogers peered at me with concern.

"I'm fine." I glanced at my watch and yelped. "But I'm late for Amber's sports day. Nice to see you both," I added as I turned to head back up the stairs. I'd have to check the genealogy records another day.

◊ ◊ ◊ ◊ ◊

When I arrived at the school, the sports day was in full swing. Father, Hannah, and Ben had arrived a full ten minutes earlier. Father was deeply engrossed in a discussion with two elderly men dressed in identical trousers and waistcoats. They reminded me of slender bookends on a lean. From the intent expression on Father's face, I suspected he was on the case. I was pleased, especially if this helped the transition from active cat burglar to retired.

Ben was questioning an elderly woman. From the way he kept stepping back she was either coming on to him or had a bad case of morning breath.

Hannah was presiding over a cake stall designed to generate funds for the school. I had duly placed my name on the duty roster and so made my way through the throngs of excited children and anxious parents to Hannah while searching for Amber. I caught sight of her and a friend. They were speaking with a tubby man in a suit. Alarm surfaced until I saw Amber's teacher walk up to them and escort both girls to the line for the children running. *Must have been a parent*, I thought in relief.

"There you are," Hannah said. "I thought you'd gotten lost." She sliced a piece of Madeira cake and competently placed it on a paper plate for her customer.

"No, I was thinking about planting a new garden," I said, "so I went to the library to do some research."

"You should have asked me," Hannah said. "Since the computer course at the senior citizens' hall, I can find anything. Besides, it's senior citizens' day at the library. The place is mobbed on a Wednesday."

I stepped behind the stall and accepted a lacy white apron from the woman I was replacing. "I wish I'd known that before I wasted my time."

Her eyes lit up with enthusiasm. "I've been telling Charles and Ben that I can help them. You're more progressive."

From that, I read since I was a female, I'd be on her side. But I didn't laugh. The concept had merit. And perhaps I could think of a way to get Hannah to do some research for me. I poured a mug of tea for a frazzled-looking teacher while I considered the idea. I'd have to be crafty, but I wasn't my father's daughter for nothing.

Once our stint at the cake stall was done, Hannah and I set off to the field where they were holding the children's running races. Amber had been looking forward to this for the last two weeks, and I hoped she wasn't disappointed. But I worried needlessly. Each child who finished a race received a shiny medal, although those that placed first second or third received a special certificate in a ceremony afterward.

"Just like the Olympic Games," Amber said. "The fat man said I looked like a runner." She beamed bright enough to light up Oakthorpe and save us money on the electric as she clutched her precious second-place certificate.

"Shall we go and find Grandfather and Ben?"

"They had plans," Hannah said. "They were working on their investigation."

The fat man. I don't know why, but I felt a distinct warning prickling at the back of my neck. Experience, maybe, but there was nothing I could do to halt the

escalating sensation that felt close to panic. The man I'd
seen talking to Amber might have been totally innocent. I
glanced around the faces and my gaze lit on the man. It
was as though he were waiting for me to see him. When
he was sure he had my attention, he pulled his right hand
from his pocket and fired a pretend gun at me. I knew then
I was right to worry. Today was a warning. Tomorrow, we
might not be so lucky.

◊ ◊ ◊ ◊ ◊

We found bedlam at Oakthorpe when we arrived home.
The police car parked out front should have prepared me.
It didn't.

"Oh, my stars," Hannah said, her hand fluttering to
her chest.

Inwardly, I had a few quivers too, but I wasn't about to
confess. What did they want? I'd covered my tracks the
other night while I was at the Moning house. I was sure
of it.

I pushed the front door extra hard to compensate for
the way it stuck in warm weather. Unbeknown to me,
someone on the other side tugged it at the same time I
pushed. I flew inside like a champagne cork gone wild.

"Whoa, there." Strong, masculine arms caught me before I fell.

Startled, I looked up into a pair of chocolate-brown eyes.

"Hello, Kate." Laughter lurked in his husky voice. "Told you I was a good detective."

I swear I forgot to breathe for an instant there. I definitely had the lightheadedness that went with oxygen deprivation.

"Let go of my mama."

Surprise widened the chocolate-brown eyes. And I suspected this was a first. Not many things surprised the Kiwi cop.

"Are you married?" He loosened his hold and stepped away. I wanted to grab a handful of his linen shirt and drag him close so I could overdose on his wicked, wicked aftershave.

"Kate?" His disapproval finally pierced the spell he'd cast on me.

"I'm not married," I whispered, hurt he'd think that of me when he'd known I was going out with Seth. He'd even asked me about Seth. I guess in the heat of the moment, the appearance of a daughter had really shocked him.

Amber stood plastered to my side, sensing my turmoil. I gently nudged her away so I could walk without danger of tripping. "This is my daughter, Amber," I said. I didn't offer any explanations. I never did since all he needed to know was that I had responsibilities. If my wildest dreams ever came true, he'd have to factor Amber into the equation before I moved an inch further. My gaze arrowed to his face in an effort not to miss any flickering giveaway signs. He regarded me with a somber look. I couldn't read it and didn't have a clue what the man was thinking. Then he smiled, a slow moving smile that crept across his face, highlighting his cute dimples and making the brown eyes sparkle. He crouched down beside my daughter.

"Hello, Amber. I hear you've had a sports day today." He glanced at the second place certificate that my daughter still clutched in her left hand. At least two fingers of her right hand were tucked inside her mouth, a sign of hesitation. "You must have done well."

The beam I'd spoken of earlier reappeared, and just like that, he was her friend. She started chattering in her half-French, half-English patois, and Kahu didn't blink an eye. He chattered back to her.

"What's this? A meeting of the unemployed?" my father groused. A tic worked at the corner of his left eye, a dead giveaway that the appearance of a police car had rattled him. "I thought we'd answered your questions."

Kahu straightened and displayed his earlier gentle expression. "I wanted to speak with Kate."

"She won't know anything. She didn't know that Moning woman."

Kahu's eyes narrowed to slits. "Yes," he said. "She did."

"Why don't we go out to the garden and have a cold drink," Hannah inserted into the sudden silence. "I know I could do with one. How about you, Amber?"

"Lemonade," she said.

"Please!"

"Please."

Hannah and I both spoke at once.

Amber nodded, her pigtails bobbing up and down. "Please."

"Kate, why don't you show the policeman out to the garden, and I'll bring the drinks."

Was it my imagination or had she stressed the word "policeman"? "Sure. You coming, Amber? You can show Kahu your rabbits."

Another test. I admit it, but I'd learned wariness since I'd given birth to Amber. If Kahu wanted recreational sex he was out of luck. The men I'd met since *the* night had done nothing to shift my opinion. Until Kahu. Of course, Seth didn't count since he existed in the category labeled friends. I followed my daughter as she skipped down the passage and through the door that led to the gardens out the back. Kahu walked behind me and I was acutely aware of his presence. My hips developed an extra sway, and the friction of fabric sliding against my skin when I walked sent my awareness to heady heights. I sucked in a deep breath. Mistake. Eau du Kahu assaulted my senses, twirling around inside my head until I felt giddy with it. I burst out of the dim, cool passage into the sunshine.

Amber stopped and turned to Kahu. "Do you want to see my rabbits?"

I held my breath, waiting for Kahu's reply. Would he

pass the test?

"My brother and I used to have rabbits."

Amber cocked her head, her interest caught. "What color?"

"Mine was white and my brother had a black rabbit. We called them 'Salt' and 'Pepper'."

Father pushed past and plunked down on a white garden chair, the air puffing from the padded cushion expressing his outrage.

Ben took possession of the seat beside Father. They looked like twins with lines of disapproval bracketing their mouths. The lines became even more defined when Amber took Kahu's hand and tugged him down the cobblestone footpath to her rabbit hutch.

"You're consorting with the enemy!" Father fired the first shot.

"But such an eye-catching package," I countered.

"Buy another package. Shop around," Ben growled.

Hannah thumped a glass jug of lemonade on the table in front of Father. "Give the girl a chance to explain. I'm sure she has a reasonable explanation for putting the family in jeopardy."

"Mmm." I paused for a beat. "Good old-fashioned lust."

"What about Seth?" Father demanded.

"Yeah, he has a good package," Ben muttered.

We all turned to stare at Ben.

Ben's cheeks turned a dull red. "Well, he's male, isn't he?"

"Enough. There's nothing going on between Kahu and I." *Liar, liar, pants on fire.*

"Kahu, is it?"

Oops. Busted. There was nothing left but to brazen it out. "I have my reasons for associating with the law. All will become clear in time." Oh! Good countermove, Kate. "I need some privacy so I can put my plan into motion." Yep, a stroke of genius.

The terrible trio stared at me with identical expressions of horror and confusion on their faces.

Hannah smiled without warning. "I understand. You're going to use him to help. Inside knowledge."

Father glared. "Huh! Pillow talk, more like."

"Since I'm *it* now, we'll do things my way." I reached for the lemonade jug and carefully avoided meeting inquisitive gazes. The idea of sleeping with Kahu or any man simply for the purpose of extracting information sickened me. And I wouldn't do it. Not even for *The Shadow.*

"Shush! He's coming back," Hannah warned. She poured two more glasses of lemonade and whisked the jug away. "Charles. Ben. I need some help in the kitchen."

A heavy-handed way of leaving us alone. Luckily for me, I still had Amber as a chaperon.

"How were the rabbits?" I smiled at Kahu and Amber, my eyes becoming trapped in Kahu's chocolate-eyed gaze. Warmth and something else, admiration maybe, blazed from his eyes. My skin heated all over, and I found myself

98

fidgeting.

"The rabbits were fine," Kahu replied.

"Amber!" Hannah hollered out the kitchen window. "I've got some lettuce leaves for the rabbits. Would you like to feed them now?"

My chaperon flew off into the kitchen. My heart skipped a beat, my palms moistened.

"Alone at last," he murmured, and he scooted his plastic chair nearer to the one I sat on, close enough that warmth from his hard thigh burned through my black trousers.

Breathing. I'd noticed it had become a problem whenever I was in Kahu's vicinity. Something about him zapped the oxygen from the air, leaving me panting. Yep, that was the problem. I refused to entertain an alternative.

"If you wanted to ask me questions about Perdita Moning, all you needed to do was ask." Focus. Ask relevant questions. Worm information from the man. "Are you close to solving the crime?"

His teasing smile faded. "We have a few leads. I came to ask you out to dinner."

Guilt made me glance toward the kitchen. Three shadowed silhouettes stood at the window, peering out at us. No surprise there. "Dinner?" I repeated, stalling.

"Yeah, you know. Man. Woman. Table. Food."

Longing to experience a slice of normal nipped at me. The man knew I had a child, and he was still asking me out. The cynical devil who'd taken up residence in my soul shrieked loud warnings. *He thinks you're desperate. A sure-fire bet for some fun in the sack.*

"I'm sorry, I can't tonight. I have . . . a meeting." I managed to meet his gaze head on without hesitation. Part of me knew that gentle discouragement was the right way to respond. He presented too many problems.

Kahu frowned. "I know it's short notice. Another night?"

"Are you still going to the Harlequin ball on Friday night?"

"Yeah, I'm going."

My gaze drifted to his mouth, his sensuous lips that begged a woman to come hither. I found myself leaning toward him, attracted like a magnet to metal. Mortified, I froze in place. "I'll see you there," I whispered, lacking the energy to free myself from the Kahu spell.

"That's a promise." His words whispered across my mouth, and he moved in, closing the slight gap between us. Warm lips covered mine, and all logical brain function ceased.

CHAPTER 8

You were kissing him!"

"Give the man a prize," I snapped. Father took a deep breath, no doubt ready to lay down the law about what good cat burglars did and didn't do. I was in no mood for lectures. "Sit. Please," I added. I gestured for Ben and Hannah to take seats in front of the desk beside Father. After deliberation, I'd decided to have the meeting in the office. And I wasn't above using subtle power plays. I sat at the other side of the huge oak desk, a blank paper pad in front of me and a pen in my right hand ready to take notes.

"Right," I said. "A list of bills. Hannah?" She handed me a wad of invoices. I flicked through them, trying not to wince at the totals. "Ben?" He handed over four invoices. "Father?"

Sullenly, he handed over a pile of invoices. One or two of them looked as though they'd been rescued from the rubbish. I studied them, anesthetized to the amounts by now. "Is this all?"

"Yes."

"What about Beauchamp?"

Father muttered under his breath as he climbed to his feet. He stomped from the room.

Theatrics.

Just what I didn't need, so I ignored the distant slamming of doors and pulled out a calculator. The office remained silent apart from the rustle of papers and the tap of calculator keys. The final total seared my eyeballs. I blinked to clear my vision. Same total. I thumped the cancel button and started again. Meantime, Father stomped back into the office.

"Here." He shoved a flimsy sheet of paper at me.

A statement.

The zeros wavered in front of my eyes. Aghast, I sent an accusing glare at my father. "This is more than half a million."

"Interest."

"Tell me you've made progress investigating the garden thefts. We need the reward money."

"Not as much progress as you've made with the bobby," Father said. His tone bordered on snide—a sulky child having a temper tantrum.

102

The provoking tone signaled opinions from others in the room. Loud. They seemed to think that the winner in this competition would be the one that shouted the loudest. Little did they know.

I ignored the verbal knives to concentrate on keeping Oakthorpe and my family out of trouble. My family was important to me. Very important. Even if they argued, told me I was stupid, and stomped about muttering and cursing, I knew that when things were bad they'd be there for me. In a heartbeat. At the moment, knowing that was the only thing keeping me sane.

I coughed loudly to restore the peace. When this failed, I held my fingers to my lips and let out a piercing whistle. Each of the terrible trio turned to gawk at me, their mouths all hanging open like so many gaping carnival-game clowns.

"I've done the sums."

"And?" Hannah said.

I sighed. No point hiding the truth. "The change out of a million won't keep Amber in sweets for a week."

Father's shoulders slumped and the way he rubbed his knee when he thought no one would notice told me his arthritis was giving him jip. Ben seemed just as defeated.

"Here's the plan," I said. "We'll sell our surplus produce at the farmers' market, and I want you and Ben to keep up your investigation." While I didn't hold out much hope they'd have success, at least it would keep them out of mischief.

"What about me?" Hannah asked.

"Internet research and watching out for Amber." I was pleased to note all three had cheered up after being given a task to perform.

"I'll carry on with *Shadow* duties," I added.

My father perked up even more. "Ben and I have a lead for a possible job."

"Yes?" I said, a note of caution creeping into my voice.

"The people that moved into the old Ledbetter estate."

"The pop stars?" Hannah demanded.

Father nodded. "Exactly so. More money than sense. Although why they get paid for that god-awful wailing, I've no idea."

"They've made a right mess of renovating the Ledbetter mansion," Ben snorted. "And they call it modernizing. Butchery, more like."

"Details," I said, cutting in before the conversation diverged even further. "What sort of jewels? Do we have any orders, or can I steal on spec?" Although I'd hesitated over the word steal, I decided there was no point dressing it up.

"The lead singer's girlfriend likes to collect baubles. Prefers diamonds," Father said, "but accepts colored stones as well."

I checked my watch. "I have time to do a recon tonight." From the corner of my eye, I noticed both Father and Ben straighten to alertness. I decided to throw them a bone. "Would you like to come with me? It would speed things up if the three of us divide up the property."

Hannah gave an approving nod while the two men beamed like schoolboys anticipating a treat. A sense of rightness enveloped me. Letting them come along was the right thing to do.

◊ ◊ ◊ ◊ ◊

We parked the Mini about half a mile from the Ledbetter estate and made the rest of our way on foot, dressed in dark clothes to blend with the night.

The estate was originally Georgian with grounds de-signed by Capability Brown. We made our way past an ornamental pond and a faux temple, through a stand of oak before the trees gave way to sweeping vistas in front of the house. In the faint moonlight, the scaffolding looked like an exposed ribcage. Father was right. The modern additions offended my eye. I couldn't wait to see inside. Visions of velvet wallpaper, mirrored ceilings, and large heart-shaped beds popped into my mind.

"Split up and meet back here in half an hour. I'll go to the right. Father, you take the left. Ben, you can check out the security on the driveway."

Father and Ben both nodded. I scanned the wide expanse of lawn in front of us. An owl hooted in a tree behind, the sound low and mournful. *A premonition?* Uneasily, I scanned the open ground again. Would I ever be at ease with the family occupation? I liked to think so since with the huge debt hanging over us there were no other options.

Father and Ben moved away from the protective cover of the trees. Still the sense of unease remained. I hesitated.

A figure flitted past a window, ducking low to avoid detection by the residents of the house.

Both Father and Ben froze, seeing what I'd seen. The figure darted around the corner and disappeared from sight. As one, we melted back into the cover of the trees.

"Who the hell was that?" Father summed up the situation with a few terse words. Who indeed?

"Common garden thief?" Ben asked, scanning the area where the mystery man had disappeared.

I studied my father's reaction and what I saw worried me. I guessed at his thoughts. We didn't need the competition. No matter who it was or what they were doing.

Father's frown ran the width of his face. "We need to find out."

"Okay, what's the plan?" Although I was now *The Shadow*, I didn't mind taking advice. Father and Ben had years of experience between them, handed down by my grandfather and Ben's father and their fathers before them. If I had to take over the family mantle, I intended to do a good job.

"We need to get closer," Father said. "Watch and assess the damage. Once we know what we're dealing with we can go from there."

"Split up and meet back here in half an hour?" I suggested.

Ben nodded. "Yeah."

"Yeah." Father fairly vibrated with the need to investigate.

"Let's go." I took one step from the shelter of the trees and stopped. "Take care."

We melted into the shadows, separating once we approached the open lawn area again.

There was a camera under the eaves in front of me. I made a note of the location on the map inside my head. A pleasant jingle-jangle buzzed through my veins when I edged along the cage of scaffolding and eased into the shadows. The soft sound of a foot scuffing the ground alerted me to a presence heading in my direction. I tugged my balaclava over my face and waited.

The man flitted past me, not more than a few feet away. Dressed in black and wearing a mask that covered his whole face, he could have been my twin. My heart sank. This was no amateur. The way he held himself and moved with confidence suggested he had researched the property and knew it intimately. This person knew exactly what he was doing. I noted the small nylon bag he carried. It bulged. The cat had done his night's work.

I waited for ten minutes until I was sure he wasn't going to return, then darted along the side of the building.

An open window, on the ground floor, signified the cat's method of entry. Surely, he wouldn't be so stupid as to leave it open. That would attract attention. An owl hooted and a shiver worked down my spine even as I cupped my hands around my mouth and made an answering call. Father and Ben joined me minutes later.

"Did you see him?" Father questioned.

"The cheek of him, horning in on our territory," Ben fumed.

I didn't have the heart to remind him that this cat ranged over a wide territory. The other man probably didn't know of my existence especially since the police assumed the Moning thefts were tied up with Perdita's murder.

Father and Ben continued to mutter. I cut in with a reality check. "We might as well continue with the skullduggery. The cat's left us a window of opportunity." I gestured up at the open window with my head. "What do you think? Should I go in?"

Father stared up at the window, his eyes narrowed in consideration. Although I'd already made my decision—I was going in—the show of tact made Father and Ben feel a valuable part of the team. And when they felt important, they wouldn't be inclined to do anything stupid such as attempting a job on their own. That was the theory anyway.

"I think you should go inside."

Father nodded agreement. "We don't know what the man took. It's possible we could salvage something and come away with a prize." His eyes gleamed, and I held back an answering grin. "I'm guessing the lights are on timers. That can only make your sortie easier."

"Let's do it," I said, the slow burn of adrenaline making itself felt. For fleeting seconds, I worried about addiction to the thrill, but I forced the thought away. Instead, I immersed myself in the situation and applied everything I'd ever learned from Father and Ben.

The inside of the gutted home was every bit as bad as the outside suggested. The Victorian-period rose wallpaper had been stripped and lay in tattered piles on the floor. White sheets shrouded the remaining furniture. Cautiously, I slid my leg over the sill and slipped into the room. Immediately, I became aware of a faint thumping sound—the sort of sound that stereo speakers make when they're switched up too loud. An annoying thud that rattled the listener's ears.

I crept from the room and out into a passage. As I neared the end, I realized the thumping noise was my hosts practicing. Up close, it didn't sound much better, but at least it was keeping the occupants busy. I drifted through a series of rooms, adding details to my mental map. At the bottom of a flight of stairs, I hesitated. If I met someone walking down, I was in trouble. I decided to risk it. At the top of the stairs, I drew in a huge breath hoping to slow my racing heart. But not for long. The longer I remained inside, the greater the risk of discovery. My lips curled upward in a mocking sneer, the dark humor directed inwardly. Or meeting a dog. If I looked in a mirror, the teeth marks in my butt were still visible. No how, no way did I have a desire to repeat the undignified experience of applying iodine to my ass.

The second floor was untouched at present. Victorian wallpapers still covered the walls. The visible furniture looked more modern. Lighting was poor, and I slowed to allow my eyes to adjust. Several doors led off the landing. I chose the second one at random. A strong perfume assaulted me—something heavy and seductive, reminiscent of the Orient. I held my nose until the tickling in my nose faded. Not the time to sneeze. Taking slow, easy breaths through my mouth, I stepped through the door and pushed it to after me so it was slightly ajar, ready for a quick exit. My eyes adjusted rapidly. An empty bed. I flicked on my torch and shone it across the dresser. A jumble of expensive makeup containers and elegant perfume bottles littered the surface. I slid open a drawer and came up empty. Our mysterious friend had already relieved the inhabitant of her glittery baubles. I switched off my torch, blocked another sneeze, and edged through the door back onto the landing. I checked the rest of the rooms. All were empty apart from the last one where a baby lay in a crib. I checked my watch. Already, half an hour had elapsed. Father and Ben would be restless. I decided to do a quick sweep of the downstairs rooms farthest away from where the musicians were playing and call it a night.

I approached the stairs with caution and hurried down once I knew the foyer and the landing were clear. I ignored the room with the open window and tried the others. The kitchen. A small pantry off the kitchen. The door at the far end of the passage past the kitchen was closed. I hesitated, unsure of whether to proceed or not. Not a scrap of light shone under the door but that didn't reassure me. The door handle was metal. I bent to one knee and peered through a keyhole. I couldn't see a thing. The key was in it. Tightening my lips, I stood again and reached for the handle. The loud creak made me curse under my breath. In the almost silent house, it sounded like the crash of thunder. I opened it and leapt in fright when a broom jumped out at me, hitting me on the shoulder. Muttering under my breath, I shoved the broom back into the cupboard and locked the door.

I moved into the formal entrance way, my soft-soled shoes noiseless on the Italian marble tiles. Once again, the lights were on. I approached with caution, sliding against the painted wall and peeping around the corner before I stepped into the spacious formal dining room.

My mouth dropped open on seeing the décor. Queen Victoria would turn in her grave or at least run screaming for bolts of material to hide the naked nymphs cavorting on the walls. The interior designer had taken inspiration from Italy, using terracotta tones, furniture with spare lines and sculptures. I scanned the walls. Apart from the wall with the mural, they were bare. Strange. I took a closer look. Two small tacks were embedded in the wall—about the right distance apart to support a medium-sized painting. The burglar hadn't taken the framed pictures with him, but I'd bet he'd taken the rolled up canvases with him.

I glanced about the room, trying to work out what else he might have taken. Jewelry from the bedrooms, maybe. The paintings. I walked around a leather couch and paused by a round pedestal table. A table empty apart from a business card. I bent closer and picked it up with my gloved hand. My brows rose, and I felt a grin tug at my lips. How interesting. The business card was black with a silver cat embossed on the front. I turned it over but the back was blank. My grin widened. At least the card confirmed our suspicions. We had a competitor. A competitor with an ego.

I scanned the room again just in case I'd missed a small token to sell. But no, it didn't look like our competitor had missed a thing. After checking my watch for a second time, I decided to have a quick look in the room next door before leaving.

Easing the door open, I listened for foreign sounds. Nothing. I slipped through the door and pulled out my torch. The thin beam played over a laden bookcase and a large oak desk. An office. Once I'd ascertained the office was empty, I switched on a small desk lamp and turned slowly to check the room. I pulled out several of the desk drawers. Bingo! Our pop star was a medal collector. Each of the drawers on the right-hand side was velvet lined with a selection of medals. Judging by the neat labels inside, some of them were very old. And I hoped, valuable. I lifted out several of the medals awarded during the older campaigns and lifted the velvet lining out to wrap them inside. The need to whistle a jaunty tune sprang from no-where and I barely managed to suppress it. This would ease a little of the Fawkner financial burden and bring a smile to the children's charity I'd chosen as my benefactor.

◊ ◊ ◊ ◊ ◊

"What took you so long?" Father demanded.

"We can discuss this later. At home," Ben muttered. "We've spent long enough in this vicinity. The hairs on the back of my neck are a-pricklin'."

I agreed. "Okay." I, too, had a sensation of approaching danger. I didn't intend to dally to find out the source.

As one, we moved stealthily across the lawns and melted into the shadowy darkness of the trees. Once there, some of the tenseness in my shoulders left. We made good time to the car. At the edge of the trees, we paused by mutual consent to check there was nothing out of the ordinary waiting for us. I peeled off my jacket and threw it on the back seat of my Mini.

"What happened?" Father asked once we were driving down the road.

"How much do medals fetch on the black market? First World War and earlier."

Father's head whipped around so quickly it was a wonder he didn't suffer whiplash. "Medals? Did you find some?"

I allowed smugness to slither across my face. Probably wasted when the light was so dim inside my car, but I still savored the feeling of surprising my father. "Yeah, I did. Do you have a contact to shift them? They're inside my jacket if you want to see them."

"Better not," Father said, although it was obvious by the tone of his voice that he wanted to look. "Just in case we get pulled over by the bobbies. Best keep them hidden until we arrive home."

I concentrated on driving at the speed limit and avoided the main roads as much as possible. I let Father and Ben off at the front door and drove the Mini around the back to park in the garage.

When I walked into the kitchen, Father and Ben were already seated around the table. I pulled out a chair and slid into it.

"Tea?" Hannah asked.

"Please." I unwrapped the four medals and handed them to Father and Ben. The metal crosses and coin shapes depicting the monarch of the day looked tarnished but the writing was still visible, and I knew better than to try cleaning them. I waited until they'd studied the medals and asked, "Worth selling?"

"Good work, Kate," Father said.

I grinned. High praise indeed. "There was something else," I said.

Father and Ben looked up from perusing the medals, Hannah from her mug of tea.

"This," I said, handing over the calling card with flourish. "The burglar left it."

"A business card." Father flipped it over to study the back. "No note on it anywhere."

"They're going to be annoyed when the press doesn't mention their calling card," Hannah observed.

"Yeah." I looked at Father waiting for his reaction.

He set the card on the table in front of him and scratched the bald patch on his head, a thoughtful look on his face. Finally, he said, "The competition is going to make life difficult. No reason for us to take this without fighting back. I think we should have our own calling card. And if we double up on targets again, we'll replace this calling card." He flicked the card with his forefinger. "With a symbol of our own—a black silhouette."

CHAPTER
9

The date for the Harlequin ball rolled around. I'll admit I wasn't in the best frame of mind to attend a ball. I wanted to continue with my investigation into the mystery child. Instead, Father and Ben had me in intense training and each night we went to check out prospects that Hannah had found on the net or Father or Ben had heard about via word of mouth. In short, I ached all over from the physical toll of the jobs, the constant fitness training, and my temper having constantly simmered on steady boil.

Seth and I drifted into the private ballroom in Surrey with a group of other guests. Seth touched my left arm, and guided me around a group of friends who had stopped to chat. A woman stepped back straight into my path. Seth jerked me to a stop to avoid a crash. Pain rippled down my arm. I gritted my teeth but a small protest emerged.

"Sorry. I didn't mean to hurt you." Seth tugged me over to a piece of clear wall space, a look of grave concerned on his tanned face. "You all right? You look pale."

I nodded since I could hardly tell him I'd fallen early this morning while breaking and entering. My father had let me know about my incompetence already. "I tripped over one of Amber's dolls," I said, with barely a blink at the lie. "Do you have plans for tonight?" I asked in a change of subject. Tonight I needed to find a target and contact Father so he and Ben could start researching the job. Actually, several targets would be better since another batch of bills had arrived today. So tonight, I was the party girl. The stereotypical ditzy blonde who flirted, laughed a lot and danced with as many men as possible. *Joy*, I thought with a trace of bitterness. Right at this moment, I'd prefer to soak in a scented bath filled to the brim with bubbles.

I glanced at the attendees as they ambled past us. A matching sapphire-and-diamond tiara and necklace grabbed my attention. My gaze shot to the woman's face. I turned away, even as I marked the jewels a distinct possibility. "I don't know many people here tonight."

Seth shrugged, unperturbed. After all, he'd disappear soon. "Let's go and find a drink." He cleared the way through the crowd, and I hobbled after him. In the short time I'd stood still, my muscles had grown stiff. The aches and pains were becoming worse as the day progressed. Deep

117

down, I knew I'd have to take one of the painkillers Hannah had pressed on me. Even if I hated giving up control of any element of my life, tonight I'd have to compromise.

We made our way through the crowded passage into the ballroom. Four crystal chandeliers cast light over the occupants and a fifth, right in the center of the ballroom ceiling sparkled like hundreds of stars. Red velvet curtains shielded the windows while hundreds of vases were filled with greenery and white roses. Their scent filled the air. At the far end of the room, a string orchestra played soothing music. At least they looked like they'd stick to the slow stuff. I didn't think my poor, abused body would handle anything faster than a slow waltz.

"No bar," Seth said, turning to study our surroundings.

"There're probably waiters circulating with food and drink," I said. I, too, peered at the various exits from the huge ballroom. "I wonder where the ladies' room is located."

Seth grinned. "Can't help you there. Why don't I wait over there?" He pointed to a grouping of empty chairs. "I'll round up drinks and food while you go exploring."

Never a truer word spoken. Because exploring was exactly what I intended doing. "See you soon." I moved off, trying to keep my gait smooth and easy without too many abrupt stops. My gown tonight was a white sheath with a slit to ease walking but even so small steps were all I could take. In hindsight, probably not the best gown to wear if I ended up doing any climbing. Since money was tight, my gowns were constantly recycled and remade to look different. If I ended up hiking up the dress to my hips, then so be it. My underwear was the practical cotton type.

I drifted through the crowd, keeping an eye out for jewels and Kahu Williams.

"You keep away from that cop," Father had ordered in a terse whisper when Seth had picked me up. "You stick to a dependable man like Seth who won't give you any grief."

Little did he know, but I wasn't about to inform Father otherwise. He was old-fashioned that way.

"Kate." Like a genie summoned, he appeared right in front of me. His husky voice sent a ripple of awareness through my aching body.

"Kahu." I nodded and inhaled deeply. The woodsy pine scent surrounded me, making me a trifle lightheaded. And definitely slow-witted. "I . . . um . . . I'm looking for the . . . um . . . restrooms."

A slow grin curled across his lips, echoing in his eyes. "You've come to the right person then. Didn't your mother always tell you to ask a policeman for directions if you were lost?"

"You know where they are?" I didn't like the breathless quality to my voice, but at least I'd managed to string several words together without stuttering.

Diamond necklace at ten o'clock, I noted absently. Maureen Glasson. Hmmm. Matching bracelet. And earrings.

Kahu leaned closer. My attention wandered from the

119

scenery back to him. His lips.

"If you keep looking at me like that, I'm going to kiss you."

"Seth's here," I said. More as a warning to me than Kahu.

"Tell Seth you're going out with me."

Now that would really be thumbing my nose at Father. Although tempted, I wasn't stupid either. "Seth is my friend. I don't want to hurt him."

"But you'd hurt me?"

"I really need to find the restrooms," I muttered, edging away from the suppressed emotion snapping in his brown eyes. I was unable to hide a wince as I turned away.

"Are you hurt?" Despite my rudeness, concern shaded his voice.

"A bit stiff. I fell over one of Amber's dolls." The lie fell easier the second time.

"This conversation isn't finished." His eyes met mine and held the contact. He reached over and smoothed a lock of hair off my face, tucking it behind my ear with such gentleness it brought a lump to my throat. I wanted to cry. The wrong time. The wrong place. Sometimes life sucked. Because, if there was one thing I was sure of, it was that this man had all the qualities of the right one.

I walked away and climbed the set of stairs without replying although it cost me. My body ached something fierce. I noticed a woman walking briskly down a passage to my right. She seemed to know where she was going so

I followed. My pace was much slower, and soon she disappeared around the corner of a long passage. When I turned the corner, she was nowhere in sight.

This wasn't the way to the restrooms. That was for sure. Either the woman was familiar with the house, or she was being plain nosy like me.

A group of family portraits on the wall snared my attention. The photo I'd found in the Monings' bedroom was a studio shot, but for some reason, there had been no photographer advertising on the back. I scanned the different shots. The one at the end made my eyes widen.

Footsteps behind me made me hesitate. Did I hide or pretend I was lost? Soft voices aided my decision. I opened the door to the room just past the portraits and slipped inside. Luckily, it was empty. A guest bedroom; and judging by the disarray and the faint scent of lavender, it was currently in use by a friend or family member attending the ball. Conscious of the rising Fawkner debt, I made a rapid search while my mind returned to the photo, trying to work out what had tugged at my memory. I scooped up a pretty necklace and debated whether to pocket it. No. With Kahu around it wasn't the wisest thing to do. I set the necklace back down on the dresser and stepped over to the door. After slipping it open to ensure the passage was clear again, I limped out closing the door firmly behind me.

When I was halfway along the passage, a figure appeared at the end. There was no time to run.

"Kate, what are you doing up here?" The mystery woman from earlier was my acquaintance Jemima. It was possible she was a personal friend and staying the night.

I shrugged and aimed for a bright smile. "I'm afraid I have the sense of direction of a homeless puppy. Hence, I'm lost. I was looking for the restrooms."

"The restrooms are on the ground floor," Jemima said.

I had no idea what she was thinking. The woman would make one hell of a poker player.

I expelled my breath in a loud huff. "Can you give me directions? I couldn't find them. I asked one of the waiters. I'm sure I got the directions right."

"I'll show you," Jemima said. Although she didn't utter another word as we walked down the flight of sweeping stairs, it was clear from her body language that she wasn't pleased. Displeased with me or someone else? The thought popped into my head when I glanced across at Jemima. Her pale face still gave nothing away.

"I've been flat out lately," I said, deciding to go for the chatty, blond, bimbo self. "What with looking after my daughter and keeping up things at Oakthorpe, I don't have much time. How about you?"

"I keep busy," she said.

Doing what? I wanted to demand because it had occurred to me that I didn't know much about her. She'd introduced herself at one of the earlier balls in the season.

The music and chatter grew louder when we approached

the ballroom.

"Jemima." A man caught her by the forearm and drew her to a halt. I didn't know his name, but he looked familiar.

Jemima jerked away from his touch. "Leave me alone."

Curious, I glanced at her face. I caught a glimmer of anger before her face blanked again.

"The restrooms are through that door there." She pointed to another exit on the far side of the crowded ballroom. "The first door on the right."

She wanted to get rid of me. Actually, make that both of us, but the set frown on the man's face told me she was in for a fight if she thought she could brush him off. Questions. They pounded me. What had Jemima been doing up on the second floor? Who was this man? And why was she so eager for us to leave?

"Have you got the directions straight?" The impatience in her voice prodded me to action. And unfortunately, there was no alternative. I had to leave. Sighing inwardly, I forced a smile. "Thanks. Will I see you later? We never have a chance to chat."

She lifted one shoulder in a casual shrug. "Sure."

The offhand manner puzzled me, but I let it slide. I had more important things to focus on at the moment. If I didn't contact Father and Ben soon—

The subtle prickling sensation you feel when someone's staring hit me. I smiled at Jemima and her mystery man. "Thanks for the directions." I turned away, doing a subtle surveillance of my surroundings at the same time.

Seeing no one to account for my uneasiness, I threaded through the chattering crowds taking note of the different gemstones on the way. Emeralds. A definite possibility. An old-fashioned setting, but as long as the stones passed inspection, the piece had definite promise.

I aimed for a gap between two groups. Without warning, the opening closed. A male body collided with mine. I choked back a pained cry as my muscles tensed.

"Hello, what have we here?" a man slurred.

Drunken oaf. I grimaced at the wave of alcohol fumes and attempted to sidestep his wandering hands. He grabbed me, but I was ready for him and stomped on his foot. My captor cursed and let me go so quickly I stumbled. A familiar scent hit me at the same time a pair of hands grabbed me to halt my fall. Kahu Williams. Out of the frying pan into the fire. He gently propelled me through the crowd and through an open door leading to a small walled garden.

"You okay?"

"I'm fine." The nighttime air whispered across my bare shoulders. I shivered.

"Cold?" Kahu drew me close to his side so his body heat seared through me. For an instant, I tensed. *No one is watching.* I relaxed and sank into his embrace just as my traitorous body demanded. "Do you know," Kahu murmured, his breath wafting over my ear. "If I didn't know better, I'd say you were avoiding me."

I made the mistake of looking up at him. Oh, boy. Confidence blazed from his face. He knew the attraction wasn't one-sided. And he wanted me to know he knew. A roguish smile played across his lips. Soft lips. Masculine lips. I swallowed. Breathe! While my brain gave the order, my rebellious, traitorous body laughed. *Go with the flow, girl.* I swear my hands moved of their own accord. My brain sure as heck didn't issue orders to ruffle his dark hair and whisper in his ear.

"My father warned me about men like you," I murmured, my fascinated gaze held in thrall by his mouth. I wanted to kiss him in the worst way. As I watched, the corners of his mouth kicked up. My cell phone vibrated inside the tiny purse I had strung over my arm. Ignoring it, I studied the shape of his mouth.

"Did he tell you about the sex? How good it will be?"

My gaze jerked away from his mouth. My brain sent urgent warning signals, but once again, they were ignored. Warmth flowered in places that had no business blooming. I leaned against Kahu, my breasts colliding with a hard muscular chest. I bit back a moan as lust took hold of my brain.

"We could leave," he said in his antipodean drawl. His left hand smoothed across my bare shoulder while the right took a slight detour. One forefinger traced across the swell of my breast where skin met strapless gown. "What do you say?"

Duty battled mightily with desire and finally emerged the winner. "I can't," I said, not bothering to hide my regret. It was too late for false modesty.

Kahu bent his head until our foreheads brushed. "Somehow, I thought you'd say that."

My held breath exited with a whoosh. I'd expected irritation at the very least, but instead the ever-present humor lurked in his drawl.

"I'm sorry." The words were inadequate given the circumstances, but what could I say?

"At least let me have a kiss?" His finger made a return journey across the swell of my breast. The instinct to turn a little so my breast nestled in his hand reared up to taunt me. I trembled, and he must have taken my body's instinctive reaction for one of agreement.

Kahu stepped away but retained hold of my right hand. He led me into the dark shadows at the far end of the balcony. In the dim light, away from prying eyes, my bravado increased. Oh, yes. I wanted his kiss in the way I needed my next breath.

Kahu cupped my face in his hands. My heart spluttered briefly before bursting into a mad gallop with no finish line in sight. I wondered if I might expire before my heart learned to pace itself.

"A real kiss," he whispered against my lips.

Before I could take a breath, or answer or even think,

his lips covered mine. No tentative kiss, this, but a full-blown statement of intent. His lips moved slowly, urging me to participate. With no experience to fall back on, I went with what felt natural. My hands crept up around his neck to clasp Kahu tightly to me. When his tongue swept across the seam of my lips, I opened my mouth. He tasted of mint, he smelled of the fresh outdoors. I was in mortal danger of losing what little control remained. My breasts ached, my nipples rubbing against the silky fabric of my dress in a silent demand to yield. I kept my thoughts north of my waist. To wander any further equaled sheer madness. I valiantly ignored the masculine hardness pressing against my belly. Kahu had already stated his wants. His body only reinforced his words.

Slow. He did everything slow and easy. A problem since my body had plenty of time to savor and appreciate and hijacked me before my brain exerted control over the lust that fogged good sense.

"Is she out there?"

I gasped deep down in my throat and wrenched my lips away from Kahu's. Resentment made me frown, my hands balled to fists at my sides. One romantic interlude about to come to a screeching halt. Kahu and I stepped out of the shadows and turned in the direction of the door.

"Kate! I've been looking for you everywhere," Father snapped. He marched up to us and fixed us with an accusing glower. Seconds later, Ben stood beside him. Two of the terrible trio scowled at me, unable to do more without tipping their hand to the enemy. They looked like irritable penguins in their evening finery. *Or frustrated gargoyles*, I thought with another wave of exasperation.

"Did you want something?" I asked, even though it was obvious they did.

"I wanted to introduce you to our new neighbors," Father said.

Check.

"And Josephine Montgomery is looking for you," Ben said. "She wants you to model in her charity fashion parade next week."

Checkmate.

There was no way I could afford to turn down that opportunity. Sighing, I turned to Kahu in apology.

"It's all right." He brushed the curl I'd left to dangle loose away from my face and tucked it behind my ear. "Next time." With a last intimate smile, he walked off, disappearing into the ballroom.

"What were you doing with him? I thought we'd decided he was too dangerous," Father snapped.

"Don't hold back on my account," I said, folding my arms across my tingling breasts.

"Give her a chance, Charles. Let Kate explain before you bawl her out."

"Thank you," I said, not bothering to hold back on the sarcasm. I was so angry I didn't make excuses. I went with the truth. "I was kissing him because he's sexy, and he turns me on, and he makes me want him."

Father held his hands up palms facing me in a definite stop signal. "Too much information!"

"Well, if you want to poke your noses into my affairs, you'll get information." By this time, my lips were quivering with suppressed laughter because I'd recognized how ridiculous the conversation was. Discussing my sex life with my father and Ben. Hmmm. Laughter spilled from me in rib-tickling snorts. Father and Ben shared a speaking glance before they succumbed and joined in the hilarity.

When we finally settled down, the air was well and truly cleared. Time for business. I checked for potential eavesdroppers and when I found the coast clear, I made my report. A list of possible targets.

Father and Ben nodded at several of the names I mentioned so I presumed I'd done okay.

"Some of the guests are staying here overnight," I murmured in a low voice. "You know what these balls are like. They'll make a weekend of it. The women will have their jewels on show, but I'm betting the security won't be as good as what they have at home. Would it be possible to hit here over the weekend?"

Father nodded slowly. In the faint light that spilled from the ballroom, I saw the gleam of excitement in his blue eyes and the faint wash of it in his cheeks. I gave a mental cheer. Score one for the trainee.

"I bet that some of the women brought several outfits with them along with matching jewelry and accessories," Ben said, looking to Father. "What do you think? Send Kate to look?"

"No," Father said. "That policeman is interested in you. If he sees you leave the ballroom, he's liable to follow. I think Ben and I could handle this one."

A protest formed at my lips and died. "How are you feeling?"

"I'm a bit stiff," he admitted. "But we don't have to do any climbing. We're already inside. All we need to do is find jewels and pocket them if they warrant it. Then we can walk out as calmly as you please."

I nodded. Father was capable and since Ben was present to help, they would get the job done more quickly than I could without the danger of Kahu appearing out of the woodwork. "The only thing that worries me is if the police question all the guests once the crime is discovered."

"Ben's not on the guest list. And I've noticed a few others that don't usually get invitations to private balls."

I nodded again. The ballroom had seemed full, in old-fashioned terms—a squeeze.

"All right. What do you want me to do meantime? And how long do you think it will take?"

Father smirked. "I've been here before," he said. "Let's just say I know one of the ladies of the house rather well."

"Whoa," I said, holding up my hands in front of me.

Father chucked while Ben guffawed. I had no choice but to join in the laugh-fest.

When our unrestrained laughter had faded to smirks, we made our final plans and checked that watches matched.

Although trepidation wafted through me at the thought of letting Father and Ben do the job, I forced myself to let them wander off into the crowd. I'd seen how excited Father was at the idea of being useful. Besides, it would make it that much easier when I went off on the next job and left the terrible trio at home. They wouldn't feel quite as left out and useless.

I needed to find Mrs. Montgomery before she decided to give my spot to someone else, and next I needed to check out more jewels.

During the next hour, I resisted the need to glance at my watch every five minutes. I accepted several requests to dance but never danced more than one dance with the same man. I didn't intend the men to receive any mixed messages. My current partner and I traversed the dance floor in a sedate waltz that suited my bruises just fine. He'd asked me a question right when I spied Father and Ben arrive at the double doors that led into the ballroom.

"Kate?" The man prodded for my attention.

I gave an absent smile while I craned my neck to check out their faces during the next twirl. Had they been successful? At least I knew they hadn't been caught in the act.

"Kate?" the man asked again.

"Yes," I replied still trying to decide if the venture had garnered jewels.

"Great!" The jubilation in my partner's voice snagged my undivided attention. What had I agreed to?

"I'll ring you with the details closer to the time. You're at Oakthorpe, right?"

Sighing, I resigned myself to what sounded like at date with the man who still remained nameless. I stepped into the blond-bimbo act that I was beginning to really loathe. "That's right. I look forward to the call," I said, lying through my teeth. "What date did you say? I'll write it in my diary. Um . . . as long as it's free, of course!" Oh, what a tangled web we weave. The timeworn saying fit like my favorite pair of formal black shoes.

The music came to an end.

"Another dance?" my partner asked.

"I'm sorry," I said, determined to be gracious in my defeat. "I promised this dance to Seth. And I see my father wants me for something." I wriggled my fingers in Father's direction and let a tinkling laugh loose.

"I'll ring you," he repeated.

All I could do was grit my teeth and smile. As I walked over to talk to Father and Ben, an announcement was made that supper was ready in the adjacent room.

"I think I might go home," Father said, raising his voice.

"Don't you want to stay for supper?" I'd caught on to his ploy and the hidden message beneath. The heady taste of success brought lightness to my step. "You not feel well?"

"What do you expect? I'm old, aren't I?"

I pasted on a bright smile and silently acknowledged the sympathy of the woman beside me. "Would you like me to come home with you?"

"I'd never hear the end of it," Father muttered, playing the grump to the fullest for his audience. "Stay. Ben will take me home."

"If you're sure." I brushed a kiss over his cheek and smiled at Ben. In an undertone, I added, "I'll see you tomorrow morning.

Father and Ben made their way from the ballroom. Father walked in a slow, almost agonized gait, giving the appearance of extreme pain. No doubt about it. He was good.

I trailed after the rest of the guests into the room where they'd served supper. The first person I saw was Seth who was talking to Kahu of all people. Live dangerously. *Why not?* I thought, and sailed over to them with a vapid blond-girl grin on my face.

Kahu grinned. "You're wearing your bimbo smile. Who's been annoying you?"

My mouth dropped open in shock and both men laughed out loud. In other circumstances, it might have been funny but today, it was downright dangerous. Was I that easy to read?

"My bracelet!" A middle-aged woman dressed in a

black designer gown swung around in a rapid circle. "I've lost my bracelet. Do you see it on the floor?" she asked the circle of friends who stood nearby.

I checked the area around us but saw nothing because people kept moving. Instead of searching the floor again, I watched the ball attendees. No one looked guilty of palming it for later private use.

"The woman probably lost it," a bored voice said.

I turned my head to see Jemima. She seemed happier than when I'd seen her earlier, and the glint of triumph in her eyes made me wonder if she were meeting a man.

"Do you know her?"

"Geraldine Palmer. She has a brain the size of a gnat. The catch was probably loose and it's fallen off in her bedroom. She's staying overnight so the bracelet is probably fighting with dust bunnies under the bed."

She sounded so cynical I had to laugh. "Yeah?"

"Yeah," she said. "Lord, I hope they hurry up the food. I'm starving."

"Well, stay away from chocolate," I said, waving my forefinger in the air in a chiding manner. "It's not good for the figure."

Jemima smoothed imaginary creases on her skintight sea-green dress. "Never catch a man if my dress is bursting at the seams," she cooed.

We stared at each other for a moment before bursting out laughing.

"What's the joke?"

The laughter froze on my face. Octopus Beauchamp. That's all I needed right now when both Seth and Kahu were busy helping the hysterical woman look for her bracelet. A hand smoothed over my bottom, and I reacted instantly, shifting my high heel and placing it squarely in the middle of a highly polished black shoe. Beauchamp let out an unmanly squawk that drew the attention of most of the men and women standing around us. A faint wash of color stained his cheeks. Jemima caught my eye and smirked. I grinned back enjoying the moment. I was starting to like this girl even though she watched my chocolate intake.

"Shall we?" she asked, indicating the clear path to the buffet table.

"Definitely," I chirped, firmly in my blond-bimbo skin. "You know, I could really do with some chocolate. That man leaves a very bad taste in my mouth."

"That's not all he wants to put in your mouth," Jemima retorted.

A gasp escaped me. Not a lot I could say to that. Not a lot that I wanted to say about that. I shivered at the thought of sex with Beauchamp. No way! We'd made a start tonight on our debt-reduction plan. I'd do anything, other than sleep with Beauchamp, to get rid of our debts even if it meant *The Shadow* became a fulltime job commitment.

CHAPTER
10

What did you get?" I demanded when I entered the office the morning after the ball. The terrible trio was waiting for me.

"Good morning to you, too," Father said.

"What's good about it? Thanks to you I have Octopus Beauchamp sniffing after me like a . . ." I shuddered at the comparison that leapt into my mind and hurriedly continued past it to more important things.

"We scooped the pool," Ben burst out, putting me out of my misery.

"Plenty for the overdue payment," Hannah confirmed.

My indignation left me in a whoosh of exhaled air. I slumped into the upright eighteenth-century chair and took a moment to savor the small victory. *Enough money to make the payment.*

"We need to get the jewels and the medals to London. Alistair will sell them on our behalf."

"I'll drive down to deliver them. Emily will be pleased," I added. "She's developed a liking for exotic travel."

Hannah laughed, but Father and Ben were all business today.

"We have to hurry," Father said. "Ben and I have to sort out our produce for the market tomorrow morning."

"And we want to follow up on a lead we have about the garden thefts."

I considered the robberies. "It can't be easy getting rid of stolen plants and garden statues. Have you looked at the ads in the newspapers?"

"Or the notice boards in the shopping centers," Hannah suggested.

Ben nodded. "Good idea, that, Charles. We're checking out the other landscape gardeners in the area. Rumor is that there's a feud between Janet, the McKenzie's designer, and Carl Johnson from Garden Designs."

While I hoped that Father and Ben didn't land themselves knee-deep in trouble, it was good to see the enthusiasm and dedication they were showing for their new direction.

Hannah interrupted my musing. "Do you have a list of clients for me to check out?"

"Huh!" Ben snorted. "Clients. That's a new one. Fat pigeons ready to pluck—"

"Here," I said. No time for bickering. Although we had earned enough to cover the upcoming payment, the next one would be due before we knew it.

Father picked up a copy of the newspaper and waved it at me. "Look," he said, his voice rich with pride and more than a trace of smugness. "We made the paper."

"What?" My heart dive-bombed my ribs in sudden fear. I snatched the paper from him. "We were caught on camera?" I bent my head to read the story Father had indicated: THIEVES HIT HARLEQUIN BALL. Thieves stole thousands of pounds worth of jewelry while owners partied and danced away the night. Police are following several leads.

"What leads?" I asked in alarm.

Hannah reached over the table to pat my arm. "Relax. The police always say they're following leads." Hannah nodded sagely. "Standard operating procedure."

"That's all right, then," I said, but privately acknowledged I still had a way to go before *The Shadow* felt like a second skin. I could see myself remaining jumpy for sometime to come.

Father retrieved the paper and scanned the rest of the article. "Emeralds? Ben, we didn't get emeralds! Or sapphires. It says here the Monkton emeralds were stolen."

"Do you think our mystery competitor attended the ball?" Hannah asked.

We stared at each other uneasily.

Father slammed the paper on the desk. "That's exactly

138

what I think, and I don't like it one bit."

I wasn't keen on the idea either. It was bad enough dodging the cops and security companies without another cat burglar on the prowl.

◊ ◊ ◊ ◊ ◊

"These are your outfits for the parade. This dress is to wear afterward when the models mingle with the guests." I accepted the garments from Josephine Montgomery with a nod, and she moved on to the next model. Jemima was one of the models too. That was the only thing that kept me sane amongst all the giggly socialites. The strain of pretending to be one of them all the way through a week's rehearsal was testing my temper.

I joined the group who had received their outfits.

"What are you waiting for?" Josephine Montgomery boomed above the feminine chatter. "Try the outfits on. If anything doesn't fit come see me or Tina here." She pointed to her hovering assistant. The poor girl looked as though she thought Josephine would bite. After checking out Josephine's scowl, I decided Tina was probably right to worry.

"Come on," Jemima said. "We'd better hurry or the old girl will burst a saline implant."

I shook my head, trying valiantly to restrain my smirk. Jemima had a wicked tongue.

We found a clear space and set our clothes down. As had become my habit, my gaze surfed the surrounding area, taking in the *objets d'art*—the paintings and anything remotely valuable that appeared portable and hadn't been nailed down. I skimmed over the family portraits without registering at first. My gaze slammed to a screeching halt, and I returned to study them more closely.

"Better hurry up," Jemima muttered. "Jo-Jo is looking this way. She's frowning. She's heading over."

"Katherine Fawkner!"

I almost leapt out of my shoes at the booming shout right behind me.

"Told ya," Jemima said, hastily scrambling into a suit that looked a size too small for her.

Feeling as though I were back at school with one of the nuns, I slowly turned. Summoning up a chirpy smile I said, "Is something wrong?"

"The fashion parade is this week. Not next month."

"I was just coming to see either you or Tina." My heart knocked against my ribs as I handed her a garment still enclosed in plastic. "This won't fit me." Cripes! Josephine Montgomery was a fearsome sight in full sail. Compared to dealing with her, life as *The Shadow* was easy peasy.

"Besides, this is so not my color," I said.

Josephine grabbed the bright yellow dress to check the label. "This dress is for Katherine Walters," she said in an accusing voice, turning her wrath on her assistant, Tina.

"You've given her the wrong size."

"And the wrong color," I chirped deciding to go for broke.

"Find the right dresses," Josephine boomed again.

I swear every one of the girls near me jumped and moved a tad faster. Plastic garment wrappers crinkled, fabrics rustled, and the chatter ceased as Josephine Montgomery strode up and down the room issuing orders like a sergeant-major.

"Come with me," Tina muttered. I noticed she had a strange eye that seemed to look over my shoulder instead of matching the other one that looked at me. Weird. I regretted landing her in trouble.

"I'm sorry," I whispered. "Josephine makes me nervous. I chatter when I'm anxious. Can I help you look for my garments?"

Her smile lit up her face. "She makes me nervous too," she confided.

I decided to try to put her at ease. Her job was difficult enough without prima donnas. "Nice portraits," I murmured in an undertone, unwilling to risk bringing Josephine's wrath down on me again. But I didn't see why I couldn't take advantage and do some investigating. My lack of progress was making me irritable.

"They are, aren't they? The photographer has a real gift for bringing out the best in his subjects. I was really pleased with them."

"Do you live here?" I asked in surprise.

"Josephine is my aunt," she said ruefully.

"Oh."

"Oh, indeed."

We exchanged grimaces.

"So who is the photographer?" I held my breath and waited for the info that would lead me one step closer to the closure. "I'm sure I've seen other photos he's taken. I recognize the beach ball and bucket and spade he uses as props."

"Jasper Cooney. He has studios in Chelsea. He's expensive and you have to book ahead, but it's well worth the wait. I didn't think anyone could manage to keep my niece and nephew still long enough to take photos."

If I hadn't been aware of Josephine Montgomery in the background I would have pumped my fist in the air and whooped. Instead, I grabbed Tina by the forearm and squeezed it with gratitude.

"Thanks for the info. I hope I can book Amber in. A photo would make a great Christmas present for my father."

"Tina!"

"Oops, we'd better hurry up." Tina cast an alarmed glance over her shoulder. "I think that's Katherine over there. Let's hope she has your outfits."

Ten minutes later, I gaped at my assigned outfits in shocked horror. "Can I have the yellow dress back?" I asked in a faint voice.

"I know," Tina said with sympathy. "There's not much to cover you, but at least it's your color."

My gaze shot to her face. Although her face remained open and innocent, her words sure as hell weren't! My complaint had zapped back to bite me on the bum. Ugh!

"All right." I knew when I'd been beaten. "I'd better try this . . . ah . . ." I picked up the minuscule piece of froth and stared at a loss. "Thing," I decided finally. I squeezed into a space between two girls I didn't know and dumped my stash of clothes on a chair.

"Are your clothes as bad as mine?" The brunette to my right rolled her brown eyes toward the ceiling.

"Worse," I muttered eying the brief triangles of red that made up the bodice of my frothy dress with disfavor.

"I wouldn't even wear mine to garden in," my other neighbor said.

"But you'd blend in," the brunette quipped.

"Yeah."

"Do you like gardening?" I'd never enjoyed the digging and weeding, the backbreaking work required to make a garden bloom. There was always a chance they knew something about the plant thefts. Father and Ben had struck out so far.

The brunette shrugged. "Not really."

"It's hell on the fingernails even with gloves," her friend agreed.

Well, there went that brainwave.

143

"Aren't you changed yet?" Josephine Montgomery hollered.

The girls and I erupted in a flurry of activity. The red dress fit like a second skin. In the crowded room behind scenes, we jostled for space, tugged hems, and assembled acceptable hairstyles in preparation for our rehearsal stint on the catwalk. Several stints, in my case. I glared at my next outfit, a bikini that existed of tiny triangles and bits of string. I had no idea what I'd done to Josephine Montgomery, but it certainly seemed as though she were out to make me suffer. Or at least inflict moments of excruciating embarrassment upon me.

"Line up, girls. I want to see the outfits properly."

Dutifully, we lined up like a platoon of soldiers on parade. Josephine was the sergeant-major inspecting her troops. She stalked the line with narrowed eyes, stopping every now and then to tweak fabric into submission or lambaste the poor girl she'd halted in front of. I became that girl.

"Katherine Fawkner," she snapped. "The bra will have to go."

I looked down. The bra was the only thing keeping me decent. "I didn't think this was a show to titillate the men," I said, making an effort to keep my voice low and reasonable.

"Off with the bra." She uttered the instruction in much the tone I imagined King Henry VIII had said, "Off with her head." No way would I win this argument. I could tell that by one look at her set face.

"I want nothing to detract from the diamonds the Marconeys are lending us."

Jewels? My ears pricked at this before I wilted inside. I could hardly steal the jewels for which I was responsible. No prize for guessing who the cops would come after first. I whisked the bra off by fumbling beneath the bodice of the dress and thought that sometimes, actually quite often, life sucked.

◊ ◊ ◊ ◊ ◊

The night of the fashion parade arrived way too soon for Josephine Montgomery's liking. According to her, we had less coordination than children learning to use stilts.

Personally, I couldn't wait for the whole thing to end. The red dress filled my nightmares, both waking and sleeping, because sans bra it was downright indecent. And I didn't even want to begin thinking about the itty-bitty green bikini.

I tugged at the offending bodice, trying to stretch the material. "That diamond is going need to be plenty big to hide my charms," I complained to Jemima.

"I'm thinking your charms are gonna be flaunted, not hidden."

"That's what I'm afraid of," I muttered.

SHELLEY MUNRO

Up ahead, Josephine Montgomery, with Tina at her side, was summoning those she'd bestowed with the honor of wearing jewels. Honor. Huh! That was a joke. I ambled forward with the rest of the chosen girls feeling a bit like a lamb going off to slaughter.

"Perhaps the audience will consist of only women," I muttered, hope in my heart.

"I don't think so," one of the girls standing beside me said. "My boyfriend is attending. I know my mother was trying to get my brother to come along."

"Great." My smile was as false as the woman's boobs.

She studied me with an assessing eye. "You know, you look like my brother's type. Would you like me to fix him up with you?"

Did I look desperate? Perhaps, I conceded. *What type?* I thought belatedly. "Thanks, but I have a man."

Immediately, Kahu came to mind. Thankfully, I arrived at the head of the line and my thoughts and eyes were directed elsewhere.

The diamond was huge. I heard a soft gasp and realized the sound had come from me.

"Beautiful, isn't it?" The small man at the head of the line with Josephine Montgomery beamed like a proud papa.

I studied the sparkling facets of the diamond, the color and size, and nodded. Man, I'd bet this puppy would put a sizable dent in our debt. I sighed. If it went missing, they'd lock me up so quickly I probably wouldn't touch the

146

ground. Still, the temptation to lift the jewel simmered through me with an almost painful intensity. The itching in my palm stopped me short. I was thinking like the damned *Shadow*.

Now there was a scary thought.

The diamond felt cool as it settled between my exposed—mostly exposed—breasts.

"Since this is our most prized jewel, you get an escort for the evening," Josephine said.

Great. Not only did I have to prance around looking like an expensive prostitute, I got to have my own personal guard, which put a right crimp in my plans to scope out the jewels that arrived around the necks of the well-heeled guests.

"I hope he's intending to protect me as well as the jewels," I muttered.

A tall, well-built man in evening clothes stepped up to my side. To the man's credit, he kept his gaze at face level. Perhaps I'd reserve judgment.

"Girls, your escorts will meet you when the parade is finished and it's time to mingle with the guests. All right." Josephine Montgomery clapped her hands together and hush fell over the large room that served as a changing room. "Places, everyone."

"Is my lipstick okay?"

"Zip me up."

The excitement level seemed to ratchet upward while

147

a corresponding herd of butterflies stomped around inside my stomach. The opening notes of a pulsating rock ballad blasted through the room. Backstage, we took our places.

Josephine stood by the door that led to our makeshift runway. "Right. One . . . two . . . and go."

*Oh*s and *ah*s from the crowd floated backstage. I stood fifth in line.

"Don't forget to smile, girls!"

My turn arrived before I was prepared. I sashayed out onto the runway. A piercing whistle rent the room, audible even over the music.

"I want one of those!"

Blond bimbo. *Blond bimbo.* My smile blazed wide and bright. By the time I'd sashayed from one end of the runway and back, my jaw hurt from the fixed smile. One outfit down. One more to go. I stepped off the runway and hurried to change into my bikini for the swimwear parade.

◊ ◊ ◊ ◊ ◊

"Thank goodness that's over," Jemima said. "Remind me to never ever let myself be talked into a charity do again. Please."

"At least you don't have to run around for the rest of the night half dressed," I said, referring to her sleek black suit.

"Stop complaining and go mingle." A cheeky grin lit Jemima's face. "You have a diamond to display."

148

The crowd that stayed for drinks and canapés were well behaved. At first. I think my silent security escort kept them at bay. At first. Plied with alcohol and only tiny morsels of food to soak it up, the men became more vocal, more pushy, more everything. Octopus Beauchamp led the baying pack.

"Nice . . . diamond," he said, his piggy eyes lingering over my exposed flesh. I suppressed a shudder.

"Only two hundred fifty thousand pounds from Mahoneys," I said, as instructed by Josephine Montgomery.

"Do you come with the diamond?" one of the wits asked.

"No," I said through gritted teeth that were bared in a requisite smile. "You'll need to discuss that with Jasper."

"That's enough, Katherine. You're meant to circulate," Josephine Montgomery boomed across the Lancaster Hotel ballroom.

My escort offered a smile of sympathy and offered his arm. "Let's keep moving," he suggested in a low voice. "We'll only stop if there is a woman present along with her husband." Once again, his gaze remained on my face, and I was intensely grateful for his gentlemanly manners.

We paraded the length of the ballroom and back several times, to show the diamond off and entice people to buy. The other girls who were modeling jewelry were receiving about the same amount of attention. Two hours later, sick of having my bottom pinched and my breasts ogled, I handed over the diamond with alacrity and changed into my own clothes. Judging by tonight's attendance and interest, I'd say the Wishes charity stood to receive a hefty chunk of sales commission along with a slice of the ticket sales. At least something good would come of me parading about half naked.

CHAPTER

11

As usual, I stayed the night in Seth's Knightsbridge flat. Seth arrived home midmorning looking tired but happy, his blond hair standing up in spikes. He clutched a pot with some kind of frilly green plant in it.

"Didn't you comb your hair this morning?"

Seth placed the plant on the bench and dropped into the wooden chair next to me. I inhaled a breath of spicy citrus aftershave as he pressed a kiss to my cheek. "It's windy outside."

"Hmmm," I said. "Cup of coffee?"

Seth leapt off his chair. "I'll get it. I brought you a present." He gestured at the pot. "I should have brought two. It looks good in the kitchen."

"Go back and buy another," I said. "I'm not giving

up mine."

"Brought it from some guy in the Bunch of Grapes. They sold out pretty quick."

I stilled, my coffee cup halfway to my lips. Surely not? "Just plants?"

"All sorts of plants. The guy was selling statues and urns." Seth poured a cup of coffee into a stoneware mug and topped up mine for me. "You interested?"

"Not me. Father and Ben are the gardeners in our family." I sipped at my coffee while my mind filed through the possibilities. I kept coming up with the same scenario no matter how I looked at it. Either the men who'd sold the plant to Seth were moonlighting or else they were shifting stolen goods.

The second option sounded more likely.

"From what they said, I think the sales last night were a one off. What time did you want to leave for Oakthorpe?"

I opened my mouth to fire further questions. What did they look like? How many people were there? Had Seth seen them before? And that was just for starters.

"I'm ready whenever you are," I said. The sooner I returned to Oakthorpe, the quicker I could get the information to Father and Ben. They could come up with me tonight and check out some of the pubs while I staked out the Patterson mansion in Chelsea. I also intended to visit the photographer while I was in the neighborhood.

I wasn't sure of what action I'd take when I arrived at

the photographers. *If he's at his studio, I'll talk to him. If he isn't . . .* I gave a mental shrug. I'd decide when forced to.

"Give me time for a quick shower, and we'll go." Seth halted by the kitchen door. "You up for the Warrens' ball this weekend?"

I nodded, trying to look enthusiastic about another ball. They blended together in one endless blur after a while. "Sure. I think I have an invitation somewhere."

"Don't bother looking," Seth said, his mouth creased in a wide smile. "My invitation is for a partner as well."

◇ ◇ ◇ ◇ ◇

We pulled up outside Oakthorpe minutes after one o'clock. A late-model sedan was parked outside the front entrance when we pulled up.

"I won't come in since you've got visitors," Seth said.

I tugged at his arm. "Don't be silly. At least come in for a cold drink and to say hello. Amber misses you."

A dark shadow passed over his face, and I silently berated myself for my tactlessness. I hugged him tightly. "Parents still nagging about marriage?"

"Yeah." He attempted a laugh that didn't quite come off. "Continuing the family line. I mean, hell, what do I tell them?"

I hugged Seth hard, trying to show him how much I cared, how much I empathized without words. "You could start by telling them how much you love them."

"Huh! Can't do that. Stiff upper lip and all that."

"Kate! You're home." Hannah dragged me inside the foyer. "About time. I thought I'd have to wade in and referee."

"What are you talking about?"

"Perhaps I should go," Seth said.

"No—"

"That would be best," Hannah agreed.

Exasperated, I rolled my eyes at Seth. Not another drama in the Fawkner household. We seemed to lurch from one to the next.

I said goodbye to Seth, stubbornly walking him back out to his car while Hannah hovered. My curiosity was well and truly stirred by this time.

"Families," I muttered when I stood on tiptoe to kiss Seth. "I'll talk to you during the week."

"Hurry up, before Charles bursts a blood vessel," Hannah called.

I followed her down the passage. Instead of entering the den or the kitchen, she carried on to the formal lounge. My brows rose, and I hurried to catch up. "What's going on? Can't you at least give me a clue?"

"Police," she muttered in disgust. She halted at the door and made shooing motions with her hands. "Go."

Heck, she could have told me a bit sooner to give me time to prepare. Nerves jumped to life in my stomach as

I tried to think how I'd given us away. I came up blank. Lordy, every Fawkner ancestor was probably turning in their graves, and those that hovered in the in-between were most likely making plans to punish me for stupidity. The urge to run rode me hard, but instead, I lifted my chin and sailed into the formal lounge, my full skirt rustling to highlight my silent aggravation.

Two men sat in the uncomfortable antique chairs that furnished the room. I bit back a hysterical laugh. Father and Charles sat opposite, both wearing identical glowers.

Each of the men seemed to come to attention when I strode into their presence. The two visitors stood and turned to face me.

"Kahu," I murmured.

"Detective Walsham and Detective Williams." Father's voice held silent warning, and I thought I heard a trace of panic.

Okay. The best thing to do was to wait for them to speak. I wasn't about to give them information that would lock me away. All the time, I kept wondering what I'd done to clue them in. What could I have done differently?

"Have a seat," Kahu said.

Good idea. If I stood much longer, I'd keel over. My knees were doing a real number on me. I tottered over to the nearest chair and sat.

"We need to ask you a few questions," Kahu said.

I nodded, not trusting myself to speak. His expression,

calm and businesslike, told me nothing.

"Where were you last night?"

I sent a frowning glance to Father. He lifted one shoulder in an imperceptible shrug, and I turned my attention back to the cops.

"At Josephine Montgomery's fashion parade." I marked up several mental points for my cool tone since inside I was a mass of writhing nerves. "Why?"

"A few more questions, first." Detective Walsham consulted a small black notepad and fixed me with a speculative stare. "Did you have an invitation? What time did you leave?"

"I was one of the models. I left about one this morning."

Instinct told me both Kahu and the officious Detective Walsham already knew that. I clasped my hands in my lap and waited.

Detective Walsham stared, looking as though he wanted to know what made me tick. I boomeranged the look. "Were you one of the jewelry models?"

"Yes," I said, a picture of ladylike calm and dignity. Inside, the nerves still rock and rolled, but I felt quietly satisfied with the front I presented.

"Which jewels did you model?" An edge of frustration coated his voice and echoed in his face.

"A diamond pendant," I said. "With matching earrings."

"Tell us about what you did toward the end of the evening," Kahu interrupted his coworker. His eyes twinkled with humor when he spoke, making me imagine they played a version of good cop/bad cop.

"I paraded around the room, showing the jewels. Sorta like a prize heifer at an agricultural show," I added as an aside.

Kahu's mouth quirked upward. Detective Walsham didn't react at all.

"Or at least I was pinched and manhandled about the same," I said. "I showed the diamond and the designer dress off for the evening with my security escort in tow. At about one people started to leave, and the models returned the jewelry they were wearing to the central collection point. It was behind scenes in the room where the models changed their outfits," I added before I was questioned on this point. "Once the jewelry was returned, I changed, and caught a taxi to the flat."

A tic started in Detective Walsham's left eye. "Did you see anyone suspicious when you left?"

"All the suspicious characters I needed to watch out for had left with their wives," I said in a dry tone. "I was tired. I hailed a cab and left. Look, are you going to tell me what this is about?"

From the corner of my eyes, I noticed the terrible trio lean forward in their seats. No wonder they were so on edge. They didn't know what was going on either.

"The jewelry you wore last night was stolen."

I jerked upright in my seat, staring at Detective

Walsham in total disbelief. "Stolen?" Who? Where? How? "But the security was tight." His very lack of expression made me draw in a sharp breath. "You can't think I did it."

"The necklace you wore is missing."

"I heard you the first time," I snapped, bounding to my feet. "I had nothing to do with the disappearance of the pendant. Check with my security escort. He was with me the whole time."

"Overnight?" Detective Walsham inserted smooth as silk, so smooth it took me a while to register.

"No!" Why did every man assume I was a loose woman because I was an unmarried mother?

"Why don't you tell me where you went when you left the fashion parade?"

My glare should have burned holes in the detective but it seemed to glance off him. He waited for my answer, eyebrows raised.

"I stayed at Seth's flat in Knightsbridge," I said with dignity, already guessing what his reaction would be to that little snippet.

His dark brows rose higher, however Kahu asked the next question.

"Seth can vouch for your whereabouts since one this morning?"

Lordy, what did I say to that? Lie, I decided. Seth's secret wasn't mine to tell. "Yes," I said meeting Kahu's gaze without flinching.

"We will of course, confirm that with Seth."

"Of course," I agreed. "Will that be all? I have things to do."

"We'll contact you should the need arise," Kahu said.

I nodded abruptly, disappointment searing my gut. The sparkle had disappeared from Kahu's eyes, and I couldn't shake the feeling that I'd blown it with him. I straightened my shoulders and pushed away the sensation of hurt. I'd told myself a romance with a policeman wouldn't work but faint hope had stirred anyway. Now I saw what Father had tried to tell me. The gulf between us was too big to bridge.

Hannah showed the policemen out, and we remained silent until their car drove down the drive and the purr of the motor receded.

"I didn't steal the diamond," I said.

Father exhaled loudly. "Then we have a problem."

"The competitor," Ben said.

Hannah wrung her hands. "The cat who left the business card?"

Father scowled. "The competitor is going to make our lives difficult. Security will tighten. And the press will jump on the story."

"The papers are full of the thefts already—the roses and the calling cards." I turned away from the window, the need to move a necessity. Conflicted feeling bounced around inside me like a ping-pong ball gone off course. Regret. Alarm. More regret. "This isn't a competition."

"Maybe not," Hannah conceded. "But mark my words. It will become a competition between the newcomer, the police, and us. There can only be one winner."

I kept a lid on the retort that bubbled to my lips. The fear that nipped at me was an old one. What if neither the mystery competitor nor *The Shadow* won? What if the winner in this jewel duel was the law?

CHAPTER
12

Breakfast was a silent affair with nothing more said than requests to pass the marmalade and the rustle of the newspaper. We'd discussed matters into the wee small hours of the night until it felt as though we were chasing our tails.

"We need to make a decision," I said suddenly, my voice a flash of lightning in the silent kitchen. When Hannah flinched, I said in a defensive tone, "We either stop or we carry on. Those are our only options."

"There is a third," Father countered, throwing the paper away with a sound of disgust.

"Yeah," Ben said. "We can find the cheeky blighter and put a stop to his high jinks. This is our territory. We've never put up with usurpers before, and I don't think we should take this lying down."

I grinned. "Fighting words."

Father screwed up his face in a frown. "I say we carry on with our plans and keep an eye out for the impostor. Of course, it's going to make life difficult but a Fawkner always rises to the occasion."

I laughed. I couldn't help it. That sounded fine and dandy for the Fawkner men, but it hardly applied to the women.

Ben waggled his finger in front of my face. "Laugh all you will, missy, but this is serious."

"Of course it is," I managed before cracking up again.

A knock on the door interrupted my mirth, and I decided, after glimpsing the faces of the terrible trio, that I should answer the door. Another round of pounding fists hurried me along.

Humor still wreathed my mouth when I opened the door.

"What can I . . . ?" My voice trailed off when I got an eyeful of the two goons on our doorstep. One was half a head taller than my five-foot-eight with a clean-shaven head. No doubt he thought it made him look tough. In my opinion, he just looked ugly with his cauliflower ears sticking out like handles from the side of his head. The other man was shorter than me by a few inches and running to seed. His belt strained at the waist. They wore cheap black suits made of shiny material. The trousers of the bald man on the left were too short exposing a pair of white sports socks.

"Can I help you?" I asked cautiously. While I knew I could take out one of the men, two might present a problem.

"Beauchamp wants his money," Baldy said. His voice matched the gangster image—low and gravel-like.

"It's not due until tomorrow." We'd had to juggle our funds and had ended up a few thousand pounds short on this payment after all. Not that I intended to spill that little gem.

"This is like a friendly reminder," Seedy said.

I inclined my head in my best lady-of-the-house style. "Thank you." No sense stirring things up with bad manners. "I'll be at his office tomorrow morning to make the payment."

Baldy nodded, and I was impressed. Maybe this was a friendly reminder and not the sinister gangster moment I'd imagined.

"Will I see both of you next month?" I asked.

"Sooner, if you don't make good your payment. You have a lovely daughter. I spoke to her at the school-sports day."

My pleasant smile faded. They'd talked to Amber. I remembered seeing her with a stranger for an instant before her teacher had intervened. A sick sensation cramped my belly, and it was difficult to squeeze out words. "I don't want any problems, boys. You'll get your payment."

Baldy nodded again. "Good. That's good."

"There was one other thing," Seedy added before I could close the door. "Beauchamp said you should reconsider his

163

proposal, and he'd knock some money off the total. He said you'd know what he was talking about."

The dirty old man. Although I wanted to slam the door in their faces and stomp off, I forced a smile to my face and stuck out my chest. Since the neckline was low, their gazes zoomed straight there like kids scrambling for lollipops. "You tell Dicky Beauchamp I'll keep that under advisement," I cooed, blinking my lashes in full-out bimbo mode.

Seedy and Baldy nodded without taking their eyes off my breasts.

"Bye-bye, then." I waggled the fingers of my right hand and closed the door with a soft click. I waited until I heard footsteps and the rumble of their car leaving, before narrowing my eyes and letting the insipid smile die.

"Shit," I muttered in total understatement.

"Mama!" Amber appeared at the bend on the stairs. "Mama said a naughty word."

"Yeah, I'll have to wash my mouth out with soap."

"Does it taste nice?" Amber wanted to know.

"I doubt it. From memory it tastes like Brussels sprouts."

"Eew." My daughter wrinkled up her cute button nose.

"Exactly," I agreed. I checked my watch and let out a very bimbo-like shriek. "Look at the time. We're going to be late for school."

I hustled Amber down the passage to the kitchen and pressed her into a chair.

"Who was at the door?"

"Tell you later," I muttered in an aside to Father.

Hannah handed me two plates of scrambled eggs, and I placed one in front of Amber. "Eat," I said, "but not too fast. I don't want you to throw up over my dress."

Amber grinned and I grinned back, inwardly marveling at my beautiful, well-adjusted daughter. As always, the past slithered through my mental barricades. My good humor dissipated while I stared at my plate of scrambled eggs. What if Amber's father had a hereditary disease . . . or . . . or suffered bad-hair days? How could I help her if I didn't know her history? It wasn't as if I enjoyed lying to her about her father dying in a plane crash.

"Finished!" Five minutes later, Amber's chair scraped the tiles in protest when she shot to her feet.

I pushed away my uneaten breakfast and stood, glad she'd dragged me from my worries.

"Go brush your teeth. I'll wait out front for you."

"The small wiggling ears have gone," Father said. "Who was at the door?"

"Beauchamp sent goons to impress upon us the need to make payment on time."

Hannah set down the china teapot with a thump. "They didn't hurt you?"

"I distracted them with my breasts. But they said they'd talked to Amber."

"Told you the bimbo act would work," Father said leaning back in his chair and looking smug.

SHELLEY MUNRO

"And I still say it's sexist," Hannah muttered. "I don't know why you agreed to go along with their crazy scheme. You should have a husband, more children."

"On that we agree," Father muttered. "Not that you're doing a bad job as *The Shadow*. But you should marry a good man and produce children to carry on the family occupation."

"Like you did," I snapped. The moment the words left my mouth I wanted to drag them back. Father had loved my mother, and I knew they'd lost several babies before and after me stillborn. Mother's health had never been robust, and she'd caught pneumonia one particularly harsh winter and died. Father had never remarried, and if he went out with other women he was discreet about it. But I was becoming tired of the parental guilt trips. I know the terrible trio wanted to see me settled, but did they have to go on and on trying to push me at Seth? I noted we were all avoiding the goon subject, hoping it would go away.

"Not a cop," Father said, shaking his head. "Imagine having a copper for a son-in-law. I don't know what you see in him. If you think walking a tightrope is a turn-on, don't! I would have thought being *The Shadow* was dangerous enough. Seeing that copper is not only dangerous, it's madness."

"I don't have time for this." I picked up the car keys. "I want to do a recon of the Patterson property in Chelsea tonight and there are a couple of other possibilities in

Knightsbridge. If you and Ben would like to help, I'd welcome your input. I need to pick up the last bit of money from Alistair so we can make the payment to Beauchamp tomorrow." I turned to leave, then snapped my fingers. "I almost forgot. The garden thefts. Seth purchased a plant at a pub in central London. Maybe you can check out some of the pubs tonight and see if it's a one-off or if someone is flogging off stolen goods? Ask a few questions."

I left the kitchen and hurried out to my Mini. Amber was waiting at the front door.

"Sorry, sweetie. Grandpa wanted to tell me something. What are you doing at school today?"

"Painting." Amber climbed into her car seat, and I fastened her in. The scent of baby powder and little girl filled my senses. Not so little anymore, I reminded myself.

The ten-minute drive to the school passed quickly. I pulled up outside the small brick building right on time.

"See you later, cupcake." I kissed her and watched Amber run off to join her friends and enter the brick building.

When she disappeared from sight, I backed the Mini up and tore back to Oakthorpe. One thing I was sure of—the photographer's studio was the first place I intended to visit tonight.

◇ ◇ ◇ ◇ ◇

I had the devil's own job getting rid of Father and Ben. Frustrated, I wondered if they could read my mind, or expected me to meet up with the enemy.

Inspector Kahu Williams.

They lingered like flies in a stable dung heap until I lost my patience. "If you don't hurry, the pubs will close before you get to the West End. I thought the pair of you wanted to be big-time detectives."

Father glared at me, not appreciating the dig. "It's not our fault Alistair hadn't sold the merchandise yet. These things can't be hurried."

I wasn't a happy camper, and I had no intention of pretending otherwise. The debt belonged to Father. "We have to pay Beauchamp tomorrow, and we don't have all the money. We're four thousand pounds short. It might as well be a million."

"We haven't arranged a meeting place for later," Ben said.

We stood on Kensington High Street, not far from the Goat Tavern.

"Meet me back here at midnight," I said. "I'll do the Chelsea look-see; then we can do the others together. Hopefully an opportunity will present, and we'll manage to get the rest of the payment tonight."

Father and Ben nodded agreement, and the breath I'd been holding eased out in silent relief.

"There's the bus now," I said, giving them a verbal hurry along. Under normal circumstances they would have taken a cab, but with money tight, tonight they were slumming it on the bus.

My shoulders slumped when the bus pulled away from the stop. One less problem with which to deal. I slid behind the wheel of my Mini and headed for Chelsea.

The Pattersons' flat was situated in Cheyne Gardens. It was after nine and still light so I drove down the street, taking note of the pedestrians out walking dogs and general comings and goings. At the end of Cheyne Gardens, I turned into St. Loo Avenue and drove for five minutes before I parked. No sense raising the suspicions of nosy neighbors by driving up and down Cheyne Gardens too often.

The Pattersons lived in an old Victorian mansion that had been converted into expensive flats. Security consisted of a locked door. When a visitor arrived, he or she buzzed the floor they wanted to visit. Not exactly top-of-the-line security.

I strolled down the street trying to look as though I belonged. I'd even dressed the part in a demure black skirt and beige top. Flat shoes and a string of faux pearls completed the outfit. I blended like cream and strawberries, or children and puppies, especially with my mousy brown wig and brown contact lenses. Careful makeup changed the shape of my face, and I dared anyone to pick me from an identity parade and state categorically that I was Lady Katherine Fawkner.

At the entrance to the mansion, I walked up the short

path and pressed the intercom for the flat on the top floor. When nothing happened, I let out a put-upon sigh and leaned on the doorbell. Miraculously, it buzzed open seconds later. *Piece of cake*, I thought with a smug grin. Now the hard part. Somehow, I needed to look inside the flat. I had a copy of the floor plans already, but I wanted to double- and triple-check everything, especially after the last two jobs.

Instead of taking the lift, I headed for the stairs. The manse was four stories, and each flat comprised one floor. The light between the second and third floors had burned out. Or been taken out? The thought slid into my mind like a stealthy fox. My internal warning signals clanged. Instinctively I slowed my ascent of the stairs and listened for the slightest sound. Nothing. But I smelled a hint of citrus. Aftershave, perhaps?

At the doorway to the third floor, I listened for a final time before easing the door open. The soft slide of shoes on a tiled floor made me hesitate. According to my info, the Pattersons were taking a long weekend in Paris. Had they arranged for servicemen to call while they were away? Pest control? Window cleaners?

The warning chime of the lift sounded. I heard footsteps again and then the doors closed with a smooth clunk. I exited the stairwell to see the lift descending.

No need for stealth now.

My gut told me I was late to the party. Too late. Somehow, my opponent was one step in front of me again.

Still, I needed to check. After drawing a set of lock picks from my black leather handbag, I entered the Pattersons' flat. At the doorway, I pulled on a pair of gloves.

"Shit." I glared down at the floor taking no pleasure in learning I was right. The shiny black business card bearing a silver cat proved it. The opposition had been and gone. Muttering under my breath, I stomped inside, unconcerned with cameras or security. No doubt my competitor had dealt with that as well.

Quashing admiration, I sped straight to a window that overlooked the street. A BMW drove down Cheyne Gardens and disappeared from sight. A young mother pushing a baby carriage strolled the footpath, pausing to chat with another mother and toddler. I couldn't see a single person properly suited to the role of thief.

Maybe roaming the luxurious rooms was a timewaster, but in a fit of pique, I stripped off my right glove to collect my competitor's business cards. A grin grew at the thought of my competitor's puzzlement. I could almost hear their thoughts. Why hadn't the reporters pried details of the calling card from the police? I imagined the prick to his ego, and my grin turned a shade evil as I stepped into the Pattersons' designer kitchen.

My, my. Another business card.

I pocketed it and searched for more during my quick walkthrough. As I'd suspected anything of value had disappeared along with my competitor. But being an ambitious trainee cat burglar, I noted security details—bolted windows, a safe behind a painting of a dog in the small office. The alarm box in the passage leading to the bedrooms.

"The alarm," I muttered. My gaze shot to the silent red light on the front of the box. A blinking red light. I'd triggered an alarm! And if I didn't move it, I'd meet the law face to face. Apart from a mess, I'd never live down the shame. A Fawkner in prison. The probable reactions of the terrible trio, not to mention my daughter, Amber, spurred me to speed.

I sprinted for the door, only pausing to snatch up another of the taunting calling cards left by my competitor. I jammed it deep in my handbag and charged for the stairs at a full-out run. "Damn and double damn," I cursed in a low, fierce whisper. This was not meant to happen. Father would have a cow when he heard. As I hurried down the stairs while trying to make as little noise as possible, I flirted with the idea of not confessing. Temptation blazed to life before it died a rapid death. I'd confess all.

By the time I reached the bottom of the stairs, my breath hissed from my mouth. Life as I knew it would change if the police captured me. I couldn't let that happen.

Pain seared my lungs, clogged my throat. No time to get my breath. I had to move. The door cracked open, my sweaty palms leaving a smeared, wet print on the wood. Cursing my stupidity, I scrubbed at the print with one of the wet-wipes I carried to clean up my daughter. Hopefully, the police would think the scent was caused by an overzealous cleaner. I yanked my left glove off and stuffed it into my bag.

I peered outside. No activity. Yet. Taking a deep breath, I eased out the door and shut it quietly behind me. Since the alarm was silent, none of the neighbors were perturbed. Yet!

I walked through the marbled foyer and let myself out the heavy glass paneled front door. A woman pushed a carriage up the path just before I let go the door. Smiling, I held the door open for her.

"Thanks."

"No problem. Nice night," I said, counting on the typical English attitude when chitchatting with strangers. The woman's cautious smile wavered.

"I'll hold the door until you maneuver the carriage through," I said. The woman smiled, nodded but didn't hold my gaze for longer than polite. Not that it would have done her much good. I smoothed my right hand over my mousy brown hair. Any description she gave the cops would describe a woman bearing little resemblance to Kate Fawkner.

A car pulled up near the mansion. I glanced casually toward the road. My gaze swept the road before darting back to the vehicle and freezing in shock. Police. And not just any cop, but one I knew. Inspector Kahu Williams.

My stomach turned in a slow somersault, fear freezing me to the spot. Would he recognize me despite the disguise? He strode up the footpath toward me and for a time, I felt as though I were in a movie. An old Western shoot out where two protagonists fired at each other with blazing guns until one lay on the ground bleeding to death. A faint tremor shook my knees. A lump formed in my throat the size of a walnut and just as dry.

Kahu pulled ID from his pocket, as did the man with him. "Police," he said. "Inspector Kahu Williams. The Patterson flat—which floor?"

"The third floor," I said. Truth to tell, I was surprised I managed to squeeze the words past the lump in my throat. I maintained the small interested smile by thinking of Amber and how much I wanted to see her grow to adult-hood, but it was a close-run thing. I caught a whiff of Kahu's familiar spicy scent when he brushed past me. The other policeman entered the building, and I carefully let go the door. They disappeared into the waiting lift before I allowed a breath to ease the tight band around my chest and lungs. Phew, that had been close. *If I hadn't walked out into the passage and seen the warning light . . .* A shudder moved through my body.

A marked police car pulled up with a shriek of brakes, reminding me I'd better move before Kahu returned and started adding facts together. The man was no slouch in the brain department, and I couldn't risk him seeing me again even though I wore a disguise.

I tottered down the short drive way to the road. The greater the distance I put between the Pattersons' flat, Inspector Kahu Williams, and me, the stronger my legs became. By the time I'd made it halfway down Cheyne Gardens, my gait was a smooth hip-rolling amble. I'd finally exerted control on my breathing and things were looking up. Best of all, I was pretty sure I'd snaffled up every single calling card my egotistical competitor had left. *The Shadow* lived to see another day free of bars.

I breathed even easier when I arrived at my Mini. I collapsed into the driver's seat, my legs doing the weird jelly thing all over as I momentarily relaxed. I'd made it to the car without a hand grabbing by the shoulder and a voice saying, "You're under arrest!"

A wobbly grin appeared at the thought. Maybe I watched too much television.

I tugged another wet-wipe from the packet in my handbag to dab the nervous perspiration from my face and hands.

"Let's hope the visit to the photographer isn't as hard on the nerves," I muttered, starting the car, indicating and pulling out into the stream of traffic. It was much darker now and the streetlights had popped on. I'd looked up the location of the photographer's studio in the phone book. It was located on Kings Road, not far from Brompton Cemetery. As was my normal custom, I drove past Jasper's studio for general scouting purposes, parked several streets away, and walked back.

The studio was part of a block of businesses. And it seemed the owners lived in flats above. Either that or they were let out to tenants. Irritated at my run of bad luck, I stomped past Jasper's studio to the business at the far end of the block. I counted the shops as I passed, assessing the degree of difficulty for this self-imposed mission. At least I wouldn't have competition. That was about the only bright spot on the horizon. Optimistic about my half-baked plan to steal . . . ah, *borrow* Jasper's database, I wasn't! But I didn't have an option. I peered into the window of a chemist. The lights burned brightly inside the closed shop for security purposes. All the premises had security lights of varying brightness making entering the shops by the front impossible. I sauntered past again but kept walking this time. Loath to attract attention, I decided to walk right around the block and find the rear entrances. That's when inspiration hit. Jeez! I'd been acting the blond bimbo too long. There was no need to break into the studio. If Jasper lived above, logic said he'd have an office in his living space. He'd need the downstairs area in order to have studio space to snap his photos.

"Bingo," I whispered. "Stupid blonde. That's if Jasper lived above and the flat isn't let out to someone else." I decided it was worth the gamble.

A muffled snigger jerked my head up. Two teenagers,

a boy and a girl, were laughing at my frenzied muttering.

Right. I'd give them something to laugh about. The sensible half of my brain screeched "mistake"! But blond bimbo didn't care.

"Men," I muttered, thinking specifically of Kahu blinkin' Williams and the way he'd scared several years off my life. And probably added gray hair. "You give them an inch and they take a bloody mile. I'll kill him, I will." I paused to glare again at the giggling teenagers. "Or snip his doodle off for straying. Mark my words, missy. Men are trouble! If you're not careful," I snarled, adding some spitting for good measure, "you'll end up like me with more kids than a body can feed. Lowdown lazy git." I shuffled close, pushing my face up to theirs. "Lowdown lazy gits, the lot of 'em."

As I'd intended, they backed off rapidly. Seconds later I heard running, and my laughter burst free like a lanced boil. *Good analogy*, I thought. I laughed harder, letting every bit of frustration out in the process. I pushed away from the brick wall I'd subsided against during the weakness of hysterical laughter to take a deep breath. Feeling much calmer and in control, I walked down the small lane that ran behind the block of shops, keeping to the shadows cast by a large oak tree. I wasn't doing such a stellar job in the investigation department. Still rattled by Kahu's presence and the antics of the teenagers, I hadn't checked to see which of the upstairs occupants were at home. Not that a lack of lights meant they weren't home—it narrowed the field.

Four of the six flats had lights burning from upper-floor windows. The flats above the chemist and Jasper's studio were dark. My smile was wry as were my thoughts. With the way my luck was going tonight, Jasper would be tucked up in his bed and that bed would be in the same room as his computer. I checked my watch. I had half an hour before I was due to meet Father and Ben back on Kensington High Street. A sigh escaped. If I arrived there late, I'd face all sorts of questions.

"Better get on with it," I whispered.

A fire-escape ladder clung to the outermost wall of the building. I shucked my beige shirt and black skirt, deciding that the singlet and dark leggings I wore underneath would be better for both climbing and avoiding detection. Deciding to keep my bag in case I needed the lock picks, I adjusted the strap to the long length and slung it over my shoulder. I tucked the discarded clothes under a hedge that ran parallel with the flats and marked off the parking area behind. I'd collect them on the way down if time allowed.

After checking my surroundings, I ran for the fire escape above the chemist's shop and shimmied up. At the top, I paused again to survey the vicinity. Apart from the blare of the TV in the end flat, nothing raised my suspicions. I scampered along the narrow ledge thankful that fear of heights was one vice I lacked. Father and Ben insisted on a daily workout in the gym they'd set up in the basement. Although I protested each training session, the practice was beginning to pay off. I'd hardly raised a sweat with my exertions. The first window I tried was firmly locked. I chewed my lip debating whether to break in here or to try the window in the flat above the photographer. Heads for the chemist; tails for the photographer's studio. I mentally tossed a coin. Heads it was. I tugged the lock pick from the handbag slung over my shoulder. Ten seconds later, the latch moved, propelled upward by the thin metal hook I'd inserted between the window frame and the window. I flinched at the scraping sound the catch made as it dropped against the inner frame but when no one screeched after three long tortuous minutes, I opened the window and sprang inside, light on my feet like the cat I was. I wanted to holler and cheer. My first attempt at a window and it had worked! Things were looking up.

It took a moment or two for my eyes to adjust to the dimmer light inside the flat. A small studio. A couch that converted to a bed sat against the wall while I made out the fat boxy shapes of two chairs against the other wall. No one was home. I sliced through the dark and collected my shins on a low metal coffee table. Agonizing pain galloped up my legs to my frozen brain as I picked myself up off the floor. I wrinkled my nose and scrubbed my hands down my leggings. Eew! The tenant wasn't big on cleaning. The rug honked like a rubbish bag overdue for collection. But more important—had someone heard? While I waited for the axe to fall, so to speak, I ruminated on my bad luck. I'd lurched from one mishap to another today. Maybe tomorrow would be better. Then I remembered Octopus Beauchamp and the shortfall in our payment. Yeah, right! Somehow, I doubted the Pollyanna concept would apply to *The Shadow*.

I waited another long minute and when nothing stirred, I inched through the room on the lookout for furniture traps and anything else that would land me flat on my face kissing the smelly floor. Definitely no one home. Step one complete. Now for step two.

I let myself out the chemist flat door. The lock was a deadbolt so I stuffed a thin pillow I'd grabbed from a cupboard in the doorway to make it remain open. With the way my luck was going, I decided a means of escape was only sensible. With the pillow in place, I unscrewed the bulb in the landing light. Hopefully, anyone arriving home would assume it had blown.

Right. I sucked in a breath to battle the sudden influx of nerves. Next stop: the flat above Jasper's studio.

The wooden door was shut. I tried the obvious—turning the handle and pushing, but it remained firmly closed. Another deadbolt. I nibbled on my lip. Father and Ben were the best in the business, and they'd trained me. I should ace this exam.

I hadn't counted on nerves doing such a number. My

palms sweated and a fine tremor shook my hands. But this was important. My first real lead. I persisted, barely breathing so I could hear the tumblers slot into line. The last tumbler lined up with a soft click. Success! I was so shocked I nearly dropped my lock picks. A pleased smile swept across my lips. If Father and Ben were good at their jobs, then so was I. I was their star pupil. I shoved aside the smart-aleck answer that popped into my head—I was their only pupil.

"Have a little faith," I whispered, and holding my breath, I slid inside the flat.

Another studio. It was easy enough to establish that this one too was empty. Much the same in layout as the other, but cleaner. I hovered by the light switch in indecision. There were no curtains at the window. Was it worth the risk? Yes, I decided. My search would take half the time, and if I found a computer, I'd need to see what I was doing. I had a small torch in my handbag but needed both hands to operate the computer. Decision made, I hunted out a pair of gloves, pulled them on, and switched on the light. No computer!

Jeez, could this night get any worse? The refrain was becoming my theme song.

The flat consisted of a small kitchenette. The counter area was spotless with not a piece of dirty crockery in sight. A double bed filled most of the space; and over against the far wall, by a window, was a small wooden desk. I hurried over, eager to begin my search. The desk, like the rest of the flat, was tidy and well organized. Mindful of the need to hurry, I checked the contents of the desk drawers. I still took the time to make sure I left things neat. Business cards. Letterheads. A pile of envelopes. At least they proved this flat belonged to Jasper. But where were his records? His database? I yanked out the larger bottom drawer. Inside, he had a small wooden box. I opened it. Bingo! Small index cards with client names, addresses, and details of the jobs he'd done for them. Great. I'd take this and go through the cards later at home. I jammed the lid back on the wooden box and picked it up. It didn't fit in my handbag. Probably better to remove the index cards anyway. I crammed all the cards in my bag and just managed to get the zipper shut. I only hoped Father and Ben didn't ask any questions. While their limbs might need repair, they were both quick and agile when it came to brain function.

I replaced the wooden box in the drawer and made sure everything was exactly as I'd left it. By the time Jasper discovered his database was missing, I'd be long gone. Databases were sensitive and valuable commercial property. With luck, he'd blame his loss on a competitor. I switched off the light and let myself out of the flat. After a quick stop to remove the pillow from the neighboring flat and toss it inside, I made my way down a narrow set of steps and let myself out the door that led to the parking area out the back. I collected my clothes and hurried back to the Mini. Unfortunately, traffic on the way back to Kensington was heavy, and I arrived twenty minutes late.

"Where the devil have you been?" Father's words greeted me like the lash of a whip.

I switched off the ignition, jumped out and pulled back the seat to allow Ben to scramble into the back. Meanwhile, Father laboriously clambered into the passenger seat.

"I said, *Where the devil have you been?*" His aching joints did nothing for his temper.

"I heard you the first time," I snapped while merging with traffic. "I ran into problems." My confession was terse and settled Father's irascible temper.

"You're only half an hour late," he conceded.

Ben leaned forward between the driver and passenger seats. "What happened, Katie?"

"I managed to get in okay, but our mystery competitor beat us to the prize."

"Who is it?" Father demanded.

"I've no idea. But they'll be pissed. I collected up all their calling cards. They left more this time."

"Good job, Katie," Ben said.

Father studied me closely. "And?"

He knew me too well. I let out a sigh, gathering courage to confess my blunder. "I tripped a silent alarm." No point giving the truth any window dressing. I knew I'd messed up and wouldn't make the same mistake again.

Father scrutinized me closely until I started to feel like a bug under Amber's toy microscope. "At least you realized."

"I held the door for the cops when they arrived," I admitted, my tone wry.

In the back seat, Ben spluttered.

"They didn't recognize you."

Hearing the pride in Father's voice, I took my eyes off the road for an instant. "No."

"That's my girl," he said. "Ben and I can tell you what to do in any particular case, but it's experience that's the best teacher. You did good, keeping cool under fire." He nodded his head. "You did good."

CHAPTER 13

Praise indeed! I didn't try to restrain the smile of triumph that curved my lips as I drove down Kensington High Street past Prince's Gate. Father was sparing with his compliments so I savored the words. I'd take compliments wherever I could get them.

"How did your investigation with Ben go?"

"We split up and tried most of the pubs around Covent Garden and the Strand. I got lucky in one of the Soho pubs."

My lips twitched at Father's wording. I wanted to tease so badly. "Did you?" I can restrain myself when the need arises. I indicated right, heading onto Brompton Road upon the light turning green.

Ben guffawed, having no such compunction. "Blonde or brunette?"

"Get your mind out of the gutter," Father growled, but I heard the humor under the bark. "I met up with the bloke who's doing the selling. He said he expected another shipment in a few days. Gave me his card, he did."

"Great job," I said, impressed in spite of myself. I hadn't expected them to get results. "Did you manage to get anything out of him?"

"The man was cagy but greedy with it. By the time I'd told him about my garden-expansion plans and the type of plants I required to make my dream a reality, I had him eating out of my hand."

"Like Amber's bunny," I said.

"Just like Amber's bunny," Father boasted, smacking his hand against his thigh in his appreciation of the joke.

I pulled up in a small mews belonging to an acquaintance who was currently in Europe enjoying the sailing on the Mediterranean. My car would be handy but out of sight of prying neighbors.

"So, what are you going to do next? You don't know for sure that this is the thief." I included Ben in my question.

Father reached over to squeeze my shoulder. "Don't worry your pretty head about the details. Ben and I will take care of everything."

"That's what I'm afraid of," I muttered. "You are keeping away from the poker games, aren't you?" Heck, I hoped so! With Beauchamp staring over our shoulders, our finances were decidedly sick, despite the strict budget

I'd imposed.

Father snorted as he struggled from my Mini. "With the pocket money you give us?"

Father's indignation and plain ingratitude stoked my temper. I was the one pulling his ass from the flames. If it weren't for the huge debts, *The Shadow* could retire. I could take a shot at a normal life or as normal as possible living in the same house as the terrible trio. I opened my mouth to spew forth a few home truths before clamping down on the hasty words. Father wasn't the only one at fault here. I had run off to France to wallow in my shame instead of facing up to the truth. The gossip. I hadn't taken a responsible stance and stayed home to watch him when I should have.

I climbed from the car and pulled back my seat to let Ben clamber out. "Let's get this show on the road."

It was a silent procession that walked down the road, each of us engrossed in our own thoughts. Father stalked ahead, his pride ruffled judging by his stiff, erect posture. Ben kept his own counsel while I followed up the rear.

Father came to an abrupt halt. Deep in thoughts of the past and should-haves, I walked right into him. Seconds later, I was a sandwich filling hiding behind a convenient mailbox.

"Cops at nine o'clock," Father whispered tersely in explanation.

"Oh, look! The boyfriend," Ben murmured.

My heart knocked against my ribs. "He's not my boyfriend." Although I wanted him. There! I'd admitted my impossible dream. For the first time since my giddy teen-age years, I felt the urge to get close to a man. Skin-close. My stomach pulled tight while a tingle sprang to life on my lips. I had a great imagination, and one or two kisses could springboard my fantasies into great works of art.

"Then why does he keep ringing up and coming 'round?" Father countered.

My cheeks heated as I struggled to maintain compo-sure. "That was business. An investigation."

"If you say so." Ben smirked. I couldn't see it but I heard it in his voice.

"A right pretty pickle this is. You say Williams has seen you tonight in that getup?"

I gasped, getting the picture. Different clothes but the same hair. If Kahu saw me here, he was likely to add two and two together and come up with the right total.

"We don't want him to see any of us," I said, peering around the red mailbox. "That's the house I intended to check out." My hands curled to fists. "God damn it! Our mystery cat is a pain in the ass."

"We don't know for sure if that's the problem."

"Why else would the cops arrive at the very house we want to check out? At exactly the same time? I don't like co-incidences." Father scowled. "We need to do something."

I tugged on Father's shirttail and squeezed Ben's fore-arm. "We'd better head back to the car. No point trying anything here."

We backtracked to the mews in silence. I unlocked the Mini, Ben climbed in the back, and Father and I settled in the front.

"We'll try the other house in Cadogan Square," I said.

"If I were a betting man, I'd say we might find our mysterious cat there before us."

You are a betting man, I thought, but I bit back the thought before it became verbal. "They have to be part of the same social circle."

Father grunted, and a remarkably similar sound came from the rear seat.

Ben cleared his throat. "We have to up the tempo and get serious. Beauchamp expects a payment tomorrow."

Did they have to remind me? "Yeah, it's a problem. Those two goons he sent around to the house were tame this morning, but I wouldn't count on them continuing in the same vein if we miss a payment. And I didn't like the way they'd talked about Amber."

Father sighed, loud and gusty before biting off a frustrated curse. "Beauchamp will use the money shortage to blackmail you, Katie." He scrubbed his hands across his face. "Hell, I'm sorry."

In the light cast by the streetlamp, I saw the lines of fatigue and worry spliced with what I guessed was guilt.

I took my left hand off the steering wheel and reached over to touch Father on the arm in a gesture of comfort, forgiveness. "You never said what you spent the money on."

Father sighed again and this time when I glanced at him, he looked every year of his age. "Maintaining Oakthorpe is expensive." His voice was matter-of-fact and void of excuses. I knew he saw maintaining Oakthorpe as a sacred trust. It was the Fawkner way.

"Keeping the business going is expensive." Ben's gruff voice held a definite frown. "Skimp on equipment, and it's jail quicker than a dog after a bitch in heat."

"Charming," I said, merging with the traffic on the A24.

"But true," Ben asserted.

Father managed a weak chuckle before lapsing into a brooding silence.

I decided to broach the subject at a later time. No doubt there was more to the story. I'd worm it out of one of the terrible trio somehow. I wasn't a Fawkner for nothing.

◇ ◇ ◇ ◇ ◇

Hannah greeted us at the door, light from indoors spilling out to light up my battered Mini in the driveway. "You're back earlier than I thought you'd be."

"A few hiccups. Nothing we couldn't handle," I said. "I'll let you out here and park the car."

Father nodded. He massaged his hands and arms in a furtive manner when he thought none of us were looking. My heart ached for him. He must find it difficult to have his freedom curtailed. I knew I would.

I watched Father hobble inside followed by Ben before I drove around the back of the house to park in the garage.

A typical summer's night, I thought with irony as I headed for the rear door that led into the kitchen. Full moon. Mild weather. The scent of honeysuckle in the air. A night made for romance and whispering sweet nothings, yet all I got was drama. Go figure.

Hannah was in the kitchen when I walked in. The kettle whistled and clicked off.

"How's Amber?"

"Measles," Hannah said, reaching for the kettle and pouring it into a blue china teapot.

Damn. "Is she all right?" Guilt assailed me. What sort of parent was I? I'd known she wasn't well but had assumed she'd overdone things at the after-school party.

"I've finally got her off to sleep. She's running a bit of a temperature but the doctor says she'll be fine. The fever should drop as soon as the spots come out."

I hurried from the kitchen and bolted up the stairs, my heart thudding.

Amber was asleep just as Hannah said. Her rosebud mouth gaped a little and each breath she took sounded like the fairy whistle that my aunt used to tell her about. I tiptoed toward the bed, my heart aching with a fierce tug of love. Her cheeks were flushed and her blond hair damp and messy, telling me she'd tossed and turned a lot before drifting off to sleep. She'd kicked off the bedcovers, and I bent to tug them into place. I smoothed a lock of hair away from her face and felt her forehead. Hot, as Hannah had said, but not too bad. I trusted Hannah implicitly with my daughter, but I'd still deserted her when she needed me most. Tears of helplessness formed behind my eyes, and I swallowed to dislodge the knot in my throat. Bottom line: I should have been here for her.

Soft footsteps sounded behind, and Hannah stepped up beside me. After one look at my face, she placed an arm around my shoulders and hugged me.

"It's all right, pet. Amber's going to be fine. Don't cry."

Of course on hearing that, my tears fell harder, faster. I sniffed inelegantly—certainly not blond-bimbo dignified and pretty.

Hannah hugged me harder to her ample bosom and when my tears eased, patted me on the back.

"Come downstairs. Ben and Charles muttered about a meeting for the terrible trio and you. We might as well join them and help drink the last of the good Scottish whiskey."

I let out a half-gasp, half-hiccup and pulled away to stare at her smiling face and twinkling eyes. "You know what I call you?"

"Of course I do. You're not the only one with intelligence around here."

My eyes narrowed as I ran through the possibilities.

"You read my email to my godmother."

"Yes," she confessed unrepentantly. "How else would I know what was going on? I like to keep in the loop."

The modern jargon sounded natural on Hannah's lips. My eyes narrowed even further. "I'm frightened to ask what else you do at the senior citizens' computer club."

Amber stirred, her legs kicking out before she settled again.

"Don't worry. The best thing for her now is sleep. Come downstairs. I need someone sensible to control those old coots. I can't do it on my own."

With those words, the band of helplessness that encircled my chest eased. Hannah, in her own sweet way, had made me realize we were a family. The four of us functioned as a family and we'd fall as a family if I didn't lead from the front.

"You see more of your daughter than most parents do," Hannah said, ushering me from Amber's room. "You visit her sports days, help out with the PTA and read her stories most nights. You're a good parent, Katie. Don't beat yourself up."

I kissed Hannah's cheek. "Thanks. You always know what to say."

We entered the den together. Father and Ben were sprawled out in their favorite armchairs, glasses of whiskey in hand. Their animated chatter died the instant we stepped into the room.

Hannah arched a brow. "Hatching mischief, boys?"

The idea of Father and Ben being called boys tickled my funny bone.

"Humph," Father said.

I grabbed two crystal glasses from an old, battered sideboard, and poured Hannah and I generous measures of whiskey. Hannah dropped onto an old leather couch, a sigh of relief at being off her feet gusting from her. I took up a position, leaning against the wall. I wanted to see them all at the same time

"We need to shut our competitor down," Father said.

I nodded. No arguments there. "How? Any ideas?"

"Ben and I have been discussing it. We need to set a trap. I hate to admit it, but your boyfriend in the force might come in handy."

"He's not my boyfriend," I protested automatically.

"How come he rang for you twice tonight and once at lunchtime?" Hannah asked, not attempting to hide her smirk.

"What did he want?" Father demanded.

"Did he leave a message?" Ben asked a split second later.

"He's not my boyfriend." *Big, fat liar*, my conscience shrieked with fiendish delight. "He's not!" Somehow, the terrible trio had wrested my position of power from me and were thumping me over the head with it.

Hannah waited until calm was restored to drop her bombshell. "He left a message. Two, actually."

I was going to kill them. A slow, painful manner would work best.

Ben waggled his eyebrows. "What did they say?"

"Where are they?" Father narrowed his eyes.

"Don't you dare give my messages to them," I said, trying a glare to subdue them even though I knew it would fail.

"I didn't like to leave any evidence." Hannah grinned, and I knew she was enjoying my predicament. "I memorized them. Now let me see . . ." Her brows squeezed together while she held one pudgy hand to her forehead like a damn psychic.

"Don't I get any privacy around here?" I didn't have to force the belligerent note. It crept in by itself while I thought about the temptation that Inspector Kahu Williams presented. So far, I'd turned down his requests for dates but that didn't mean I was happy about it. I wanted a normal life, but what were the chances of that? A normal life . . . I'd obviously committed a bad, bad crime in a former life and was still paying big-time.

"He can help us with our problem," Father said, breaking into my thoughts.

"Let me give Katie her messages before I forget the exact wording. It's so important to get things right."

My hands itched with the need to wrap around her neck, to throttle her. And judging from the twinkle in her eye, she knew it. She was doing it on purpose, trying to cheer me up.

"The first phone call was to touch base, to say hello and ask Katie out for dinner and drinks tonight if she were free. The second was a plea to ring back on his cell phone, and the third message was sorry that he hadn't caught up with you. He wanted to wish you sweet dreams, and he'll ring again tomorrow." Hannah sighed dreamily. "That is so romantic. Ben, you could take a few pages out of his book. He has such a nice manner on the phone, and that voice. So sexy!"

By this time, each of the terrible trio was eyeing me with various degrees of interest.

My father coughed loudly. "That's enough of that, Hannah. Ben has everything you need. You don't need to stray."

"My father, the advice columnist," I mocked. "We're drifting off topic. Your plan? You know, the one to oust our competitor and leave the field clear for us. That's if there's still an 'us' after we short Beauchamp tomorrow."

As always, reality exerted a calming influence on the terrible trio.

"I've been turning the idea over in my head all day," Father said. "How about this? Let out a rumor that we've found a Celtic dagger while we were digging up a new garden."

I straightened from my casual pose. "Not bad. Not bad at all. How are we going to bring the police into it?"

"That's where my plan gets sticky," Father admitted.

"We're going to have to let that man into our house." Father expelled a heavy sigh. "You're going to have to accept a date or two with that cop. We might even have to let him stay the odd night."

I spluttered in my shock. To their credit, Ben and Hannah buttoned up and left Father and I to slug out the details.

Father's cheeks reddened. "In a spare room, of course!"

Surprisingly, it was me that fought against the idea the hardest. "Won't it make things difficult for *The Shadow*?"

Ben shook his head. "I don't think so. In fact, the idea has merit. Beauchamp's goons will keep away if they know we have an in with the police."

"Have you all lost your minds?" I shouted. Senility. That was it. Somehow, because we lived in such close proximity, the senile gene had hit the terrible trio at the same time. They did everything together. Was it any wonder they were synchronized?

CHAPTER

14

The next morning, I wiped my sweaty palms on my jeans and picked up the phone to ring Inspector Kahu Williams. I'd been outvoted. Phase one of the plan was contact, according to the terrible trio.

The scent of bacon and toast hung heavily in the air. I should have been hungry but nerves were making my stomach dip and dance. I was a step away from nausea and food would only aid the process.

"Get on with it," Father snapped. As I glared at him, he speared a piece of crispy bacon and dipped it in runny egg yolk. I hurriedly looked away. The deep breaths I sucked in were full of breakfast smells. I puffed them out in a hurry.

"I can't understand what's so difficult about ringing the man," Father said.

Yep, he was genuinely confused. Forehead pleated. Brows drawn together. The whole nine yards.

"Men," Hannah muttered, plopping a piece of whole-wheat toast on a plate and handing it to me. "Eat," she ordered. "It will settle the nerves."

Anything to put off the phone call, I decided. I set the phone down with a click and dragged out a chair to join the terrible trio at the table. I stared at the toast with disfavor but picked up a knife and some of Hannah's homemade marmalade.

"Amber is much better this morning," I said.

"Poor lamb. She's upset about missing pet day at school. She wanted to take her rabbit." Hannah sipped at her cup of tea.

A pang of sympathy got me. I'd wanted to attend the pet day too. "The spots are out this morning," I said. "I'd say quite a few of her classmates will miss the pet day."

"The phone call." Father dragged another piece of bacon through his egg and looked up with a grimace. "I can't abide all this waiting around."

I picked up my toast and crunched down. Better a full mouth than saying things that were unforgivable. Hannah had mentioned this morning in Amber's room that Father's arthritis was acting up again. I tried to make allowances but sometimes he made it difficult.

"Fine," I muttered after swallowing. I leapt to my feet and grabbed the phone off the kitchen counter where I'd left it. Kahu's business card sat beside it, his name and details taunting me. I dialed the number to his mobile and listened to the ring-tones with a sinking sensation in my stomach. The idea came to me that this move was irrevocable. My family unit would change forever because of this one phone call.

Get a grip, I instructed myself. It's only a phone call, a date. But it still felt as though I were playing with fire.

The phone rang for so long I almost hung up. The ringing cut off abruptly.

"Williams."

I swallowed and transferred the phone to my other hand. Stupid nerves again.

"Hello?" He sounded impatient, making me suspect he might hang up if I didn't speak soon.

"It's me," I said quickly to allay disaster.

"Kate?" This time pleasure shaded his voice. "Hang on. Let me grab a towel. You got me out of the shower."

Too much information, my brain screamed. I swallowed. Again. And my mind dived right into the fantasy. Man. Naked. *Oh-la-la!*

"What is it?" Hannah whispered. She'd seen my face, no doubt, which felt hot enough to cook any number of fried foods.

I glanced toward the breakfast table. Big-time mistake! Each of the terrible trio had leaned forward, eyes bright with curiosity.

"He's . . . ah . . . getting a towel!"

Father led the chuckle session at my expense.

"I'm back," Kahu said, his voice low and husky. My confidence took a nosedive. Who was I kidding thinking I could control this situation? I was floundering and way beyond my comfort level.

"I missed you last night. I kept thinking about kissing you. I wanted to . . . very badly."

Phone sex. He wasn't. He couldn't! In front of the terrible trio!

"Actually licking came into the equation as well," he murmured with a wicked laugh.

Oh. My. God.

"I'm not alone!" I shrieked.

"Not Seth?"

"The terrible trio," I blurted, whirling away so I couldn't see their smirking faces.

"Ah," Kahu said. "I can see your problem. Were you out with Seth last night?"

Was that jealousy I heard? Something occurred to me then. My arrangement with Seth would create problems. Although I'd already admitted to Kahu there was nothing between Seth and I, I still attended lots of balls and parties with him. I'd have to ask Seth if I could tell Kahu the truth. It was either that or not seeing Seth again for the duration of the plan.

"No, I visited friends with Father and Ben," I said.

"We arrived home late."

"That's all right, then. There are no obstacles to me kissing you." The slight inflection on kissing told me the man's mind was way ahead.

"We'll see," I mumbled in the distinct school-miss-like tone I used with Amber when she was being naughty.

"Ah, character plays. Very good. I can see fun ahead for us."

I squeezed my eyes shut. Lord, save me from sexy men with jumped-up opinions of themselves.

"You rang me," I reminded him. I wasn't having much luck maneuvering the conversation.

"So I did," he mused. "Are you busy tonight? Would you like to go out to dinner?"

"Where would we have dinner?" I prodded. I realized I had no idea where Kahu lived. In London, but where? "And does this mean I'm still the main suspect in the necklace theft? If this is business we don't need to go for dinner."

"You've been cleared, and we're chasing down a few other leads. This dinner is purely personal."

The smoky tone of his voice made a shudder sweep the length of my body. I almost missed his next words.

"I've got to visit Shalford," he said, naming a village not far from Oakthorpe. "Why don't we eat somewhere down your way?"

"Have you had measles?"

"Is that a trick question?"

202

"Amber has measles so if you didn't have them when you were a child, we should leave dinner to another time."

Kahu laughed, low and rich, reminding me of picnics on a lazy summer day, sleep-ins, breakfast in bed—*Whoa! Stop the train—I wanna get off.* It was ludicrous combining Kahu with those thoughts. Not to mention dangerous to my sanity.

"I managed to catch all the usual childhood ills when I was younger. My brother and I just about drove my mother mad the time we had chicken pox."

I pictured two small boys with brown eyes and mischievous grins. Actually, strike the grins—they had chicken pox, and I recalled experiencing acute itchiness and being covered with pink splotches of calamine lotion.

"What time works best for you? Around seven?"

"Seven is fine. The local pub does a good meal." Thank goodness he'd interrupted my runaway thoughts. *Concentrate on keeping Amber safe. That's all you need to do.* Do not get your emotions involved! My chest heaved as I sucked in a breath and turned to lean my butt against the kitchen counter. The terrible trio. Yea, gods! I'd forgotten about their presence. I was in deeper trouble than I'd suspected.

"See you later."

I nodded even though Kahu couldn't see. "Seven."

"Seven," he confirmed again, but when he said it, it sounded like a caress.

Aghast, I pulled the phone away from my ear and

stabbed at the talk button. My heart pounded and the moistness had returned to my palms. Inside, anticipation surged, strong enough that alarm bells rang in my sluggish brain.

"Good job, Katie," Hannah said. She bustled past me to grab two slices of toast freshly popped from the toaster. She propelled me to my chair in a silent order to sit on her way back.

I applied myself to a slice of toast, but I might as well have been eating sawdust. Dropping the toast back on my plate, I dabbed the crumbs from my mouth with a linen napkin and placed it on my plate. After a deep breath, I looked up to face the inquisition of the male members of the terrible trio.

"What?"

"You'd better not go soft on that man," Father warned.

Stung and more than a little guilty because of my wayward hormones, I murmured, "It wasn't my idea in the first place."

"True," Ben agreed.

"More toast, anyone?" Hannah asked.

"No, thanks," Father said, speaking for all of us.

Hannah joined us at the table with a fresh pot of tea and went about the business of refilling cups.

"I keep thinking about the mystery cat," Hannah said, a shade of puzzlement in her voice. "We use the social whirl to scout targets. What if we managed to get hold of the guests lists of as many social gatherings as we could and I cross-reference them to work out a list of suspects?"

Silence greeted Hannah's suggestion. I know I felt awe. Not at the idea, but on learning she had the skill to carry out her suggestion. I caught the stunned looks on Father and Ben's faces and laughed.

"And here I thought those computer courses you were taking were a waste of time." Admiration shone on Ben's face as he stood and walked around the kitchen table to where Hannah sat. He planted a smacking kiss on her mouth, leaving Hannah blushing and wearing a beam at the same time.

"Way to go!" Father scratched his head. "Complicated things, computers. Give me a set of blueprints to decipher anytime."

◊ ◊ ◊ ◊ ◊

Kahu arrived right on time. I peered out my bedroom window to confirm the car pulling up in the drive belonged to him before turning back to cast a rueful glance at the mess of clothes all over my bed. They bore mute testimony to my inner panic. A date. It was only a date. I tried to remind myself of the fact even though deep down I knew this was a step into murky waters. Far away from my prior, safe relationships with men. I wouldn't be human if I didn't let memories of my rape affect my present. Rape is the ultimate indignity a woman can face, and it is impossible to go through the experience without change. I was no longer the trusting, open person I'd been at eighteen. But even so, I was one of the lucky victims—if you could call a victim lucky. Because I'd been drugged, I didn't remember any of the experience. My first memory was waking up in the empty hotel room. But I was wary, shy of men. This date, with Kahu Williams, was a new departure. The only man I'd trusted so far was Seth. Being gay, he didn't have a sexual interest in me so he rated safe on my measuring scale.

In the distance, I heard the doorbell chime. One of the terrible trio would answer the summons. In truth, they were as nervous as I was, although none of them had admitted it. They knew this was a big step for me, especially with the added pressure of the *Shadow* mantle, and the trap we hoped to spring.

"Katie! Your dinner date's arrived." Hannah knocked on my bedroom door and stuck her head through the door to make sure I'd heard. Her gaze swept the tangle of clothes littering the bed and the pile of shoes by the wardrobe. She stepped inside and shut the door with a firm click. "Don't worry. Nerves are natural. He's a lovely young man. Thoughtful, too. He brought a present for Amber: a puzzle she can play with while she's confined to bed, and a painting set for later. You'll be fine with him. Besides, you're on home territory down at the local. If he steps out of line, even a little, just give the nod to Reg behind the bar. He'll sort him out for you."

"Thanks." Summoning a weak smile, I added, "Are my nerves that obvious?"

Hannah tugged me into her arms and patted me on the back in the same way she used to when I was a child. "You look beautiful. Black suits you," she said, referring to my full black skirt and matching sleeveless blouse. "I look washed out in black, but you—you look lovely. Inspector Kahu Williams won't know what's hit him."

I sighed. "I feel guilty. I don't want to lead him on, to give him ideas about a future. I mean, how can we have a future when we work on opposite poles of the law?"

"Go with the flow, Katie. Don't worry about the future. Take one day at a time. That's all we can do at the moment. Besides, despite what Charlie and Ben say, *The Shadow* can go into retirement."

Grateful for the feminine support, I hugged the woman who was mother to me. "I'd better not keep him waiting."

"He's in good hands. Charlie and Ben are with him."

"That," I said dryly, "is what I'm afraid of."

◊ ◊ ◊ ◊ ◊

The drive to the Wheat Sheaf pub was conducted mostly in silence with a little small talk sprinkled in. We'd covered the weather—unseasonably warm heading for a heat wave—and the terrible trio. An apology for their overprotectiveness from me, and amusement but total understanding from Kahu. A summation of the conversation since leaving Oakthorpe.

"Thank you for thinking of Amber," I said, desperate to fill the yawning silence before my nerves got the better of me. "It was kind of you to bring a gift for her."

"She's a good kid," Kahu said, taking his gaze off the road to look at me. "Is her father around?"

"No." Even though I tried to keep inflection from my voice, the one-word answer emerged short and terse.

A thoughtful frown creased Kahu's brow before he pulled into the Wheat Sheaf's crowded car park. I could almost hear him processing my response and formulating an opinion.

"And Seth? Where does he fit into the picture?"

"I've told you before," I snapped. "We're friends. There's nothing romantic between us. Seth is like a brother."

Kahu switched off the ignition. "I wanted to clarify things," he said, his voice even and controlled. "Again. People have told me different."

"You should have asked me," I said, not bothering to hold back on the flash of temper. "I'm the one in the know."

Kahu turned to me and picked up my right hand in his. My senses narrowed to the point of contact. His hands were callused, confirming he sometimes worked with his hands. Warmth sped up my arm settling around my heart.

"Of course you are," he soothed, a soft smile curving

208

THE SHADOW

his mouth. Eyes shone with echoed amusement. "That's why I wanted to check with you. Don't want to get too carried away with thoughts of kisses and licking if—"

"I get the picture," I said hastily, attempting to tug my hand from his grasp. "We'd better hurry or they'll shut the kitchen before we order."

Kahu laughed and took his sweet time about releasing my hand. "Just so I have things clear, Seth is your brother and Amber's father is not in the picture. I'm the only man you're seeing."

Intent stated concisely, so clear a child could understand. Blond bimbo deserted me, unable to think of a suitable answer for Kahu, leaving Katherine Fawkner, to deal with the fallout.

"Come on. Forget about the kisses," he said, laughing. "Dinner and conversation, that's all."

Kahu read my confusion with an ease that made me fidget in the passenger seat. Jeez, I was so out-of-date with this dating stuff. Well-meaning advice from the terrible trio fluttered around inside my head like a flock of monarch butterflies on speed. Flirt. Make eye contact. Stroke his ego. Men like that. Smile. Wear a low-cut top.

Oh, boy.

"Sure," I said. Agreement came out low and breathy. Unintentionally sexy. *Take a deep breath*, I instructed myself. The man's hardly going to jump you in a pub full of neighbors and friends. The extra intake of air helped calm me. I opened the door of Kahu's sedan and climbed out.

Kahu stood at my side before I could shut the door. Hannah was right. The man was a gentleman. Instinct told me I had nothing to fear.

The Wheat Sheaf was packed to capacity. When Kahu opened the door for me, a low rumble of chatter greeted us, spliced with music from the jukebox and the rattle of a slot machine paying out.

"Looks busy," I said. "We'll be lucky to get a table."

"I booked one earlier," Kahu said.

"Oh."

We weaved through the crowd of locals standing at the bar, heading for the dining room. The Wheat Sheaf has always been a favorite of mine. Apart from the friendly locals, I loved the ambiance of the pub. Bric-a-brac lined shelves, ranging from a collection of toby jugs to chamber pots and old books of varying sizes. Each shelf had a different theme. The pub was children- and pet-friendly during the day, and Amber loved to visit the beer garden for lunch on a Sunday. She invariably spent time petting all the dogs in attendance. We hadn't visited much recently since we were on a strict budget. And the safety aspect was always at the back of my mind. I didn't like Amber leaving the security of Oakthorpe. Every minute of the day she was at school was an exercise in torture. I worried.

"Nice pub," Kahu said, his hand in the small of my back, guiding me in the direction of the dining room.

"Lady Katherine! We haven't seen you for a while," Reg, the Wheat Sheaf owner, said.

"No. Amber can't wait to visit again. She's in bed with the measles."

"Aye. Seems to be doing the rounds in the village."

"This is my friend, Kahu Williams. We're here for dinner."

"Good enough," Reg said, eyeing up Kahu in the way men measure strangers. "Try the special. Roast beef with all the trimmings. Gravy. Yorkshire pudding. Can't go wrong with the special." Reg laughed, a loud booming sound that made everyone listening want to laugh along with him. "I'm hoping for roast beef myself tonight. Don't suppose I should recommend it," he confessed, a twinkle in his eyes. "Pleased to meet you," he said, nodding at Kahu. "You from Australia?"

"New Zealand," Kahu answered.

"Ah! I know the countries are a distance apart, but you all sound the same to me. Catch up with you later, Lady Katherine."

I smiled and nodded. No matter how many times I asked Reg to call me Kate, he stuck with the more formal Lady Katherine. I had the notion he liked the status of a regular with a title so I let it go.

Kahu checked in with the dining-room hostess, and she showed us to a table overlooking the river.

"I'm going with the roast beef," Kahu said after he'd

seated me and ordered a bottle of sparkling water and a glass of wine for himself.

"Fish and chips with salad," I said, not bothering to check the menu. "It's my favorite." I glanced at his face, shadowed in the lowered lighting and candle glow. "Where do you live? I don't know much about you at all."

"I have a flat in Fulham. Don't spend much time there with my work."

"And where do you live when you're at home in New Zealand?"

"Wellington."

The evening passed so quickly I thought I'd blinked and missed it. I'd assumed I'd never feel relaxed with a man again, but I was wrong. After the initial getting-to-know-you questions, our conversation flowed freely.

"I hate to rush you, Lady Katherine, but we're about to close," the dining room hostess said.

My head jerked up, away from Kahu to travel the dining room. Where had everyone gone? I checked my watch, stunned to see it was almost eleven. "I didn't realize it was so late."

"No problem. Would you like coffee? There's time for coffee before we close."

"I'd like coffee," Kahu drawled.

The hostess blinked at his smile. Not that I blamed her. I was a little dazzled myself and heading down the path toward a stronger emotion. The notion should have scared me silly, but I barely hesitated.

The drive home to Oakthorpe sped past in silence again, but this time it was a comfortable one—until my thoughts turned to the concept of a good-night kiss. Would Kahu expect one? Did I want one?

Okay. I knew the answer to the second question. I'd feel cheated if I didn't get a kiss. I wanted to taste him again, to find out if our last kiss, which had made my heart pitter-patter, was an anomaly.

Kahu turned the sedan into the driveway and pulled to a stop by the house. The air seemed to vanish from the car interior, sucked away by anticipation. My tingle-meter leapt to the top of the scale when I risked a glance at him. Chocolate-brown eyes sparkled with sensual heat as he met my gaze. He switched off the ignition, and the silence was a living thing. Kahu's aftershave with the spicy undertones drew me, as it had all night. Like a magnet, I was helpless. I felt myself sway toward Kahu across the console between the driver and passenger seats.

"I've thought about this all night," Kahu murmured. In the dim light, I saw the naughty twinkle in his eyes. His right hand cupped my cheek while his lips curled up in a soft smile. Without warning, my skin was suddenly ultra-sensitive. I shivered.

Our lips met. Parted. He nibbled his way down my neck, small bites that sent miniature earthquakes rippling across my skin. My heart thudded so hard I thought it might leap from my chest. Or at the very least, Kahu would notice my excitement and comment. Embarrassment city. My peripheral vision caught a flicker of light from the house. The terrible trio. Watching our every move, no doubt. And still muttering under their breaths about the necessity of using a cop to spring their trap in the first place.

"Fawkners will roll in their graves," Father had said minutes before Kahu arrived. The knowledge we were watched tempered my lust—a fraction. But no way did I intend to leave the car or Kahu without a decent kiss to commit to memory, a memory I could pull out and relive whenever Father decided to lecture.

"Are we being watched?" Kahu asked in a voice full of lazy amusement. Luckily, he didn't seem to mind. "Should we give them something worthy to look at?"

He didn't wait for my reply, merely lowered his head and captured my lips with expertise that should have frightened me. But who was thinking? I was too busy assimilating taste, touch, and smell. A masculine hand threaded through my hair. A flicker of tongue across my lips made me gasp. My hand, which had somehow managed to undo several of Kahu's shirt buttons, inserted itself inside the parted fabric. I felt the subtle rise and fall of Kahu's chest as silent laughter played out. The taste of coffee and Kahu exploded on my senses. His slow and thorough exploration sent ribbons of need curling through me. With frightening speed and a total lack of common sense, I wanted more. Much more.

214

The sensation of naked skin sliding against naked skin. The freedom to explore masculine muscles . . .

For so long, I'd suppressed my sexual urges, keeping my heart wrapped up tight. *Safe*. With one kiss, Kahu had ripped the protective cover away and made me want to live again.

Kahu eased up on the kiss and feathered a trail of tiny nibbles across my cheek, making me laugh.

"You'll go out with me again?"

"Yes." Hard to tell anything from his voice, but I knew what I wanted. "Do you want to come in for coffee?"

"Not this time. I need to drive back to Fulham tonight." He exuded a dazzling smile in the dim light of the car interior. "I'm not sure of my schedule but once I know, I'll call you." The back of his hand smoothed across my cheek in a gesture of farewell, leaving a pleasant tingle.

I managed a nod, hastily removed my hands from Kahu's chest, and fumbled for the door handle. Embarrassment caught me without warning. Why didn't I just throw myself at him and have done?

"Good night, Kate."

"Night."

I made the top of the steps leading to the front door before I succumbed to temptation and peeked to see if Kahu watched me. He did. I lifted a hand and waved before turning back to open the front door. It flew open before I had a chance to grasp the handle.

"Aw, man," Ben said. "Look at the goofy grin on her face."

"I knew this would happen. Females can't keep their minds on the job when romance jumps into the equation."

I gaped at Father in shock. "You told me to go out with Kahu," I said in a studied voice. "Mission accomplished."

"But we didn't tell you to get up close and friendly," Father spouted in outrage.

"Let the girl inside," Hannah said, using her elbows to clear the way and give me a path to the kitchen.

The trio herded me subtlety in that direction—one standing on each side and Hannah bringing up the rear. I guess someone had called a meeting and hadn't bothered to inform me.

In the kitchen, Ben pulled out a wooden chair and indicated with a jerk of his head I should sit.

Indignation ruffled my temper. "I'm not a prisoner to interrogate."

Father took the seat opposite. "We just want to know how things went."

"We're concerned about the plan," Ben said hovering over me.

"Quit treating Katie like a circus freak. I'll make tea," Hannah said.

"Are you going to tell us what happened?" Father's brows drew together so they resembled a long, furry caterpillar. "Did he ask you out again?"

THE SHADOW

I felt my mouth firm, my eyes narrow. I wasn't the only stubborn member of the Oakthorpe household. This scenario was way off-kilter. I wasn't a teenager out on her first date, but I could tell the male members of the trio weren't going to give up without feedback.

"Enough," Hannah said. She punctuated her directive with a firm thump of the teapot on the tabletop. "Both of you are acting like policemen. Give Katie breathing space, and maybe she'll quench your raging curiosity."

Though she buttoned their lips, their eyes demanded answers. Silently conceding that I'd best offer up details for the sake of peace, I said, "Yes, we're going out again, but I'm not sure when. Kahu is going to ring me."

"Excellent." Ben settled back in his chair and glanced from the teapot to his wife. "How's that tea coming along?"

"Humph," Hannah snorted.

Father continued to frown. "You'll play the man just as we discussed. You won't go girly and fall for him."

Enough. I wasn't in the mood to deal with them tonight. I'd enjoyed my evening, and the more time I spent with Kahu, the more I liked him. I stood abruptly, almost knocking over my chair. "It's late. I'm going to bed."

"But we want to go over our plan again," Father protested.

"Then do it without me," I said, and I marched out of the kitchen ignoring the protests that floated up the stairs after me.

CHAPTER
15

A mber, my wee croissant," I said, early the next morning. "You can't go to school yet. You've still got spots on your tummy." I lifted her shirt to show her, and when her bottom lip started to tremble, I skimmed my fingers across her ribs to make her giggle.

When the laughter stopped, her small mouth tightened to a pout. Her bottom lip stuck out. *No need to search far to find where that came from*, I thought with a wry glance at my father.

"I don't wanna stay in bed," Amber said, stamping her foot on the kitchen floor.

"You don't have to stay in bed today. If you're good, Hannah might let you help her today. I'm sure I heard her say it's baking day."

"That's right." Hannah stacked the last of the breakfast dishes in the dishwasher and wiped her hands on a towel. "I thought I might make gingerbread men to take to the senior-citizen club tonight."

Tantrum averted. I ruffled Amber's brown curls. "Grandfather and Ben might let you help pick peas for dinner."

The phone rang, and I reached for it since I was closest. "Hello?"

"Charles Fawkner."

"Can I say who's speaking?"

"None of your business, sweetheart. Just get him."

I held the phone away from my ear and grimaced. "For you," I said to Father, not bothering to lower my voice in the slightest. "I don't know who it is, but he needs to work on his manners."

Father accepted the phone from me. "Fawkner." He listened for a time and nodded while we watched with burning curiosity. Not one of Father's answers gave us a clue. Finally, he hung up. "Yes!" Father pumped his fist in the air. "You'll never guess," he said.

"Not unless you give us a clue," Hannah said snidely.

"The man we met in the pub and talked to about the plants. He's rung to tell me he has the plants I wanted."

Interested in spite of my self, I stopped clearing the breakfast table. "How are you going to handle it?"

"Ah," Father said. "We discussed it last night while you were out with the cop."

"He has a name," I muttered.

SHELLEY MUNRO

Father ignored my comment, intent on getting to the point. "We'll give him a call and ask him how to proceed. Get on the cop's good side. Where's his business card?"

I could see that Father's mind was made up, no matter what I said so I extracted it from my handbag and handed it over without further comment. But before Father could ring Kahu, the phone rang again.

"It's for you," Father said with not much more than a grunt. "It's Seth." He glared at me, but I wasn't entirely sure why. It could have been because he wanted to use the phone, or maybe he thought Seth threatened my budding relationship with Kahu. Who knew? I ignored him and picked up the phone.

"Hi, Seth! What's up?"

"Do you want to go to the ball at Hawkins House on Friday night?"

Bother. A scheduling conflict already. "Do you have time to meet me at Ye Olde Tea Shoppe in the village? Say, around ten?"

"The terrible trio up to their tricks again?"

"You could say that," I said, my tone cagy.

"Ten is fine. I'll tell my secretary I'm interviewing a witness for next week's court case."

"Are you scared of your secretary?"

"Hell, yes," Seth said with a laugh. "Talk to you later."

The phone disconnected abruptly, and my grin widened. No doubt Sara had walked into Seth's office with a load of

220

messages. Seth had inherited Sara and was convinced she bore tales to his father. He claimed there was no other way for his father to keep so up-to-date with the goings-on at Winthrop, Brown & Mason, the local law firm.

At ten prompt, I pushed open the wooden door to the village teashop, the tinkling of a bell over the door announcing my arrival. I spotted Seth at a corner table. Seth stood to pull out a chair for me.

"Good choice," I said as I brushed a kiss over his ruddy cheek. "Too far away from the cash register for Mrs. Fletcher to eavesdrop on us."

Seth rolled his brown eyes, the movement of his head flopping his fringe over his forehead. "That didn't stop her trying to interrogate me when I arrived," he muttered.

"She probably compares notes with Sara."

"No doubt," he said. "And speaking of Sara, she asked when to expect me back in the office. I'm on a strict schedule."

"I'll get right to the—"

"Are you ready to order yet, Mr. Winthrop?"

Seth managed a polite smile. I was tempted to snarl. Mrs. Fletcher, the owner of the teashop, loved to gossip and spent lots of time indulging the passion. In fact, the terrible trio called the teashop Gossip Central instead of by its real name, Ye Olde Tea Shoppe.

"Another few minutes please, Mrs. Fletcher."

She nodded and bustled away but couldn't resist a

glance over her shoulder.

I leaned toward Seth. "You can almost hear her take notes."

"Here." Seth shoved a menu at me. "Pick something and start talking. I have to be back at the office in an hour."

We ordered pinwheel sandwiches and scones warm from the oven, along with a pot of Ceylon tea. The scones arrived with a bowl of homemade strawberry jam and Devonshire cream. I'll say one thing for Mrs. Fletcher. The woman could cook up a storm and regularly took honors at the village fete.

"Now, what's the problem?"

"I went out on a date with Kahu Williams last night," I confessed in a rush. All the way on the drive into the village, I'd practiced what I would say.

"I wondered how long it would take," Seth said, grinning.

"I wanted to tell you before anyone else did."

"Too late. Mrs. Fletcher told me before you arrived. Said she didn't want me to get hurt and thought I should know."

"No wonder she's hovering," I said, making no effort to hide my indignation.

Seth placed his half-eaten sandwich back on his plate and reached across the table to pat my arm. "Don't worry, Kate. I knew you'd meet someone eventually. You're so pretty, it was only a matter of time."

I grabbed at Seth's hand and squeezed hard. "But what

will you do now? I feel as though I'm letting you down."

Seth shrugged off my worries. "We'll still be friends. I can't see what the problem is."

"Yes, of course we're still friends."

"I'll make alternative plans for this weekend," Seth said. "No problem."

"I'm not sure if Kahu will ask me to go with him or if he's working. He said things are busy at the moment, and he's not sure of his schedule."

"All right. I'll leave it up to you. I don't want to come between the two of you," Seth said.

"Thanks." Wow. That was a relief, although I felt a trifle guilty since I hadn't told the truth in its entirety. I'd managed it without having to explain why I was dangling after Kahu. Seth thought the attraction was a romantic one. It was my job to make sure Kahu, along with everyone else, thought the same.

◇ ◇ ◇ ◇ ◇

I arrived back at Oakthorpe to find Kahu in residence. It appeared Father had acted with uncharacteristic speed, and the police had jumped at the chance to capture the thief. I climbed from my Mini, my fingers crossed behind my back. Hope they caught the crooks and paid out on the reward lickety-split. We needed the reward money yesterday! The goons had stayed away so far, but I wasn't

223

holding my breath. The situation felt like a trap waiting for the unwary victim.

"Good to see you, Kate." Kahu kept his words simple, but one glance at his mischievous eyes told me he was thinking of our goodnight in his car. Kisses. Touching. And if he were like me, thinking about where the seductive path might lead.

All at once, a herd of butterflies stampeded through my stomach. *Keep it casual*, I ordered my leaping libido. It was still early in the courtship process. Unfortunately, my heart didn't pay a single bit of notice. Although I kept telling myself nothing could come of this relationship, that going out with Kahu was a ploy to further *The Shadow*'s career, my heart insisted otherwise. The antipodean hunk had crept into my sleep-befuddled brain this morning, and I hadn't had much peace since.

"Good morning," I said.

"I'd hoped I'd see you. I wanted—"

"Are you going to stand there and make doe eyes at each other?" Father demanded. "Don't you have some crooks to catch?"

"Father!" To say I was embarrassed was an understatement. Wasn't Father the one who had forced this travesty on me? The one who'd insisted I consort with the enemy? After glaring at Father, I took Kahu's arm. "We can talk in the garden."

A smile lit Kahu's dark eyes and his gaze drifted to

my mouth. Man, he pushed buttons I never knew I had—without breaking a sweat. I was drifting into dangerous territory yet n thing I did seemed to halt the fall.

We walked around the corner of the ivy-clad house, and I led Kahu toward the rose beds, mainly because I knew they weren't visible from the kitchen. I caught sight of the terrible trio when we ambled past the kitchen. Yep, they were definitely treating us like the hottest show of the week. A novelty for their viewing pleasure. Feeling quietly satisfied, okay—smug, I admit it—I savored the scent of the roses and enjoyed the novelty of walking beside a handsome male.

Kahu slowed his steps and turned to grin at me. "Are we out of sight yet?"

Heat bloomed in my cheeks. "How did you know?"

"I'm a policeman," he murmured, running his fingers across my cheek, all the while looking at my mouth. "I'm paid to observe."

A timely reminder to keep me focused on the job at hand. "No, they can't see us here."

Kahu stepped closer until I felt his body heat and smelled his spicy aftershave. I swallowed my sudden unease at the dangerous game I played.

"That's good," he said, "because I want to kiss you so bad, I ache."

I looked at him, startled by his directness. A mistake. His lips descended and claimed mine before I could do more than take a breath. My mind ceased its turmoil of right and wrong and the shades of gray in between, to concentrate on the man who had his lips locked on mine. He tugged me off balance, and I landed against Kahu's chest, clutching his shoulders while his lips plundered mine. Tongues dueled. Tasted. Lingered to explore and savor. My nipples puckered to hard points against my lacy bra, suddenly aching. Astonished, I pulled away from Kahu to stare. "How did you do that?" I blurted.

"Do what?"

I noticed he had trouble taking his eyes off my lips. And luckily my brain engaged once we were no longer touching. I censored the unsaid words hovering at the tip of my tongue. Way uncool to blurt out the first thing to come into my mind.

"Do what?" he repeated.

"Ah, nothing," I muttered.

A roguish grin played about his lips as he witnessed my discomfort. Another thought occurred. I hope he didn't guess my thoughts.

Kahu's dark eyes crinkled at the corners. "Good." Before I knew it, I was plastered against his chest in another lip-lock.

Hmmm. Hands on skin. A shudder of pure desire shot to my belly. My hands tightened on Kahu's shoulders and drifted up to rest behind his neck. Things were moving at breakneck speed, and for once, I had no inclination to slam on the brakes.

"Phone!"

I jerked away from Kahu so quickly I almost fell.

"Phone!" Father again hollered. "Did you hear?"

"Yes, the first time!" I snapped, peeved at the rude interruption. Things had just been getting interesting. I glanced at Kahu and intercepted a wink.

"I'd better go. I'll ring you later."

Like a mannequin, I nodded, my thoughts still wholly involved with our kiss.

"Are you going to take the phone or not?" Father asked with a trace of impatience.

I whirled away from Kahu, ready to tear a strip off my father. It was then I noticed his pale face.

Forcing a smile, I said to Kahu, "That would be great." I waved and hurried toward the kitchen. Father arrived not long after, and the terrible trio and I all stared at the phone, treating it like a mythical beast about to eat us. Swallowing, I picked it up, noting at the back of my mind that my hand was trembling. I covered the receiver. "Make sure Kahu's left."

Ben trotted off to undertake the assignment. Back seconds later, he nodded and the tension seeped from my shoulders. One less thing to worry about.

"Hello. Lady Katherine Fawkner here," I said in a pleasant voice.

"I don't have all day," a familiar voice snarled.

I sighed. Goon number one. "I'm very sorry," I said. "I had the police here undertaking a local investigation. Did you want me to tell them sorry, I have to go? I have goons waiting to speak to me on the phone?"

"Lady, you have a smart mouth."

"So I've been told," I said, not sparing the snide tone.

Father tapped me on my shoulder and mimed something.

"What?" I mouthed, not understanding the frantic hand actions. Ben started up too—his version, no doubt, because they didn't match.

"Your payment is late."

My eyes rolled. Tell me something I didn't know. I considered saying that out loud but judging by the sound of his voice, I'd annoyed him enough already.

"Yes, I'm sorry," I said, trying not to sound too meek or too condescending. It was a difficult assignment when I wanted to ream him out for frightening the terrible trio. They might have enough sass and sheer pigheadedness for six but they were getting on in years. And quite frankly, I was pissed by the situation. "I would like to speak to the man in charge," I said.

"Who am I? Chopped liver?"

Cow dung described him better but I didn't voice that thought either. Phew! A whole lot of censorship goin' on.

"I would like to speak to your boss," I stated with quiet dignity. "The man to whom we owe the money."

"He won't be pleased. He pays me to deal with the likes of you."

"What do you think you're doing?" Father whispered.

Ben was making frantic no-no movements with his hand along with slashing signs across his throat.

"Could I have a phone number to ring you back?" I asked the goon.

"No! My boss told me to get the money, and that's what I intend to do. No money, no commission. Simple as that. This, lady, is a business transaction. It's nothing personal."

"Nothing personal?" I shrieked down the phone. "You make threats against my daughter and say it's nothing personal?"

"There's no need to get screechy, lady." He rattled off his number. "If I don't hear back from you in exactly fifteen minutes or less, I will take that to mean you do not have the payment owing and will take steps to extract said payment. Do I make myself clear?"

"Crystal." I repeated the number back to him and slapped the phone back in its cradle. I hoped it hurt his ears because he'd given me the mother of all headaches.

"Are you mad?" Father hollered.

Hannah took one look at my face and hurried to the drawer where we keep odds and ends. She yanked out a packet of headache tablets, popped open the bubble pack, and handed me two pills along with a glass of water.

I downed the tablets straightaway. "Thank you. Have

you contacted Alistair today?" I asked.

"Yeah. No good news there. He can sell the goods today, but the price won't be a good one. He has feelers out with another collector from the States. Seems to think we should wait a week or so and the chance at a better price."

"Logical. If it wasn't for the money due, we'd wait. Okay, this is the plan. I'll ring back the goon and say we're short on the payment."

"Oh, that will make him happy," Father said.

"I'm going to point out that my new boyfriend is a cop who takes a dim view of his latest squeeze being harassed."

"Latest squeeze," Hannah said with delight. If she'd been younger, I'm sure she would have given a feminine squeak. "Oh, that is good news. The two of you look so right together. I can't wait to have more children in the family."

"Cut the—Children!" Father roared, the lines on his forehead very evident since he glared at Hannah so hard. "Are you stark raving mad? I thought we'd decided this was a ruse to get rid of our competition. The rumors are circulating in the village about the dagger already."

"I told you that clinch looked personal. Way personal," Ben said, waggling his eyebrows.

"All I said was it would be nice to have more children about the house. Katie needs someone."

"She has us."

Hannah sent a grimace in my direction while I did

a mental eye roll. Living at Oakthorpe with the terrible trio didn't keep me warm when I lay in the single bed I'd slept in as a kid. I noticed that even Ben gaped at Father this time.

Father cleared his throat and looked at us as if to say, *What?*

Hannah let out a snort of disgust and advanced on Father. "Katie has every right to a sex life. With a male of her choice. And if that man happens to be that hottie, Kahu Williams, then good!" She punctuated each sentence with a finger jab at Father's chest.

Father's face paled.

Ben shook his head in disbelief. "A hottie? Just what do you do down at the senior citizens' hall?" He winked at his wife. "Should I worry, sweetcakes?"

Sweetcakes? I was so not going there. Time to change the subject.

"I'm going to contact Beauchamp, assuming he's the mouth behind the goons, and try to work out a deal. We'll offer to pay what we have right now and see what he says. But I'd better ring the goon first." I picked up the phone and dialed.

"That was longer than fifteen minutes," the goon snapped.

I ignored the attitude and put out one of my own. "I don't appreciate your threats." Might as well start at the main point of contention.

"If you paid on time, I wouldn't have to make threats."

Good point. "Do you work for Beauchamp?"

"What's it to you?"

"I want to talk to him. Discuss things."

The goon laughed with a smug snigger that raised my hackles. If I'd been in the same room, I'd have flattened him. Or at least have made an attempt. Instead, my hand gripped the telephone and I gritted my teeth.

"That little girl of yours is mighty pretty. Amber, isn't it?"

Fear kicked me in the ribs. The implacable tone of his voice indicated a willingness to follow through with his threat.

"I'll go to the cops," I stated.

"Oh yeah? And what kind of story are you going to make up to explain the circumstances? What are they going to do to your father? No, I think you're going to get the money and pay up. On time."

Fury whipped me, but the fear cut deeper.

The man was deadly serious. He'd really hurt Amber if we didn't pay. My curse was short. Sharp. Not particularly original. And it didn't relieve any of my frustration with the situation.

"Are you going to tell us what he said?" Father demanded once I'd hung up.

"He's insisting we pay the full amount. I guess he wants his commission." I pushed back my chair, wincing at the screech of wood against tiles, and stood.

"Where are you going?" Father's voice held an edge of fear.

A contagious condition, it seemed.

"I'm going to find the phone directory."

"It's in the office." Hannah shot to her feet. "I'll get it." She hurried from the kitchen before I could protest.

The truth was I wanted time alone to think. No. That wasn't the truth. I'd already decided on what had to be done. It was carrying it out that jammed my throat. I tugged open a cupboard and pulled out a glass. After filling it with water, I returned to the table and sat. One swallow of water. Two. The dry, choked sensation remained.

Footsteps heralded Hannah's return.

"Here," she said, handing over a slip of paper with a phone number written on it. "I looked up his home number for you."

Richard "The Octopus" Beauchamp.

I wasn't exactly looking forward to this call, but I had to make it. I crammed the number into the left hip pocket of my jeans.

"I'll take the portable phone upstairs and make the call from there."

"What are you going to say?" Father asked, a troubled expression on his face. It made me realize how fragile they were despite the gutsy front they all presented. I made a silent vow. I'd get us through this mess somehow. I'd make sure they behaved and didn't get out of line again, that they behaved in a manner more befitting a senior citizen. Hysterical laughter—a little crazed and carrying more than a bit of irony—screeched through my mind. Correct behavior. Huh! Cows might fly.

"Katie," Hannah stepped around the table to stand in front of me. She placed a hand on each of my shoulders and studied my face. "Don't do anything that makes you uncomfortable. The three of us were here, not you. The blame for this debt lies with us." She squeezed my shoulders. "Really, we realize how difficult the rape was, how it ruined your plans for the future, your dreams. Make sure that any decision you make is for the right reasons."

The sudden blast of silence in the room was deafening. No one ever mentioned the past. We all sort of swept it under the table and ignored it as best we could. Of course, Amber was a visual memory since she didn't resemble me, but she had such a strong personality it was easy to ignore the circumstances of her conception.

"I don't think we need to bring up *that* subject," Father said in his stuffy aristocrat voice.

Hannah loosened her grip on my shoulders and turned to glare at Father. "It won't change—"

"Enough," I said. "We're not going to muddle through this mess if we snipe at each other. We're a family. We need to pull together and act like one." I didn't wait for comments. I'd had enough, and besides, I had to confront

Beauchamp and sort out terms of payment. The schedule we were trying to keep to at the moment was near impossible.

I entered my bedroom and closed the door to keep the world out or the terrible trio at least. I wouldn't put it past them to try to eavesdrop.

CHAPTER

16

My bedroom hadn't changed much since I was a teenager. I studied the faded floral curtains, the single bed with its frilly lace cover. The posters had long gone but the darker patches on the wallpaper signaled where they'd hung. With a sigh for the past, I picked up the phone and dug deep into my pocket to find the piece of paper bearing Beauchamp's number.

Perhaps I'd ask Amber what she thought about redecorating. It could be a mother/daughter project. Not a bad idea, I mused, especially since she can't go to school. Hannah was highly skilled on the sewing machine and with all the stuff in the attic, we were sure to find something to give the room a facelift.

Procrastinating! I scolded firmly. I smoothed out the phone number and dialed. The phone rang for a long time before an answer machine picked up. I hesitated before deciding to leave a message. There was no time to waste after I'd hung up on the goon. Talking to Beauchamp was a priority.

"This is Lady Katherine Fawkner." My voice sounded crisp as I rattled off pertinent details and started to state my number.

"Hello, bimbo! Bit of cheek leaving a message. You can tell Dicky from me that he can stuff his privates where the sun don't shine."

"Certainly," I said cool as a slice of cucumber floating in a glass of Pimm's. "As soon as you tell me your name, I'll pass on the message." The person on the other end of the phone, I'm presuming they were the hired help, was drunk and almost incoherent. They sounded like they were crying.

"Got a mouth, ain't cha? Bet you know how to use it."

My jaw dropped upon hearing the insinuation. The cheek. I didn't like talking to Dicky. The thought of being close and intimately personal with the man was enough to make me puke. *Now if the woman had said Kahu . . .* My thoughts screeched to an appalled halt. Oops! *I was not going there.*

"Who is speaking?" I asked, infusing my voice with hauteur. Father wasn't the only one who knew how to play the nobility angle when it suited.

"Stay away from Dicky!" The phone crashed down hard enough to make me wince.

Well, that had certainly improved things for the Oakthorpe household. Not. I'd have to ring Octopus Beauchamp at his office or maybe make an appointment with his secretary if I couldn't speak to him.

◊ ◊ ◊ ◊ ◊

I ended up making an appointment, and even that hadn't been easy. His secretary had pit bull running in her veins, and she guarded Beauchamp in a possessive manner that raised my curiosity. I couldn't wait to see if the picture in my imagination matched reality.

Beauchamp Industries was housed in one of the new, modern buildings in the Docklands area. Lots of chrome, steel, and huge plate windows that caught the afternoon sun. I strode through the automatic double doors, ignoring the fact that I was way underdressed for a joint this classy. No doubt the pit bull would frown upon my faded jeans and formfitting red T-shirt that bore the words "Sex Kitten," but I was determined. She'd met her match in me.

The heels of my boots tapped when I made my way to the receptionist. She sat behind the large black marble counter wearing the city uniform of a black suit. Her brown hair was blunt-cut to jaw level.

"Yes?" She arched a delicate brow in a silent prod to get me to spill the reason for my presence. Her makeup looked impeccable making me wonder if I shouldn't have taken the time to run a lipstick across my lips. Once again, I'd failed in my blond-bimbo disguise. Perhaps I should give it up and take a chance on being me. Now there was a novel concept.

I cast aside my thoughts of *Shadow*-type work and smiled in a professional manner. "I have an appointment to see Richard Beauchamp."

Her gaze ran across my face and down my body. It was easy to see the clear disbelief on her face. It was obvious I didn't conform to the correct image of Beauchamp's visitors.

"There," I said, leaning over the counter and jabbing at the diary with my finger. A bite of impatience infused my voice, along with attitude. *Look out, lady. Stand aside. I've arrived.* I didn't have time for this palaver with the goon breathing down my neck. "Lady Katherine Fawkner."

A gasp escaped her perfectly sculpted lips, and her eyes widened as she studied me. A trace of envy showed in her hazel eyes. I wanted to say, "It's only a title. It doesn't make me a better person," but centuries of conditioning made people covet titles. I felt like a mannequin wearing the latest designer wear in a shop window. I pushed away my annoyance. Heck, I wanted to get this meeting done. The load of apprehension and uncertainty weighing me down was crippling. "Should I go up?" I gestured at the lift.

"Oh, no!" She looked at me in horror, making me think I'd committed the worst faux pas imaginable. "Someone will come down and escort you up to Mr. Beauchamp's office."

"Right." What sort of business was he running anyway? Apart from locating the phone number and address of Beauchamp Industries, I hadn't had time to research the company. I'd set Hannah on the job before I left while the other members of the trio were discussing how to find their next case. They'd tasted success and wanted more. I glanced around the luxurious foyer with its marble floors and walls, the ceiling to floor windows and the tasteful arrangement of flowers. The surroundings didn't yield a single clue. I turned back to the receptionist. "What does Beauchamp Industries do?"

"Importing and exporting," a frigid voice from behind me said.

The pit bull, I presume? I turned slowly to give myself time to control the smartass quip that sprang to my lips. I hadn't reached the inner sanctum. Yet. "That's interesting," I drawled and left it at that. My inner child kicked and screamed, but I closed my mouth firmly.

"Lady Katherine Fawkner?" the pit bull asked. Her lips pursed, the only reaction to my casual jeans.

I inclined my head, acknowledging that she'd found the right person.

"Come this way, please." Her high heels tapped a strict beat on the floor as she glided to the waiting lift.

I followed more slowly and wondered why the woman was so protective of her boss. In truth her appearance had surprised me. I put her age around late twenties, early

240

thirties. And she was attractive with a cool, classic beauty like Grace Kelly. Jealousy, perhaps? I glanced at my worn jeans. I was no threat. You couldn't pay me enough to become romantically involved with Beauchamp.

The lift rose to the top floor with stomach-swooping rapidity. After a deep breath to resettle my innards, I followed the secretary into the office suite. With my connections, I'd seen opulence up close, but this was luxury personified. My boots sank into soft woolen carpet while my eyes popped out on stalks at the view. Ms. Secretary stopped walking, but I was so busy gawking, I ploughed into the back of her. Color scorched my cheeks. Hello, blond bimbo! Nice to have you back.

A door opened behind me.

"Ah, Lady Katherine. Good to see you again." Richard Beauchamp swaggered toward me. He grasped my hand and pressed a moist kiss on my knuckles. Eew! I fixed a vapid smile to my lips, hoping I didn't crack under the smarmy pressure and say something I shouldn't. Softly, softly and all that. *What I need*, I thought, *is a combination of the bimbo and the brain.*

With the smile still intact, I rescued my hand before it received another coating of slobber and flicked a strand of blond hair over my shoulder. "Thank you for seeing me today, Richard. I know you're very busy at the moment." I nodded at his secretary in firm dismissal. "Thank you for your help."

"This way, my dear." Richard slid an arm around my waist. It felt like a piece of slimy seaweed, and I found it difficult to restrain my reaction. He paused at the open door and ushered me inside. "Coffee please, Rita."

"Right away, Richard." She bustled away with a whisper of silk stockings.

"Take a seat, Lady Katherine."

The view from Richard Beauchamp's office was simply stunning. He overlooked the Docklands area with a panoramic view of the Thames winding its way out to sea. I wondered how he managed to get any work done. The desk backed up the supposition: clean blotter and a single silver pen. No messy piles of files, but perhaps Ms. Secretary was big on neat and tidy. Yeah. That would be it.

Richard stepped behind his desk and sat in his executive leather chair. With the massive wooden desk between us, I felt immeasurably safer. Probably a bad illusion but I'd run with it.

"I wanted to talk to you about—"

A sharp tap on the door interrupted me. Ms. Secretary opened the door and an elderly woman in a royal blue trouser suit walked in bearing a tray of coffee. She set it down before glancing at me.

"How do you take your coffee?"

Nonplussed by the ceremony my simple visit attracted, I blurted, "Black. No sugar."

A thin lemon-colored china mug appeared in front

of me.

"Biscotti?"

"Ah, thank you."

Two small biscotti were placed on a matching lemon plate and set in front of me.

"Your usual, Richard?"

"Thank you, Janice."

Bemused, I wondered if Richard romanced all the women, the way he'd come on to me at the ball so long ago. They all seemed to adore him—apart from the maid who'd answered the phone when I'd rung his house earlier.

Finally, Janice arranged everything to her satisfaction and left the room, shutting the door quietly behind her.

"I wanted to talk to you about the money my family owes you," I said before we had further interruptions.

Richard sipped at his coffee—white and heavy on the sugar—before saying, "Ah! I wondered if that might be the case. My employee did mention your particular loan earlier this morning. You realize, of course, that I don't concern myself with the day-to-day collection of debts." He offered a toothy smile along with the lie.

The man looked like a crocodile ready to take a bite. Uneasiness assailed me. Too late now. My course was set. I'd come to plea for leniency, and I had no alternative but to play his little games. "Yes, I spoke with your man this morning. He seemed reluctant to accept part of the payment so I suggested to him that I speak with his boss."

Beauchamp preened a little, but his eyes remained watch-ful—the eyes of a determined and successful businessman. I had to remember that. He hadn't gotten where he was today without being hardnosed and ambitious. Ruthless.

"We don't have enough money to make full payment," I said in a clear voice, refusing to cower.

"I see."

I was pretty sure that was glee I saw in his blue eyes and a figurative rubbing together of hands. My mind wandered the possibilities and came up with the probable answer.

Sex.

"We will be able to make the payment next week when the sale of my mother's jewels is finalized."

"Hmmm." Beauchamp scratched his chin, his manner thoughtful. "Seems a pity to sell heirlooms. Don't you want to hand them down to that pretty daughter of yours?"

I sucked in a hasty breath even as I battled to maintain my composure. The man was pretending lack of knowledge, but he knew exactly what was going on in his monetary empire. And I was betting he knew word for word the con-versation I'd had with his goon. I leaned back in my chair and waited. I was not going to plead no matter what sort of hold the man had over me. The silence stretched, and I started thinking of it as a game of one-upmanship.

"It doesn't do to set a protocol like this."

"Is that a no?"

"Merely thinking out loud, my dear. Merely thinking

out loud."

I wanted to mutter that he should get on with it and put me out of suspense. I would have except saying that would put me at a distinct disadvantage, so I waited.

Beauchamp regarded me closely until I felt an unladylike sweat forming all down my back. He picked up his coffee and took a long sip before picking up a biscotti and toying with it. The wait was slowly prodding me beyond the limits of my control. I gripped the edge of my seat, taking care to keep my hands out of sight. The phone rang in the outer office; then the intercom buzzed. Beauchamp picked it up, watching my face all the while. I felt an urgent need to squirm.

Beauchamp listened to the person on the other end of the phone and said, "I'll deal with it. Talk to you tomorrow." He dropped the phone back in its cradle, still without taking his eyes off me.

Creepy. And I still had no idea what his answer would be. I decided to push. No one ever said I was a patient person. I admit it. I'm an instant-gratification princess. That's why my lack of progress on my own investigation was so irritating.

"When will you have an answer for me? Today? Tomorrow?"

Beauchamp steepled his hands in front of his face and looked at me over the top. "I gave you the opportunity to talk a few weeks ago. You didn't show."

"I wasn't in possession of all the facts at the time," I said, working at keeping my tone even. Calm. Because I was remembering the other part of the conversation—the part about us becoming good friends. I did not intend to go that route. No way. No how.

Beauchamp's gaze lingered and it irritated me. A scowl sprang to life. I felt it, but too late to counteract.

Beauchamp smirked. He leaned back in his chair. The chair didn't so much as squeak a protest. "All right. Here's what I suggest."

My heart jumped in my chest, my stomach contracted while I waited to hear my fate.

"I'll wait until next Friday for payment of the installment due."

A smile of relief curled my lips. "Thank you! That's great." I stood ready to leave now my mission was completed.

"Wait." Beauchamp held up his right hand in a "stop" motion. "There's a condition you might like to hear before you agree."

Oh-oh. This didn't sound good. I sank back onto the hard chair and clasped my hands on my lap, imagining I were out for a Sunday drive. But it was pretense this time. Calm, I was not.

"I have a business meeting in Edinburgh this coming weekend."

And you're telling me because? Get to the point, I wanted to snap at him.

"I need a hostess."

My jaw dropped betraying every inch of the confusion I felt. "I don't understand," I said finally after I'd snapped my mouth shut.

"I want you to be my hostess." A smile played around his lips.

I didn't trust that smile. "Spell out exactly what being your hostess entails," I suggested in a hard voice.

Beauchamp smirked, his gaze drifting slightly to scan my breasts before returning to my face. "You would need to travel up to Edinburgh with me on Thursday night, and we'd return Sunday afternoon. We stay at the Sinclair in a suite." He paused to grin with real humor. "Separate rooms, if you insist."

"Go on," I said.

"The two men I'm doing business with are bringing their partners with them. I'd want you to take the women shopping, sightseeing, or whatever else they want to do. Help me when we have cocktails and dinner. That's about it," Beauchamp said. "Nothing too onerous."

If there was a trap here, I wasn't seeing it. The duties didn't seem unreasonable. I'd attended finishing school in Switzerland. I could hostess with my hands tied behind my back even if my skills were a little rusty.

"And if I refuse," I asked.

"Then I'm afraid my employees are likely to carry out their threats," Beauchamp said gravely.

CHAPTER 17

I don't like it," Father said, lifting his chin in a belligerent manner.

The argument had raged all last night, and frankly, I was sick of it. I didn't see any other alternative. Father hadn't seen the determined look on Beauchamp's face. I had.

"But you won't have any backup. Ben and I should go too." Father looked like a testy elf. Any moment now he'd stomp his foot.

"We can't afford it," I said, settling the argument with those four words. "Besides, I need you here to help keep an eye on Amber. One of you needs to drop her at school and pick her up afterward." I looked at Father and noted how slowly he moved today. The arthritis had flared up again two days ago. Perhaps he wouldn't stomp after all.

"Actually, it might be safer if both of you go. And there is another reason. We need the money you bring in at the weekly market."

A pleased look flashed across Father's face while Ben beamed.

"True," Father conceded.

No hidden pride in this family! I grinned at him because I was proud of the way they'd made the Oakthorpe stall a success. They sold out by ten most mornings, and the locals had started ringing with vegetable and flower orders when it wasn't market day.

"Did Charles tell you we might have another case to investigate?"

Great! I thought. Keep 'em busy and out of my hair. "That's good. The reward money from the last one came at the right time." Perfect timing to stop our power from being cut off.

Hannah bustled in with a garment bag held over her arm. "I've pressed the Chanel suit for you along with the Trelise Cooper outfit. I like that New Zealand designer," Hannah commented as she draped the bag over a chair. "Nice lines."

"She shouldn't be going," Father growled.

"Katie doesn't have an alternative. We don't have the money so she has to pay the piper," Hannah declared.

"The piper's a stupid ass."

"Look on the bright side," I said, trying to minimize

the dangers of a weekend away with Beauchamp. "We haven't hit any targets in Edinburgh. They do have society bashes up there so we might need to consider Scotland as an option."

Father brightened, and I sighed in relief. Firestorm number six averted.

"I can do some research on the internet this afternoon," Hannah volunteered.

Ben shot an alert look at Father. "Isn't the Mackintosh estate up that way? The Tiger Sapphire."

Father dropped his testiness to nod with enthusiasm. "I'd love to get my hands on that. Top-line security from what I hear."

"I'll look into it," I promised. "And anything else that looks promising so the weekend away won't be a total waste of time."

"What time do you need to be at Stansted Airport?"

"By four this afternoon." I ran a brief mental check to make sure I had everything I needed. Two dressy outfits for dinner. Several for outings that were more casual, and some comfortable cat-burglar clothes. Translation: black tracksuit. Appropriate shoes, undergarments, makeup, and costume jewelry. Check. All present and accounted for.

I turned to Father. "Can you drop me at the railway station? I thought it would be easier than paying for parking at the airport."

"We'll pick up Amber from school on the way to the

station so she can say goodbye."

I nodded, feeling a wrench at the idea of being parted from Amber again. The only time I felt she was truly safe was when I could see her.

◊ ◊ ◊ ◊ ◊

Beauchamp ushered me from the taxi and escorted me into the hotel foyer while porters organized our luggage. The foyer was minimalist. Elegant, and exactly what Beauchamp would need to impress his guests. I wondered why he hadn't asked his wife to hostess before remembering that the two had gone their separate ways. A modern marriage of convenience. I frowned at the thought. Should I ever decide to marry, my union would run along the lines that my parents' had. A partnership with decisions made together. Although my mother had died when I was young, I remember them laughing together, soft and intimate. Hannah had told me recently, how Father had never had a serious relationship with another woman since. If I ever trusted a man enough to commit, I intended to have a partnership. No half-measures for me. My thoughts drifted to Kahu while Richard registered. I hadn't seen Kahu for the last couple of days, not since Father and Ben had summoned the police to tell them about their investigation findings and Kahu had turned up at Oakthorpe. Part of me was glad since I hadn't wanted to lie to him about this weekend trip to Edinburgh. I knew it would look bad to anyone who didn't have inside information. And I wasn't about to tell Kahu about our debt. Some stuff was private. *Fawkner family business in particular*, I thought with a flash of dark humor.

"Penny for your thoughts," Beauchamp said.

The smile fled my face when I registered his flirtatious grin. "Just thinking that Seth would love this hotel. He doesn't like clutter."

"Ah, yes. The boyfriend. What does he think about your weekend away?"

I took pleasure in seeing his jovial manner burst like a bubble. Naughty of me, but I'm only human. Beauchamp's stricture to act as his hostess was nothing short of blackmail, so I felt the small digs were payback.

"Seth is away this weekend," I said, without thinking.

Beauchamp's smile returned, slow and steady like a flower blooming. "Keeping secrets isn't good for a relationship."

Well, he had me there. I ached to tell Kahu even though our relationship was one date and a few kisses long. "I agree," I said, keeping it cool. "Which is why I'll tell Seth when I next talk to him."

Beauchamp's expression told me he thought I lied. My eyes narrowed. Maybe he expected me to partake in a little horizontal tango this weekend. "Is our room sorted? There's so much dust on my face. I'd like to freshen up." I reverted to blond bimbo to cover my anger. The man was in for a rude awakening when he tried to make a move on me.

"This way, my dear."

I suffered through the hand in the small of my back again, taking care he didn't see my moue of distaste.

The glass lift sailed up the edge of the building to the very top floor. I moved away from Beauchamp's touch, ostensibly to look out the window.

"Great view," I said, and it was nothing less than the truth. The city panorama stretched out before us with the castle dominating the skyline. Absolutely stunning. I decided I'd have to visit the castle and purchase Amber a small souvenir.

"Our guests are arriving later this evening," Beauchamp said as he slid the keycard into the lock and opened the door. "I'd like to have a late supper and drinks when they arrive. Can you organize that?"

"No problem." I stepped over the threshold and turned to Beauchamp. "Which is my room?"

"You can choose," he said. "Either one will be fine with me."

I took him at his word and strode across the luxurious oatmeal-colored carpet to inspect the bedrooms. They looked pretty much the same. Both had king-sized beds with en suite bathrooms. No locks on the bedroom, but a lock on the bathroom door. I took comfort from that. I walked back out to the lounge area where Beauchamp waited. Our luggage had arrived while I inspected the bedrooms.

"This one is fine," I said.

Beauchamp, ever the gentleman, picked up my leather overnight bag and carried it into the bedroom for me.

"I'll arrange supper now," I said. "What time would you prefer?"

He frowned as he considered. "Their flight arrives at nine."

"Actually, the time doesn't matter. I've had an idea that will work. Are we meeting them at the airport or here?"

"Here."

I nodded. "That will give me time to contact my friends."

"You're up here to act as hostess, not gallivant around with friends."

"I know why I'm here. I don't believe there's any mis-understanding," I snapped. "I'll have everything ready for nine, myself included." Ice dripped from my words and it was a wonder I didn't trip with my nose held so high in the air. The need to slam the door was an angry pulse thrum-ming through my blood. I resisted.

In the privacy of my room, I punched my hand through the air in a series of crosscuts and uppercuts, imagin-ing Beauchamp's face as my target. Pompous jerk. I ran through another series of punches and added kicks to my routine. My imaginary Beauchamp looked a beaten man by the time I'd finished.

Feeling immeasurably better, I headed for a quick shower before dealing with the hotel's catering service. Half an hour later, I clocked off Beauchamp time and decided to look up my friend Jaycee. I hadn't seen her for years. Not since the night.

Pushing aside trepidation, I dialed the number I'd retrieved from my handbag.

"Jaycee?"

"Speaking." Her voice contained a hint of Scotland.

"It's Kate Fawkner."

"Katie!" she screeched down the phone.

Grinning, I held the phone away from my ear until the din reduced to normal range. "Are you free for a couple of hours tonight?"

"Hell, yes. But not at home. Mum's house is jam-packed with family. My two brothers are here with both their broods, and—Well, it's madness here."

"I'm at the Sinclair Hotel," I said. "Can we meet at a pub?" I wanted to keep Beauchamp away from Jaycee.

"Good idea. How about the Poachers Pocket? That's on Jennings Street. I can be there in . . . say, half an hour?"

◊ ◊ ◊ ◊ ◊

Jaycee looked just the same. Tall with brown eyes, an hourglass figure, and a mane of dark curls.

She gave a girly shriek when she saw me and ploughed

through the crowds between the door and the bar to throw herself at me. We both laughed.

"It's great to see you," I said and meant it.

"You're lucky you caught me in Edinburgh. I work for the Foreign and Commonwealth Office as an interpreter."

"Never," I said, arching my brows. "Miss Peterson would be so proud!"

We exploded into a fit of giggles. Miss Peterson, our much maligned French tutor, had despaired of Jaycee managing to order her dinner in French let alone work in a position requiring extensive use of a foreign language.

"Let's get a drink and grab a table," I said. "I have to be back at the Sinclair by nine."

With our drinks in front of us, we got down to the business of reminiscing and becoming reacquainted. Somewhere along the line, I needed to work the Christmas party into the conversation and see if Jaycee could help me. I hesitated, letting the conversation drift. For an instant, I wasn't sure I was ready for the truth. Finally, I stiffened my backbone and asked the question I needed answered.

"Do you remember the Christmas party held at the Grosvenor Hotel? At the end of our final year at finishing school?"

"Was that the party that Matt proposed to Suzie?"

I sipped from my glass of sparkling mineral water and scanned my memories of the party. Still a big blank even after all this time. I set my glass down. A bit more candor required. "It was the party where I got pregnant," I said bluntly.

Shock flashed across her expressive face followed by sympathy. "I wondered," she said, reaching over to squeeze my hand. "But you were withdrawn and you disappeared off the face of the Earth. I did ring Oakthorpe, but Hannah wouldn't say anything. All she said was that you weren't well."

"You knew I had a daughter?"

"Yeah, but I didn't know how old she was." She paused and studied me closely. "Tell me to butt out if I'm being nosy, but who's the father?"

Even though I'd assumed she'd ask the question, I was unprepared for the jolt of fury that lashed me. "I don't know," I said in a hard voice. "But with your help, I intend to find out."

"Hello, ladies."

Two men dressed in suits stood by our table. They looked as though they'd stopped off at the pub after work, and the drinks they'd imbibed had given them the courage to try a tired chat-up line.

One whistled. "You're the most beautiful women in the room."

"Thank you," Jaycee cooed. "We'd better watch out for the best-looking men in the room so we'll be matching pairs." She turned back to me and said, "I'm not sure that I remember much. It was such a long time ago."

"I know, but I needed time to put the past into focus."

I sensed the men's confusion and fought a smile. Jaycee obviously had more experience than me in the pickup-line department. They walked away, heading for another table of women on the other side of the pub near the fireplace. *Good luck to them*, I thought.

"Can you remember which men were with our group or joined us over the course of the evening?"

Jaycee traced the rim of her wine glass, a frown of concentration on her face. "Peter and Jeremy. Aidan. Ah, Kate, honey. My memory's a little fuzzy. Let me think on it overnight."

Hiding my bitter disappointment, I nodded. It had been a long shot anyway. "What about Simon Grenville?"

Jaycee snorted. "Him I remember. He was paralytic drunk by nine, and they had to carry him from the hotel. Believe me, the man wasn't capable of sitting, let alone—" She broke off abruptly. "Have you tried contacting some of the other girls?"

"Yeah. I've struck out so far. Vivienne isn't talking to her parents so I don't know where to contact her. Her mother told me in a frosty tone that they had disowned their daughter."

"Always was a lot of friction there."

"You can say that again."

"Always was—"

I grinned, enjoying the old camaraderie we'd fallen

258

into. "Figure of speech, old girl."

"Humph! Not so much of the old thanks! I found my first gray hair last week. I'm still in shock." Jaycee gestured at my empty glass. "Time for another drink?"

I checked my watch. "I'd better not. I need to get back to the hotel. What are you up to tomorrow? Any plans?"

"Not a thing," Jaycee said. "Although I intend to sleep in. That's a given."

"I'm not sure what I'm doing tomorrow. I'm meant to baby-sit the partners of the men Beauchamp's doing business with. Shopping or sightseeing, or both."

"Beauchamp? Is he related to Matthew?"

I shrugged and bent to pick up my black leather purse. "It's Richard Beauchamp I'm working for this weekend."

"Oh! Oh! I've just had an idea."

"I wondered about the smell," I retorted, putting on my posh upper-class accent.

Jaycee grinned. "Ach, I know the city well. Why don't I come with you tomorrow?" Her accent was soft with the burr and rolling "r"s of Scotland.

My grin spilled out to a laugh. "That's a great idea! I'll ring you in the morning when I know what they want to do. Thanks!"

We stood, and I hugged Jaycee hard before I left. It was great to talk to her, and I wished I'd plucked up the courage to face my past a little earlier.

◇ ◇ ◇ ◇ ◇

As soon as I arrived back at the hotel, I rang Oakthorpe to check on Amber.

The phone was picked up after two rings.

"Hello?" The slow, careful greeting made me pause. Hannah sounded reluctant to answer the phone. My instincts roared, adding two and two and coming up with a grand total.

"Hannah, it's Kate. Has that goon rung sprouting his threats again?"

"Worse," Hannah muttered. "Kahu rang wanting to speak to you. I didn't know what to tell him. In the end, I said you were away for the weekend with friends."

I pulled a face at the phone. "What did he say?"

"He didn't say much at all, but I think he was a bit put out."

"Damn," I muttered. I'd known I was running a risk not telling Kahu, but since he hadn't contacted me with firm plans, I'd assumed he was working.

"I told him, I'd get you to ring him when you returned home. I didn't give him your cell-phone number. Was that all right?"

Hannah's concern came across loud and clear. "Don't worry," I said. "There was nothing else you could have done without alerting his suspicions. I deliberately haven't given him my number, in case he connects it to you know what."

"Ah," Hannah said. "Good point. I'll make sure Charlie and Ben don't give it to him either. How are things going up there? Has Beauchamp made a pass at you yet?"

"Not yet, and he won't if he knows what's good for him."

"Is Amber all right?"

"She's fine, Katie. Don't worry. That painting set that Kahu gave her last weekend has kept her busy. She spent the evening decorating eggcups. Your daughter has a real artistic bent. The eggcups looked so good, Ben asked if she'd like to sell them at the market for some pocket money so she could buy more."

"They that good?" I asked with a trace of surprise. "I can't draw a straight line."

"I resisted the impulse to point that out," Hannah said in her dry manner.

A thump echoed through the suite to my bedroom.

"Oops, someone's at the door. I'd better go. I'll call you tomorrow morning."

"Take care, Katie."

"I will," I promised. "Good night."

I hung up the phone and raced to answer the door. A room service attendant stood on the other side with a trolley of hors d'oeuvres for our late supper along with four bottles of Moet champagne.

"Great," I said, standing back to allow him entry into the suite. He wheeled the cart through to the small kitchenette and unloaded it for me.

After he'd gone, I checked my watch and saw I had time for a quick shower before Beauchamp arrived with his guests.

◊ ◊ ◊ ◊ ◊

A tap sounded on my bedroom door before it opened. Beauchamp stepped inside without waiting for an invitation.

I plucked the toweling robe off the king-sized bed and pulled it on. After tightening the belt around my waist, I said, "Was there something you wanted?" A shiver of distaste worked its way up my backbone. The man had seen me naked. The need to jump back in the shower and scrub my skin clean of his gaze almost overwhelmed me. I forced myself to look at him and cringed inwardly at the heat in his eyes. "Yes?" My voice sounded chilly and imperious, a lady of the manor speaking to a servant.

"Are you sure you won't change your mind?" he said hoarsely, and I knew he was talking about his proposition. He wanted me and was reminding me of the fact.

"Quite sure. I'm involved and I don't fool around." The same answer I'd given him when he first asked. A chilling thought occurred. I hoped he didn't intend to try physical force to gain his desires.

Richard nodded, and I thought I saw a flash of regret. "My guests have arrived. They've gone to their rooms to freshen up and will be here shortly."

"Everything is ready," I stated. "I'll be out in five minutes."

This time his look contained clear doubt. An affront to my timekeeping. "Five minutes," I repeated. "If you leave the room." My stare was pointed.

Richard shook his head. In the moment, he seemed immeasurably older, and I felt a second of sympathy. I wondered if his marriage had ended up the way it had because of him or Mrs. Beauchamp.

"You're on a timer," he said, and he turned to leave, shutting the door with a faint click after him.

I let out my breath in a soft whoosh. He wouldn't walk in again if his guests were expected soon. I hoped. I cast an uneasy look at the door and discarded my robe to pull on the high-cut black lace briefs and matching bra I'd set out earlier. My black knit dress was simplicity itself. It covered me from neck to ankles and clung to my figure like a second skin. My shoes were black embroidered slippers that my godmother had given me—a souvenir of her trip to Istanbul. I released my hair from its tight braid and pulled a brush through it. In the interests of speed, I decided to leave it loose, but anchor it away from my face with a pair of jeweled combs. I left my gold studs in place. Makeup tonight was simple—a swish of mascara on my lashes, and a quick brush over my face with a tinted powder that gave my skin a glow. After a brief check in the mirror, I opened the door and stepped into the main suite area to join Richard Beauchamp.

"You look beautiful," he said, taking my hand and planting a lingering kiss on my knuckles. "Classy but not too dressy. Perfect. Can I get you a drink?"

"I'll get one," I said. "I want to take the covers off the hors d'oeuvres."

He looked as though he might argue but someone tapped on the door so I escaped while I could. The guests had arrived.

Although I hadn't asked Richard about the men he was doing business with, I'd pictured them in my head. They pretty much tallied with my imagination. A bit like Beauchamp. Older men with polished veneers and figures that suggested too many long lunches. The third man took me by surprise. Richard introduced him as his brother, not that they looked alike.

I shook his hand. "Matthew." I racked my brain trying to think if I'd seen him before but came up blank. "Pleased to meet you," I murmured.

The women on their arms were a different story. Young. In their early twenties, I judged. Tiffany and Jules.

Richard held out his hand to me, and I smiled, doing what was expected even though I loathed touching him. I reminded myself that being here was buying us time to make the payment and let my grin widen.

Richard did the introductions. Theo Henry and Reginald

Mitchell. I nodded and slipped smoothly into social chitchat, a skill drilled into me at finishing school. Richard poured drinks while I handed around smoked salmon tarts, olives, cheese, grapes, and dried apricots and kiwi.

"What would you like to do tomorrow while the men are talking business?" I asked Jules. "We could do some sightseeing and a little shopping."

"Shopping," Tiffany said, clapping her hands together.

I groaned inwardly. Great. Retail therapy without the money to back it up. And Tiffany sounded like a dedicated shopper.

"My friend lives in Edinburgh. Would it be okay if she came along? An insider's knowledge will be helpful."

Tiffany lifted one pale shoulder in a shrug. "Doesn't worry me."

"Sounds good to me," Jules said. She had a faint twang that made me think she'd lived in Europe for a time.

"I'll arrange a cab," I said. "What time would you like to start?"

"As soon as the shops open," Jules said in relish. "I want to buy one of those darling little tartan skirts."

CHAPTER 18

The weekend passed rapidly despite the endless shopping. Jaycee's local knowledge was a godsend and her company kept me sane. And since we had an extra man to our party, I suggested to Richard that we invite Jaycee to make up the numbers.

"I don't know," he said. "This is business."

"But Matthew is coming to dinner with us. It won't look good if he flirts with the other women."

Richard understood my not so subtle point, and I pushed my advantage. "Jaycee attended finishing school with me in Switzerland. She knows how to act around people with money. Her family has money. The Carris-brookes," I said, shamelessly namedropping. "The girls got on well with her when we went shopping today." Of course, I refrained from mentioning that they were too enthralled

with purchasing darling little skirts—kilts to you and I—
to worry about much else.

Richard's eyes narrowed into what I privately called his
shrewd-businessman persona. Finally, he nodded. "Okay."

Instead of letting loose the whoop that trembled at
the back of my throat, I gave a ladylike smile and a nod.
Mission accomplished. I hadn't relished fighting off two
Beauchamp brothers.

◊ ◊ ◊ ◊ ◊

We were a veritable advertisement for designers when we
left the hotel. I wore slinky black while Jaycee, Jules, and
Tiffany wore blue, innocent white, and siren red respective-
ly. The men looked magnificent in their suits. It promised
to be an elegant evening at White's Restaurant. White's,
according to Jaycee, was the place to see and be seen.

"Ohhh, Theo!" Jules said in a breathless little girl voice
when the hostess showed us to our seats. "This is beautiful."

Theo beamed, no doubt thinking about scoring later
back at the hotel, I thought with a flood of cynicism.

Richard guided everyone to his or her seats without
seeming to take over. I doubt anyone noticed they were
organized. I ended up seated between Richard and Matthew—a Beauchamp sandwich. Theo and Jules sat across
the table from me.

A bottle of Moet appeared almost magically along

with a glass of sparkling mineral water for each of us. I was glad of the water since I didn't like to make an issue of my non-drinking status. It inevitably led to nosy questions.

"I've seen you somewhere before," Matthew Beauchamp commented when Richard's attention was claimed elsewhere.

"Probably at one of the balls this season," I said without a lot of interest. Another tired pickup line. "I've attended most of them."

"No," Matthew said with a thoughtful smile. "I don't think so."

I shrugged and smiled at Jules across the table. Theo looked up and intercepted my smile.

"Thank you for looking after the girls so well. I know Jules had a wonderful time yesterday, and she's glowing after another enjoyable day today."

"It was my pleasure." *The man is rather sweet*, I thought.

"Business went well because Reginald and I knew the girls were enjoying their time here. You must come to the States with Richard, and the girls will reciprocate."

Not in this lifetime, I thought, but I managed a smile.

Dinner was surprisingly good. I'd expected the reputation to exceed the food, but the rack of New Zealand lamb I ordered tasted delicious—pink and succulent with glazed carrots, tiny roast potatoes, fresh peas, and delectable gravy. And I dropped any pretense of blond bimbo to order and savor the crème brûlée, a decision I didn't regret since it melted in my mouth.

The only sticky moment came when Richard left the table to take a phone call and the other couples adjourned to the dance floor. Jaycee had wandered off to talk to a friend at another table, leaving me alone with Matthew Beauchamp.

"So what are you doing with Richard?" he asked. "You could do better."

"I suggest you ask Richard," I replied coolly. Heck, both brothers were equally obnoxious. Trained from birth? Maybe.

"I have a cottage in the Cotswold," he said. "How about visiting for a weekend? We could have a lot of fun."

"I don't think so," I said, struggling to keep my anger under control. I had no difficulty understanding the sub-text. *A private weekend for two with drinking, sex, and*, I thought, glancing at Matthew, *maybe designer drugs.*

"Perhaps another time," Matthew said.

Arrogant baboon. His manner suggested he thought I was merely playing hard to get and that eventually I'd succumb. The man had a lesson to learn. Unfortunately, I didn't have the time or inclination to teach him to respect women.

◊ ◊ ◊ ◊ ◊

We checked out of the hotel at ten the next morning. All in all the weekend hadn't turned out as badly as I'd feared. Richard had behaved and his brother had refrained from repeating his invitation.

A taxi screeched to a halt in the hotel forecourt. Jaycee bounded out and rushed up to me breathless in her hurry.

"Thank goodness," she gasped. "I thought I'd miss you."

"I'm pleased to see you," I said, "but we said our good-byes last night."

Jaycee pulled away and rifled through her handbag. I smothered my amusement as she muttered to herself about meaning to clean out her bag. Jaycee had always carried the equivalent to the kitchen sink along with her. It was no surprise to me that she couldn't find anything.

"Ah! Here it is." She pulled a rumpled sheet of note-paper from her bag. After a quick glance to see if anyone was paying attention, she handed it to me. "The list," she said in a soft voice. "I remembered last night that I hadn't done one for you so I did it when I arrived home after dinner. I thought of a few extra names, so hopefully there's something there that will help."

I hugged Jaycee tight. "Thanks."

"Don't be a stranger," she murmured against my ear. "I've given you my email address so keep in touch."

"I will," I promised and meant it. The sharing of my sordid past had lightened the weight on my shoulders, and even though I'd discovered little to help me to date, I knew Jaycee cared and supported me in my search.

I waved to Jaycee as she climbed back in her cab and drove away.

"Nice girl," Richard said, stepping up beside me. "Glad you suggested her joining us for dinner. Matthew seemed keen."

Jaycee had confessed that he'd made a pass at her too, offering the same weekend away in the Cotswold. The man sure lacked in the imagination department when it came to women.

"Is he married?" I asked. In the group I socialized with, affairs were the norm. Beds were treated like trains. On and off. It wasn't how I wanted to live but who was I to judge?

"Yes, he married a French girl—Veronica. They have three children."

I nodded and moved away from Richard's hand that had snuggled into the small of my back. Despite the success of the weekend, I had no intention of encouraging him.

Across the busy street, a shriek of brakes sounded followed by the long, fluid curse of the driver. A figure in dark clothes, hat pulled down low over their face, dodged between the moving vehicles.

"Idiot," Richard said. He turned away to signal the doorman.

A loud bang echoed in the street. A car backfiring. I scanned the area and saw the pedestrians on the other side of the road scattering in all directions. *Like a swarm of ants*, I thought.

"They've got a gun!" a man hollered.

Another shot rang out.

A woman screamed and toppled to the ground.

"Jesus!" Richard shouted. "The garden tub. Over there! Get behind it and keep down."

He didn't need to tell me. I was already on my way. Keeping low, I darted toward the stone urn that stood in the hotel forecourt. Two shots rang out in quick succession. I heard a whine to my right just before I ducked behind the urn. A fragment of stone flew through the air and embedded in my cheek. A drop of blood fell onto my white trousers. My pulse thundered, adrenaline sending fear swooping through my belly.

In the distance, I heard a siren. As I cowered behind the potted palm, another shot fired.

The window behind me exploded, fragments of glass raining down on my body. I hid my face in my hands and hoped for the best. When the glass had settled, my hand explored the stinging wound on my cheek. Thanks to my trousers and jacket, apart from the cut on my cheek, I'd emerged unscathed. I swallowed, acknowledging how close I'd come to being hit. I smelled exhaust fumes, the damp soil in the urn, and the sickly sweet designer perfume of the woman crouched behind a cab not far from me.

The sirens sounded closer now. More than one police car, judging by the racket.

I turned to see if Richard was okay but couldn't see him.

My cheek stung and bled profusely. I wiped a trickle from my jaw with the back of my hand.

The sirens were deafening now. A screech of brakes announced the arrival of the police. I hadn't heard a shot for a while. I poked my head up cautiously, scanning the area around the hotel for movement. Apart from the cops, I didn't see anyone moving. Everyone was still hunkered down, hoping like hell they didn't get shot like the poor woman lying in the middle of the footpath on the other side of the road.

I stood, ready to drop to the ground should the need arise. Police swarmed around the woman who lay on the pavement. An ambulance pulled up.

"Officer, is it safe to stand up?" a man called.

Somewhere else, I heard a woman sobbing.

I sighted Richard in the hotel foyer.

"Are you all right, miss?" A policeman approached me. "You're bleeding."

"I wasn't shot," I said. "A fragment ricocheted and hit me."

"Come with me. We'll get it looked at while I talk to you."

I followed him to the ambulance. A medic took control. After a closer look, he said, "Doesn't look too bad. I'll clean it up for you, but it won't scar." The young man grinned at me. "Won't spoil your stunning looks."

I couldn't help but grin back, even though it hurt to

smile. "Thanks," I said.

"You from around here?"

"Just up here for the weekend."

The young man grimaced. "Pity," he said. "I'd love to take you to the pictures."

His wide smile and easy manner went down a lot better than Matthew Beauchamp's innuendo. "I'll let you know if I'm ever up this way again."

The dark-haired policeman sauntered over to me after he'd finished questioning an elderly man. "Are you up to answering a few questions?"

"Sure. Now would be best since I'm meant to catch a plane in an hour." At the thought, I glanced about for Richard.

Already the crowds were building and the police were roping the area off. It was a wonder they hadn't diverted the traffic.

Almost as soon as I formed the thought, I heard a senior policeman holler. "You and you." He emphasized his shouts with finger jabs in the air. "I want you to stop traffic at both ends of the street. No one comes in and no one leaves before we've talked to them. Clear?"

"Yes, sir."

"Yes, sergeant."

The two policemen held a brief conference and trotted off, one to either end of the street.

"Tell me what you saw," the dark-haired policeman said.

My gaze snapped to his face. Judging by his impatient tone this wasn't the first time he'd asked the question.

I cast my mind back, letting the picture replay in my mind. "At first I thought it was a car backfiring. I heard a scream. Someone across the other side of the road shouted that they had a gun. I saw a figure in dark clothes. I've no idea whether they were male or female. Everything happened too quickly."

"How tall were they? What color hair?"

I frowned as I tried to remember. "I think they were taller than me, but I couldn't tell you exactly. And they wore a hat. A black one and it was pulled low over their face."

The policeman jotted this down in a small spiral-bound notebook. "Anything else?"

I thought back again and shook my head. "No, nothing else. It all happened so fast."

The ambulance officer who had remained quiet during the interview, eased up on the pressure on the pad he held to my cheek. He removed the pad and gently turned my head to look at my cheek. "Bleeding's stopped," he said. "Looks like it might bruise. You'll look colorful for a few days, but you'll live."

"Thanks," I said.

"I'll give you a card. Ring us if you think of anything else. It doesn't matter how small or unimportant you think it might be."

I accepted the business card. "All right," I said, but

didn't think I'd be ringing them. My powers of observation were pretty good due to my occupation. I'd told them everything I knew.

"Kate! Are you all right?" Richard rushed up to the ambulance, red-faced and out of breath.

"She's fine," the ambulance officer said. "Just a small war wound."

Richard's eyes opened wide with shock when he spotted my cheek. Obviously it looked as bad as it felt. Now the adrenaline had fled my system it ached and whined like a freshly stubbed toe.

"Are you up to flying home today?"

"Of course I am. I'm cleared to leave. The police have interviewed me."

Richard's face held relief at my reply.

"Quite an exciting weekend," I said.

Richard grunted. "This last bit, I could do without."

◊ ◊ ◊ ◊ ◊

The taxi ride back to Oakthorpe took forever. By the time I arrived, a vicious headache throbbed at my temples and played a duet with the ache in my cheek. But at least I was alive. The woman shot during the incident had died on the way to the hospital.

The front door opened and the terrible trio and Amber spilled down the steps before the cab came to a halt.

Hannah opened the door for me, took one look at my abused cheek and bit her bottom lip. Amber stroked my leg, a sympathetic expression in her brown eyes. "Does it hurt?" she said in a hushed tone.

"I'm all right," I said, climbing from the cab after paying the driver. I bent to give Amber a quick hug. "What I want to know is how you're feeling. All the spots gone?"

Amber nodded, but I cast a quick glance in Hannah's direction for reassurance. She gave a brief nod, and the knot of nagging worry inside my stomach dissolved.

Father and Ben retrieved my luggage from the boot, and we walked inside together. It felt as though I'd been away for weeks rather than three nights. So much had happened.

"The money came through from Alistair," Father said.

"That's good news," I said and grinned. A shard of pain told me to quit with the facial expressions. "How did the market go this morning?" As much as I hated to pressure them, we still needed money to make the next payment.

"Business was so brisk all four of us worked the stall. We could have sold twice as much. But nothing has happened on the dagger front, which is disappointing."

Amber pushed between Father and I, and hugged my hip to snare my attention. "People paid for my eggcups."

"Did they? How many did you sell?"

Amber held up ten fingers.

"Ten!" I exclaimed. No pretending necessary. I was seriously impressed.

SHELLEY MUNRO

"They were a big hit," Father said, ruffling Amber's hair. He looked pleased enough to have painted the egg-cups himself.

"I'm painting more for next week," Amber said. "Come see."

She dragged me through to the kitchen, and the terrible trio followed. Amber had a small desk set up near the windows looking out over the gardens. Small tins of paint and brushes covered the table. Six freshly painted eggcups were drying.

Hannah walked straight to the kettle, filled it with water, and plugged it in while I admired the eggcups. Amber had painted bright flowers and trees on some while others bore houses and stick people. They were adorable, and it was easy to see why they'd sold so well.

Hannah slapped a packet of painkillers on the table along with a glass of water.

"You're a lifesaver," I said, reaching for the painkillers. "And a telepathist. How did you know?"

"You're forehead is wrinkled up like a prune," she said. "Thought I'd better do something quick before the wind changed."

"Love the description," I said dryly, but I made a conscious effort to smooth my frown. I popped two tablets from the foil pack and swallowed them down.

"Beauchamp behave himself?" Father inquired.

"Yes, surprisingly."

The phone interrupted, and Hannah answered.

"It's for you." She clapped a hand over the receiver. "Kahu Williams."

My stomach dropped with sudden foreboding. "Hi, Kahu. How are you?"

"I'll be there in five," Kahu said without preamble. The phone slammed down leaving me feeling ill at ease.

"He'll be here in a few minutes."

"Shit," Father said.

I went with sarcasm to temper my spiraling fears. "I couldn't have said it better myself."

CHAPTER 19

What are you going to tell him?" Hannah asked.

"I don't know." And I couldn't think. The brain cells that weren't aching were tearing around in a mad panic, too ruffled for logic thought.

"You'll have to tell him something," Father snapped. "We need him around in case our competitor decides to show."

"That's hardly likely now. Our competitor seems to have disappeared into a vacuum. I haven't heard news of any thefts all week, apart from the job I did."

"A week's not long," Father countered.

I saw his point but didn't have time to think about it now, not when I had to face Kahu. Nerves hummed through me in a way that hadn't happened for a long time. I don't know exactly how it had happened but Kahu figured large in my heart. I knew he had the ability to hurt me.

"I'll talk to him out in the garden," I decided out loud. I paced the length of the kitchen while I practiced what I might say.

"He might not know you were up there with you know who," Hannah said, ever practical. We'd kept details from Amber, merely saying that I'd visited a friend, in case she innocently spilled the beans.

I considered briefly and shook my head. "No, it was his tone. He knows."

"He's not bad for a cop," Father conceded.

Praise indeed! Despite the gravity of the situation, my eyes widened and my lips twitched in the beginnings of a smile. "Really?"

Ben nodded, missing my attempt at subtle humor. "He hurried up the reward money for us."

"That was nice of him." And it didn't surprise me.

The doorbell rang. I whirled about to face the terrible trio in a silent bid for encouragement. I received it in spades but nerves still jiggled in my stomach warning me the worst was yet to come.

The doorbell rang again—three short bursts.

I wiped my hands down the legs of my white trousers. They still bore splotches of blood, making me realize I should have changed. But it was too late now.

"Don't let me catch you trying to spy out the window or heaven forbid, eavesdrop," I warned.

"We wouldn't think of it," Father said in an affronted

manner.

I walked down the passage to answer the door, still none the wiser about how to handle an irate Kiwi cop. When I opened the door, I noted that my palms were sweaty again. I wiped them on my trousers while staring wordlessly at Kahu.

His brown eyes narrowed. I felt his policeman's gaze, intent, noting everything about my appearance. The bruised cheek. The splatters of blood on my white suit.

"It's true," he said. "You were there in Edinburgh."

"Come around the back into the garden. We can talk there."

I shut the door and stepped past him, heading for the narrow path that led to the gardens out the back. My ears strained to hear if he followed. The edgy feeling inside told me he did but I was unable to hear any actual footfalls.

A thrush sang over to my right. The heady scent of the old-fashioned red climbing roses filled the air. All the ingredients of a romantic meeting—apart from the man. When I arrived at a stone bench overlooking the valley below, I sat. Kahu remained standing, controlled anger evident in the slight flush in his cheeks, his taut stance. He didn't intend making this meeting easy for me.

"You lied to me. You were up there with Richard Beauchamp." He said Richard's name with a slight sneer, but I already knew he disliked the man. He hadn't mentioned his brother's death to me, and I didn't like to ask.

Words and explanations danced around inside my head, but I knew I'd never admit the truth. I'd never verbalize a single one of my thoughts. It would give rise to questions I wasn't prepared to answer.

Kahu studied my face, waiting for an explanation that would make everything all right. I fidgeted inwardly but resisted the urge to squirm. His quiet, intense scrutiny probably worked well in the police sphere. He had my nerves worn ragged.

"Not going to talk?" he asked. "You could start by telling me about your friend."

I don't think so, I thought. My heart seemed to stall, a fist closed over it preventing a beat. I felt wretched. My head pounded, the relentless sun accelerating the ache. The prickly sensation behind my eyes told me tears were not far away.

Kahu frowned down at me. "I don't like liars."

That made me feel heaps better. My life was one big lie. I mean where did I start? I felt a spurt of hysteria rising to the surface and rushed into speech. "I don't think there's much more to say," I said, feeling sick to my stomach.

"I thought we had the makings of a friendship." Kahu's voice held no expression, sounding as though he'd locked all his emotions away.

"We do," I protested. Unable to look at him because it hurt so much, I studied a flock of white sheep grazing in the neighboring fields. A tear slipped down my face and I scrubbed it away, concentrating fiercely on the sheep.

"Not without truth," Kahu said. "I asked you if there was anyone else in your life. You said no." He turned to stare out at the valley as well. "I believed you."

I fumbled in my jacket pocket for a hanky, and when I couldn't find one, resorted to an unladylike sniff. "So what happens now?" This was goodbye, but I needed him to tell me, to put it in words.

Kahu laughed, the sound bitter and harsh. "Truth is important to me. It's part of what I am and how I live. You lied and as far as I'm concerned, that's it. No second chances."

I bowed my head and studied my hands and short nails. "I'm sorry," I whispered. Another tear fell. Then another.

"Goodbye, Lady Katherine."

The lump in my throat had grown so much I couldn't force a polite reply. Or any reply. The teachers at finishing school would have been horrified if they'd witnessed. I heard soft footsteps as he left, taking my heart with him.

◊ ◊ ◊ ◊ ◊

The next few days were difficult. I made it through by focusing on the important things.

Amber.

And revenge.

I spent as much time with my daughter as possible.

In the evenings, Amber painted eggcups while the terrible trio and I carried out research into possible jobs. When Amber attended school, I carried out research into special interests—the search for Amber's father.

I placed the last index card down on my bed and sighed. My search through the photographer's records had yielded nothing helpful. All the drama breaking into his premises for naught!

Next on the agenda was a comparison of Jaycee's list with the photographer's cards. Six names on Jaycee's list: Allan Grayson, Quentin Sparkes, John, Patrick O'Finnegan, Duncan Urquart, and Jason.

The names were all familiar, and when I checked faces in my old photo albums, my memory matched the likenesses to the names. None of the young men bore any resemblance to my daughter. I threw the album down on the bed in disgust and stormed from my bedroom, slamming the door so everyone at Oakthorpe knew of my bad mood.

What the heck did I do next? If there were an easy way to solve this mystery, I'd missed it.

The terrible trio sat at the kitchen table taking morning tea. The hum of the dishwasher, the low conversation, and the clatter of cups and saucers from Hannah's tea preparation comforted me, soothing my ruffled temper.

"Talking about me?" I asked while I slid into an empty seat.

They shared a glance and seemed to vote for Hannah

in the silent conversation.

"Only in passing," she said, shunting a mug of tea in my direction.

"I thought I'd ring Seth to see if he's going to the ball this weekend at the Sheraton." I speared a glance at Father. "Why don't you find a date and help me narrow down our list of prospects?"

"Can't," Father said. "Ben and I have another case to investigate."

Ben let out a sudden guffaw that lengthened into a full-out belly laugh, the type that has your lips twitching and wanting to join in. Tears formed at the corner of his eyes and trickled down his face. He raised a gnarled hand to wipe them away, still chuckling. "You're gonna love this, Kate."

"They've hired us to recover stolen jewelry!" That set him off again, with Father joining in this time.

Hannah and I shared a silent roll of eyes that covered everything from the fact that men are such little boys at times to the ironic truth that they were right. This new job they'd signed on for was a hoot.

"Was the theft reported to the police?" I asked, interested in spite of myself.

"It's the Martins' at Rose Manor," Father said.

"Ah!" I reached for a piece of shortbread. That explained everything. The Martins were strange, although harmless. They didn't trust the police. "How much are they paying you? How's the job going? What was stolen?"

"One question at a time, Katie." Ben pulled a small burgundy notebook from his shirt pocket and flicked through the pages. "Two Victorian brooches with sentimental value. They were passed down through the family," he added. "And a tiara. Another family heirloom. None of it insured since they don't think much of insurance companies either. At least that's what they told me over the phone. We have an appointment to see them this morning."

"They're offering one thousand pounds if we recover the items." Father leaned back in his chair until the front two feet left the ground. He clasped his hands behind his head. "I'm thinking it might be an inside job."

I studied his posture, his bright eyes, and uttered up a silent thanks to both the Martins for hiring them and the new medication the doctor had prescribed.

"Guess it's just me at the ball," I said. "Hannah, do we have a recent statement of what we owe Richard Beauchamp?" Since Hannah was such a whiz on the computer, I'd asked her to keep track of our money.

"I'll print you one out," she said. "It's looking better. If you can do another three jobs that net us the same as this last one we'll break the monkey on our backs."

"That's if the other cat doesn't turn up and rain on our parade," Father groused. "Damned nuisance. And damned strange that no one on the inside is talking. I've asked every contact I can think of and none of them knows a thing. Not even Alistair."

"Did you check with Emily?" I asked, only half joking. Emily seemed to know everything that went on in the community.

"Emily's a gossip," Father growled.

"Exactly. Besides, don't knock it. Gossip might help you recover the stolen brooches and tiara."

Ben checked his watch. "Point taken. Time for us to visit the Martins. We don't want to arrive late. That woman is damned peculiar. Would hate to rile her and lose our job. I haven't had so much fun in ages."

Father bounded to his feet and after landing a quick peck on my cheek, trotted after Ben.

Hannah stood as well and started to gather the dirty cups. "It's good to see them both so happy again. The forced retirement didn't go well."

"No. It makes them feel as though they're contributing. They get a kick out of the market stall as well, even though they complain about getting up so early."

"And that it's not an upper-class activity," Hannah added in a low, gruff voice, much as she'd mimicked Father's initial objection when I'd suggested the idea as a means to raise funds.

"It was a good idea, full stop. Amber gets a real kick out of her sales. Do you have a minute to help me? I need to go over the ball plans and try to find a list of who's attending."

Hannah rolled up her sleeves and wiped the table down.

"Are you asking me to do a little hacking?"

"Who, me?" I clapped a hand to my chest and tried to look mortally wounded. Then I laughed. "Could you?"

CHAPTER
20

I n the end, I attended the ball on my own. Seth was away on business in Lucerne, and I'd left it too late to find a date. All the good ones had been snapped up, leaving the dregs. In other words, the ones that would cling like a second skin all night when I had work to do. Solo sounded easier.

I left my car in Kensington at Alistair and Emily's house, since I intended to stay there the night, and caught a cab to the Knightsbridge hotel where the ball was being held. The cab deposited me outside the hotel.

A red carpet stretched the length of the walkway from the road to the ballroom entrance. Security guards kept the public at bay while a man wearing a turban and Indian silk checked tickets. High security here. I scanned the public out of habit, checking for familiar faces.

A photographer snapped shots of guests before they entered the ballroom, creating a slow-moving line.

"Ticket, love?" While the costume looked exotic, the accent was pure East London.

I handed over my ticket.

"No partner, Lady Katherine?" His eyes twinkled as he grinned and offered a wink.

"Too many to choose from," I said blithely. "Trying to pick brought on a headache so I decided to attend alone."

Ah! The blond bimbo had decided to burst out in full glory. *Probably the best way to go tonight*, I mused.

"Thank you," I said when he handed my invitation back to me. When the line in front moved, I drifted along the red carpet with them.

"That's Lady Katherine Fawkner," I heard one of the public bystanders say.

"I like her dress. I wonder who designed it."

I forced back my amusement and worked at keeping a straight face. Hannah and I had found four new outfits for me to wear to balls and charity functions at a second hand clothes shop in Kensington. The dress was made from midnight-blue silk that suited my blond coloring perfectly. It skimmed my curves and dipped low in the front, giving any male with height a fairly good view. Hannah and I had discussed the low bodice and concluded that it was another weapon in my arsenal.

The line moved closer to the photographer. I considered

trying to duck around and miss this important step but saw there was another security guard. Photos were not optional.

A voice from the crowd piped up. "That's Lady Katherine. I wonder who her escort is tonight. She's got a young daughter. Unmarried, you know."

This time, I had trouble finding amusement. Why did I have to attend with a man? There was nothing wrong with going solo, and what business was it of theirs if I were an unmarried mother? Ugh! Some people were pretentious snobs!

The line moved again, and I came face to face with the photographer I'd stolen from—Jasper Cooney.

"Stand over here please." He glanced past me, and then his gaze zapped to mine. "Where's your partner? I don't have time to wait for him. Surely you can see I have others waiting?"

"I don't have a partner tonight," I stated in a loud voice. Too loud since the guests behind me heard and started murmuring to each other. I felt my cheeks heat but lifted my chin and ignored the gossip in session in the line behind me. "Where would you like me to stand?"

"Over there, please, Lady Katherine."

I stepped into a leafy bower and gave a big toothy smile for the camera. The photographer snapped several shots and lowered his camera.

"Thank you. I was wondering," he said, visibly hesitating.
"Yes?"

"Would you save a dance for me later on?" he blurted.

He wasn't my type. He wasn't tall. He wasn't dark, and he didn't speak with an exotic accent that sizzled through me each time he spoke. In short, he wasn't Kahu.

"That sounds lovely," I said with a gentle smile that I hoped put him at ease. *Get over it*, I told myself firmly. Kahu doesn't trust you. "I look forward to it."

Finally, I was allowed into the ballroom. I paused in the doorway to give everyone a chance to see my arrival and the lack of an escort. Might as well get the hard bit out of the way first.

The organizing committee had gone full out to arrange a different theme, something the jaded attendants hadn't seen before. Swathes of colorful silks billowed from the walls. Large urns of feathers and flowers decorated alcoves and corners, and the subtle scent of sandalwood permeated the air. In the other portion of the huge ballroom, the part that led out to a small private balcony, the committee had created an outdoor feel with potted trees and lush tropical plants along with hundreds of fairy lights.

The staff were dressed in turbans and silk suits or flowing saris. They distributed glasses of champagne and tiny samosa, pakora and cubes of fresh melon and berries.

As my gaze took in the decorations and acquaintances in attendance, I cast my mind back to the conversation I'd had with Alistair and Emily. It seemed rubies were still in demand.

Propelled into the ballroom by the guests arriving behind me, I drifted closer to a waitress dressed in a bright orange sari to check out the offerings on her tray.

Ohhh! Bite-sized chocolate treats and tiny lemon tarts. As I reached for a napkin and one of each succulent mouthful, a sense of déjà vu filled me.

Jemima.

I did not want her horrified screeches drawing attention.

My hasty glance didn't see her in the near vicinity. Safe, I reached for my chocolate treats and went in search of a nonalcoholic beverage. There must be a bar around here somewhere.

In the back of my mind, I catalogued the jewels being paraded tonight. The usual assortment. Diamonds and more diamonds.

I tried to think when I'd seen Jemima last. A frown formed. Not since the ball where I'd run into her and she'd been uncharacteristically snappish. Nothing like her normal self at all, and that strange mystery man . . . My frown deepened to a scowl. No, she'd been at the fashion parade. That had been the last time I'd seen her. A sneaking suspicion formed. Was it possible Jemima was my competitor? I catalogued the thought to mull over later.

"Is there a bar around here somewhere?" I asked a passing waiter.

"Yeah, over there." He gestured with a sweeping wave of his hand and disappeared between a chubby young lady in a skintight black dress and an older woman who looked enough like her that I guessed they were related. Even standing on tiptoes, I couldn't see a bar.

"Hello, Lady Katherine."

The voice started my heart racing even though I'd decided earlier in the week, that I was wasting my time thinking about a man. Or men full stop.

I turned slowly, with what I hoped was a poker face. "Kahu." Damn, he looked good. My hands itched to touch his face, to run my fingers through his hair. "How are you?" Scintillating conversation, it wasn't—but it was all I could manage.

His chocolate-brown eyes were serious, lacking their normal sparkle and hint of humor. "Busy with work," he said.

"Caught any crooks lately?" I don't know where that came from, and suddenly I felt ashamed of myself. My gaze slid away to study my black shoes. No wonder Kahu had told me he didn't want to see me anymore, the way I shifted from character to character hardly ever letting the real me shine through.

I darted another quick look at Kahu to gauge his reaction. He surprised me with a grin.

"Nope, the crooks are still running loose."

I found an answering smile on my lips before I'd even formed the thought. Scary, the way he prized reactions from me.

He gestured at my uneaten lemon tart. "Are you finished or would you like to dance?"

"I didn't think you wanted anything to do with me," I said bluntly. My heart did a series of excited leaps at the idea of being close to him. I knew I was setting myself up to be hurt again but the reality didn't seem to matter.

He closed one brown eye in a wink. "I'll take a chance."

I searched for a place to stash my lemon tart. Kahu reached for it, plucking the tart from my hand. "Open up," he murmured.

My eyes widened and conveniently, my lips parted. Kahu nudged the tart against my mouth, his eyes intent on watching me.

I opened my mouth and at the same time, reached to hold the tart by myself. My hand collided with Kahu's. Our eyes met, and just like that, every single one of my good resolutions regarding men faded into oblivion.

Somehow, I swallowed the tart, and we joined the other dancers on the dance floor. A four-piece band played easy-listening music, the saxophone throbbing a solo that made my blood sing with awareness of Kahu.

"Are you here on business?" I needed to put the brake on my runaway emotions somehow. Talking about police work seemed a fine solution.

"Mostly."

What did he mean by that?

A finger touched me under the chin, forcing me to

look up to meet his gaze. "And I wanted to see you," he said with stark honesty.

A lump the size of Ben Nevis formed in my throat. Probably just as well since his words made me want to shout and scream with happiness. Another chance? Yes! Yes! *Yes!*

Kahu twirled me into a spin, and I caught a glimpse of red. A beautiful ruby choker with a matching bracelet.

Reality check.

Our relationship remained full of potential conflicts.

"I've missed you," I confessed. Who wanted sensible? Me, I conceded with an inward sigh.

"I—" Kahu stopped dancing. "Sorry, Kate." Frustration simmered over his face when he pulled a pager from his inside jacket pocket. He scanned the message and looked back to me. "I have to go. I'll call you."

I watched him fade into the crowd, a sense of regret inside. Okay. So he'd left. It was for the best since I needed to concentrate on work. The sooner I raised funds to pay off our debt to Richard Beauchamp, the better. The minute the debt was paid off Amber would be out of danger.

Safe.

That's what I was working for. I left the dance floor and prowled about making small chat with friends and acquaintances while I checked out the jewels. The good news was that Marilyn Ransome and Fifi MacIntyre were both wearing rubies. An embarrassment of riches.

I retired to the gardens to find a quiet spot to ring Oakthorpe.

The phone rang twice before Hannah answered. "Two possibles," I said. "Ransome or MacIntyre."

"I'll start doing preliminary work right now," Hannah promised.

"Is Amber all right?"

"She's fine. Very excited about the market tomorrow morning."

"I hope last week wasn't a fluke," I said. "She'll be crushed if the eggcups don't sell."

"They'll sell," Hannah said.

Richard Beauchamp stepped outside. "Kate! There you are."

"I have to go," I said to Hannah. "Talk to you later."

"Just checking on my daughter," I said.

"Would you like to dance?" Richard asked.

"Sure." While I wasn't thrilled with the idea, I still needed to keep on his good side. I just hoped he kept his hands to himself because I'd have take action if they wandered.

Richard snared my hand when my attention was on a rather splendid emerald tiara. His clasp was gentle yet tenacious. I wasn't likely to get my hand back anytime soon.

We stepped on to the dance floor as the band started a new segment of slow dances. I suppressed a sigh when Richard's hands slid around my waist, pulling me close.

Strange. His expression was serious, and the sexual gleam absent for once. Perhaps I'd been wrong about another proposition in the wind. His mind seemed miles away.

"Your cheek has healed up." Richard trailed a hand over my abused cheek.

"Ouch," I mumbled, jerking from his touch. "I covered the bruise with makeup."

Regret chased chagrin across his face. "Sorry."

"It's all right."

"No, I mean sorry for putting you in danger. You could have died."

Huh? What had they done with Richard Beauchamp? This wasn't him. "A bus might run me over when I leave tonight. It was no one's fault. We were in the wrong place at the wrong time."

Richard didn't seem convinced. "Maybe." He turned me into a tight turn to avoid a collision with another couple. "You did a top job for me. I appreciate it."

"Enough to knock some of the interest charges off the loan?" I shot back.

"Ring me during office hours, and we'll talk about it. I wonder . . . would you consider helping me out again next month?"

If it meant being debt-free quicker, I'd consider anything. "Let me think about it."

The music faded and the lights flickered signaling the business side of the evening. Speeches.

"We'll talk about details when you ring me," Richard promised. He squeezed my hands and kissed me on the lips. "I need to go," he said. I'm presenting a check to the committee on behalf of Beauchamp Industries. Talk to you later." He pressed another kiss to my uninjured cheek and strode off leaving me looking after him with my mouth open. Aware that men and women around me were studying me with a great deal of interest, I left the dance floor for a more private place where I could rehash the last five minutes. I finally found refuge behind a huge potted palm at the far end of the ballroom.

But my refuge didn't remain private for long.

"You said there was nothing going on with Beauchamp. It doesn't look like nothing to me." Kahu's eyes flashed dark and dangerous. I found myself taking a step backward before I realized and planted my black heels firmly to stop my retreat.

Kahu kept coming, only stopping when we were so close I felt the heat emanating from his body and smelled his intoxicating scent. Instantly my hormones jumped to high alert.

"I don't know what you're talking about." My voice sounded breathless as if I'd recently run a four-minute mile or participated in a horizontal tango on silken sheets. I sounded guilty. Defensive.

"That kiss," Kahu snapped.

Emotion rippled off him in waves. Anger. Determination. Maybe a hint of confusion.

"It didn't mean anything." Truth rang in my voice. I only hoped it convinced Kahu because the last week had been hell. My emotions hadn't experienced such a roller-coaster ride since Amber's conception. Funny thing. Both instances involved a man.

"Stay away from him. He's involved in illegal activities."

Now there was a surprise. "What sort of illegal activities?"

"Money laundering. Gambling rings." He paused clearly hesitating about what he'd intended to say next.

"What?" I prompted, following my question up with a soft touch at Kahu's nape.

"Maybe murder," he said.

I stared. I didn't need to pretend shock. "Why hasn't he been arrested?" I demanded.

"Because I can't prove that he's responsible for my brother's disappearance." Both bitterness and determination warred within him. He sounded as though he believed himself at fault.

"I'm sorry. I didn't know you had a brother."

"Step-brother," he said tersely. "Look, we can't talk here. Why don't we go for coffee somewhere? My flat?"

I'd seen enough in the way of jewels tonight to have a range of possibilities available for *The Shadow*. If my market wanted rubies, then rubies they would have. "All right, but just for coffee." I didn't want to have any undignified

SHELLEY MUNRO

struggles and decided to make that clear up front.

The old familiar cocky grin slashed across his face for
an instant before it disappeared.

My mouth firmed. "That wasn't a dare," I snapped. "It
was a condition."

Kahu sobered completely. He placed both hands on
my shoulders, making sure he had my complete attention.
"I don't use force with a woman. Never. And I'll explain
that in greater detail later too, if you insist."

What girl could resist that sort of carrot dangling before
her? Besides, I had to admit I felt a burning curiosity about
this man from New Zealand. A man's home provided a lot
of clues for a girl. I nodded decisively. "All right."

Kahu gave me a quick kiss that left me tingling and
wanting more. He grinned. "Let's go."

We weaved through the crowd of people who were listening to the speeches and the verbal shoulder thumping
that goes on at charity fundraisers.

Outside, it was much cooler. A light fog had descended over Knightsbridge, giving the streetlights an eerie glow.
"You wait here, and I'll organize a cab."

Before Kahu took three steps out the double doors of
the hotel, his pager beeped.

Kahu turned, a wry smile on his face. "Sorry. Business calls." He headed back into the hotel lobby.

I followed a little more slowly. By the time I found
Kahu, he'd finished his call.

"Work," he said. "I have to go. I'll call you."

I nodded, afraid to read too much into his promise. I lifted a hand in farewell, but he ignored the hand to kiss me again. Hard. Like he meant it. My right hand crept up to touch my tingling lips. Wow, that man packed a punch. Before I could react further, he'd walked away.

"Is he yours?" a red-haired woman in a flowing black dress asked. Her blue eyes held avid interest, none of it directed to me.

I felt a frown pucker my brow. The need to direct her gaze off Kahu's butt simmered through me, fueling my indignation. That was my man she ogled.

"My man," I agreed a touch aggressively.

The woman laughed and held up her hands in a message received manner. "Just admiring the view. Can't blame a girl for looking."

I nodded, deciding not to utter the words trembling on the tip of my tongue. My reputation was bad enough as it was. A deep breath later, I was calm enough to notice her diamond-and-sapphire necklace.

Payback.

Childish, I know, but very satisfactory. I decided to place this specific piece of jewelry on my personal shopping list.

When two women joined us, I took the opportunity to slip back into the ballroom.

From the corner of my eye, I glimpsed a man and woman

leaving the ballroom. Normally, I wouldn't have thought anything of it, but the woman didn't look well. A closer look made me decide to follow. She looked out of it. Drunk. My mouth firmed, and I hurried after them, but not too closely that the man would notice. If he thought he could take advantage of that poor woman, he could think again!

The man maneuvered her out a small backdoor that I hadn't noticed earlier. A shortcut to the hotel's underground car park. He headed for a white sedan and seemed to hesitate when it came to unlocking the car because he couldn't hold the woman up and get the keys from his pocket at the same time.

"Can I help?" I planted my hands on my hips and glared, incensed at a man taking advantage.

"What? Oh, yes! Would you?"

Huh? The man seemed pathetically grateful at my offer of assistance. I studied his pale face and his brilliant green eyes. I'd seen those eyes before.

"Do I know you?" I asked, then snapped my fingers. "Rufus Geraghty!"

"And you're Lady Katherine. Are you going to help me or not? Jocelyn drank too much champagne. I told her to lay off, not to mix the pain pills with the alcohol, but did she listen? No!"

He sounded so put out, I knew he hadn't intended her harm. I grasped the hapless Jocelyn by the scruff of the neck and balanced her against the car while Rufus found his keys.

"I thought you were kidnapping her or something equally sinister."

"Me? Kidnap Jocelyn? You have to be joking! She's my younger cousin, and I'm always having to get her out of scrapes." He pushed a button on his remote and the car chirped as the locks disengaged.

"I wish I'd had a cousin like you to look out for me," I murmured.

He speared an intense look my way. "Did something happen to you?"

"Yeah."

He scrunched his brows together. "I might be talking out of turn here, but a friend of my brother was mouthing off about you. It was a few years ago . . ."

I sucked in a deep breath. What happened? I wanted to demand. And, more importantly, who?

"Now who was it? Mark—no, Matt. I have it! It was Matthew."

"Matthew who?"

His shoulders slumped. "Sorry. Can't remember."

The girl groaned feebly.

"Suppose I'd better get Jocelyn home. She's gonna have a hell of a head tomorrow."

I fished a card from my bag. "If you think of anything else, give me a call. Please," I added.

"I promise," Rufus said. "Men like that should be

tarred and feathered and then paraded down the street."

"That's exactly what I intend to do," I said sweetly. "The minute I catch his sorry arse."

"I'll ask my brother when I talk to him next," he promised while he stuffed Jocelyn into the passenger seat and fastened the seatbelt.

He waved as they drove away. I sighed, hoping he'd get back to me. Time to go home. I checked my watch. No, I'd better do a little more homework since it looked as though Kahu were back in my life, and windows to research targets could become minimal. I strolled up to one of my potential donors. She stood by a buffet table that had appeared while I was away with Kahu. I glanced at her plate and saw she loved chocolate. Score one for the lady. She knew how to open a conversation.

"Hello. That looks delicious." First, a look of guilt flashed across her face. An expression of suspicion swiftly followed as she glanced at my figure.

I'm a victim of genes. Good when it comes to the figure department, not so good in occupation choice. I ignored the suspicion and carried on with my prattle. "Chocolate is my favorite." I pursed my lips in what I hoped was a thoughtful expression rather than a prune face. "I like it more than lemon."

The suspicion cleared like a cloud swept away by a gale-force wind. She believed I was a member of the closet chocolate brigade. Which, in truth, I was.

"I prefer chocolate myself," she said, leaning toward me in a confidential manner. "With caramel as my second choice."

I nodded, feeling very much in charity with this woman. In the world we lived in it took a brave woman to admit to a secret vice like chocolate. I don't know why, but a sex or alcohol addiction was regarded as more acceptable. Chocolate was a secret you kept hidden. Weird. "What would you recommend?"

"The chocolate gâteau," she said with firm authority. "Definitely the chocolate gâteau."

I nodded and reached for a plate. The lady was older than me, a bit on the plump side but it suited her. Her jet-black hair cascaded in casual curls down her back, over silky blue fabric of a dress similar to mine. I imagined that a painter from an earlier age would have loved to depict her on canvas. My gaze wandered to the all-important jewelry. The rubies were splendid at close quarters. But I couldn't do it. I liked this lady since we had a common bond. I decided to keep her as a backup and try one of the others first.

"Nice to meet a fellow chocolate lover," I said. "I'm Katherine Fawkner."

"I've seen you at other balls, Lady Katherine. I'm Grace Montville."

"Pleased to meet you, Grace." I clicked my fingers suddenly as my memory slipped into gear. "Ah. Married

SHELLEY MUNRO

to Thomas."

She nodded. To her credit, she reacted with calm and poise even though her husband jumped in and out of beds like other people boarded buses. She must have known that people gossiped and laughed about her. That made me feel protective.

"If you're ever down near Oakthorpe, pop in to see me," I said impulsively. "Our housekeeper makes the best chocolate brownies I've ever tasted."

She seemed startled by the suggestion but suddenly she grinned. "Thank you. I'd love that."

I tugged a pale blue business card from my purse. "Here's my number."

The look of delight on her face set the seal on my decision. I wouldn't steal this necklace.

"I need to speak to a friend of Father's," I said. "Are you going to the Sterling ball next weekend?"

"I think so."

"Great. I'll make a point of looking for you." I waved and headed off, my plate clutched protectively to my chest. Half of me expected Jemima to jump from the woodwork, her lips pursed in a manner guaranteed to bring my guilt to the fore.

Now, where were the other sets of rubies I'd spotted earlier on? Ah! One was at ten o'clock on the dance floor. I turned slowly in a circle and spied another set of rubies at about seven o'clock. My breath stalled in my throat. These

. . . these were the ones! A big, fat ruby the shape of a tear dangled from a delicate necklace of diamonds and rubies. My fingers tingled with the need to caress the glowing stone. Jeez! *There must be more Fawkner in me than I'd realized*, I thought in awe. I tore my gaze away from the mesmerizing sight, my heart pounding in excitement at the idea of the chase. Definitely too much Fawkner blood!

I glanced at my watch. Nearly midnight. Already, the crowds were thinning out as people moved on to other parties and nightclubs in Soho and Piccadilly. Might as well leave too.

I wandered from the ballroom, stopping to chat with a friend of Seth's when I collected my cloak from the coat check. One of our neighbors waited for his coat, too.

"Good to see you home again," Mr. Forbisher said in his gruff voice.

I'd known him since I was a child and remembered him fondly because he used to produce peppermint sticks from his pockets for me each time we met.

"No peppermint sticks today, Mr. Forbisher?"

He gave a bark of laughter. "You always were a minx, Lady Katherine. Good to see you haven't changed."

"Katherine! Are you still trying to coax candy from Julian?" Amusement colored the voice behind me.

I chuckled as I walked into outstretched arms. "You were just as bad," I said. "Plying me with chocolate. I've never grown out of the chocolate fixation you started!"

"You must—"

A loud explosive bang echoed throughout the hotel foyer where we stood.

"Oh, my stars," Mrs. Forbisher said, her hand fluttering at her chest. "That sounded like a gun."

"It was." Her husband sounded grim, and I caught the note of worry.

Another shot sounded. A scream.

"Call an ambulance!" someone shrieked.

People ran in all directions. Mr. Forbisher swept both his wife and I back against a wall out of the path of the panicked people pouring through the door from outside.

In the distance, a siren sounded. Another scream rippled through the pandemonium.

A car pulled up outside. A police car. The blue light reflected in the window.

I heard a policeman fire questions before silence fell, an intense silence that was frightening and strummed along my nerves.

"Are you all right, dear?"

Mrs. Forbisher nodded.

"Katherine?"

"I'm fine," I mumbled, but in truth, I didn't feel so hot. Gunfire seemed to figure prominently in my life lately, and I didn't like it at all.

CHAPTER
21

I was up early the next morning since I'd had trouble sleeping. I tried to tell myself it was the strange bed but knew it for a lie.

Last night's murder had kept sleep away.

Emily and Alistair were already in the kitchen, with the scent of toast and the crackle of a new newspaper battling with an oldie playing on the radio.

Alistair looked up from the *London Telegraph* when I walked in and pulled out a chair to join him at the table. "Were you there?"

I didn't ask for an explanation. Unable to speak, I nodded.

"And you were present at the drive-by shooting in Edinburgh."

Again, I nodded.

Emily placed a plate of scrambled eggs and crispy bacon in front of me. My stomach roiled, and I gave up any idea of eating. I looked away from the laden plate. Perhaps a cup of tea?

Alistair shook his head and made a *tsk*ing sound at the back of his throat. "I don't like it. I don't like this situation at all."

"A more suspicious person would think the two were related and you were the target," Emily said. She pushed my plate toward me to silently indicate she expected me to eat. "I think I'll consult the cards before you leave."

"Not on my account," I said hastily. My bottom started to smart, and I wriggled around on the hard chair in distinct discomfort. I still remembered the last time she'd predicted my future from the cards. I'm sure the dog remembered too. When Emily nudged the plate again, I picked up a knife and fork and cut a corner off a piece of whole-wheat toast.

"I don't like coincidences," Alistair said. "But it can't be related to *The Shadow* because if that were the case, the police would turn up at Oakthorpe. You'd be locked in jail before you could shout boo."

The picture he called up made me cringe. Jail? No, thank you! "Do you think it would be wise for *The Shadow* to fade into the background for a few weeks?"

Alistair shook his head. "A judgment call, I'd say. It depends on how much people panic. If they start to stay at home that might crimp your style."

"Yeah." The last thing I needed was stay-at-home jewel owners. Or becoming an unwitting voyeur forced to listen to kinky sex! That rated high on my hate list. With an inward shudder, I stood in a decisive manner. "I might head back to Oakthorpe early. After last night, I have lots of research to do."

◊ ◊ ◊ ◊ ◊

"Thank God you're all right! I've worried all morning." Hannah hugged me so hard the gold charm I wore suspended on a chain around my neck felt as though it might pop out my back or at the very least leave a tattoo.

"I should have rung," I said, contrite. Hannah worried enough without me being thoughtless. "Where's Amber?"

"Upstairs. She wanted to make her bed and get ready for school on her own without help."

"I'll go up and see how she's getting on." I wanted to hug her and reassure myself she was happy and safe.

"You have a visitor."

I stopped mid-step. "At this time of the morning?" Glancing at my watch, I saw it had only just turned eight.

"He's in the kitchen with Ben and Charlie."

He. Kahu? The nuances in her voice made me think it wasn't a good idea him being on is own. Instinct made me rush to the kitchen.

313

"What are your intentions toward my daughter?"

"Father!" I shrieked from the doorway. Mortified, I offered Kahu a weak smile of apology. "I'm sorry about my nosy family. Forget you heard the question."

Kahu closed one chocolate-brown eye in a wink and grinned. He didn't seem too upset.

That should have calmed me. I mean, if he wasn't worrying, then why should I? But instead, my pulse jumped around all over the place, breaking new land-speed records.

"Is this . . . ?" I coughed to clear my throat and steady my nerves. "Is this business?"

"Mostly," Kahu answered. The teasing glint disappeared from his eyes making me suspect he wanted to talk about last night. The few mouthfuls of breakfast I'd swallowed down to placate Emily danced a lively jig in my stomach.

"Okay," I said, fighting to keep my voice even and panic-free. I sank into a chair and smiled at Hannah when she placed a mug of strong tea in front of me. I doubted I'd manage to drink it but it might come in handy as a prop to hold.

"What color was the dress you wore last night?"

Of all the questions I'd expected, it wasn't this one. "Blue," I said.

"Dark blue," Kahu corrected, his eyes narrowed with concentration.

My head dipped in a nod. I reached for the mug of tea

but realized my hand was shaking too much to avoid spills. I jerked my hand back and hid it on my lap.

"The woman who was shot was wearing a dark blue gown almost the same color as yours. She wore a matching cloak that covered her hair when she left the ballroom."

Shocked silence met Kahu's statement. I concentrated on breathing, controlling the nausea that threatened to overpower me. A blue dress. His words kept echoing through my mind, along with the implications.

I was the intended target.

"Katie?" Father asked Kahu. "You mean Katie was the intended victim?"

"That's where the facts point. Any idea who hates you enough to shoot you?"

Wordlessly, I stared at Father. He shook his head in an imperceptible no. Of course, he was right. Telling Kahu about *The Shadow* was a no-no. "I can't think of anyone," I said, and it was the truth. Apart from the goon, but I couldn't talk about him either.

"What about Amber's father?"

Hannah drew in a sharp breath at the question. Me— I was too numb to react.

Luckily, Father answered for me. "He's not in the picture."

"He's dead," I blurted, mainly because I could see the next question forming on Kahu's lips. A question I didn't want to answer so I fired off the only answer I could think of that would bring questioning to a halt.

"I'm sorry," Kahu said.

Lively curiosity danced in his eyes, and I averted my gaze so that I too was blind to the silent questions. My quest for revenge . . . I was closer to the truth now. I sensed it in my gut. The names James had given me drifted through my mind.

"Can you think of anyone else who might want you dead?" He repeated his earlier question, and I grappled with suspects in my mind.

The owners of the jewels. Maybe. But they had no idea who I was, so that seemed unlikely. But perhaps it was connected with jewels indirectly. I thought back to the night Perdita Moning had died. Had her murderer seen me leave?

"No, I can't think of anyone," I stated firmly. No way could I tell Kahu about that night. Not now.

"I don't want you to attend any more balls."

My head jerked up, my eyes widened. "What?" I gasped. Impossible. I had to leave the house on *Shadow* business. We still needed the money. "I can't put my life on hold just because you think some loony is after me."

"What about Amber?"

I froze at the possibility. Damn. The only argument he could have used to make me hesitate. "Do you think she's in danger?" *More danger than she is already*, I added silently. The goon had taken to ringing again, despite my in with Beauchamp. *Probably on commission*, I thought with a touch of black humor. Earns extra money for each threatening phone call.

Kahu shrugged. "I don't know, but do you want to take that chance?"

"No." I thought furiously, trying to think of a solution to keep Amber safe.

"We can put you under police protection," Kahu said.

"No," Father snapped.

Silence enveloped the kitchen at the abrupt answer. Ben and Hannah eyed Kahu uneasily.

"What Father means is that we'd feel better without strangers around," I added to counteract Father's rudeness. We did not want to give Kahu any reason to suspect us of a crime. A policeman on site would represent a problem.

"It was a suggestion," Kahu said. "That's all. I understand you'd prefer to maintain your privacy. Think about it, anyway. I've got to go back to London. Kate, walk me out?"

"Are you sure it's safe?" Father asked in a snide tone.

Kahu met his scowling face without a flinch. "She's safe with me."

"Humph!"

Father's bulldog expression told me he wanted to argue. And I wasn't one-hundred-percent sure they were talking about the shooter anymore.

"I'll walk you out," I agreed.

Kahu stood back to let me pass and followed me from

the kitchen. I rolled my eyes on hearing the fierce whispering that broke out the second we left.

"Kate?" Kahu's hand on my shoulder stopped me. I turned.

Kahu hauled me into his arms, moving so quickly I didn't have time to blink. The charm pressed into my chest again. His spicy green scent filled my senses, and his arms wrapped around me offered the illusion of safety. He pulled away, his eyes fierce and warrior-like as he stared down at me. "Hell, when I heard about the dress . . ." He trailed off and kissed me hard. Tongues fenced and parried, teeth clacked. Our mouths mated with savage disregard of our nearby chaperons. All I knew was that his hand on my breast felt as if it belonged.

"Mama!"

Kahu pulled out of the kiss with apparent lack of enthusiasm. I felt the same way at the interruption, but this was countered by guilt.

"Hi, sweetie. I was about to come up and say hello."

"I dressed myself."

The bright green T-shirt clashed with the purple jeans; her socks didn't match, either. "You've done great," I said, my eyes misty with tears. My little girl was growing up in leaps and bounds. I owed it to her to make sure she had the chance to have children of her own. A plan formed in my mind to guarantee her safety.

"Why are you kissing Mama?" she asked Kahu. The way

she bit her bottom lip looked so cute a grin bloomed across my face. Kahu grinned too as he crouched beside her.

"I was kissing her goodbye," he said in his Kiwi accent. My insides quivered. His accent stirred pure wanton need every time.

Amber regarded him with a serious expression and offered him her cheek. From where I stood, I saw her tiny rosebud mouth was pursed.

"You can kiss me goodbye too," she said.

For an instant, I worried about Kahu's reaction. I shouldn't have. The man was a natural with kids and slid into the parental role without missing a heartbeat.

He kissed her on both cheeks in the French custom. Amber beamed.

"I am having toast and cornflakes for breakfast," she announced, and she skipped off down the passage, lopsided ponytail flapping, without looking back.

Kahu climbed to his feet. "Can I see you one night soon?" A silent question throbbed within his words.

One night soon.

Lord, I wanted that. I wanted a normal life where I wasn't paralyzed by the thought of sex. His kisses didn't repel me so I had hope about progressing to the next stage.

"Okay," I whispered.

After another kiss that left my blood singing and my legs shaky at the knee, I wobbled back to the kitchen.

Hannah moved away from the kitchen door without

a trace of embarrassment. Even my glare brought nothing more than a grin. "I'm thinking that man knows how to kiss."

My nose shot into the air and after an indignant sniff, I changed the subject. "I'm going to send Amber to France for a while."

"Good idea." Hannah nodded at my announcement. Her agreement echoed in Father's and Ben's faces.

"But who's going to take her? We're all needed here," Father said.

"I've thought about that. I'm going to ask Emily if she'd like to take a break in France."

A grunt escaped Father. "Good plan."

"I've washed my hands." Amber held up hands that still dripped water.

"Well, I can't dispute that," Hannah said, inspecting the trail of water that went from the small cloakroom off the kitchen to the spot where Amber stood. "But how about we dry them too?"

Amber trotted off to the cloakroom with her, and we could hear them discussing the lack of towel. Father's fault, evidently.

"Feeling henpecked?" I asked, fighting a smirk.

"Humph!"

My father—a man of many words.

"Alistair's still asking for rubies," I said, angling to the cloakroom so I could halt the discussion the minute Amber returned. "There were several paraded for show last night."

"Tell her our news!" Ben interrupted. He looked as though he might burst if he had to wait much longer.

"I couldn't tell her while that man was here," Father said.

"We've solved the crime," Ben exclaimed. "Our second one already!"

I popped two slices of toast in the toaster and reached for a carton of cornflakes.

"I'm dry now," Amber informed us in a loud voice.

The expression on Ben's face was priceless. Frustration combined with impatience to form a truly unique look. Like he'd eaten a sour apple. I decided to take pity on him.

"Would you like to escort Amber and I to school this morning? We can chat on the way home."

In the end, both Ben and Father accompanied us. The trip to school was quick and without major mishap. I walked Amber to her classroom and headed back to the car.

"I'll drive," Father announced. "You listen."

I scooted into the back of the Mini and clicked the seatbelt into place. "I'm a captive audience."

"We found the missing brooches and tiara hidden in the floor of their spare bedroom, along with . . . get this! A cache of jewels."

"They fit the descriptions of the jewels our competitor stole," Father added. "I'm hoping our problems are over."

No wonder they were excited. "I don't suppose you

321

were able to stash some of the loot for later use?"

Father chuckled as he pulled from the school. "Our use, perchance?"

"Well, yeah." Attractive thoughts of being debt-free started to float through my mind. The idea that maybe *The Shadow* could go into retirement.

"Afraid not," Ben muttered, a trace of disgust in his voice.

Enough to prick my bubble of a happy, *Shadow*-free future. "What happened?"

"Our clients came running when Mr. Bigmouth here started hollering."

"I was in shock," Ben muttered, shame-faced. "Not every day you fall over a cache of jewels."

"The clients were in shock too since it was the room used by their niece. The good news is that we're entitled to a finder's fee. We rang the local cop shop, and they hoofed it over and took the sparklers away with them."

The thought of the local cops hoofing anywhere raised a smirk. They were all older and nearing retirement. Crime rocked their boats, and they took emergencies as a personal affront.

"How much?" I asked. "Will it cover the next payment?"

"Each owner decided to fork out five thousand each."

There was no mistaking the smug satisfaction emanating from Ben. Father, too.

"Well done. Two for two. That's a pretty good strike rate."

"We're hoping for more jobs via word of mouth. It's weird being on this side of the law, but the money's just as satisfying."

"Who is their niece? Do we know her name? And are we sure this is our competitor?"

"Jemima Cameron. I felt sorry for them. They—"

"Jemima Cameron? I met her when I first came back from France. We met up at most of the balls, but I hadn't seen her lately. I was wondering about her last night. Are you sure?"

"The jewels pretty much prove she did it, so we won't need to worry about our Celtic-dagger trap anymore. She has to be the culprit. Her uncle and aunt aren't capable, and I've heard they have alibis for most of the dates on which the thefts occurred." Ben hopped up and down with excitement. "They haven't seen her for weeks. Evidently she's done a runner to Europe with a man."

Father chuckled at my frown. "What? Didn't she fit the stereotype? Did she look like a bimbo?"

Touché. "Point taken," I said dryly. I thought about the chocolate episode at an earlier ball. She'd acted the part of debutante well. She'd fooled me, which made me uneasy. I wouldn't be fooled again.

CHAPTER
22

Early the next morning, the phone rang. I shoved my head under my pillow and pretended not to hear.

"It's for you!" Ben roared from the bottom of the stairs.

Unable to miss the thunderous summons, I groaned and climbed from bed, rubbing the sleep from my bleary eyes. *This had better be good*, I thought, irritable at being woken after working into the small hours on a foolproof plan to snare a ruby necklace.

I stomped down the stairs and snatched up the phone. "Hello!"

"Katherine, it's Rufus. I've remembered the guy's surname. Beauchamp. Matthew Beauchamp."

I drew in a sharp breath, my hand tightening around the phone. Rage engulfed me and I wished my hands throttled Matthew Beauchamp instead of the phone. They fair itched to commit the crime.

"Are you there?"

"Yes." Anger pounded my brain in waves of red and black. *The lowdown rotten . . .* The man had flirted with me up in Edinburgh, propositioned me. Part of me wanted to stomp from Oakthorpe and tear off in the Mini to confront him. But that would be a mistake. I needed proof; then I'd nail the bastard's hide to the closest wall.

"Do you know him?" Rufus asked. "From what I hear, he's a bit of a womanizer. Married, but that doesn't seem to stop him."

I hadn't recognized him even though I'd thought he was familiar. "I met him recently." And I intended to meet him again soon. On my terms.

"You . . . you're not going to do anything silly?" Rufus asked.

I grimaced. I'd tried to keep the hate from my voice but had obviously failed. "I think you watch too much telly," I teased. My face felt frozen by the effort I put into making my voice sound normal. "I'm not going to murder him in his bed!" But I might chop off his masculine equipment and make a eunuch of him, I added on a silent snarl.

"What are you going to do?"

A good question. "Gather my facts," I said after a long hesitation.

"Okay." Rufus's response lacked confidence in my

SHELLEY MUNRO

answer. "Thanks for helping me the other night. If I hear anything else, I'll ring you."

"Thank you," I said. I hung up abruptly, the receiver crashing back into position with a thump, and headed for the kitchen. There was no way I could go back to bed now. The need to strike out, to act immediately sang through my blood with a heady adrenaline rush. Revenge. I craved it bad.

Hannah and Ben were at the table, an early cup of tea brewing in the china teapot.

"What's wrong?" Hannah demanded.

"Nothing," I muttered, unwilling to explain my desperate need for payback. A part of me had always felt so naïve for being duped, and I wasn't about to explain the depths of my stupidity after all these years.

"Are we going to do a preliminary recon tonight?" Ben took me at face value, but I noticed Hannah's thoughtful look and knew a grilling lay ahead.

"Yes." I collected three china mugs from the cupboard and placed them on the table in front of Hannah. "I thought I might take a drive past now since I'm wide awake. What is the time anyway?"

"It's just gone six," Ben answered.

I groaned. "Way too early to be awake."

"Who was on the phone?" Hannah's grilling commenced.

"A friend I met at the ball the other night. I haven't seen him for years."

326

Hannah finished pouring the tea and shunted mugs in front of both Ben and I.

"Strange time for him to ring," she mused, watching me steadily with hawk-like intent.

"Hmmm." I took a mouthful of tea and nearly spat it out. The liquid scalded its way down my throat, bringing tears to my eyes.

"When's Amber going to France?" Ben asked.

"I rang Renee last night. She was fine with Amber staying for a few weeks. I thought I'd drop in on Alistair and Emily later this morning."

"I haven't seen Emily for a while," Hannah said. "Why don't I come with you?"

Checkmate!

I sucked it in, rolling with the punch. She'd fenced me in neatly. Now I'd have to do the recon just as I'd told them. "Can you be ready in half an hour?"

"No, on second thoughts, I'd better stay here. The boys are picking beetroot today, and I wanted to make my prizewinning pickle for them to sell at the stall. My contribution."

Suppressing my cheer with difficulty, I managed a restrained nod. "If you're sure." Please don't change your mind!

I picked up my mug and blew before taking a cautious sip. I glanced at my watch and stood. "Last chance to change your mind."

"Maybe next time," Hannah said.

Yes! I'd passed the test. Cat-burglar training came in handy sometimes. I plucked my keys off the hook in the pantry and hurried upstairs to change. A pair of jeans and a black T-shirt were the first clothes at hand. I bunched my hair in a ponytail and fastened it with a black fabric scrunchie.

My plan . . . well, I didn't have one. But I was a quick study. I'm sure I'd come up with the perfect punishment. Confronting the man would be a start.

On the way out, I stopped to check on Amber. She lay curled on her side, her hair spread over the pastel pink pillowcase. I tried to superimpose my memory of Matthew Beauchamp over her face. It didn't work. Apart from the same colored hair, Amber didn't look much like him. To my mind, she had her own identity.

I smoothed my hand over her brow and pressed a kiss to her cheek, a wave of love for my daughter making my throat clench. Despite the circumstances of her conception, I didn't regret being a mother.

In the end, I decided to drive via the Stanhope premises. I wouldn't put it past Hannah to quiz me on my return to Oakthorpe.

The Victorian house was in the Cotswold, near Burton-on-Water. Large oaks and beech screened the house from the road. Good for privacy, not so good for security since I'd become an expert at entering buildings from the second floor. Surprising how many people didn't bother alarming the upper floors of their houses.

I followed normal procedure and parked my Mini a five-minute walk away in the actual town of Burton-on-Water. It was nearly seven o'clock by the time I reached the driveway. I marched past the imposing brick mailbox without giving it a second look, my pumping arms and legs making me appear a woman intent on a rigorous keep-fit regime. A hedgerow ran parallel with the road creating a natural barrier. I kept moving, maintaining my brisk pace. To any onlooker, I'd seem focused on my goal. And I was. It's just my goal was to steal the Stanhope jewels.

I passed a small thatched cottage with whitewashed walls and a more modern bungalow. At the curve in the road, I jumped a ditch and ducked through a wooden gate that led to a field. If the maps Hannah unearthed were correct, a shortcut across this field should end in the Stanhopes' back garden. I peered through a convenient gap in the hedge where one of the plants had died. Right on target.

The first thing I looked for were dogs. No kennels visible. No rubber balls or chew toys. But I wasn't about to take chances this time. I made a thorough investigation of the grounds. I'd thought surveillance cameras might scan the garden area but they were only out the front recording visitors at the entrance to the property.

By the time I left, I was confident I'd have the knowledge to answer any question Hannah threw my way. *Pick a question*, I thought with a grin. Any question. Number of trees. Type. Windows—number thereof.

My grin felt smug as I climbed into my Mini and headed for London. First stop—Alistair and Emily . . . and then I intended to stalk Matthew Beauchamp.

◊ ◊ ◊ ◊ ◊

Matthew Beauchamp's house bordered Holland Park. Well, a few streets away. I parked the Mini so I could observe the comings and goings. This time, I didn't care if he saw me or not. In fact, I preferred him to know I watched. And I'd make a point of breaking up any of his liaisons I came across.

A black taxi drove up and a woman emerged. Tall and well groomed in a charcoal-gray Armani suit, she didn't look familiar. She juggled five or six shopping bags and rang a buzzer until someone let her into the Georgian building. I wasn't sure if this was Matthew's wife or not.

Best I find out. I exited the Mini and strode up to the front door. I pressed the buzzer.

"Yes?" a tinny-sounding voice intoned from an intercom on the wall.

"It's Lady Katherine Fawkner here. I've come to see Mrs. Beauchamp about the East London children's charity luncheon." Yes, it was the truth. Yes, I was on the committee. I hoped that it would work and she would let me inside. I'd swing the conversation around to children with little trouble since that was what the charity was all about. Actually, maybe I wouldn't have to if they had photos of their children displayed in a prominent place.

"I'm sorry. Mrs. Beauchamp is not feeling well. She's unavailable at the moment," the voice squawked through the intercom.

"I'm sorry to hear that," I said, infusing sympathy. "I'll ring in a few days."

"Thank you, Lady Katherine."

I stepped away from the door and made my way back to the Mini. The woman hadn't looked sick when she strolled up to her front door with all the shopping bags.

I studied the bay windows on the lower floor and the windows on the upper floors. Hmmm. No security cameras here. I caught a flash of white curtain when I returned to the car. Neighbors might be a problem. But nothing a good cat burglar couldn't handle.

◊ ◊ ◊ ◊ ◊

"Kahu rang," Hannah said, the minute I walked in the door.

"What did he want?" I asked, pretending an indifference I didn't feel.

"I don't know," Hannah retorted. "Why don't you ring him back to see?" Once again, it appeared as though she could read my mind and knew of both my joy and

331

trepidation at hearing from Kahu.

"I'll wait until you've finished in here," I said.

"Oh, phooey," Hannah said, a big grin stretching from one side of her face to the other. "You're no fun at all. Is Amber still going to France?"

"Yeah. Emily jumped at the chance to visit Renee. I'm going to spirit Amber out tonight and drive her down to London. Alistair is organizing flights for them and will see them to Heathrow."

Hannah sighed. "As much as I'll miss her, I'll feel a lot better knowing she's out of the clutches of that goon. He rang again, about an hour ago. Just to discuss the weather, he said."

My curse was short and pithy, but insulting his mother didn't make me feel much better. I hated the thought of not seeing Amber. But even more, I needed to know she'd be safe.

"Was the threat specific or was he just being annoying?"

"Both."

I nodded knowing I was doing the right thing in sending Amber to France. "I'll go and start packing for Amber. I'll have to keep it to one bag in case the goon has posted surveillance."

"Renee will take her shopping," Hannah said dryly. "Renee loves an excuse to shop."

And that meant I'd have to find a bit more money from somewhere. Not that I hadn't considered the money angle.

Because I had. Money worries were a daily occurrence.

"I'll be upstairs in Amber's room," I said.

"Don't forget about ringing that nice young man," Hannah said. "I don't want him thinking I don't pass on messages."

"I won't forget." How could I? Kahu constituted part of my problems. I knew I wanted to take the relationship further. I felt right when we were together. I even trusted him, but I was frightened, too.

I trudged up the stairs, the weight of my thoughts both heavy and worrying. Thoughts of Amber, of money, of holding the family together. And the biggie.

Revenge.

I intended to settle my past if I died in the doing.

The phone rang when the packing was almost done.

Hannah shouted from the bottom of the stairs. "Katie! Your young man is on the phone."

"Why don't you tell the whole village," I muttered as I stomped past her to pick up the phone in the kitchen. From the corner of my eye, I caught sight of Father and Ben making a move toward the kitchen, ostensibly for afternoon tea. I wasn't stupid. I knew it was to eavesdrop. One day soon, I promised, I'd splash out on a phone in my room or at least a modern model that I could take to another room. And maybe a new cell phone that did everything except wash the dishes. I'd lost mine while supervising the shopaholics in Edinburgh.

"This is a private conversation," I snapped. As much as I loved the terrible trio, there were times when I had the urge to throttle them.

"Don't mind us," Ben said with a cheerful grin. He had the nerve to aim a sly wink at Father. My eyes narrowed in warning. Unfortunately, not one member of the trio took a whit of notice. The two men seated themselves and looked expectantly at Hannah. She froze beside me, gave a delicate sniff that only I heard, and marched over to join them at the table.

"It's your turn, Charles Fawkner."

I rolled my eyes and picked up the phone. Sometimes I wonder who the children are in this household. I'm pretty sure it's not me or Amber.

"Hi, Kahu." I didn't bother trying to lower my voice. Their hearing was excellent when it suited them. They wouldn't miss a word.

"Did I get you at a busy moment?"

"No. I've just had a tussle over who gets to listen in on our phone call. And I lost," I said in a gloomy tone, my gaze slicing to the three interested parties. "Honestly, you'd think they were at a rugby match."

Kahu's laugh soothed my ruffled mood, heating me from the inside out. Damn, he was good.

"Would you like to go to dinner and a movie tonight?" He hesitated. "It would have to be here in London, but you're welcome to stay the night at my flat."

334

My heart stuttered before bounding into a rapid beat to make up time. I tightened my grip on the receiver and resisted the urge to run clammy hands down my jeans. "I . . . ah . . . that sounds good," I said in a rush. "I have to drive down to London tonight anyway."

"What do you think he said?" Ben asked in a loud whisper. "Do you think they're having this phone sex?"

Heat slashed across my cheeks, and I turned my back to the trio. But that didn't stop the comments.

"I read an article about phone sex in *Marie Claire*," Father said gruffly. Judging by the tone of his voice, I knew he was looking at my back.

"You read woman's magazines?"

"It was the only magazine I could find without pages torn out in the doctor's surgery."

No missing the defensive tone there.

"Well? Do you think it's phone sex?"

"It is not phone sex," I hissed, turning to pin them with an intimidating glare.

"Who's having phone sex?" Kahu asked. His amusement came through loud and clear.

By this time, my cheeks were fiery red.

"I can do phone sex," he said in his sexy drawl.

My stomach swooped at the thought. No one had ever suggested it to me before.

"What are you wearing?"

"Jeans," I murmured.

335

"There!" Ben slammed his hands on top of the kitchen table. "If it walks like a duck and squawks like a duck—"

"It must be a duck!" Father and Ben shouted together.

I scowled at the oldies. "I'm gonna kill you."

"Are you threatening a police officer?"

"Not you," I snapped. "A triple murder, here at Oakthorpe." I turned and pointedly offered my back to the audience again.

"Ah, shame," Kahu said. "Never mind. We'll try kinky when the terrible trio isn't around."

Be still my heart. The man wasn't even in the same room and I was a quivering mess. An aroused, quivering mess. I tugged my T-shirt away when it started to cling to and shape my breasts, almost like a pair of hands. What I needed was a cold shower.

"What time and where should I meet you?"

We arranged details and I hung up. The terrible trio was silent. Too silent. They were up to mischief. Slowly, I turned to face them, inwardly braced for a series of personal remarks.

"Do you find telephone sex fulfilling?" Ben asked. A definite twinkle lit his blue eyes.

Embarrassment blossomed into pissed off. My hands curled to fists. I stood lightly balanced on the balls of my feet, ready to get physical.

"Sit," Hannah ordered. "Can't you see they're winding you up?"

"I can feel the key in my back," I retorted, following her instructions with an abrupt drop onto the nearest chair. My jaw was so tight I thought my teeth might crack. I unclenched it at the thought. We didn't have money to spare for dental repairs. "I surveyed the Stanhope property earlier today. Have we ascertained what security system they have inside?"

Father straightened, as did Ben. Their grins faded into a business-like mien. They looked like a pair of matching bookends. The urge to laugh faded when I remembered their teasing. My teeth ground together again.

"I've got the blueprints and rest of the details in the office," Hannah said.

"Charles, are we getting our cup of tea before night fall?"

"It's Ben's turn."

"Oh, for goodness sake!" I jumped to my feet. "I'll make it. I only have half an hour before I need to pick up Amber from school."

That's all the time I had to come up with an explanation for Amber. She was her mother's daughter and wouldn't take kindly to being shipped off to France. I'd have to think of an original slant before I reached the school.

CHAPTER 23

I t's Renee's birthday," I said. "And she especially asked
that you be allowed to stay with her."

Amber's button nose crinkled as her chubby hands
pushed the seatbelt home with a loud click. "I like
school."

My daughter got her stubbornness from my father.
Ben and Hannah played an equal part in forming her need
to know the why of everything. I scowled in the driver's
mirror. The terrible trio went out of their way to make my
life difficult.

"But Renee is looking forward to seeing you. And
Aunt Emily."

"I like Aunt Emily. She gives me chocolate."

I thought about that for a second. She'd given me
chocolate too. Helped get me hooked on the stuff. "Good

chocolate," I agreed. I backed the Mini out of the small garage.

The terrible trio stood inside the house. I knew they were watching because I saw the curtain in the front room flap. We'd said our goodbyes inside since we didn't want to alert anyone to our departure.

My gaze traveled to the rear vision mirror often. No one following that I could see. I merged with the motorway traffic still keeping wary watch. The nerves jumping inside my stomach didn't settle until I'd pulled up outside Alistair and Emily's house.

The hunter green door flew open, and Alistair hustled us inside.

"I'll get Amber's bag," I said. I was back in minutes, feeling fairly sure that no one had witnessed our entrance to the flat.

I found Emily and Amber in the kitchen. Telltale chocolate marks outlined Amber's face already.

"You look nice," Emily said in approval.

I should do. Even though the final result looked casual, I'd spent two hours going through my wardrobe discarding one outfit after another. I recalled the jumble of clothes on my bed with a slight frown. Hannah didn't need to be a psychiatrist to pick up on the message laid out in my bedroom. Make no mistake: I was nervous about my date with Kahu.

"Mama's going out with the cop."

Emily's gasp rivaled thunder. Right now, dozens of neighbors were peering out their windows and expecting black rain clouds. I squeezed my eyes shut and waited for the storm to hit.

"You're going out with a cop?" Emily shrieked. Her double chin bounced up and down to highlight her agitation.

My eyes popped open. I sucked in a calming breath. "Yes."

Keep it simple, I thought. No point disclosing facts that Emily didn't need to know.

"Alistair," Emily said. Her arms flapped through the air, and I took a step back out of the range of fire. "Katie's dating a cop. I mean of all the men, in all the world, why did she pick a policeman?"

Alistair gave an uncharacteristic grin. "I know."

"You know?" She clapped her hands over Amber's ears and whispered loudly. "What sort of example is that to set for a young, impressionable cat burglar?" The end of the sentence came out as a loud wail.

"I hardly think it's the end of the world. In fact, there are things Katie could learn from a policeman."

"Ah! Pillow talk."

"Mama, what's pillow talk?"

I rolled my eyes. What was the fascination with my sex life? I mean, heck! I didn't have one.

"Mama, what's pillow talk?"

"Emily will explain it to you," I said. My eyes shot a

"take that" at Emily. She greeted it with a grimace.

"Would you like another chocolate bunny?" she asked Amber. "Then we'll go upstairs, and I'll show you where you're sleeping tonight."

I checked my watch. It was still early but I'd decided to use the time furthering my private investigation.

"I have to go now, sweet pea." I squatted in front of Amber and enfolded her in a crushing hug.

"Mama, too tight," she protested.

I lightened up on the hug, but the lump of emotion in my throat grew. I tried to persuade myself that sending Amber away to France was for the best. I mean, I'd come to the decision using logic and clear thinking, but now the moment for goodbye had arrived I wanted to snatch my daughter up and tell her she wasn't going anywhere.

"You ready to go upstairs and find your surprise?" Emily asked.

Unwillingly, I let Amber go, my hands dropping to my sides. Amber skipped over to Emily, clasped her hand and trotted off without looking back.

Regret ached inside me as I climbed to my feet like a much older person.

"Don't worry, Katie." Alistair patted my shoulder in an awkward manner. "Amber will be safe with Emily."

The stupid lump had come back to clog up my throat and I swallowed loudly. "I know she will," I said, my voice thick with tears. "But I'm going to miss her so much."

"Of course you will," Alistair said in his crisp upper-class accent. "But you can't do a proper job if you're worrying about your daughter's safety. It's better this way. You can concentrate on the job at hand, pay off the debt, and get rid of the element of danger."

Of course, he was right. A light switched on inside my head. "What do you know about the debt?"

"Charles told me last week. He feels bad about letting you down. I think he needed someone to talk to."

"He could have talked to me."

"Ah, but he feels guilty for putting you under pressure."

Okay. I could understand that. But he wasn't the only who attached blame. I shouldn't have lingered in France hiding from my problems for so long.

"He shouldn't," I said. "I'll talk to him about it when I get home." That's all it took. A conversation with someone outside the family to make me see that we needed to communicate a bit more.

"Off you go to meet your young man."

"No horrified comments?" I asked, unable to resist.

"Not from me. I'm reserving judgment."

"Thanks, I think." I waved and headed for the door.

Once again, I surveyed the street, the vehicles parked in front of the block of flats and men, women, and children who strolled along the pavement. No one stood out as suspicious; but then, I probably didn't look like a cat burglar, either.

I drove directly to Matthew Beauchamp's house in Holland Park. My timing was perfect. I arrived just as Mrs. Beauchamp pulled up in a black cab. Once again, she was laden down with shopping bags; the cabbie who had staggered into the flat carrying the day's purchases was so obscured by them that I couldn't surmise if he were blond or brunette. Matthew Beauchamp was notable by his absence.

I hadn't seen him since Edinburgh. And since this was pretty much a spur-of-the-moment visit, I wasn't sure how I'd approach him. Whether I'd take a confrontational stance or a more clandestine approach. While I considered the matter, the cabbie exited the building and drove off.

Without a solid plan in mind, I climbed from my car and strolled across the street.

I leaned on the intercom.

"Yes?" The smooth, cultured tone gave away the expensive education and moneyed background.

"Lady Katherine Fawkner to see Mrs. Beauchamp."

A click sounded when the lock of the outer security door disengaged. Well, that was easier than I'd expected. I pushed my way through and came up with my first snag. Which flat? The Georgian building housed four flats—two on each level. Cripes, not even a discreet nametag below the flat numbers on the lift. The woman had probably done it on purpose. She obviously hadn't met up with Fawkner determination, if she thought I'd give up that easily.

I marched over to the lift and once inside, pressed the

button for the flat on the top floor. My assumption was that this flat would have a view of Holland Park and therefore would have a higher price tag. My decision was simple. I considered the snob factor.

The lift opened to a luxurious, well-lit area with thick woolen carpet, an expensive-looking sculpture—my brow crinkled as I tried to work out what it was trying to say—and several potted palms.

I strode up to the wooden door that led into the flat and thumped my impatience with the runaround. If this was the wrong flat, I'd try the next one down.

Veronica Beauchamp stood in the open doorway. "Lady Katherine. How nice of you to call."

I stretched out my hand in greeting. "I'm pleased to meet you at last."

"You should have rung first." Censure repeated in her frown. "I'm on my way out."

"This won't take a moment," I said firmly.

Her face wasn't familiar. Tall and lean, with jaw-length hair in a blunt cut, she moved with a dancer's grace. She also smelled like the inside of a bottle of whiskey. Must have been a long liquid lunch because she'd only arrived home ten minutes ago.

Her delicately arched brows rose and her right foot tapped an impatient tattoo on the cream carpet.

"I'm involved with the children's cancer charity, Wishes. You might have heard of us."

The foot tapped harder. "No."

My mouth strained to drop the friendly smile I'd adopted. "We were wondering if you would care to donate—"

"No."

Okaaay. "Thank you for seeing me. If you change your mind—"

"I won't."

I forced a brighter, saccharine-sweet smile, accepting the rebuttal with good nature. Inside, I railed. I'd hardly stepped one foot inside the flat.

"Goodbye." I turned and headed for the lift. So, my first approach had failed. But I'd seen enough to learn entry into the flat would be fairly simple.

So be it, I thought as I made my way back to my car. My senses screamed that inside the flat I would find the clue I needed to solve the mystery.

Deep in thought, I drove to the restaurant where Kahu had suggested we meet.

Pacifica was fairly new on the scene, and they specialized in Pacific Rim food. Translation: lots of seafood and vegetables with a hint of Kahu's Kiwi roots. The menu was fleshed out with New Zealand and Australian wines or so I'd been told when Kahu suggested we meet here.

I arrived late, and that made me flustered. Along with escalated nerves. A great combo for a girl wanting to look cool and in control.

I walked slowly into the restaurant foyer. Soft music

played—I couldn't have told what it was, but it should have soothed. It didn't. I slid my damp hands down my dress in a clandestine manner, and fixed a smile on my lips. A bright and confident one, hopefully.

"I'm meeting Kahu Williams," I said to the young girl behind the desk.

"You're with Kahu?"

Another Kiwi. The accent was distinctive. *What's wrong with me?* I thought belatedly.

I must have looked put out because she said, "Kahu is over in the far corner. I'll show you over."

I followed her through the restaurant, winding between diners and tables and skirting the pocket-sized dance floor.

Kahu stood when he saw me.

"Hi," he said and kissed me. The soft glow I saw in his eyes when I pulled away help set me at ease. Even though his gaze hinted at sex, there was nothing off-putting about his interest. My heart resumed its racy beat of expectation.

"Would you like a drink?" Kahu asked as he pulled out a chair and seated me.

"Mineral water, please."

"Sparkling?" At my nod, he added to the hovering hostess, "And a beer. Steinlager, thanks."

The hostess frowned over her shoulder as she walked away.

"Do you know her? Or have you been involved with her?"

346

"Carly?" Kahu sat opposite me and reached across the table to grasp my hand. His touch started a lively tingle in my palm that spread down my arm and sent blood to my cheeks.

"Carly's family lives next to mine. She was the first person I looked up when I arrived. Carly is like a sister."

"Oh." Carly wanted more than friendship, but familiarity had Kahu wearing blinkers.

A different waiter arrived with our drinks and poured them into glasses with a flourish.

"How's work going?" I asked, dodging the more personal for refuge in casual chitchat. "The woman who was shot at the Knightsbridge ball."

"We rounded up a few witnesses but it was fairly dark. No one saw where the shot came from."

A shudder snaked down my body. "So you're not even close to charging anyone?"

"No."

"That isn't comforting." And it wasn't. But it wouldn't stop me from carrying out my investigation.

"Let's change the subject," Kahu murmured, gathering up my hand again. He ran his calloused finger across my palm. I suppressed my shudder with difficulty. "I don't know much about you. I want to."

I went all gooey inside before reality intruded. I couldn't tell him about my past or my present, should it come to that. I looked into his brown eyes. "Why don't

347

you go first?"

"Are you ready to order?" Carly bounded up to the table.

"Give us another five," Kahu said.

He handed me a red, leather menu. "The lamb is good; so is the fish." A lopsided grin appeared. "Most anything on the menu is good."

I glanced down the menu. "I'll go with the lamb medallion and tamarillo sauce."

The waitress returned, and stood with an expectant look on her face, her pencil poised over her order pad.

"The seafood taster for me. The one with the green-lipped mussels."

Carly paused and looked up. "Wine?"

"No wine for me," I said.

"Another glass of sparkling water, and one of Gisborne Chardonnay."

Carly strode off in the direction of the kitchens.

The evening passed so quickly, I was surprised to glance across the restaurant and find that we were among the last diners left.

"I didn't realize it was that late," I said. My nerves had settled, and I'd enjoying chatting so much I'd forgotten about the end of the night.

The conclusion.

Carly approached the table with our bill while I dithered and generally rebuilt my apprehension to pre-dinner levels and beyond.

Kahu pulled a credit card out of his wallet and gave it to Carly.

"Did you drive here or catch a cab?" he asked. "I caught a cab."

"I drove. Would you like a ride back to your flat?"

Brown eyes studied me in silence. "You don't have to give me a ride home. There's no pressure. No matter what you decide, I'll still talk to you, still ask you out again."

The silence lengthened while we stared at each other. I weighed his words, studied his face. He seemed sincere. All I needed to do was give my trust. A precept that seemed simple, but whose execution might prove tricky after having not trusted any men for all these years. Out of sight under the table, my fingers curled to dig into my thighs. The prick of fingernails forced me to concentrate.

I stood. "Are you ready to leave?"

"Sure," Kahu said easily. "I'll say goodnight to Carly on the way out."

I carried on a silent debate all the way to Kahu's flat, interspersed with the odd snippet of casual conversation.

"It's the block of flats opposite the park."

The park in question was one of the small fenced greens that the tenants had keys to and could use when they wanted. Kahu caught my glance at the park when I switched off the ignition.

"Would you like to go for a walk in the park before I make you coffee?"

Good idea! I turned to offer my agreement. My words jammed against Kahu's lips as he stole a kiss. And just like that, my panic seeped away.

Kahu's hands tunneled into my hair tugging strands from my chignon until locks fell to my shoulders. I didn't care. I was too busy savoring the rich and heady taste of his mouth.

His lips wandered to the tender skin of my neck.

Teeth!

I jerked, but not in pain. Kahu soothed the love bite with his tongue and repeated the bite. The second bite wasn't such a shock but sent a jolt of pleasure shooting down my body. A moan escaped, and I felt heat surge throughout my body converging in a single spot. Greedy, I sought more, burrowing closer to Kahu's hard, muscled chest. My hands slipped between buttons desperate to touch skin, to run my fingers across warm, masculine skin.

Kahu lifted me, dragging me closer. My head connected with the car roof. The gearshift dug painfully into my thigh. "Oomph," I muttered.

Kahu chuckled, but his hand swept down to massage my upper thigh. "Perhaps we should take this inside."

I crawled back to the driver's seat, taking a deep breath. Instead of clearing my head, I dragged in Kahu's scent. It was just as heady as his taste.

"Kate?" A question hovered between us.

I nodded, unable to express my feelings or my agreement to take our relationship further. I dipped my head in another nod.

Kahu opened the passenger door and unfolded his rangy body from my car. I followed suit, glad of the fresh air to cool my heated skin.

Kahu curled his arm around my waist and led me up to his flat door. He fumbled in his right trouser pocket for keys, the only sign of nerves I saw. Perhaps not, I mused. He managed to slide the key into the lock easily enough. He'd make a great cat burglar with his athletic build. The way he moved told me he'd be a natural. After all, I was in a position to know.

Oh-oh. And I was also nuts. If it were anyone else speaking, I'd have said they'd been drinking. Here I was weaving happy ever after and the man didn't have an inkling of the truth. Cat burglar—yeah, right! The man would probably clap me in cuffs so quick I wouldn't see him move. Then he'd shove me in jail, and my worst fears would come to bite me on the butt. I'd never see Amber and witness all the firsts a good mother should.

The door creaked when it opened. The cat burglar in me diagnosed the problem. It needed oiling. Kahu flicked a switch and the single bulb burned bright, making me squint against the sudden light. The place was old but tidy.

I wasn't sure what to expect, having never visited a bachelor pad before. But I'd heard stories so that didn't stop me from have a good imagination.

"I don't spend enough time here to get the place messy," Kahu said with a twist of his lips.

Galling he could read my mind with such ease. I hoped that was all he'd seen.

"Come in. I don't bite. Not straight away anyway."

The man oozed sexual magnetism and self-confidence. Every time his gaze met mine, my heart somersaulted in response. Any minute now and I'd be hyperventilating.

"That's good to know," I said in an attempt to concentrate on something other than my insecurities.

"I'll put on coffee." Kahu moved purposely into the small kitchenette.

Although the brown linoleum and the lime green–painted cupboards were dated, the area was scrupulously clean. The man kept his dwelling much tidier than my room. The last glimpse of the jumble I'd had of my room before having shut the door passed through my mind. Hmmm. Definite potential for conflict there. I wandered over to the lounge area where a small television set stood in the corner of the room along with two well-used armchairs—the sort that retains the butt imprint of the last person who sat in it. A few sports magazines were strewn on a glass-topped table. Mostly rugby, but when I looked more closely, I saw there were magazines relating to police work.

"Why are you so nervous all of a sudden?"

The soft drawl right behind me made me jump in fright.

"Don't do that," I whispered, holding the palm of my right hand to my heart. "I swear I just parted company with my shoe "

"That's not answering my question. If you've changed your mind, all you need to do is say. I don't do rape."

I couldn't prevent a flinch at the horrid word. Rape. A shudder swept through me.

"I never thought you did," I said, trying for a light tone and not doing a bad job. "Is the coffee ready?"

"Don't change the subject," Kahu growled. There was none of his easy charm visible on his face now. Instead, I read determination to force the truth from me.

"I haven't changed my mind." My eyes met his and held. Messages passed between us, but I'm not sure they had much in common. I tried to infuse my look with certainty and confidence while in truth I was feeling more cautious and insecure. Definitely uneasy about the whole situation.

"Come here," he ordered.

A test.

I sauntered up to him with my best come hither smile fixed to my lips.

"Sometimes I have trouble reading you," he confessed. "The proverbial iceberg with seven-tenths below the surface."

"I'm here," I murmured, forcing the air to my lungs and trying not to sound too breathless, too unsure. I lifted arms that suddenly felt heavy like bags of wet sand, and ran them across Kahu's shoulders. His cotton shirt was light enough for my hands to feel the heat that rose from his skin. At once curious, my hands went to the tiny white buttons that fastened his shirt. I slid the first one free and moved my hands at snail's speed toward the next while keeping my eyes firmly on Kahu's face. His dark eyes gleamed, allowing a spark of passion free.

Following instinct, my hand slid through the gap made by the gaping buttons. Warm skin greeted my tentative touch, and I felt the steady thud of Kahu's heart.

I squeezed my eyes shut, aware of my lack of experience. In my panic, I froze not sure of what to do next.

Kahu saved the moment.

"Can I take your hair down?" he asked. "I've already messed it up." A rough cadence shaded his words and I sensed he struggled with deep emotions.

For me?

My eyes flew open to register his bold appraisal. I stared back, powerless to resist him.

Without waiting for my answer, he dealt with the combs and pins that held my hair away from my face. When my hair finally toppled down around my shoulders, he made a murmur of appreciation.

"Beautiful," he said in a reverent tone. "I knew it would be. It'll look even better spread across my pillows."

The implication sent waves of excitement lurching to all points of my body. My body moistened, preparing for him, and I gave a silent cheer. Everything would be all right. Everything was happening as nature intended. Kahu and I would be good together.

CHAPTER 24

Kahu swept me off my feet without warning, cuddling me against his larger frame without even breathing hard. He moved through the lounge heading for another room. The bedroom, I presumed as my pulsed quickened.

Guess this meant coffee was off. My mouth dried, suddenly in fierce need of a cooling liquid.

The room was dark, but Kahu negotiated chairs, doorways and a cane basket in the hallway. In the room at the far end of the passage, he stepped inside but kept walking. He leaned down letting me fall onto a large bed. I bounced several times while I stared through the gloom trying to make out his features.

I couldn't see his face. Sudden fear twisted my insides, threatening to flare into outright panic. It's Kahu, I tried to tell myself.

It didn't help.

Instead my mind conjured up all sorts of terrifying monsters with unscrupulous acts on their minds.

A bedside lamp flickered on, and Kahu's face came into view. My breath eased out with a relieved hiss.

I could do this. I wanted to do this, I reminded myself.

As I watched, Kahu shrugged out of his shirt and let it drop to the floor. His hands moved to his leather belt. He hesitated then shrugged and unbuckled the belt, tugging it from his trousers. It clunked to the floor.

Appreciation hummed through me. Nice. Very nice. I plucked up the courage for a grin.

"Is that as far as you're going?"

He looked puzzled—and no wonder. I was switching off and on with the frequency of a light bulb.

"I knew you'd look good in my bed," he replied.

No denying the satisfaction there.

"I'm lonely," I whispered. Also terrified I'd muck up this chance with Kahu. But that was a whole other story.

"Can't have that." Kahu sat on the edge of the bed and removed his shoes. He peeled off a pair of black socks. I watched the process with fascination. Oh, I'd seen Father's feet. And Ben's. But they weren't sexy. Kahu made me "hot," for want of a better word.

He stood, lithe and limber, and stripped his black trousers off with economical movements.

My breath stalled at the back of my throat. *Wow!* I thought, enthralled with the man's muscles, his tanned skin, his almost hairless chest. A thin line of hair disappeared beneath closefitting black boxer shorts. I made a soft sound of approval at the back of my throat.

A grin bloomed on his face. Masculine and cocky. "You like?"

"Oh, yeah."

"You can touch if you like."

A challenge. I was never one to resist a challenge.

He kissed me, the taste of his after-dinner brandy as delicious as the man. My hands ran across his shoulders, my fingernails digging lightly into his flesh. Smooth. And smelling of a hint of the great outdoors—a Calvin Klein aftershave, if I wasn't mistaken. Delicious. I nuzzled at his neck, a combination of kissing and nibbling.

Kahu lay beside me, our bodies barely touching, letting me set the pace. It made me feel safe and cherished.

I skimmed my hand down his side and discovered he wasn't ticklish. If he tried the same move on me, I was likely to let out an un-cat burglar–like squeak.

Actually, this reminded me a little of the necking sessions I used to have with my boyfriend. Before the event. We'd broken up shortly before the Christmas ball so I'd gone on my own. I tensed inwardly at the thought.

Kahu seemed to sense my turmoil. He took over and kissed me slow and thoroughly. My mind fogged, the past disappearing into the mists of my memory.

My breasts were sensitive, and I wanted more than anything to feel Kahu's skin against mine. I struggled to remove my dress, my hands bending behind me to get the zipper.

"Let me," Kahu said.

He dealt with the closure to my dress with competence. Competence gained from experience. The thought made me frown when his hand smoothed down my spine. The first foray skipped over my bra closure but the second released it with a minimum of fuss.

A thread of unease rippled down my spine, fighting the magical mood I'd been basking in. I forced it away, planting a smacking kiss on Kahu's lips. He stilled, halting the undressing to participate. Tongues twirled. Touching. Tasting. Exploring.

My dress disappeared without me even realizing it. Cool air caressed my naked upper body and all that separated us were my briefs and Kahu's boxers.

That was the moment when I realized that as much as my head and body wanted Kahu, I couldn't go through with it.

I wasn't ready.

Who knew if I'd ever be ready?

I started to fight his grip on my shoulders, scissoring upward and away from his touch. My heart hammered. My skin grew clammy. Panic set in.

"I can't," I gasped. "Let me go! Let me go!"

Kahu froze. He fixed a frown on me. "What's wrong?"

God! I could never explain this. Never in a million years. I felt like a fool. Half a woman.

"I—I have to go!" I leapt off the bed, grabbing up my dress as I ran from the room. At the front door to the flat, I yanked the dress over my head, half expecting Kahu to come charging after me. Furious because I'd aborted our lovemaking. After snatching up my handbag, I fumbled with the door and flew outside.

The pebbles on the edge of the road dug into the souls of my feet, making me realize in my hurry to flee, I'd left my shoes. Too bad. I didn't intend going back for them. I'd be lucky if I could face Kahu Williams again. Regret chased my panicked thoughts as I revved the Mini and took off down the road with a crunch of gears.

If ever there was a man for me, it was Kahu. Too bad fate had to step in and mess everything up.

◊ ◊ ◊ ◊ ◊

I stalked into the Oakthorpe kitchen to find the terrible trio taking tea even though it was twelve-thirty at night. Great. One question-time, coming right up. I marched over to the cupboard to pull out a clean mug and spun to face them. "I don't want to talk about it." I drilled my gaze at each of the terrible trio, my lips tight and shoulders tense. Just in case they hadn't heard clearly, I repeated my words. "I. Do. Not. Want. To. Talk. About. It."

Hannah wiped floury hands on her floral apron. "Has something happened to Amber? Was there a problem departing for France?"

"No," I responded. "Amber's fine. She couldn't wait to get on the plane."

"Ah," Ben said.

"What do you mean, ah?" I snapped.

"Man trouble," Hannah said with a sage nod.

"I do not have man trouble." My shoulders slumped and tears pricked at the back of my eyes without warning. I squeezed my eyes shut and told myself to quit being such a girl. Cat burglars didn't cry. And especially over men. "I don't have time for a man," I stated, taking the vacant seat at the table. My mug made a grinding sound as I pushed it across the tabletop to Ben. "May I have a cup of tea, please?"

They shared a concerned glance, both men looking at Hannah with expressions that said: *You're a woman. You do something.*

"I've decided to hit the Beauchamp place. Richard's wife wears some good quality jewelry. His brother, Matthew, also seems to have plenty of money. I propose to check their security this week.

I turned to Father feeling more in control now I was doing something concrete for our future. "Do you have the paperwork you signed for the loan?"

He nodded. "It's in the library—in the desk drawer. But you won't find anything suspicious about it. I showed it to a lawyer friend. He said it was legal."

"No," Hannah said, excitement in her voice. "I get what Katie's driving at. I think she's suggesting we obtain any other copies of the document and destroy them. Since it's a gambling debt, there shouldn't be anything in our way."

"I can't do that," Father protested. His face had whitened in shock on hearing my suggestion. "It's a debt of honor."

"Get with the times," I snapped. "Neither of the Beauchamp brothers have an honorable bone in their bodies."

"I'm with Katie," Hannah said.

I looked to Ben. "What about you?"

"I think it's a good idea to hit Beauchamp. Both brothers, if you think it's doable. And, if you should come across documentation in the course of your foray, I say grasp the opportunity."

My brows rose. That was a long speech for Ben.

"Okay. Done deal. That's three votes to one."

"I know when I'm beaten," Father muttered. *Ungraciously*, I thought. "I guess it's worth a try, but he's probably got all his paperwork locked in that office of his."

"Maybe," I allowed. "His secretary is a real pit bull too. But I'm sure I could manage to enter the building at night."

"Wait and see," Hannah said. "I'll power up the computer and start research." She stood and automatically started to collect the dirty cups.

"Wait until morning," I said. "We need our sleep since it's going to be a busy week." I glanced at Father. "You and Ben still planning on attending the Wishes ball tomorrow night?"

Father nodded. "We'll be there in the background as planned."

"Good. I'll see you in the morning." I marched from the kitchen only allowing my shoulders to slump when I was out of sight in the passage. I hurt inside. Was it possible to die of a broken heart? I sure as hell felt ill even if it was my own fault. Maybe if I'd told Kahu the truth things would have been different. Maybe . . . Yeah, I was full of maybes, and they didn't help one bit.

"She's obviously had a fight with that man," Father said. "I knew it would end badly."

"Kahu Williams is a lovely man," Hannah said. "If I were younger—"

"You're not," Ben said.

"I've said it before and I'll say it again, the man's a cop. How could he be anything but a problem?"

I sighed, once again fighting the onslaught of tears, and dragged myself up the stairs to my lonely bedroom. Like I said before, maybe if things had been different.

◊ ◊ ◊ ◊ ◊

I arrived at the ball fashionably late, dressed in body baring black and dangling from Seth's arm.

The ball was a mad crush. Just the thing to make the Wishes committee rub their hands together in glee. Lots of money for the cause.

"I'm going to run out on you before the end of the night," Seth said as we made our way through the well-dressed throngs to get to the bar. "I'll meet you in the morning at my flat."

"New man?" I asked in a low voice.

"No. Same one."

Envy rose in me and I noted the way Seth glowed with happiness. Before I dropped into blue mode again, I thought about my plans for the night. My backbone stiffened, buoyed by a sense of purpose and a goal to achieve.

"That's great," I said, and I really meant it. Seth was like the brother I'd never had, and I cared about his happiness. "I hope you'll introduce us soon."

Seth grinned and bent to kiss me on the cheek. Interesting, I felt none of the excitement I'd savored with Kahu.

"Usual?" Seth asked me as we finally reached the bar.

I gave an absent nod while I scanned the faces and the jewels of the people standing around me.

After noting the icy-blue glow of a sapphire tiara, my gaze moved on, settled.

Kahu.

He lifted his hand in greeting and started toward me. Grief, raw and primitive pierced my heart. What was the point? I'd spent the last few days dodging his calls. How could a relationship work if I couldn't bear my partner to make love to me? Relationships were difficult enough without the weighty emotional baggage I carried. I turned away, accepted my drink from Seth, and told him I needed to speak to one of the committee members about a donation to the cause.

I'd taken five steps when a hand grasped my upper arm. Kahu spun me around to face him. "Kate. Wait, please. We need to talk."

At my glare, his hand dropped off my arm.

"I don't think there's anything left to say." I swallowed, fearing I'd burst into tears if I didn't get away. The worried, concerned look on his face brought the tears a step closer to reality.

Fear gripped me, freezing my legs in place. Sounds of gaiety battered my bruised heart making me aware of how lonely I felt. My godmother had suggested seeing a professional. I'd resisted. Fawkners didn't break under strain. They reveled in challenge. But a tiny voice at the back of my mind asked if getting help was such a bad idea. My gaze skittered over Kahu Williams, not settling but needing the comfort of his solid presence even if I wished he'd disappear. Go figure. The indecisive, stupid bimbo makes a stunning return.

I glanced at him again, teetering with indecision. The firm chin and flashing-yet-steady gaze clued me in. Determination floated off him in waves. Kahu would talk to me whether I wanted it or not.

"Tomorrow at Oakthorpe," I said.

His hot eyes swept over me. A frisson of awareness skidded across my skin, leaving my nipples hard and achy, my stomach quivering for his touch.

Kahu gave a decisive nod. "I'll be there at ten."

He stalked away without looking back, leaving me with doubts the size of China.

An elbow dug me in the ribs. "Quit gawping at the man. Get your mind on the job," Father snapped.

Resentment stiffened my shoulders. Even though he was right. "Have you seen Richard Beauchamp?"

"Last I saw he was heading outside with some woman."

"The gardens?"

"Affirmative."

I held back my snort at Father's version of spy-talk. Without deigning to reply, I pushed my way through the crowds using my elbows mercilessly when people responded too slowly to my requests to pass.

It was a relief to exit the overheated ballroom and step into the cooling breeze. Potted lavenders filled the air with their pungent scent. Strings of fairy lights ran the length of the knee-high hedge. *Amber would love the lights*, I thought, watching them twinkle, fade, and spring to life again.

I scanned the gardens for Richard. The same gardens in which I'd tried to hide from him. Kind of ironic the way life went 'round in circles.

Same circle.

Different choices.

I picked a path at random and hurried down, listening for telltale signs of heavy breathing. The first couple I came across were strangers. It took me ten minutes to find Richard and another ten while I waited for his assignation to finish. I followed Richard as he ambled between two hedges. When no women intercepted him, I decided it was safe to make my move. Somehow, I had to get him to talk about his brother.

"Richard?"

Richard turned at the sound of my voice. He smiled with what looked like genuine pleasure. "Lady Katherine. Kate!"

"How are you, Richard?"

"Missed me?"

I fought to control my instinctive shudder of horror. Although the man hadn't stepped out of line in Edinburgh, I wasn't stupid. I still didn't trust him.

I shrugged, a loose tendril of hair moving across my bare shoulder with a soft tickle. "I've been busy."

Richard's eyes moved to rest on that lock of blond hair. I felt nothing but distaste.

"Doesn't your brother come to any of the social functions?"

"My brother? You're after my brother?"

I cursed my impatience and forced a placating smile. "Merely conversation."

His frown said he wasn't convinced. I wracked my brain for words to ease his suspicion.

"I've been meaning to contact you, my dear. I'm sorry I had to put our meeting off. I—"

"Richard! I've searched for you everywhere."

Richard and I sprang about to face the woman advancing on us. My breath hitched when I felt Richard's jerk of apprehension. He was frightened of his wife? Although I found it hard to believe, the evidence was in front of me. I filed the knowledge away. Who knew? It might come in handy at some stage.

"And now you've found me," he said.

I'll say something—the man recovered quickly.

"With your bimbo," Mrs. Beauchamp snapped, looking down her nose at me as though I were a rodent eating her cheese.

Righteous indignation sprang to the fore. "I am not a bimbo."

"Could have fooled me."

No mistaking that tone for anything but snide. The woman could talk how she liked to her husband, but I didn't have to take it. My nose shot upward, my jaw firmed, and I debated stalking off.

"You knew I wanted to leave early. I have the headache!" she snapped like a heroine out of a regency novel. She turned her glare on me, her thin aristocratic nostrils twitching in disdain.

Right. I didn't need this crap. "Don't let me keep you," I said. My smartass words were probably not the wisest course but at this point, I didn't care. The woman was accusing me of sleeping with her husband, of getting my greedy hooks into his fleshy body. Eeeek! I'd rather eat a plate of worms from Father's vegetable garden.

"Let me call you a cab, Millicent," Richard said in a soothing voice.

His words didn't soothe. She puffed up like an indignant snake. I swear I heard her hiss as she prepared to strike.

"Leave you with this scheming hussy," she snarled. "Give me a little credit."

"I'm outta here." I turned away from what looked like the start of a marital spat. As I strode up the narrow concrete path toward the ballroom, I heard the couple start to snap and snarl at each other in earnest. Here's hoping that Hannah scored with the internet research because I'd found out jack at the ball.

An inspirational thought struck before I stepped back into the crowd. The Beauchamps were both at the ball. I could leave now and hit their house. As soon as the thought occurred, I discarded it. I'd have to wait until I spoke to Hannah.

But the idea wouldn't leave me alone. I retreated to the

garden to ring Hannah.

"Hannah, it's me."

"Has something gone wrong?" Alarm rang down the line.

"No. I've had an idea about moving my search forward." Mindful of being overheard, even in this quiet corner of the hotel, I framed my questions with care.

"Oh. Okay." I heard the rustle of papers and the thud of something dropping to the floor. "Won't be a moment," Hannah said.

"I did a search on the brother. Not much on the net. I rang an old friend who used to temp as a housekeeper to see if she knew of the family. Bad news, she said. The man's a skirt-chaser."

"I already knew that."

"Two children. The marriage was pretty much on the rocks when she covered their regular housekeeper's holidays."

Children.

The word was like a kick to my gut. I cleared my throat. "Boys or girls?" I aimed for casual.

"Why?" Hannah demanded, obviously alerted by something in my voice.

"I am not ready to leave," Richard said.

Strike one. Their angry voices carried to me.

"I refuse to take a cab."

"I have business to attend to. I told you attendance at the ball wasn't for pleasure."

"I am not leaving you when that hussy is around."

Sounded like a stalemate to me. And this hussy was going while the getting was good. I decided I would visit the Beauchamp residence tonight. Ever the opportunist, I decided I might be able to gain entry to the property while the fight raged on at home. Because that looked likely with the way they sniped at each other.

Inside the crowded ballroom, I scanned faces looking for either Father or Ben. When I couldn't find them, I decided I'd check in with Hannah en route. I collected my coat, and mindful of the shooting at the last ball, scanned the hotel foyer, the hotel frontage, and the area across the road for anything the slightest bit out of place. Apart from a higher police presence than normal, there was nothing to raise my antenna.

In the hotel forecourt, I signaled a black cab. The driver pulled up and waited while I climbed in.

"Where to, love?"

"Knightsbridge. Brompton Road, near Harvey Nichols," I said, giving the address of Seth's flat. I'd packed a change of clothes in my bag along with a set purely for cat-burglar purposes. A bit of forward planning.

My mind whirred with plans and possible scenarios I might find at Richard Beauchamp's residence in Chelsea.

"This all right, love?"

I glanced out the window to see the well-dressed mannequins in Harvey Nick's window. Thick winter coats and furs reminded me that frigid weather was only a few months away.

"Just around the corner please. Yes, that's fine," I said when he pulled up outside Seth's home. I paid the driver and watched him drove away.

I clattered up the stairs, ignoring the lift because I wanted to ease the adrenaline that arced through me. Five minutes later, I rang Hannah to let her know my plans, changed into suitable cat clothes, and was good to go. Once again, I took the stairs so I didn't bump into any residents. I headed directly for the Knightsbridge tube. Although time was of the essence—I wanted to arrive before the Beauchamps—the tube to Chelsea wouldn't take long.

My luck was in. I managed to get to Kings Road in Chelsea quicker than I'd envisaged. Memory of the dog episode dimmed my grin. It reminded me that things could and did hit blips even with the best of planning. After that, I walked toward the Beauchamp residence with less of the cocky attitude and more gritty determination to get the job done. I was tired of living on edge, waiting for the goons to spring from the woodwork and hurt Amber— or even worse, spirit my daughter away.

When I reached the end of Gardonne Place, where the Beauchamp residence took up a goodly portion of one side of the road, I slowed my steps. The River Thames flowed past the back of the house, creating another boundary. From my research and casual questions while up in

Edinburgh, I'd ascertained that a towpath ran between the river and the fence that enclosed the Beauchamp property. I decided to approach the property that way. Less chance of being seen by neighbors peering out there windows or passing pedestrians and motorists.

Now that the Beauchamp property was in sight and I'd made my decision, calmness descended on me. I was doing the right thing hitting the problem at source. A part of me wondered why I hadn't done it before.

I reached the end of the street and turned left. Although I still couldn't see the river, I knew it was there. I found a property with no lights burning and a low fence that told me if there were pets in the family, they were inside. I stepped over the fence, and keeping to the shadows cast by a bushy shrub, I hurried through the section to the rear of the house. I skirted a small vegetable plot where the weeds had grown wild.

Exiting the property was a more difficult proposition. I had to scale a fence with vicious points to discourage visitors. I scrambled over with a distinct lack of grace but escaped injury or death by impalement. I checked my watch under a handy lamppost. Behind on my self-imposed schedule. I sped up into a trot, the dirt towpath dulling the sound of my footsteps.

Ah! There it was. The Beauchamp residence. And another bloody fence to scale. Taking a deep breath, I shimmied up like a well-trained monkey, mentally thanking

SHELLEY MUNRO

Ben and Father for their insistence on at least an hour's training every day.

I crept through the well-manicured garden and hoped like hell no one was looking out a window that overlooked the lawn. Although I'm sure it looked breathtaking during the day, the lack of large trees and shrubs made my life difficult.

I scrambled for cover. When I reached the building, I flattened against the brick, panting lightly, a fine sheen of sweat coating my body. The hot day had transformed into a muggy evening. Only my goal of separating the Beauchamps from some of their wealth and my search for proof stopped me from turning around and heading for the nearest icy cold shower.

Once my rapid breathing dropped back to normal, I circled the building, trying to decide on an entry point.

The open window didn't register at first. My gaze scanned the whole wall before snapping back to the white window frame with a sense of shock. Surely, it couldn't be that easy?

I climbed up a drainpipe to second floor level and edged along the window ledge to peer inside.

It was a bedroom, complete with slumbering resident—an elderly gentleman who snored loudly enough for Amber to hear in France. Let's hope he was on the deaf side as well because I was going in.

Keeping an eagle eye on the slumbering man, I crawled

374

through the open window and eased to my feet. I waited to let my eyes adjust to the different light levels and headed for the closed door. I couldn't wait to see if the bloody thing creaked fit to wake the dead. Or in this case, a slumbering gentleman. My clammy hand reached for the door. I wiped it on my black leggings before I attempted to turn the knob. No wonder he had the window open. A trickle of sweat ran down my neck and seeped between my breasts. It was awful hot in here.

I sucked in a breath and turned the handle. As I suspected, it let out a sharp protest. I froze. The snoring halted mid-trumpet. *Don't wake up. Don't wake up.* A long snore-free pause ensued. *Was he awake or not?* I waited a bit longer before I boldly turned the knob a full rotation. Without waiting to see what happened, I whisked the door open wide enough for me to fit through. The room opened out to a dimly lit passage. At the far end of the passage, a light burned in a wall sconce. The carpet was plain—a serviceable dark blue. Light blue paint covered the walls and I saw no artwork to relieve the large expanse of space. I'd definitely entered the servant's wing of the house. I carried on, moving slowly and cautiously, ready to run should the need arise. The low hum of voices gave me pause until I worked out the sound was a television. A sliver of light crept under the door. *Another employee*, I thought. *This one's awake. Not so good.*

I crept past the door. The passage turned to the left.

A flight of stairs led to the floor below. I hesitated before carrying on down the passage.

The surroundings changed from Spartan to luxurious. The carpet thickened miraculously. Perhaps it had eaten a hair tonic and bloomed. Silk wallpaper covered the walls. A group of three small watercolors depicting seaside scenes enlivened the plain color. A marble urn filled with artificial sunflowers stood in an alcove. Bingo. This wing belonged to the Beauchamps.

I paused at the first door I came to. This one stood slightly ajar so I decided to risk entering. It was darker inside the room than outside in the passage. Just inside the door, I stopped to listen. Nothing alarmed me so I stepped further inside and slowly let my eyes adjust. I felt for the torch I carried in an outside pocket of the pack I wore. Taking a deep breath, I turned it on.

The beam hit an empty double bed. My breath eased out and my shoulders relaxed. I hadn't realized how tense I'd felt.

Shaking away my unease, I played the torch over the room. I tugged open a wardrobe door. Empty. A guest room, I decided.

I switched off my torch and peered out the door into the passage to make sure it was clear. The door of the next room I came to was firmly closed. I watched my hand reach for the brass knob. Inexplicably, trepidation slithered through me. I wiped my hand down my black leggings—getting to be a bad habit—and let my hand drop to my side. Butter-flies scurried about inside my stomach. Shaking my head, I forced myself to focus. I listened. Sweet silence greeted my ears. Stupid. Just do it. Before the Beauchamps returned.

I entered the room, my footfalls soft yet decisive. Another bedroom, but not a guest room. This one smelled faintly of roses and a floral perfume that reminded me of lily of the valley. The beam from my torch confirmed my guess. I'd struck gold. Millicent Beauchamp's room. I started my search at the bedside cabinets. A thick romantic suspense novel and a watch lay on top. Nothing worth my while. The torch beam played over a bunch of apricot roses, a combination of buds and full blooms, in a crystal vase. Next a brush with a mother-of-pearl back and a matching hand mirror came into view. A picture frame. Surely the woman had left something interest—my sudden gasp broke through the silence like a stone through glass. Unsteady hands swung the torch beam back to the photo in the small gold frame. I picked it up and sank onto the lace cover on the bed, my legs as unsteady as my hands.

A copy of the same picture I'd found at Perdita Moning's house.

I traced my forefinger over the girl's face. Inside, I felt . . . I shuddered. I wasn't sure what I felt. Anger. Betrayal. This time I didn't intend to creep around the truth. Richard and Millicent Beauchamp knew this child's identity. Suspicions ran through my mind, thick and fast. Answers clicked into place, but I wanted—needed—to know for sure.

I walked from the room, not bothering to shut the door after me. At the top of the stairs, I hesitated again. A split second later, I headed down the stairs. I chuckled without much humor. Too bad if I triggered the alarm. At this point, I didn't give a damn. The need to learn the truth burned strong. But not strong enough to melt the icy cold that surrounded my heart.

If I'd set off an alarm, it was a silent one. And I didn't care about any consequences.

I marched into a formal lounge near the main entrance to the house. Picking a chair at random, I perched on the edge and prepared to wait.

I'm not sure how long I waited before I heard a car outside. My stomach muscles clenched. My eyes narrowed while I waited for my victims to walk through the door.

I heard the door open. No key in the lock. The thought that I could have walked up to the front door and just stepped inside nudged my temper a notch higher than the simmer it was on currently. A light flicked on. Footsteps sounded moving toward me. I eyed the doorway, waiting to see which Beauchamp I'd have the pleasure of questioning first.

I caught a flash of black. Richard. For a moment, I thought I'd have to chase after him. I half stood, prepared to do just that. Then he wheeled abruptly and walked back; right into the room where I waited.

CHAPTER
25

Hello, Richard," I said coolly. "Nice of you to drop in."

"Kate? What the hell are you doing here? Millicent will be here any moment. She can't see you. She went ballistic outside the hotel when we were leaving." Richard shuddered, and I noticed a shiny film of perspiration coated his face. He glanced over his shoulder and winced when I kicked a footstool that stood in my way. The man looked . . . frightened, for want of a better word.

"Anyone would think you were frightened of Millicent," I said tartly.

"You've broken into my house. That tells me the reason you want to see me is important. Spit it out and leave."

I ignored the rudeness, but agreed with his sentiments. I came straight to the point. "The girl in the photo. Who is she?"

Before Richard could answer my question, the front door opened and slammed.

"It's Millicent. Hide!" Richard said with clear panic.

I folded my arms across my chest, balanced lightly on the balls of my feet and waited.

"Kate," he pleaded. "Please. She's not well," he whispered.

He should tell someone who cared. I wanted the truth and after all this time, I wanted it now. "No. If you won't talk to me, I'll talk to your wife. I'm not leaving without the answers I came for."

"But I don't know any—"

"Who are you talking to Richard? Who's there?" Staccato footsteps sounded on the marble entrance tiles. Seconds later, Millicent Beauchamp appeared in the doorway.

"You," she said, pointing a dramatic finger at me. Her black leather bag dropped to the floor at her feet.

I stared.

Richard's jaw dropped.

Millicent Beauchamp's silver-gray dress was covered with red splotches that looked like blood. When I'd seen her earlier in the evening she'd looked immaculate, not a hair out of place. Now locks drooped from her chignon and her mascara was smeared down one cheek. I took a closer look at the red and took a hasty step backward. It was blood.

Richard must have come to the same conclusion I had.

At any rate, he looked distinctly uneasy.

"Are you all right, Millicent?" he said. "Have you had an accident?"

"Don't try to change the subject. I told you earlier. I'm sick of your extramarital affairs, and I refuse to put up with it any longer."

"But Millicent! I'm not having an affair with Lady Katherine. You tell her, Kate."

"It's true," I said.

"Then why is she here?" Millicent screeched. "I don't believe you."

I heard the slam of a car door outside. The doorbell chimed in an exact replica of Big Ben.

"Richard, the door," Millicent said as we all stared at each other.

"I'll get the door," Richard said.

Probably my cue to say I was leaving too, but I still hadn't received answers. I remained right where I stood, keeping a wary eye on Millicent. I'd picked up on Richard's panic. Inner alarm bells clanged, doing a real number on my nerves.

"Now is not a good time," I heard Richard say to whomever was at the door.

"Veronica's kicked me out."

Veronica? Sure enough, Matthew Beauchamp entered the room, an overnight bag held in his left hand. My eyes narrowed, and I felt a feral grin bloom. All the players in the same place at the same time. How provident. I couldn't have planned it better if I'd tried.

Matthew stepped further into the room. "How about a whiskey, old boy? I could do with one. Millicent, you're looking . . ." A transparent look of astonishment passed over his face when he studied his sister-in-law at closer quarters.

I couldn't prevent a snicker escaping. Matthew whirled about, his brows rising when he saw me.

"Well," he said. "Fancy meeting you here."

I studied his face in light of my new knowledge. Maybe the look around the eyes was similar. Niggling doubts nipped at me. Was he or was he not Amber's father?

"Veronica finally woke up and kicked you out," Millicent said. "Clever lady."

"She'll take me back." Confidence oozed from Matthew, and he sauntered over to sit on a leather couch, full of masculine bravado. "Make that a double, old chap."

"I could do with one myself," Richard said with a quick glance at his wife. He scurried from the room leaving the three of us in a prickly silence.

"I won't overstay my welcome," Matthew said. "Veronica will come to her senses soon."

"Damn right you'll be leaving," Millicent snarled. "Tonight."

Something in her tone made me edge even further away, putting the leather couch and a matching oversized chair between us.

"I say! That's not very hospitable. I've nowhere else to go," Matthew protested.

Millicent's face hardened so much it was a wonder her jaw didn't crack. "You're not welcome here." She bent to pick up her bag, and pulled a black object from inside.

Holy shit. The woman had a gun.

Tension filled the room without warning. My gaze darted left and right as I worked out which way to jump. The woman's hands clutched the gun without shaking. In my opinion, it wasn't a case of if she'd shoot, it was when.

"What? If I refuse to leave, you'll shoot me?"

"Men like you make me sick," Millicent snarled, and she calmly pointed the weapon at Matthew and pulled the trigger.

Shock took me in a strangle hold, paralyzing me for precious seconds. The gun fired again. I dived behind a chair and dropped to the floor. My heart thudded loudly, reassuring me I was alive. The truth looked me in the eye. It hadn't been my quick reaction that had saved me. I could chalk that up to pure, dumb luck. But what about Matthew? He'd been much closer to Millicent—an easy shot.

Running footsteps sounded. I wanted to shout for Richard to stay away. The words jammed in my throat and nothing came out but a croak.

"My God! Millicent. What have you done?" The horror in Richard's voice told me she'd hit Matthew.

"Pest control." Millicent sounded calm and in total

control. "Someone had to do it."

The distinct sound of the hammer pulling back on the gun pulsed a fresh wave of shock through my traumatized body.

"Don't shoot, Millicent. It will be murder."

The gun fired.

I heard Richard fall. A groan. Then nothing.

"Good," I heard Millicent say. "I think I'll have a cup of tea. Now where is that wretched housekeeper? Always slacking off. She's never here when I need her."

I heard nothing for a time, then the tap of high heels on the marble tiles. Finally, I risked a peek around the corner of the leather chair. When I didn't see Millicent, I stood cautiously. Matthew Beauchamp lay slumped on the leather couch, a large pool of blood forming under his head. With trembling legs, I forced myself to go to him. No pulse point. The man was dead. Horror rose up my throat. The pungent, coppery scent made me want to throw up. But I couldn't. I scanned the room for Richard.

I found him behind a green two-seater. This time, I felt a pulse.

"Richard," I whispered, shaking him gently. When he didn't answer, I searched him for a cell phone. God, no phone. I swallowed and looked at Matthew. Squelching my unease, I searched his jacket pocket for a phone. When my hand closed around a small object, I sent a silent prayer winging skyward. I grabbed it and headed for the nearest window. No way was I staying inside the house with Millicent Beauchamp.

Security bars blocked the first window I found. A sob tore from my throat. I heard footsteps. My heart leapt in alarm. Hell, she was coming back for me. Wheezing pants squeezed from my lungs. I fumbled with a set of French doors. They refused to budge. The footsteps sounded closer. In total panic, I searched for a hiding place. At the last minute, I scrambled behind a curtain. I trembled, my hands shaking so much I almost lost my grip on the cell phone I clutched in my right hand.

"Now where did I leave my bag?"

I froze, scarcely daring to breathe.

"Ah, there it is." I heard a satisfied sigh and a click-click of a retreat. I slumped against the cool glass of the floor-to-ceiling window, relief and lack of oxygen making me weak. I had to get out of here. Before the woman remembered I'd witnessed her shooting Matthew Beauchamp. And Richard. He needed medical help. I followed the window along and tried the French doors again. This time I noticed the security locks. Seconds later, cool night air drifted across my face.

I opened the cell phone and dialed 111, the emergency-services hotline. With one eye on the house, I relayed the details. "Police and ambulance." I answered the operator's questions in a cool, detached voice.

"Stay on the phone," the operator said.

A shiver worked down my body. No. I wasn't going to chitchat with the operator. I hung up and dialed Kahu.

He answered almost immediately.

"Kahu, it's me. Kate." Reaction had set in and my whole body trembled. I swallowed again in order to get my plea out. "Can you come? I need you."

Even though it was late, the man sounded alert. "Where are you?"

I rattled off the Beauchamps' address. "I'll wait for you out on the road."

Easier said than done. I staggered down the driveway, trying to keep out of the light.

When I reached the road, I loitered, desperate to see Kahu. I wished he'd hurry. The need for a comforting pair of arms was like a fever in my blood. Not just any pair of arms either. I needed someone I trusted and cared for. I needed Kahu. After pacing backward and forward several times, my gut in turmoil, I sank down on my haunches and leaned back against the low stone wall that separated the footpath and the Beauchamp property. Immeasurably weary, I hunched up in a ball and hoped like hell Millicent Beauchamp didn't come after me with her gun. Cold from the stone wall crept through my black long-sleeved T-shirt sending a shiver goose-stepping across my skin. I wasn't sure how much time had passed since I'd rung the police. I hoped the ambulance would arrive soon. Although I didn't think much of Richard Beauchamp, he didn't deserve to die.

Finally, the wail of the siren filled the air, the sound bringing with it a sense of urgency. A plain car was first on the scene followed by two pandas.

Kahu jumped out of the first car and hurried over to me.

I hurled myself at Kahu desperate for human contact. His arms came around me, giving me a hard hug before he pushed me away to arm's length.

"Are you hurt?" He rubbed his fingers across my cheek, his brown eyes full of concern. "Where's the blood coming from?"

I stared up at him blankly until I saw the blood-smeared fingers that came away from my face. Eew! Nausea rushed up my throat and I gagged. Kahu spun me around just in time for me to throw up in the gutter. Kahu waited until I'd finished and then turned me to face him.

"We need to know what we're going to encounter in there. You told the . . ." The ambulance siren drowned out his final words.

The siren switched off mid-roar.

"She shot them," I said into the silence, shock from Millicent Beauchamp's weird behavior still ricocheting through my horrified mind. I felt the policemen around me tense at the news and I inhaled deeply, trying to steady myself. "She shot Matthew and then she shot Richard. Matthew's dead."

"And Richard?" Kahu asked in an urgent tone.

"He was still breathing, but he didn't look too good."

"Okay. Wait there." Kahu strode over to a group of policemen to relay orders.

He turned back to question me further.

"Did she still have the gun?"

I thought back, trying to remember. "I don't know. Sorry." All I could think of was the pool of blood around Matthew. I turned away abruptly, my hand jammed up against my mouth as I dry-heaved.

"I'll call the armed defenders," a voice said.

I turned back to see Kahu nod. "We'll wait until they arrive."

"What about Richard?" I said. "He might die if he doesn't get help." Strain sounded clearly in my voice, and I noted the exchange of glances between several of the men.

A young Woman Police Constable walked up to Kahu. "Sir, I'll look after her."

My gaze swung to Kahu, words of protest trembling at my lips. I didn't want to be foisted off on someone else.

Kahu's look speared through me. He thought I was involved with the Beauchamps. The conclusion hurt. But then again, the times he'd seen me with Richard—and after the way I'd left him earlier in the week . . . maybe he had reason for his suspicions.

I waited silently while the armed defenders arrived and they and the rest of the policemen moved closer to the house. The man and woman who'd arrived in the ambulance waited until the police announced it was safe to move inside.

Time for me to leave. I turned and walked away, intending to head for my car.

"Wait!" The WPC grabbed my elbow. "You can't leave."

I turned to glare at her and she took half a step back. "Am I under arrest?"

"No," she said slowly. "I don't think so."

"Then I don't have to stay here," I said, and I turned and kept walking.

◇ ◇ ◇ ◇ ◇

It was five in the morning when I pulled up in front of Oakthorpe. Never had home looked so welcoming. I dragged myself out of the car and up the front steps. The door opened before I reached it.

"You're home," Hannah said. "Thank goodness. I was starting to worry. The boys arrived home ages ago."

I stepped past Hannah, feeling bone weary to my soul. This was a day I never wanted to repeat.

"You've got blood on you!" Hannah shrieked right next to my ear.

"Yeah. So I've been told."

Hannah closed the door and put an arm around me. "Your smartass tongue is still working. You can't be that badly hurt. Come into the kitchen. The light's better there."

She propelled me into the kitchen. Not that I put up

much of a fight. I was tired, yes, but what I wanted more than anything was the sense of family and knowing I was loved. The terrible trio gave me that unstinting love.

Father and Ben were sitting at the kitchen table when Hannah and I stepped inside. The china teapot with its ridiculous woolly cozy sat in front of them along with a plate of toast and two blue, china mugs. The scene looked so ordinary after what I'd just witnessed that tears came to my eyes. I squeezed my eyes shut but a tear escaped and trickled down my cheeks.

"What's wrong, Katie?" Father asked in alarm. He stood so abruptly his wooden chair toppled over. "Is that blood?"

"Yeah. I'll wash it off later."

Hannah pulled out one of the empty chairs, and I subsided into it gratefully. Father righted his chair, and Hannah bustled about getting a mug and pouring me a cup of tea. Finally, they all looked at me expectantly.

"Matthew Beauchamp is dead." There was no other way to say it except straight up. "And Richard was shot too. I don't know if he's still alive. He was when I saw him last."

"Dead?" Ben asked.

"Who shot them?" Father demanded.

"Not you?" Hannah's brows arched to emphasize her question.

"You know I don't have a gun," I said indignantly.

"Millicent Beauchamp."

The doorbell rang insistently before they could ask further questions.

I sighed, not sure whether I was ready to face Kahu but knowing I'd have to. "That will be Kahu. Can someone let him in? I don't think I can move." A flash of pure misery shot through me to settle in the pit of my stomach. I was so not looking forward to this interview. Already Kahu thought the worst. I wondered how he'd feel when I spoke the truth instead of avoiding it and skirting around my past. No matter how he reacted, I knew it was time for me to face the truth. And I knew something else as well. It didn't matter how Kahu reacted to the horror of my past. Sure, it would hurt, but I knew the terrible trio would support me, would continue to support me and see me past the worst until I was ready to face the world again.

"You were meant to wait," Kahu growled from the doorway. "I was worried, dammit." He prowled into the room with the attitude of a big cat, rattled and ready to attack.

Father remained silent for once. Actually, none of the terrible trio said peep. Hannah gestured at an empty chair beside me and found another mug. She pushed a mug of black tea at Kahu and joined us at the table.

Kahu's brown eyes rested on each of the terrible trio before coming to rest on me. He'd obviously decided it was pointless trying to get rid of them. Wise move.

My hand tightened around my mug of tea as nerves

skipped around inside me. My other hand rested in my lap, my nails digging painfully into my palm, the only way I had to control the dull ache of foreboding and the desperate need to run away and hide.

"Tell me what happened," he said in his deep, husky voice.

Despite my inner anguish, I responded to the sexy note. *How would it feel to wake up next to him in the morning?*

"Kate?"

Cognizant that I was playing for time, I glanced up and met his gaze. Instantly, the nerves turned to something else. Awareness. He reached for my hand and heat engulfed me. Briefly, I closed my eyes. I took a deep breath and opened my eyes again to stare down at the table.

"This started six years ago," I said, forcing the words out. "I went to a Christmas party with a group of friends. At some stage during the night—"

"Kate," Hannah said urgently. "You don't have to rehash the past. It's been and gone. We understand."

I gulped at the compassion in Hannah's voice, the unreserved support, and knew I was the lucky one. I stared at her through glistening tears, a smile on my face. "It's time," I said simply.

A glance at Kahu told me he was confused, but he remained silent and I carried on.

"At some stage during the night, someone spiked my champagne. I don't remember much of the night, but I woke up naked in a hotel room."

Kahu's hand tightened on mine to a painful grip. I don't even think he was aware of his reaction. His expression remained neutral. "Cop mode," Ben called it. But I noticed his eyes. They glowed with intense fury on my behalf, and that gave me courage to continue.

"I had no idea what had happened, but it was obvious I'd been raped. I tried to find out who had paid for the room from the hotel staff, but they wouldn't tell me. And after that, I came home. Instead of telling Father and Hannah what had happened, I ignored the whole thing. About six weeks later, I couldn't ignore it anymore. I was pregnant."

"Rape?" Father spluttered. "You let us assume . . ."

"I was eighteen and frightened. Besides, what could you have done?"

"I would have found the bastard and shot him. That's what!" Father shouted, jumping to his feet.

"Let her finish," Hannah snapped, her own eyes fierce with emotion.

Father sat. "Carry on," he muttered.

"I went to France to live with my godmother, Renee. The plan was to have the baby and put it up for adoption. I agreed, but when I saw Amber, I couldn't part with her."

Kahu's hand flexed. "How does this connect to tonight?"

"Until this year, I hadn't returned to England. I stayed in France. When I was at one of the balls, I saw a picture of a child who is Amber's double. And I wanted revenge,"

I whispered.

"Hell," Kahu said. His gaze arrowed to my face. "But you didn't shoot the Beauchamp brothers. Millicent Beauchamp did, according to Richard."

I nodded. "It took me a while to put the pieces of the puzzle together. No one knew anything, and I couldn't ask openly without tipping my hand."

"Who's Amber's father?" Father demanded. He leapt to his feet again and pranced up and down the kitchen in a high temper. "Which one of those Beauchamp weasels do I go after?"

"Amber's father is dead," I said.

"Matthew Beauchamp is Amber's father," Kahu said, putting the pieces together quicker than any of the trio.

"I hope he suffered," Father spat, doing another circle of the kitchen.

"Millicent Beauchamp shot him point blank in the chest," Kahu said, "and then she shot her husband. What we aren't clear on is why. I'm hoping you'll be able to help me."

Remembering the hate in Millicent Beauchamp's voice made me shudder. And the horror of knowing how close I'd come to being her next victim . . .

"She took exception to Richard's infidelity. Matthew's wife had kicked him out of the family home for the same reason. He wanted to stay with Richard until he could talk his wife into taking him back. Millicent said no, and she took a gun out of her purse and shot him. Then she shot

Richard. She seemed to snap."

"Katie," Hannah said. "We're lucky you're still alive."

"She shot at me too. I think she thought she'd killed me, but she didn't check." My laugh sounded strained as I recalled the woman's actions. "She wanted a cup of tea, and I heard her muttering about the housekeeper. I don't know what happened after that because I left. Richard told me to go to get help so I did."

Kahu nodded. "Your story matches Richard's."

The terrible trio rounded on him as one.

Father glared. "What do you mean by that?"

"You can't think Katie would shoot them," Hannah snapped.

"The girl wouldn't hurt a fly," Ben muttered.

"I didn't say she was a suspect," Kahu said. "I'll need you to come into the station and sign a statement." He paused to study the terrible trio. "Can I talk to you in private?"

"Katie's been through a bad time. She needs her rest," Hannah said.

Ben narrowed his eyes. "You said she wasn't in trouble."

"Can't you leave my daughter alone?" Father glowered fiercely.

Kahu ignored them all. "Kate?"

While part of me wanted to talk to him, the other part of me felt like a kid frightened of the dark. I stood upon trembling legs. "We can talk on the way out to the car."

Kahu stood and followed me from the kitchen. A spate

of indignant chatter broke out when we left the room.

By common consent, when we exited the house we turned for the gardens instead of the car. I led Kahu to an area I knew wasn't visible from the kitchen. We rounded a huge camellia bush and stopped. I turned to face Kahu and found myself snatched to his chest and held so tightly I could hardly breathe.

"God, Katie," he murmured into my hair. "I nearly lost it when I found out that the address of the shooting was the location from which you'd rung me earlier. And when you disappeared . . ." He pulled away and gave me an abrupt shake that rattled my brain. "Don't ever do that to me again. I swear I aged ten years. God, I love you. I don't know how the hell it happened, but it has, and I want you in my life."

"You love me?" I echoed, a faint stirring of hope unfurling. "But what about—"

"I don't care about the past," Kahu said passionately. "We can deal with it together. All I know is that when I came to England to search for my brother, I didn't expect to find you. And now I've found you and Amber, I'm not about to screw up and lose you."

"You really love me?" I asked, unable to get past his declaration.

"Yes." He kissed me, his lips hard and searching before they gentled. When he finally pulled away we were both breathing hard. "I haven't made much headway on my search for my brother, but I'm not letting you go without a fight. I want you to marry me."

I closed my eyes, my heart pounding so hard that I wondered if I'd survive. Kahu had handed me a dream—the possibility of love and a future. Security. I wanted to say yes so badly, I shook.

"You do love me?" he asked, his chocolate-brown eyes glinting with humor.

I nodded abruptly. Hell, yes! I loved him. "I thought I'd make an appointment to talk things through with a professional."

"Whatever you want," he said. "We'll take things slow. As long as I know you're mine. Together, we can do anything."

I thought about it. The main obstacle was the family business. Father would have a cow when I told him I intended to marry the cop. But the glimmer of an idea had brewed at the back of my mind for the last week. Father and Ben had lucked out with their newfound business. There was no reason why we couldn't take up the investigation business full time.

The other problem was the debt to Beauchamp. My mouth firmed as I thought about the answer to that. The Beauchamp family had put me through enough. I intended to have a private talk with Richard when he recovered. I had no doubt that he knew the how and the why of that night. Once I had my answers, I'd blackmail him. One forgiven loan in exchange for silence. Not particularly nice of me, but hell, revenge was a bitch.

"Katie? You've gone all quiet on me."

I wound my arms around Kahu's neck and grinned up at him. "You realize that you'll not only be marrying me, but you'll get Amber and the terrible trio into the bargain."

Kahu chuckled, the look in his eyes making me weak at the knees. "What I'll be getting, sweetheart, is an adventure."

I laughed, feeling deliriously happy. "I love you, Kahu. I love you so much." I reached up to kiss him. The poor man didn't know how right he was. Life at Oakthorpe was certainly an adventure . . .

Don't miss Shelley Munro's
first novel from Medallion Press:

THE
SECOND
SEDUCTION

SHELLEY MUNRO

ISBN#1932815198
Jewel Imprint: Sapphire
US $6.99 / CDN $9.99
Gothic
Available Now

I

East Sussex, England, 1720.

Lucien studied the elderly man standing by the window—the man who claimed him as son.

The family, the faithful servants, all backed up the Earl of St. Clare's assertion, but the role didn't feel right. Not to Lucien. Living in the gloomy pile of rocks they called Castle St. Clare made him edgy. Uneasy.

They were mistaken.

He was not the Earl of St. Clare's son.

The idea was laughable. Him, the long lost heir, Viscount Hastings. He recalled none of what they told him.

"Hastings, the carriage is coming." The earl stepped away from the window. "Your betrothed has arrived."

Lucien rose from a square-backed chair and flicked the lace at his cuffs. "My name is Lucien."

The earl ruffled up like a feisty bantam cock. "Stuff and nonsense! You were christened George. If it's good enough for the King, it's good enough for you."

Lucien strolled past shelves of books and paused to finger an amber figurine from the Orient. From what he'd heard since his arrival in England, people disapproved of the King who hailed from Hanover. The man didn't even speak English. Lucien looked the earl straight in the eye. "My name is Lucien," he repeated, his tone implacable and determined. "Lucien. Not George. Not Hastings."

"Dammit, boy. You have the look of the forebears. Why do you persist with your gainsaying?" The Earl of St. Clare's voice held a trace of pleading. "Can't you see it in the family portraits?"

Lucien grimaced. If he studied the portraits with one eye shut and the other squinted, certainly there were similarities. He replaced the figurine and stalked across a blue Persian rug to gaze out a window overlooking the courtyard.

The study door flew open. Lucien whirled then relaxed when the honorable Charles Soulden bounded in. "Hastings . . ." He faltered as he intercepted Lucien's glare. "I mean, Lucien! The carriage comes with your betrothed."

"So I'm told." Lucien sauntered toward Charles, his newly discovered cousin. "By all means," he murmured. "Let us greet the woman brave enough to wed me . . . the man with no memory."

❦ ⤜◗❖◖⤛ ❦

The carriage swayed and bounced over the uneven road. With each successive pothole, the driver cursed more colorfully. Rosalind gripped a carriage strap, the excessive jolting doing

2

nothing for her frazzled nerves. At the completion of this journey, she would meet her betrothed — for the first time. Questions pounded inside her head. Would he like her? And would he accept her, despite her . . . faults?

Beside Rosalind, her childhood friend and maidservant, Mary, pressed her nose to the carriage window. "Oh, miss! I think we're almost there."

Rosalind tensed at the news. She forced a smile then bit back a cry of alarm as the carriage lurched. Grabbing the seat to avoid a tumble to the floor, she righted herself and slid along the seat toward Mary. "Can you see Castle St. Clare?" She peered out the dusty window.

A snarling gargoyle appeared inches from their faces. Rosalind's breath escaped with a horrified gasp. Beside her, Mary trembled and jerked away from the window.

She clutched at Rosalind's forearm, her voice rising to a squeak. "Miss Rosalind, do you think we should turn around and return to Stow-on-the-Wold?"

Mary's dread, her frenzied thoughts, bombarded Rosalind and she shrugged from her maid's grip to break the connection.

"The earl is expecting us, Mary. We can't go back."

They sped past a rundown gatehouse, the carriage jolting from one pothole to the next. As they clattered through a stone gateway, Rosalind glimpsed the gargoyle's twin. It leered from atop a stone wall and seemed alive, as if it could step from its granite prison on a whim.

The carriage made a sharp swing to the right, the coachman cursing his team of straining horses as the gradient increased sharply. The whip cracked. Without warning, the interior of the carriage turned pitch black. Mary yelped and clutched at Rosalind again.

Rosalind swallowed her gasp, rearranged the skirts of her best blue and gold-trimmed riding habit, and patted Mary on the arm.

"It's all right," she soothed, yet the hand hidden in her skirts trembled. For a moment, the temptation to turn back teased at her, then she recalled the situation she'd return to — relations who resented her presence. The reality pushed aside her fears. Ugly gargoyles or not, she silently vowed to continue her journey.

An object scraped along the carriage sides, sending a shiver down her spine. Mary's piercing shriek echoed within the confines of the enclosed space. Goosebumps rose on Rosalind's arms. Her gaze whipped about the carriage. The noise repeated with an eerie echo.

"Hush, Mary," Rosalind snapped, her heart pounding so loudly she could barely hear herself think. Mustering every shred of courage, she pressed her nose to the cold glass of the window.

This was meant to be a grand adventure, her last opportunity to seize a secure future. Rosalind, the afflicted one, the one the people of Stow-on-the-Wold whispered would never catch a husband. The cousin destined to stay on the shelf. This was her chance to prove them all wrong. *Despite her accursed gift.*

Leaves swept against the windows, followed by the same scraping sound. The cold knot of fear in her stomach twisted. A flash of ghostly fingers waved before her startled eyes. A branch. That was surely a branch. The fear clogging her throat lessened, and she relaxed against the plush cushions of the St. Clare coach with a tremulous sigh of relief.

"It's a branch," she said to Mary. "We are driving along an avenue of trees. I fear they need trimming to let in the sunlight."

"Are you sure, Miss Rosalind?"

"Of course I'm sure." Rosalind made her voice firm and decisive. "Look out the window. You can make out the branches if you look hard enough." As she spoke, the darkness in the carriage lifted. Then they were in daylight again. "There, what did I tell you?"

Mary grabbed her arm. She tugged. Frantically. "Miss. Miss. Look!"

Rosalind turned. Her mouth dropped open. This was where she was to live? She swallowed as she studied the fortress that perched on the cliff top like a menacing monolith. The castle was built of stone, solid and strong to withstand the winds that howled across the English Channel. Arrow slits glared like malignant eyes. Hardly the welcoming home she had envisioned.

"We're almost there," Mary announced. "I can see the gate and the courtyard beyond." She turned to Rosalind, her eyes huge brown rounds in her freckled face. "There are people waiting to meet us."

Uncertainties assailed Rosalind, threatening her fragile composure. Repeated swallowing did little to clear the lump in her throat. They said Hastings was mad. Perhaps she should have refused to marry him, but she had promised her uncle. The papers had been signed when her cousin,

Miranda, and she were babes. One of them had to marry Hastings. Miranda had flatly refused so it was up to her to fulfill family obligations. At least she would have a home of her own. Her hands crept up to check that her lacy cap sat straight. That was what she wanted, wasn't it? A home of her own. A husband, and if she was fortunate, lots of chubby, laughing babies.

Security.

"Whoa, there!" the coachman bellowed. A horse snorted. Harness jangled, then came a piercing screech as the coachman hauled on the brake to halt the ponderous carriage.

The door flew open, and a footman dressed in green livery placed a step down for them to alight. Rosalind pushed aside her apprehension, swept up her skirts in one hand and placed her other into the footman's to descend. She released his hand instantly. Seconds later, Mary exited and stood beside her, blinking in the early afternoon sun.

The earl, much older than she recalled, bowed before her. Tall and thin with stooped shoulders, his clothing hung loosely while his powdered wig drew attention to his extreme pallor. "Lady Rosalind, it is good to see you again."

Rosalind sank into a deep curtsey, her eyes modestly lowered to hide her sudden nervousness. Her betrothed was here, standing right behind his father, but she was too frightened to look. Her cousin's frenzied words rang through her mind. Viscount Hastings was an ogre. A beast.

The earl interrupted her panic. "Child, let me look at you."

Rosalind straightened and met the frank gaze of the elderly earl. "Lady Rosalind, you have the look of your grandmother."

She smiled. "Thank you, my lord. I count that a compliment indeed."

Certainly, her grandmother had been the one person who understood how Rosalind felt, since she suffered from the same family affliction. Rosalind had found the past three years since her grandmother's death difficult and lonely.

The earl urged her forward. "Let me introduce you to my son and nephew. You will meet my sister, Lady Augusta, later."

A chill swept through Rosalind and her lashes lowered to screen her fears. The moment she had both looked forward to and dreaded — the first meeting with her betrothed.

"May I present my son, Viscount Hastings, and my nephew, Charles Soulden?"

Viscount Hastings thrust out a hand, and Rosalind placed her trembling one in his, wishing she had remembered to pull on her gloves. It was too late to worry now. She sank into another curtsey, too nervous to look up at his face. She registered his size first and then a number of erratic pictures flickered through her mind. She shoved them away, concentrating on the tangible man. He towered above her by a good ten inches, making her acutely aware of her own lack in that area.

The calloused hand that held hers tightened, and Rosalind looked up, startled. Her breath caught when she saw her betrothed clearly. Clad in a somber black jacket and breeches, and dark as she imagined the devil, he disdained the fashionable wigs and powder the other men wore. Instead, his hair tumbled in loose, disheveled curls about his head. His face was tanned, as if he spent many hours outside under the sun. But what really caught her attention was the angry scar that slashed his face, running from just below his left eye to his jaw. Puckered and red, it drew the eye.

Rosalind swallowed and looked away, but her gaze clashed with that of her betrothed before she could politely withdraw. His eyes were a mahogany brown, so dark they were almost black, and they openly mocked her reaction.

Confusion and embarrassment fought within her. She tensed under his sardonic gaze. She'd known the viscount had suffered an injury while on Grand Tour in Italy. The gossip of his miraculous return from the dead had spread rapidly through the ballrooms of London. Her stomach churned uneasily, and she averted her eyes to the weathered gray wall that surrounded the courtyard.

"Lady Rosalind, enchanted I'm sure." Hastings' low, gravelly voice sent a surge of alarm through her veins.

She inclined her head and valiantly tried to hide her agitation, but she suspected few fooled Hastings. "Thank you, my lord."

Sensations bombarded her mind, fragments of pictures, pieces of a larger puzzle. They were faint at the moment, but she knew from experience more details would come with time. A frustrated scream lodged in her throat. She tugged to free her hand, but he held fast. Why now? Why her betrothed? She'd thought — hoped — her betrothed would be one of the people for whom her accursed gift did not work. She had felt nothing when she touched the Earl of St. Clare.

The picture of a woman formed in her mind. Dressed in a flowing white gown with a tumble of dark curls about her shoulders, she walked arm in arm with a man. Rosalind gasped. Her left hand clutched her skirt, and she yanked her right from her betrothed's grasp. The man she saw in her mind was her betrothed, and the woman with him was heavy with child. She fanned her face vigorously, fighting for control. "It is hot today."

"Come inside, Rosalind," the earl said. "You must be tired after your long journey."

"Yes," she said, still aware of the viscount's mocking countenance. Her chin rose. "I am a little weary."

"Allow me." Hastings offered his arm. Rosalind caught the beaming smile on the earl's face as he and Charles Soulden turned toward a flight of stairs leading inside the castle.

"It's not too late to call off the wedding," the viscount murmured.

Rosalind went cold inside. If she backed out of this wedding, she would be a laughingstock. A failure. And she would have no home.

No chubby, laughing babies.

The gravel in the courtyard crunched underfoot, the only sound breaking the sudden hush between them.

She would end up on the shelf, a charity case depending on her uncle's largesse. A shudder swept through her body at the thought of being prey to her waspish aunt again. No. She didn't want that, which meant the wedding must go ahead. Despite the fact the man walking at her side was in love with another woman.

Lucien studied the young woman chosen for him by the earl. Pretty enough, in a bland English way, but he'd need to be dumb and blind not to realize she was frightened of him. She'd turned as pale as his white linen shirt when she'd noticed his scar. And she'd kept her gaze averted ever since, preferring to study the crumbling North tower, the departure of the carriage, the stable lads scurrying about. She watched anything instead of him. Even now, her whole body trembled with fear. If he made a loud noise, the woman would be off running, probably screaming all the way back from whence she'd come. Dammit, if he had to marry, he didn't want to marry a mouse. All he wanted was Francesca, and since she was dead, he couldn't have her. The familiar burning pain of loss seared through his chest. Francesca . . .

"No." Her voice was barely audible above the pain that roared through his head. "I will marry you."

Surprise, nay, shock, made his brows shoot toward his hairline. With eyes narrowed, he turned to study her face. Dammit, if he hadn't missed the stubbornness in her small pointed chin. He cursed inwardly. At least he couldn't be accused of marrying a copy of his deceased wife. Blond curls peeked from beneath the lady's lace cap, while pale blue eyes shied from his gaze. She was petite, and very dissimilar from Francesca's dark, Junoesque beauty. He tried to imagine her in the marriage bed and failed dismally. Time to play his trump card. He continued with his lazy saunter, up a flight of stairs into the Great Hall with the English mouse at his side.

"They say I'm mad," he offered, observing her reaction.

"Y . . . yes." She stumbled at the final step.

Ah, the girl had heard but remained set on her course. "I have no memory of my past. Does that not disturb you?" She

10

said nothing, but Lucien found her transparent. The rumors bothered her. Then without warning, her generous mouth firmed, her chin lifted defiantly, and her left hand screwed up into a fist, quickly hidden in her blue skirts.

She wasn't going to change her mind.

An unwilling surge of admiration filled him. He shoved it away. He wanted nothing to get in the way of his plan. Someone had ordered the killing of his beloved Francesca. That someone must pay. Not only Francesca had died on that dark night, but also his unborn child. Vengeance would be his.

Lucien's heart hardened. If Lady Rosalind wanted marriage to Viscount Hastings, she would have it. After all, it mattered little. Nothing mattered except revenge.